GW00455857

Money Death Chainsaws & Curry

HD McTie

© 2018 HD McTie

All rights reserved.

ISBN: 1979036837

ISBN 13: 9781979036832

Prologue

"Why do you want to be a solicitor?"
"Well, it's money for nothing isn't it."

Chapter One

Mandy Brighton was naked.

Deakin had a broken nose.

Her lack of clothing hadn't been an invitation for sex, hence the broken nose.

She knew it was broken, because that's what happened when the outside of her foot came into collision with a face at over 20 miles an hour.

Deakin yelping "You bitch! You've broken my nose" was rather academic.

Breaking a nose wasn't intended to knock someone out but disorientate. Blood, a blinding pain between the eyes and a problem breathing, tended to confuse most people when they experienced all three in the space of a millisecond. Normally the argument ended there. But Deakin was drunk, horny and full of rage. It'd taken two more blows to put him down Was she getting old?

She nudged the side of his face with her foot, he was still breathing, so she hadn't totally lost it. It was a fine line between hitting hard enough to knock a person out and hitting them too hard with the result they never got up again. Mandy was capable of doing both. She was 25. There'd been a time when two strikes would have been enough. Now was not the time to contemplate her failing fighting prowess however. The shiver that ran through her was a reminder she was naked and still wet.

She also had a Chief Inspector of the Metropolitan Police unconscious on the floor.

She picked up the towel which had fallen when Deakin attacked her and vigorously rubbed her hair and body. She quickly pulled on knickers, t-shirt and track suit. Deakin was lying face down in a shallow pool of water. He probably wouldn't drown, but the man was her boss and having to go through some fairly major rhinoplasty was probably enough punishment. As she moved his head, she noticed the jaw flop at an unusual angle. Something else was broken, she started to curse at the fact she couldn't recall the name of the bone. The curse though turned to a grin, her forgotten anatomical knowledge was really the least of her problems.

This was not the evening she'd planned. A 10K run, hot shower and an even hotter curry with Ben and Tim Farrington were what she wanted. Rape and a drunken assault by her boss had not been on the agenda.

It was well known that Deakin was something of a sexual predator around the Police station. His wife had kicked him out and he was sleeping with one of the female PCs.

Deakin apologised when he came into the locker room, clearly a mistake, but he didn't leave. Mandy's

'Marbella brown' body wearing nothing but a wet towel brought his eyes out on stalks. From the subsequent words, he'd grunted, she gathered he'd been dumped.

"All you fucking bitches are gagging for it" wasn't one of Mandy's favourite chat up lines. When he refused to go, and grabbed her towel, there was only one way it was going to end.

She'd hoped the broken nose would have been enough, but Deakin never could understand the meaning of the word no.

She could leave him in the locker room, but that would only give rise to a major internal investigation when he was found. Although Mandy was the innocent party, she doubted her superiors would see it that way. Whatever the police might say about equal opportunities, there were still enough Neanderthals in positions of authority who would say that a police constable who took showers naked was asking for trouble. Knocking out a superior officer just because he was trying to rape you was completely unacceptable. Better she dropped him at the casualty department of the local hospital. Mandy picked up her mobile and dialled.

A voice at the other end answered. "Mandy, where are you?"

"I'm still at the club, I'm going to be late."

"Ben is frying the Bhaji's. You should have been here ten minutes ago, what is it? Have you met a man?"

Mandy looked down at her feet. "In a manner of speaking."

"Well if you're having a shag make it quick."

"Tim, he won't be shagging anyone, I need to get him to casualty"

"Jesus Mandy, is no man safe with you. What happened?"

"He wouldn't take no for an answer so I hit him."

"And?"

"He still wouldn't take no for an answer."

There was silence on the other end of the line. "He is still breathing isn't he Mandy?"

Chapter Two

"Do you love me Harry?"

Harry Trent looked into the pale blue eyes of Annabelle Brown. What was not to love? She was witty, clever, tanned and great in bed. Her father was rich and owned a brewery, Harry loved the cliché. She was without doubt the most fantastic woman he'd ever met. He loved her, madly, so much that sometimes he though his heart would burst.

The only problem was the screwdriver. The large one with the yellow handle firmly embedded in the table in front of him. Harry hadn't appreciated the damage you could do with a screwdriver until Annabelle had shown him.

Her screaming and the sound of the screwdriver thudding into the table turned many heads in the pub, but not those behind the bar. The staff acted as if nothing happened, it was one of her father's pubs. It didn't go unnoticed with Harry they hadn't turned a hair. Was this the first time she'd screamed "You won't ever leave me, will you?" as she stabbed the table with the screwdriver.

The image of the screwdriver hadn't left Harry's head as he lay in bed that night and Annabelle fellated him in a way that would normally have driven him almost insane with ecstasy.

It was 2.00 AM by the time they stopped having sex, Harry driven by a mixture of fear and lust out performed himself. Annabel finally falling asleep groaning and weeping. He looked at her still form, one uncovered breast slowly rising and falling as she slept.

Harry lay in silence until he was sure she was in a deep sleep. Gingerly he moved aside the covers and swung his legs over and on to the floor. As he stood they folded underneath him and he collapsed to the ground. Crawling across the floor he found his trousers, and shirt. After five minutes of struggle he had the trousers on. Holding his shirt, he left the bedroom. The house was in darkness. He managed to descend the stairs and walk through the kitchen to the back door. As he opened it the cold night air slapped his face and chest. He stumbled through the door and as his bare feet hit the concrete path he realised he'd forgotten his shoes and socks. He stood shivering until the cold kicked his brain into gear and he pulled the shirt on. Looking at his watch he saw it was 2.00 AM. He stumbled his way to the edge of the drive and began to walk. Reluctantly he looked at his mobile phone. He would have to call him.

"Hello, Dad?"

"Wha? Who's this?"

"It's Harry."

"What time is it?"

"It's 2.00 AM."

"Who is it?" said Harry's mum.

"It's Harry."

"Is he okay? Has there been an accident? Is it Annabelle? Is she pregnant? I told you to give him those condoms."

"Will you stop? Harry, are you okay?"

"Yes, I'm okay."

"He's okay."

"Well it must be Annabelle then. Are they getting married, I'll need a new hat? Oh, God they've eloped and got married without us!"

"Your mother wants to know if you've eloped?"

Harry looked around, the moon giving a faint glimmer of light. He was freezing.

"I don't have any shoes; can you come and pick me up?"

"You want me to bring you a pair of shoes, its 2 O'clock in the morning".

"Shoes?" said his Mum.

"Dad, I'm freezing, please."

Harry's parents looked at each other questioningly.

"What's happened?" said his mum. "Is he married or not?"

"He just keeps going on about being cold and having no shoes."

"Oh, my God! He's taking drugs, my poor baby! Annabel is pregnant and my son is a drug addict!"

"Don't be daft Harry wouldn't take drugs, he must be drunk."

Harry pulled the phone away from his ear and strangled it wishing it was his parents. He lifted his left foot off the ground getting momentary relief from the biting cold and then hopped onto the other foot. He put the phone back to his ear.

"Harry, Harry are you there?" it was his mum.

"Hi mum."

"Are you okay? What's wrong with Annabelle."

"Nothing. We've split up. I know its the middle of the night. But I'm freezing, please can you pick me up?"

He could hear his parents speaking in subdued tones. His father muttering that it was 2 O'clock and an hour's drive. His mother that he should stop moaning and get his coat as her poor baby was freezing to death. Has he accepted the job asked his father. She didn't know said his mother and now wasn't the time to ask. It was precisely the time to ask said his father, it was time Harry stopped pissing around and acted like a proper grown up. There was silence.

"There is no need to use language like that Brian" said his mother.

"Well has he?"

"I don't know."

"Well ask him."

A short silence followed. Then his mother spoke to Harry.

"Harry, sweetheart, have you accepted that job with Clancy Burns?"

Harry looked at his feet, they were turning blue, he needed to find some shelter before he froze.

"Harry?"

"Mum I told you I'm waiting to hear from the publisher."

"They've sent your manuscript back darling. You know your dad and I, well, me anyway thought your novel was fabulous, but unfortunately the 47 other publishers you sent it to didn't. You spent all that time and Grandad's money studying to become a solicitor, it really is time you put all that hard work to good use. He was so proud when you told him you were going to be a solicitor."

The moon scudded behind a cloud and it was if a black cloak had been dropped over Harry's head. He was 26, running away from his homicidal girlfriend, barefoot and frozen.

"Yes, okay I'll take the job."

As Harry sat in Alex Small's office, that last evening with Annabelle came to mind. A strong feeling of déjà vu, rolled over him. He was sure he'd heard Small correctly when he said. "She will think herself lucky if she still has one of her kidneys, by the time we're finished." Harry wasn't a Doctor but he was pretty sure most people had two kidneys. Small had clearly indicated he was going to get his hands on one of them. His law school studies taught him when people divorced one party invariable got all the cash. There'd been no mention of body parts. Small had a gleam in his eye reminiscent of Annabelle with her screwdriver. It was a look which said 'fuck with me and I will pull your heart out and eat it in front of you.'

. It was his first day at Clancy Burns solicitors and he was working for Annabelle's 'big brother'.

Small ended his conversation and glared at Harry. "What's your problem?" He said.

"Nothing" said Harry.

Small threw a thick file across the table towards him. "Well take this and fuck off then. You're due in court in twenty minutes".

Harry grabbed the file and left the room. He'd no idea where he was going or what he was expected to do when he got there. So, began his legal career.

Leaving the building he hailed a passing cab.

"Court please." He said to the driver. Harry jumped in the back of the cab. The cab didn't move. "Is there a problem?" said Harry.

"Which one mate?"

"I'm sorry?"

Which bleedin' court, Magistrates, Crown, High Court?

Harry looked in the thick file, why was there so much paper? He pulled out a thick bundle and the rest cascaded over the floor. He picked up a document embossed with a court stamp.

"Queen's Row Magistrates court please."

As the driver zigzagged through London's busy streets, Harry opened the file. Dave Squirrel was a successful business man when sober, and a curry eating belligerent drunk, when he wasn't. A police statement in the file said Squirrel had been found sleeping in a gutter covered in vomit. That was 6 months ago. Looking at the paperwork sent to the barrister it seemed after a period of rehabilitation he'd fallen off the wagon again. The instructions went on to say that while Squirrel had been told to turn up sober and well presented this could not be guaranteed. There was a psychiatric report in the file which was to be used if Squirrel looked like he'd spent the night in a rubbish skip.

The cab stopped outside the court and Harry bounded up the steps. The place was a sea of tattooed men, shaved heads, and young girls with screaming infants. A pack of sharp suited lawyers herded them back and forth like Gucci sheep dogs. He couldn't find Dave Squirrel, or the barrister, he was supposed to meet. The sound of snoring made him turn his head. Was this sleeping drunk Squirrel? He'd asked every other candidate.

"Excuse me, Mr Squirrel?" asked Harry.

Harry's 'client' snored on. He lent in closer, recoiling as the drunk's fetid breath sand papered his face, "Mr Squirrel?" Harry gently shook his shoulder and then with a little more force, "Mr Squirrel?"

"Wha? Who the fuck es callin' me a squirrel!" demanded the drunk. Harry stepped back. The drunk looked at him through bloodshot eyes. "Who the fuck are you?" he said.

"Harry Trent. I'm from your solicitors."

"Wha? You my solicitor?"

It didn't seem the time to argue the point, though Harry would later regret it. "Yes", he replied.

The drunk looked around, his large dirty hands searching for something. He pulled a tattered bag from his jacket and examined it minutely. Finally, he tore it to pieces before being convinced it was empty. He looked at Harry accusingly.

"Where es it?" he demanded.

Harry shook his head in bemusement. He could see people around him moving into court. Where was the bloody Barrister? Was this Squirrel? He hadn't said he was. "I'm sorry, what have you lost? Are you Mr Squirrel?"

The drunk staggered to his feet, flicking dried vomit at Harry as he brushed himself down. "A am not Mr Fucking Badger! Or Mr Fucking Bunny Rabbit! And,

A am not Mr Fucking Squirrel, neither! And if you don't give me back ma whiskey am goin' to do you!'

Harry moved back, this kind of thing never happened on TV. Thankfully, an usher came across and put a hand on the drunk's arm.

"Come on Jim," he said soothingly. "Let's get you into court." The drunk looked into the calming eyes of the usher and allowed himself to be led away. Harry could hear him muttering as he did so that it wasna fair for a grown man to be called a squirrel and they should get that bastard who'd stolen his whiskey.

Harry stood slightly shaken and then realised almost everyone had disappeared. He looked around in despair. He stopped a passing usher.

"I'm looking for the court?" he said.

"Which one?"

"I don't know"

The usher rolled his eyes. "Most of them have gone upstairs" he said walking on.

Harry looked around for the staircase. It was sat in the wall on the far side of the room. he was running towards it when he spotted the second staircase off to his right. He stopped, his eyes flitting from one to the other. With a soft moan, he headed for the first staircase. Racing to the top, he saw a pair of glass paned double doors. He pushed through and found himself in an empty corridor. He ran down looking for any signs of a court room. He saw a sign saying clerks room and opened the door.

"Knock!" barked a voice from within.

Harry stood in the door way. Across from him a man sat at a desk, grey coloured folders piled on top of it.

"Sorry to....." said Harry.

"Knock!" said the man in a louder voice.

Harry shut the door and knocked.

"Enter".

Harry opened the door and entered.

"Name and matter number?"

"Er Harry Trent, I don't have a number. Will my date of birth do?"

The man glared at him. " Are you taking the piss?"

The two exchanged looks. The man took in the newness of Harry's suit and his youth. Trainee solicitors where the bane of his life. He moved the mouse on his desk and opened a file for that mornings hearings.

"Trent, you say?"

Harry nodded.

"Harry, is that short for Henry? "Memories of school flooded back, the number of times, teachers had insisted he write his name as Henry or Harold, despite his protestations it was just Harry. He stifled the desire to tell the man in no uncertain terms, it was just Harry.

The man though took Harry's look of suppressed rage as further evidence of imbecility. He finished looking down the list.

"Its not listed" he said.

"I'm sorry what isn't?

"Your case."

Harry didn't know what to say. The man glared back. "I'm looking for the court," he mumbled.

"Which one?"

Not that again, thought Harry, why hadn't he been told which one before he left the office. It had all sounded so simple. "It's the case of Squirrel." he said.

"You said it was Trent."

"No I didn't."

"Get out!" The man rose to his feet, his face now decidedly pink and well on the way to red. As he came around the desk, Harry decided it was time to go. He slammed the door hearing something heavy being thrown against it as he did so. As he emerged into the corridor, the tramp he'd earlier mistaken for Squirrel emerged from the toilet opposite. A broad smiled crossed his face as he saw Harry.

"Oh! there you ar, a wis gettin wurried. Should we no be in the court? A dinna wun ta give the Judge the wrong idea."

Harry ignored him and walked on. The tram scurried behind.

"Hey, wait for me"

Harry went through another pair of double doors and around a corner. Up ahead he could see people milling. He spotted another usher, standing at the top of what had been the correct flight of stairs. Cursing to himself Harry approached him

"Excuse me, I'm here for the case of Squirrel"

The usher looked at his list. "Court 7, third on the right" he said pointing ahead. "They will be starting in about five minutes.

Harry was beginning to regain his composure, when he felt a sharp dig in the shoulder.

"Hey pal, jest because am on legal aid es no reason ta treat me like that."

Harry swung around, almost gagging at the tramp's breath.

"I'm not your solicitor", said Harry.

"What!" spat the tramp. "You said you were!"

"Well I'm not and I haven't got your whiskey either."

At the mention of the whiskey a light seemed to come on in the tramp's head. "You've got ma whiskey?" he growled grabbing hold of Harry's lapels. "Where Is it?"

Harry only meant to push the tramp away, it hadn't registered they were standing on the top of the stairs. As the tramp began to lose his footing. His hand flew up in the air and he fell head over heel down the stairs. Harry looked on in horror. He was about to descend the stairs when the usher grabbed his arm.

"Come on. They are going in." he said.

Harry turned and looked at the man. He was grey haired, balding and had a face that said 'I've seen it all and what's more its now coming around for the third time.

"But what about? said Harry.

"He'll be fine."

"But he's just..."

"They do that all day, everyday. You need to go into court. The Magistrate doesn't like to be kept waiting."

He gave the usher a final look and got a reassuring nod. Harry moved towards the court and went in. He was guided to the second row of benches populated by solicitors and barristers. Harry hovered over his seat. Was it a good idea to have come in here? Shit, he didn't know… further thought was cut short.

"Silence in Court"

Everyone stood as the Magistrate came from behind a screen and sat at the head of the court. The first case was called, and Harry's funk began to grow. Where were Squirrel and the Barrister? The first two cases came and went and Harry's unease continued to grow.

"Call James Grange."

Harry looked up and saw the old tramp he'd thought to be Squirrel walk into the dock. he had a large ugly cut across his forehead and a line of dried blood down the side of his face. He was charged with being drunk and disorderly, and shoplifting.

The Magistrate who had been busily writing looked up and recoiled in horror as he took in Grange's appearance.

"Mr Grange what happened to you?"

"Oh this" said Grange, a smile on his face, "He caught me a right whopper and no mistake."

"Who did?"

"Ma solicitor."

"Your solicitor hit you?"

"That right yur Majesty. He said he wasna ma solicitor anymore an hit me and threw me doon tha stairs."

The Magistrate turned to the clerk of the court, an appalled look on his face.

"It's a new one on me sir" said the clerk. I've heard it alleged that police officers have thrown people down the stairs, but never by their own solicitor. Is your solicitor in court?

Mr Grange?"

"Oh aye, he'll be here all right. He's got a great right hook", he said with a grin, swiping his fist through the air.

Harry looked on in horror. Not a word of it was true, but then it wasn't exactly a lie. The usher had seen what happened, but where was he. A grey-haired man in a black cloak. He'd seen half a dozen of them that morning.

The Clerk waited expectantly for the lawyer representing Grange to rise. No one moved. He turned to Grange.

"Mr Grange, your solicitor doesn't seem to be in court. Who is it?"

"It's one of that lot", he said, pointing at the benches of lawyers. The Clerk swung round to a sea of shaking heads. The Magistrate was getting agitated.

"Which one, Mr Grange?"

Grange looked hesitantly at the double bench of lawyers. His face broke into a smile as he recognised Harry and pointed a grubby finger.

"Him!"

"All eyes turned on Harry.

The Clerk shot Harry a stare. "Mr...?" The look compelled him to stand.

"Trent... Harry Trent."

"Do you represent this man?"

"No!"

"He does! He said he was ma solicitor!"

"No, I didn't."

"HE DID! HE DID!"

The Magistrate joined in, "Did you say you were this man's solicitor?"

"Well, yes, but..."

"But what? You either act for this man or you don't."

"I don't, I'm not even a solicitor."

"What! Why did you tell this man you were?"

"I didn't!"

"He caught me a right one!" said Grange "But he shouldnna have stole ma whiskey" he added mournfully.

"Is this true? Did you assault this man and steal his whiskey!?" demanded the Magistrate.

The image of Annabelle with the screw driver flashed in front of Harry. What was happening to him?

"Well?" Persisted the Magistrate.

"No! He fell, it was an accident. I've never seen his whiskey. I did tell him I was a solicitor, but that seemed the easiest thing to do at the time."

"Let me get this straight. You impersonated a solicitor, assaulted this man, and stole his whiskey?"

"And he called me a squirrel" added Grange.

"Why," demanded the Magistrate "did you call this man a squirrel?"

"I called him Mr Squirrel", said Harry plaintively.

"Mr Trent" said the clerk trying to restore order. "It's a serious matter to pretend to be a solicitor when you're not. As for the assault, there will need to be a proper investigation of what happened, and we have the matter of the missing whisky, which should not have been brought into court in the first place", he added looking sternly at Grange. "Now, we have established you are not a solicitor."

"No."

"And you admit you assaulted this man?"

"No, but..."

"You say he accidently fell down the stairs?"

A titter of laughter ran around the court.

"Silence! I will have silence in my court!" screamed the Magistrate.

"Yes", said Harry resignedly.

"And what qualification, if any, do you hold?"

"I'm a trainee… solicitor."

The clerk turned to the Magistrate who was starting to hyperventilate, "Send… send him down," he gasped, "we'll deal with him later."

And so, two hours into his legal career, Harry was led to the cells.

Chapter Three

Mandy braced her legs against the floor of the van as it cornered sharply. There were nine other occupants all dressed in the blue body armour of the Tactical Support Squad. Intelligence said a Serbian drug dealer was at a house in Notting Hill. Her job would be to look after any women on the premises, the Serb also being suspected of sex trafficking. As she was only to look after the women she wouldn't need a gun she'd been told. So, Mandy was the only one without one. Going into a house full of armed Serbs without a gun was a bad idea so far as she was concerned

She wondered if Deakin was involved in the decision. Their paths had crossed the week before, he was back on light duties, she'd asked him how he was. He'd said something dismissive, but there'd been nothing in the way he looked at her which indicated he remembered what had happened. The official explanation was he'd been mugged on his way home, made it to casualty and then passed out.

The truth was Tim and Ben Farrington arrived at the police sports club, helped her dump the semi conscious Deakin in the back and they'd bundled him out at the entrance to the casualty department of the local hospital minus his wallet.

Mandy had been appalled when Ben removed it from his jacket.

"Mandy, it has to look like he's been mugged. We'll chuck it in a bin somewhere." Ben rifled through the wallet. There were four twenty pound notes in it. Better take these."

"Ben that's stealing" said Mandy.

"Nonsense, its petrol money and the samosas will have gone cold by now. You know they are never the same warmed through. I call it justifiable compensation."

She looked at Tim for support. He grinned, "Ben's right Mandy, look upon it as a randy copper tax."

Mandy looked around the van her gaze settled on a face she didn't recognize. From the pips on his shoulder, he was an Inspector. He must be the new guy who'd just joined the station. Great an armed raid being led by someone nobody new.

The young prostitute flicked her bitten finger nail against the white parchment skin of her arm as she searched for a vein. She couldn't find one. Indifferent to the two Serbs sitting opposite, she pulled up her skirt and jabbed the needle into her thigh.

The shorter Serb winked at the other man and nodded towards the girl. She didn't have time to bother with knickers in her line of work. The second Serb was called Gregor Vincnipovic. He'd arrived in London eight months ago and made a great deal of money. Making money was simple if you had good contacts and instilled great fear. He excelled in both.

Vincnipovic slipped the cleaning brush in his hand down the barrel of his Uzi machine pistol. "Put your chicken away, woman. Keep it for the customers," he said. The girl sat back in the torn yellow arm chair, carelessly pulling her skirt down. The other Serb giggled as he could still see up it. Vincnipovic barked at him in Serbian, and the man retreated behind his newspaper; he would practice his English. As he did so, there was the sound of smashing wood followed by the cry of "armed police". With four quick unhurried movements, Vincnipovic assembled the machine pistol and slapped in a full magazine.

The new Inspector liked to lead his men by example. The first and only example he taught them was not to burst into a room where a man was holding a machine gun. It took a two-second burst from Vincnipovic's gun for the Inspector's chest and face to turn to red papier-mâché and for his body to be flung backwards into the hall. The Sergeant, who wisely placed himself third in line, grabbed the webbing of the PC in front of him and jerked him back out of harms way. "Call for back up!" he bellowed.

Vincnipovic, slammed the front door shut and ordered the short Serb to stand guard. He pulled out his mobile phone and quickly dialled a number. When the call was taken, he said just one word "Eagle" and broke the connection.

Harry Trent sat back in the cab, the words of Alex Small ringing in his ears. 'Idiot' and 'moron' had been the more complimentary. He was aware his training contract hadn't been signed, and after the morning's events, he wondered if it would be. Small had come to the court to get him out. He'd shouted and screamed at Harry and Harry had grovelled to the magistrate. The usher who'd witnessed the incident had been found and confirmed Harry's story. They'd left the court together and Small just walked off. When Harry's mobile rang a few minutes later, he was keen to make amends.

"Harry, it's Suzy, where are you?" It was Suzy Walsh, Michael Burns secretary. Harry was meant to be working for Burns and had only been leant to Small for the morning.

"I'm on my way back to the office."

"Michael needs you to go and see someone in Notting Hill. He's a new client, a friend of Bernie Doyle's."

"Bernie Doyle?"

"Michael's biggest client, Harry. Get on the right side of Bernie and you win big brownie points. The clients name is Gregor Vincnipovic. The line wasn't very good, but it seems he has the police at his house and needs a solicitor. Michael is a bit tied up at the moment and wonders if you could go along and see what the problem is."

"Sure, I'm on my way."

Harry's buoyant mood at the chance to make good the misdeeds of the morning evaporated as the true meaning of 'he has the police with him' sank in. The taxi stopped at the end of the street and he was led through police lines.

A Superintendent, an Inspector and a Sergeant were talking in a huddle and had not acknowledged Harry's arrival. The copper who had brought him through the lines had disappeared with a "wait here."

After what seemed an eternity, but was, in all truth, only a couple of minutes, Harry felt the need to have his presence noticed. "Excuse me," he said tentatively. They ignored him and continued their conversation. "I'm here to see my client" he said in a louder voice. The Police Superintendent in charge turned and gave Harry a querulous look.

"Who are you?"

"Harry Trent, Clancy Burns Solicitors, we act for Mr Vincnipovic."

"This is a very dangerous situation, Mr Trent, one of my men has been viciously murdered. It's not a time for lawyers." Said the Superintendent

"Excuse me sir," the Inspector whispered in his ear.

"Maybe," he grunted, in response. He turned to Harry, "if you don't mind waiting over there for a minute, we will see if we can make arrangements for you to go and see your client". Mandy Brighton walked by, "Mandy, get Mr Trent a cup of tea, will you?" Harry followed her through a line of police vans, having to quicken his pace to keep up.

"Wait here, will you, sir?" she said and walked away. He could tell from the way she moved she wasn't coming back with a cup of tea. For one thing, she hadn't asked him how he took it. Harry looked around. He couldn't see where she would have got tea from, anyway. Perhaps it was just a reflex action with male coppers to presume that female coppers always went around carrying a kettle of boiling water and a box of tea bags.

Harry looked around, there were armed police everywhere. It was like something out of a war movie. He pulled out his mobile and rang the office.

"Suzy, its Harry, I've... " his voice trailed off. He was reluctant to tell her that once again he had a bit of a problem.

"Harry? Are you still there?"

"It's Mr Vincnipovic."

"Oh God, Harry! Don't tell me you've lost him as well!"

"No. That's not the problem. He's here with the police. Hundreds of them."

"Hundreds? Harry, what's going on?"

Harry could hear the voice of Small in the background, "Who's that?" That was all he needed.

"It's Harry; he appears to be having a… problem… "

Small grabbed the phone. Trent was a fucking liability! He hadn't been with the firm a day and was already causing grief for the second time.

"Trent!" barked Small down the phone, "what the fuck have you done now!? If the police have arrested you again, they can fucking keep you!"

Harry pulled the phone away from his ear as if it had bitten him.

"TRENT! TRENT! Are you there!? If I have to come and get you out of trouble again, you'll be taking your balls home in a paper bag! TREEEEENT!"

It seemed a good time to lose reception. Harry pushed the disconnect button on his phone.

"Mr Trent?" He looked up. It was the PC who had been sent to get him tea. She didn't have it, instead Mandy led him back to the three officers. The Superintendent gave him a confident smile as Harry approached, the others avoided eye contact.

"Right, Mr Trent. We've spoken to your client and have arranged for you to go in and see him."

Harry looked at the assembled police vans and cars formed in a barricade around the house. Armed police officers tensely poking their guns over bonnets and from behind car doors. Harry licked his lips; his mouth felt like sandpaper.

"Is it safe?".

"Of course, of course," beamed the Superintendent, "after all, your client is hardly going to shoot his own solicitor, is he?"

Vincnipovic lifted the corner of the net curtain and looked out the window. The police deployment indicated they were settling down for a long siege. Before moving to England he'd been a colonel in the Serbian army. He believed in planning for contingencies. If the police should raid his headquarters, he had men who would steal a helicopter. The code word was "Eagle." Stealing helicopters was not like stealing cars. But he'd indentified several locations in London from where one could be taken. How soon he was rescued would depend on how quickly it could be done. In the interim he would play for time. He'd met a man called Bernie Doyle, a major London gangster. Doyle had provided him with the name of Michael Burns. "My brief can be a handy man to have around if the coppers get nosey." Said Doyle. Vincnipovic didn't understand the reference to the 'copper's nose', but appreciated the value of having a solicitor who didn't care how his clients made their money. He'd telephoned Burns number.

The phone rang, he picked it up.

"Yes?"

"Mr Vincnipovic, we're sending in PC Brighton with your lawyer."

"No Policemen, just my lawyer."

"It's okay, it's a female officer. We'd like her to check on the girls you have in the house."

A smile crossed Vincnipovic lips, a policewoman could be a useful hostage.

Mandy Brighton was less happy about the idea than the Serb. The look she gave the Superintendent when he said she would be less threatening made him think twice about the statement.

Mandy clenched and unclenched her hands as she tried to regain her composure. Fuck the lot of them. She'd had enough of being regarded as a glorified trolley dolly.

"You all right, Mand?" She looked into the smirking faces of two male officers. She wasn't going to let those tossers get the better of her. She handed one of them her helmet and the other her flack jacket.

"Hold these." Open mouthed they took them as Mandy walked across to Harry.

Harry hadn't paid any attention to Mandy when they'd originally met. He watched as she walked towards him, she stood 5' 9" and walked with the lightness and easy poise of an athlete, her hair the colour of burnished copper.

"Mr Trent." She said in an icy tone

Harry felt his mouth go dry. "Yes....mmm, that me" he mumbled.

"Follow me."

Mandy strode out towards the house making Harry almost break in to a trot to keep up. By the time, they reached the house Harry had forgotten all about his earlier concerns.

The telescopic sight followed Harry as he crossed the road. The police had a number of marksmen situated on adjacent roof tops. PC 4753 Fox, was an expert marksman and a wife beater. Thrown out of his home he now lived with a young Russian woman, who he knew was in the country illegally and in no position to complain about his violence. He'd been due to go off duty when the siege commenced. Looking forward to an afternoon of sex, and administering a few slaps, if the slag didn't behave, and they never did, he'd taken three tablets which he believed to be Viagra. Unknown to Fox they were LSD, disguised to look like the sex drug.

The marksman liked his violence and would happily fabricate evidence to give him an excuse to beat people up. Such evidence would often fall apart in court. The collapse of a major trial now meant he faced disciplinary charges. He'd lost his house and could lose his job. All because of fucking lawyers. When he'd heard over his ear piece that a solicitor was going in to the house, the drug fuelled cells, that lurked in what passed for his brain had gone into overdrive.

From his rooftop position, he was perfectly placed. His finger twitched over the rifle's trigger; 'bang bang' he whispered. This was the prefect opportunity to kill one of the bastards. The marksman giggled. He wasn't sure what was so funny but he didn't care, he felt fantastic! God, he was hungry, he reached in his pack and pulled out a Mars bar. He just needed an excuse to start firing and Harry Trent would be a dead man.

Chapter Four

Bernie Doyle flexed the fingers of his right hand, the joints were stiff that morning. He pulled the cashmere overcoat tighter around him. He looked at the distorted shape of his trigger finger and wondered how much longer he would be able to fire a gun. Doyle smiled to himself, he'd only ever fired a gun in anger once in his life. At the time, it was pressed against the head of Billy Ronson, a notorious London gangster, it was 1979, Doyle was 19. "What you going to do son? Shoot me?" were Ronson's last words.

Doyle had never fired a gun before, and was unaware of the consequences of shooting someone at close quarters. He'd calculated his chances of hitting Ronson from a distance were slim, so he had the barrel pressed firmly against his head. He reckoned even he couldn't miss. Doyle was finding shards of skull and brain membrane stuck to his scalp weeks afterwards. The hearing in his right ear had never fully returned and as he'd reached his fifties his hearing seemed to have deteriorated

He'd scowled when his wife Bianca suggested he got a hearing aid. Similarly rejecting her suggestion, he dyed his greying hair. He knew if his hair suddenly went back from mousey grey to the strawberry blond of his youth he'd have every villain between here and Bermondsey laughing behind his back. Doyle couldn't afford to have people regard him as a figure of fun, as someone past it.

He was not a man to cross. Not if you valued the good things in life, like walking, or holding a spoon. Violence, to Doyle was a tool. When things went wrong he used it accordingly. Thirty years of using the right tools, had left him rich, feared and respected in equal measures.

It'd been a long time since he'd been anywhere near any violence carried out in his name. Such instructions passed through numerous levels before they were act-ed on. But these were unusual circumstance. Melvyn Godson was a trusted member of Doyle's inner circle. He'd known him for over 25 years. As a senior bank manager, Godson had laundered millions of pounds of money on Doyle's behalf.

Doyle said "If you can't trust your own bank man-ager, who can you fucking trust?"

Norman 'the Suit' Crawford, shrugged his shoul-ders. Norman 'the Suit' had been with Doyle since school. Age 5 Crawford turned up for his first day at school wearing a suit, his father had stolen, thinking it would do as a school uniform. He'd been known as Norman 'the Suit' since. Norman always wore the finest

Saville Row suits, or the latest cut by Armani. "If you're going to nick a suit, nick a goodun" his dad always said.

Doyle was more casual in his clothing. He dressed down, but well. A £500 hand stitched shirt sent its own message.

Now this. The million pounds, Doyle needed towards his new house purchase, stolen by his own bleeding banker. Moving house was stressful enough. If his wife Bianca discovered the money was missing a lot of expensive crockery would get broken.

The previous day Doyle had ruefully observed to Norman the Suit, that if he ordered someone dead at 9.00 in the morning, it would be done by 2.00 in the afternoon. But could he get the buggers buying his house to get their survey done?

Doyle sat in the cellar, deep below a railway arch, and squinted at the wine catalogue, his long vision was deserting him.

He looked up as one of the men in his organisation approached.

"We don't have any rope," said the man.

Doyle said. "Use something else," returning to the section on Chablis.

"Like what?"

Doyle lowered the catalogue and glared. "There's a hammer and nails over there. Use them."

As he reached the bottom step, Melvyn Godson stumbled, wincing with pain as his ankle twisted beneath him. The men jerked him upright, swearing as they did so, their words muffled by the sack covering his head. He was hot and scared. Half walking, half dragged he went forward and was pushed to the floor. His head snapped back as the sack was removed and the light struck his eyes, making him wince.

A whitewashed cellar, four men. Bernie Doyle, Norman 'the Suit' and two others, he didn't recognize.

"Bernie!" he cried. "What's going on? What's this about?" Doyle ignored him and continued to read. Godson's eyes took in the cover of what Doyle was reading, a picture of a French chateau. He looked at the three men looming impassively over him. He twisted his head from one to another looking for a sign. A hundred-watt bulb blazed from the ceiling.

"You ever had Les Close Grand Cru '64, Melvyn?" asked Doyle, from behind the catalogue.

He looked at the others, appealing for guidance. "Sorry Bernie? I'm not with you."

"It's a Chablis, Melvyn. Expensive. I thought as you'd helped yourself to a million pounds of my money, you might have treated yourself."

Godson felt his arms being grabbed, he was pulled up and backwards, his feet sliding under him as he tried to stand. His back hit something hard and he was dragged onto a flat surface. They pinned his hands down, palm open. He saw the hammer as it fell and screamed in pain as something cut through his skin. He looked as the hammer drove the nail through his flesh, and he rolled his other hand into a fist. He yelped in pain, as his fingers were prised open, the little one breaking in the process. He heard the sound of drumming feet and someone screaming "NO!", and then it all went black.

Doyle stood over the unconscious body of Melvyn Godson, area manager of Allied Scottish Bank. He should have read the signs. Godson had told him he was being shafted over his retirement package. Faced with that, and a rampant desire to keep his hands on the plastic tits of some young slag more interested in the contents of his wallet than his pants, Godson had thought he could get away with stealing from him. Doyle looked at his watch as a train rumbled overhead. He was due to meet Bianca at the estate agents in half an hour.

Godson came around as the water struck his face. He tried to sit up and screamed as the pain from his hands collided in his head. He was nailed to a table! Doyle turned to one of his men, "We got a gag? If he carries on like that he'll be heard all the way to Euston."

"It's alright Bernie, the trains going overhead drown it out."

"So, if we wait till rush hour, we can question him as much as we like!" Doyle turned to Godson. "You're not going anywhere, are you, Melvyn?"

Doyle swam in and out of focus above him. It hurt. It hurt so much. The pain made it difficult to think. Doyle knew! He must. But how? He needed time. If Doyle knew he'd taken the money, he was dead. If Doyle would let him go, for only an hour, he could sort it out. He would get the money from the luggage locker, book it in at the bank and send it offshore. He could blame it on a glitch in the CHAPS system.

"Bernie, your money's in Guernsey. I sent it myself."

"Don't lie to me Melvyn! That young slag of yours was in Bianca's salon, telling everyone you were taking her to Rio!

The stupid bitch! He'd spent thousands on that fucking slag and she'd gone into Bianca Doyle's place and opened her big gob! Still, if that was all the evidence Doyle had…

"I rang Jules in Guernsey," Doyle went on "He's not had the money."

It was looking better. "Bernie, what does that smack head Jules know? I tell you I've sent it."

A look of hesitation crossed Doyle's face. He glanced at his watch again. "I haven't got time for this. Bianca and me are seeing the penthouse in half an hour. If you were taking that little scrubber to Rio, you'd have needed a pot of money. The way you were whinging to me the other day, you didn't have enough to go to Southend."

Doyle saw the fear in Godson's eyes. Was it the look of a man who'd stolen a million or simply of someone nailed to a table?

"Bernie, let me go back to the bank, I can prove it," pleaded Godson.

Doyle looked at Norman 'the Suit', he shrugged his shoulders. "Bianca said she was boasting about flying Club Class," he said.

Doyle said. "Club Class! Get his shoes and socks off and get the blowtorch."

Godson heard the pock and roar as the gas was ignited. He tried to twist round to see what was happening. He felt a rush of air to his feet as his shoes and socks were removed. He shrank back as the blue and orange flame of the blowtorch was waved in front of his face. He couldn't scream; the fear oozed from his stomach consuming him.

Doyle pulled out his mobile phone. "Oh fuck! I can't get a signal. Look, I've got to call Bianca and tell her I'm going to be late. Tickle his toes whilst I'm gone and see what he has to say." Doyle left the room and climbed the stairs into the sunlight. He dialled his wife's mobile,

"Bianca? Yes, I know, but… look… I'm trying to tell ya, if…."

The pain sunk its fangs deep into Godson, tearing at his flesh. "It's in a locker! Please! Please God, help me! Oh Christ! It hurts! It hurts! Please stop! I stole the money! It's in a locker!"

Doyle walked back into the cellar, wincing at the smell of burnt flesh. Godson lay unconscious on the table, his feet black and blistered, the skin of his hands ripped and torn from trying to pull himself free.

"Well?"

"The money's in a luggage locker at Victoria," said Norman 'the Suit'. "He had the key in his pocket."

Doyle looked at the broken body of the bank manager. "Well, my son, it's carpet slippers for you for some time, isn't it?" He turned to Norman "Give me the key, I'll have it couriered over to Michael and he can collect the cash. I need to go. Bianca's giving me a right earful."

"What about him?"

"We may as well finish what we've started. Get the lads to take him down the incinerator."

"It's not working at the moment, Bernie."

"The underpass then."

"Construction finished last week. They still have the grass verges to do?"

"What, and have someone's dog digging him up in a fortnight. It'll have to be the factory then.......... what?" said Doyle, seeing the look on Norman's face.

"Bert's been a bit off about that lately."

"He takes all the poxed up chicken he can get his hands on to stick in his pies, and gets funny at a bit of bank manager?! Tell him not to worry; Melvyn was a vegetarian."

Chapter Five

As Harry and Mandy entered the house, a man wearing a black jacket frisked them. His hand lingered on the inside of Mandy's thigh, but she resisted the urge to knee him in the groin. They were shown into a room where Vincnipovic rose to greet them.

"Michael!" he said reaching his hand out and grasping Harry's, "Bernie Doyle tells me many fine things about you. I'm sure you can sort out this little misunderstanding for me."

Harry looked into Vincnipovic smiling eyes.

Mandy did a double take. A policeman had been gunned down and Vincnipovic was acting as if he'd been caught for speeding. He turned to Mandy and gave her an even bigger smile, "I'm sorry? Officer...?"

"PC Brighton."

"PC Brighton, would you mind if I spoke to my lawyer in private for a moment?"

Mandy looked round hesitantly. She'd been sent in with Harry to stiffen his resolve and bring back intelligence on the layout and number of armed men. She found herself shown into the hall. The man in the black jacket leant against the far wall chewing gun, giving her a leer. Mandy silently counted to ten as she resisted the desire to turn the man's testicles into a hat.

Vincnipovic turned to Harry once they were alone, "Michael, I need you to get rid of all these policemen for me."

"I'm Harry, not Michael."

"What?"

"Harry Trent, I work for Michael." Harry thought it wise to leave out he'd only been doing the job for five hours' half of which he'd spent in a police cell. He also figured words such as 'trainee' were best avoided. Not that he was to telling anyone he was a solicitor!

Vincnipovic looked at him carefully.

"Where is Michael?"

"He was… in a meeting… sends his apologies. But, what can I do to help? What do the Police want to speak to you about?"

"I shot policeman."

"Is he dead?"

"I don't know," Vincnipovic picked up the small machine gun from the table and waved it at Harry. "A two second burst from gun fires 32 bullets. I hit him in head, neck and chest.'" He shrugged his shoulders. "Whether he's dead is not important. As you can see," he waved the gun towards the window, "still plenty policeman left. Would you like some tea?"

The two men sat on a sofa and drank tea. Harry listened as Vincnipovic told him about fly fishing in the Caucasus. After ten minutes Harry glanced at his watch. Vincnipovic noticed and smiled.

"Harry, I'm sorry, you are busy man. To business. Now what do you advise me to do?"

Harry looked at him in bewilderment. The situation was surreal. One minute he was being told Vincnipovic had shot a policeman 32 times, the next they were drinking tea and discussing fishing. Harry saw the expectant look on Vincnipovic face.

"Well... er... you, you said you shot the officer? But you don't know whether you killed him?"

"When I shoot someone, I kill them. Otherwise waste of bullets."

Harry contemplated the contradiction.

"Right." He wondered if he should use the word murder. It didn't sound a good idea to call a man with a machine gun a murderer, but he had to say something and Vincnipovic didn't look that concerned about the killing. He took a sip of the tea, forgetting it was now cold and trying to avoid gagging as it went down.

"They, they could be looking to charge you with murder."

Vincnipovic nodded and looked intently at Harry. Harry had hoped for more of a response. He was out of his depth. He'd never expected his first client to be a gun toting Serbian drug dealer. Or, had that old dosser been his first client? Jesus what a day!

"It's life, if, if they find you guilty.'"

"Life? I didn't think you had death penalty?"

"No. I don't mean they take your life. They send you to prison for life. Well, about 12 years actually. You see... no, thank you..."

As Harry spoke, Vincnipovic sat back and took a silver cigarette case from his pocket. He opened it and offered the case towards Harry. It contained long thin black cigars. Vincnipovic lit one and put it in his mouth. He took a deep draw and exhaled into the air.

"......although they call it life imprisonment, its not," Harry added.

"You can tell them it was self-defence."

"Right"

"In my country, if policeman with gun burst through door, he has come to kill you. So, you shoot him."

Vincnipovic saw the confusion in Harry's face. It was clear he'd been sent the office 'monkey!' He was angry at being treated so dismissively, but he knew to conceal it. This was a situation he could use to his advantage. Harry would be far more malleable than a more streetwise lawyer. It would also amuse him to send this boy and the police on a merry dance. The helicopter might not be there for sometime and it was far better to keep the police reacting to what he did as opposed to planning their next step. "Harry, I have list of demands I want you to take to the police."

Mandy looked around the hallway. Light filtered in from a glass panel above the front door. The paintwork was off-white, heavily marked and scuffed from frequent passage. To her left, a wooden staircase rose to the first floor. Further along the hallway, the light faded as it led to the kitchen door. The man in the black jacket belched and a strong whiff of garlic wafted past her.

"I want to see the women you have here," she said.

Black Jacket shrugged his shoulders and walked towards the kitchen, Mandy followed. A thick fog of cigarette smoke hit her as she entered. Two girls in their late teens, their hair cheaply dyed, sat at a table with a man who was looking at a pornographic magazine. All three were smoking. The man looked up as she entered and said something in Serbian to Black Jacket. He said something back and both men laughed.

"I'm a police officer," said Mandy a note of steel in her voice.

The man reading the porn magazine looked up as he heard the word police. He said something in Serbian and made the gesture of holding a large penis in his hand.

"My friend wants to know if you would like to sit on his truncheon?" said Black Jacket, grinning.

Mandy ignored him and turned to one of the girls. "Do you speak English?" The girl shrugged her shoulders.

"A little."

Harry walked back to the police lines a worried man. Vincnipovic was intent on taking the piss, but to what end, Harry couldn't tell. He thought about ringing the office for help, but feared a further confrontation with Alex Small. He suspected the police wouldn't take kindly to what he was about to say.

The police officers looked at Harry expectantly.

"Where's your client?" demanded Roper.

Harry looked at him blankly. "He's in the house over there.'"

"Why isn't he with you?" demanded Roper through clenched teeth. "Why hasn't he surrendered?". Callan stepped in before Roper exploded.

"Can you tell us what Mr Vincnipovic is planning to do, Harry?"

Harry looked at them in turn, an imploring look in his eyes that said 'this really isn't my fault', "he has some demands," he said.

"Demands!" barked Roper "I'm not listening to this." He stormed off.

"What are they, Harry?" asked Callan quietly.

The demands were quite simple. He had hostages, two young girls and a bank manager from Tooting. The latter's misfortune was to have popped in for a quick bit of relief on his way home, just before the police had struck. If the demands were not met, Vincnipovic would kill his hostages. First, he wanted the release of a Pavel Sislavic. Secondly, the release of all members of the Welsh Liberation Army. Thirdly, he wanted to free Willy, and fourthly, some smoked salmon sandwiches and a bottle of Sancerre. Harry had only mentioned the third with a great deal of reluctance. The police noticed his hesitation and demanded he tell them what he was holding back, but Harry knew he would get no thanks for repeating it.

It took some time for the penny to drop with Roper. He stood with Callan in the control centre while Harry hovered outside.

"And, who is this Willy? Sounds German to me. Are we holding any German terrorists?"

"He's a whale, sir." Said Callan patiently

"A what?"

"A whale. Vincnipovic is making fun of us. *Free Willy* is an old movie about freeing a killer whale."

"So, he wants us to free a whale? What is he, some Eco-nut?"

"No, sir," said Callan more firmly, "he's taking the piss.'"

"Oh. What about this Welsh lot?"

"There isn't a Welsh Liberation Army and even if there were, we don't have any of them in prison. The only possible genuine one is Sislavic and I'm having that checked out. As for the hostages, the girls are hookers. The only genuine hostage is a Philip Robinson. Trent was given

Robinson's wallet; it's got his home address and a picture of him and his kids in it. I'm having the ID confirmed."

"I'm seeing the Chief Constable in the morning," said Roper. Callan said nothing. "We are meeting with the Home Secretary. You do know we have the worst clear up rate in the whole country?"

"I'd heard, sir."

"Well I want this sorted by morning. I've got a civic reception tonight with the Mayor, so I've got to go, but get it sorted." He brushed past Brookes as he entered the van. Brookes raised his eyebrows expectantly.

"Well?".

"We'll go in when it gets dark," said Callan, "make sure we've all got infra-red"

"And till then?"

Callan gave Brookes a thin smile. "He thinks we're a bunch of totals wankers. So, let's not disappoint him. We got the sandwiches and wine yet?"

"I've got some tuna mayonnaise and a warm bottle of Australian white."

Fox picked up Harry in the telescopic sight as he crossed the road. He was sweating profusely; his body felt on fire. Harry popped in and out of vision as the rifle jerked uncontrollably in Fox's trembling hands. He could hear children singing, a school choir singing Jerusalem, but it wasn't the words to Jerusalem, the same tune but different words:

> *"... and so, he took - her panties down - and place his hands up - on - her breasts and then he shagged – oh yes, he shagged – oh yes, he shagged her – roughly....."*

Harry walked slowly towards the house clutching the sandwiches and wine. He didn't know how much more of this he could take. It was bad enough the Serb took him for a total prat without the Police doing the same. They'd even told him they'd been on to an aquarium and were making arrangements about the whale.

Warm blood ran from Fox's bottom lip as he bit into it, straining to steady his aim. All he needed was one clean head shot and Trent was dead. That bastard not only had him kicked out of his home, he'd been shagging his missus!

Harry was reaching for the doorbell as he heard the crack of rifle fire. As he did so, the woodwork above him exploded in a shower of splinters.

Chapter Six

Ron James stood outside the *Holiday Inn,* he glanced at the screwed-up piece of paper taken from his pocket. *Interview: 2.30 pm., Harvey J Weingold III, Utah Gun Prison & Pizza Company.* Ron couldn't fathom what he was doing at a hotel if it was an interview for a job as a prison guard. He reached into his other pocket and removed the remains of a pork pie. Oblivious of the car park sticker attached to it, he rammed the pie into his mouth as his eyes flicked from the paper to the hotel sign. The reassuring taste of pastry and pork fat calmed Ron's nerves as he walked into the hotel's reception. Why someone who suffered from claustrophobia would want to be a prison guard would have been a mystery to most people. Ron however had found the cure; as long as he had a pie to eat, he could keep his fears at bay.

"I'm here to see Mr Weingold" he said with a greasy smile.

"Down the corridor, third door on the left," said the receptionist.

"Thank you." As Ron walked away from the desk, he turned and went back.

"You don't sell pies, do you?"

The receptionist gave him a quizzical look. "Pies?"

"Yes. Pork pies, chicken and mushroom, steak and kidney, or a nice pasty if you have it," said Ron with growing enthusiasm.'

"We've got salmon en croute on our lunchtime Busy Traveller menu."

"No, I'm after a pie, not a croute."

"The salmon en croute comes in pastry."

"I'll take three, please!"

"They're are only available in our Voyager restaurant. I'm afraid lunch has just finished. We start serving dinner at 5.30"

"Oh." Deflated, Ron walked down the corridor and was ushered in to see Harvey Weingold.

A large American came from behind a desk and shook Ron's hand with a warm smile as if he was a long-lost friend. He beckoned Ron to a chair and sat down behind the desk.

"Mr James, my name is Harvey J. Weingold, welcome to the Utah Gun Prison & Pizza Company"

"I like your pizza's."

"I'm pleased to hear that," said Weingold

"Have you thought of doing one with a pork pie topping?"

"Excuse me?"

"You know, pork pies," Ron could see the look of bemusement on his face and decided to change the subject. I picked up one of your job applications in the local pizza place. They said it was closing down?"

"Yes, unfortunately the business model doesn't work for us in this country, we aren't allowed to use the same marketing slogan we use back home. Feed and defend your family."

"Defend?"

"Yes, in the States you get a free gun when you have enough of our pizza points. We tried it with knives in this country, but it wasn't the same and your Government objected anyway. You see Mr James, guns, prisons and pizza makes the perfect combination. Pizza is the ideal food to feed prisoners. It's cheap to make and it's far harder for fat prisoners to escape. Although we do have the occasional problem with some prisoners who get so fat we can't get them out of their cells."

"What about the guns?"

Weingold spread his hands and gave Ron a broad smile. "Everybody needs a gun."

Ron James nodded. His eyes took in the name plate sitting in front of Weingold that announced him to be Harvey J. Weingold III.

"I had a Mark III Cortina once," said Ron, attempting to be funny. He always thought a joke at an interview was a good idea. It seldom worked.

"Excuse me?"

"Your name, Harvey Weingold Mark III. That makes you the latest model, does it?" added Ron, having no idea when to stop.

The American blinked. He'd been in the UK for 24 hours and it was his first visit. Perhaps this was how all Brits acted, but slowly it dawned on him.

"No Mr James, I'm just Harvey J. Weingold the third. I'm named after my father and grandfather."

Ron nodded enthusiastically.

"Mr James, it says on your application form that your last job was as a traffic warden. We don't have traffic wardens in the States, but we do have prison wardens, which is a pretty responsible job. He's the guy who's in charge of the whole prison."

"Yeah, that's right," said Ron, catching on quickly to the American's wholly unexpected line of thinking. "I was in charge of all the traffic... prison section."

The American looked at him quizzically.

"We don't mess around in this country. Anyone caught speeding and we lock them up no messing. I was in charge of all of that."

The American beamed and stretched out his hand. "Welcome to the Utah Gun Prison & Pizza Company. You're just the kind of man we need."

Chapter Seven

Harry jumped backwards, as the bullets struck the door, dropping the wine and sandwiches. The bottle hit the ground erupting in a shower of broken glass and wine that soaked and pebble dashed Harry's trousers. Bending over to examine the damage, he heard a zip and felt a sharp pain as if someone had drawn a hot razor blade across his back as a bullet tore through his jacket and dropped at his feet. Another bounced off the pavement and over Harry's shoulder. Jesus Christ! He was being shot at! Harry hammered on the door and screamed to be let in. Bullets whizzed off the door-way around him and through the window to his left. The shots were answered by automatic gunfire from the house. The door flew open and a blue clad arm shot out and grabbed Harry, throwing him to the hall floor. "Stay down!" barked Mandy, as she kicked the door shut and dived on top of Harry. They both flinched as bullets slammed through the door and into the wood and plasterwork of the walls around them.

Callan dived from the control centre - as the first shots were fired back by the Serbs - and ducked behind a car, a bullet zinging off the side of his helmet. He looked to his left and saw the crouching figure of Brookes.

"What the fuck is going on?" he bellowed in his ear.

"Don't know, someone started shooting."

"Who?"

The two men crouched lower as the car window above them shattered, sending a hail of glass onto their body armour.

Callan pulled the radio from his shoulder. "Cease fire! Cease fire!" he bellowed into it.

Fox stopped firing when he realised he couldn't control his trembling. He threw the gun to one side and began to sob. As the firing subsided around him, he came to his senses. They would know it was him who started it. They would come and take his gun away. He couldn't allow that. Not until he'd killed Trent. He picked up his rifle and kit and scurried across the roof. He needed a new position where he wouldn't be found.

Inside the house was pandemonium. Harry looked out from under the prone body of Mandy as the Serbs ran back and forth waving automatic weapons in the air. He twisted his head round and smiled at her.

"Thanks, I thought I was a gonner for a moment."

Mandy gave him a brief smile back, "I think its time we left," she said.

"I'm not going out there again in a hurry." said Harry, looking towards the front door.

Mandy slid off Harry and got to her feet. He felt a pang of regret. He knew it wasn't the time, but he'd liked the feel of her warm, supple body on top of him. "Let's see if there is a back way out," she whispered.

Mandy squatted by the water butt outside the back door. She looked intently around for any sign of a blue helmet she could signal to. Before she and Harry tried to exit from the rear, she needed to be certain the watching police marksmen knew it was her.

"Have you lost something?"

Mandy looked round into the smiling face of Vincnipovic who was pointing a pistol at her. "Come back inside, please."

Mandy followed him into the kitchen. Harry wasn't there.

"Where is Mr Trent?" she asked.

Vincnipovic grinned. "He is poor lawyer. Perhaps he makes better hostage. Still I keep you as reserve."

Chapter Eight

Stafford looked at the crumpled smiling specimen who sat in front of him. The buttons on his greasy shirt straining to keep his bulging gut from breaking free.

It seemed at the outset a dream job. Twenty years in the prisoner service and continually passed over for Governor. The Utah Gun Prison & Pizza Company had offered him an unbelievable salary, but that was where the good times stopped. It was explained to him by the Executive Vice President succinctly: "John, we're paying you a shit load of money, and for that, we expect you to take a lot of shit." Ron James had been sent to him as his number two. The email from Weingold who was now back in the States had explained that Ron James had run a traffic prison and was just the help he needed. Stafford hadn't a clue what Weingold was talking about until he'd seen Ron's CV.

"So, you were a traffic warden?"

Ron James nodded.

"What's all this crap about you running a prison?"

"It's not my fault, that Yank thought a traffic warden was the same as a prison warden. I tried to tell him."

"Have you got a car?"

"Yes."

"Then get yourself down to the East Cheam depot, we need Prison escorts."

"But, I thought I was going to be an executive".

"And, I thought I would be shagging Claudia Schiffer this evening! So, we were both wrong! Now clear off and don't come into my office covered in pastry again." Ron stood up, hastily brushing the flakes from his last pie on to Stafford's floor. He scurried out at the baleful look he got as a result.

Chapter Nine

Philip Robinson looked up with a start as the door opened. He'd not had a good week. Passed over for promotion, he'd felt like a little cheering up on his way home. How would he explain this?

Harry stumbled into the room and took in the picture of a middle-age, balding man handcuffed to a bed wearing nothing but his vest and one sock.

"I've got my eyes closed, I haven't seen you!" squeaked Robinson, "I haven't seen any one."

Harry looked round as the door shut behind him and the key turned in the lock. He went to the window but could see nothing. He looked over at the tower block opposite the window but couldn't see any Police on it.

"Shit, shit, shit!" muttered Harry to himself. Robinson opened half an eye and squinted at Harry. He took in his suit and age, he didn't look like any of the men he's seen earlier, perhaps he was another punter.

"Excuse me?"

Harry looked up from gnawing his fist, "yes?"

"You couldn't pass me my underpants, could you?"

"Sorry?"

"It's just, err..." his voice trailed off as he pointed at his waist. Harry hunted around on the floor and found a pair of blue boxers and threw them at the man. Robinson struggled into them. "What's going on? Before I can get my socks of all hell breaks lose downstairs, door gets kicked in and then there's shooting and next thing I know I'm handcuffed to the bed." Robinson waved his handcuffed arm in the air. A concerned look came on his face. "You don't think they'll try and charge me for extras, do you? It's normally an extra fiver for handcuffs."

Harry smiled, "I don't think so. Let me see if I can get you free." He walked over to the bed. The metal rail of the bed head ran into a post secured by an Allen key. Harry got his keys out and undid the bolt. He managed to pull the post away and slid the handcuff off the rail. Robinson got to his feet and scrambled into his clothes.

"What do we do now?" he queried.

Fox ran quickly up the flight of steps and headed for the roof. He giggled to himself at the bollocking Brookes would get for not having any one in the building. As he settled down on the roof he could see why. He was now sideways facing the house. There were windows running up the wall showing a staircase, bedroom, and a landing. From this side of the property there was no means of access or escape. He swept the stairwell and bedroom window with his telescopic site and was about to abandon his position when the vested Robinson came into view struggling into his shirt. The sight shot away from the window onto the brick work as Fox's arms began to shake and his vision blur. He stood up and head butted the wall in a desperate attempt to clear his vision. He let out a howl as his head struck the brickwork. He reached up with his hands and brought them away from his forehead, shaking and sticky with blood. His legs slowly buckled underneath him and he subsided onto the ground sobbing, "I only want to kill him."

Harry looked round the room blissfully unaware of Fox's whereabouts or intentions. His eyes took in the gold fish bowl standing on the chest of drawers. A solitary fish swimming round in surprising clean water. He picked up the bowl and gave it to Robinson.

"Stand behind the door, I'm going to try and get one of them into the room and then you hit him over the head with the bowl."

Robinson nodded enthusiastically. He stood, all 5' 6" of him, behind the door as Harry began to kick it and scream blue murder. It was unfortunate that Pytor Dagilivic was 6' 3" tall. As he entered the room to Harry's summons, Robinson leapt up behind him, realising as he did so that without the aid of a step ladder, he was never going to reach his head. All he succeeded in doing was throwing the bowl of water and gold fish over Dagilivic's back. Harry hadn't worked out a plan B. As Dagilivic turned snarling on Robinson and the poor goldfish slithered down the inside of his shirt, Harry leapt on the man's back and grabbed him by the ears. Dagilivic let out a scream of invective, reaching behind him and grabbed Harry.

Two steel pincers began to crush the bones in Harry's arms as he and Dagilivic swung round and round, Dagilivic trying to shake Harry lose. Robinson hovered to one side clutching the empty goldfish bowl. Under Harry's weight Dagilivic was bent over. As the two of them tottered towards the bed, Robinson leapt onto it and brought the bowl crashing down onto Dagilivic's head. It stunned him more than knocked him out, but as he staggered forward his head struck the iron bedpost and he went down. Harry catapulted over Dagilivic's head and ended up in a tangled heap with Robinson.

The two men ran into the corridor as Vincnipovic and Black Jacket came up the stairs with Mandy held at pistol point. Vincnipovic took in the scene and grinned. He pointed his pistol at Robinson and shot him. Then, he turned his gun towards Harry.

The trembling in Fox's hands slowly subsided. He wiped the blood from his face and settled down besides his rifle. Its sight swept across the side of the house and took in the window. He saw Harry's head, but as he squeezed the trigger a man in a black jacket got in his way. He fired two shots in quick succession.

Black Jacket screamed as the first bullet tore through his shoulder, and the second bullet struck the light fitting over Vincnipovic's head, showering him in broken glass. He let out a low growl. "Move!" he shouted to Mandy, shoving her forward. "Finish him!" he yelled to Black Jacket, who was too busy writhing on the floor to shoot anyone. Harry dived back into the bedroom as bullets tore up the floor, ceiling, and walls around him.

As the gun fire subsided, Harry took in the carnage. Robinson lay in an oozing pool of crimson, his skin a chalky white. Black Jacket lay moaning on the floor.

On the roof, Fox was oblivious to the clicking noise his rifle was making, the magazine now empty.

Harry looked up and down the corridor, which was suddenly silent. He took the phone from his pocket and considered ringing the office. But, what should he say? What about Brighton? Mandy? Yes, he was sure he'd heard the PC called Mandy. She hadn't told him her first name, but she'd saved his life; he couldn't just leave her. He saw the gun lying on the floor next to the now unconscious Black Jacket. He picked it up and ran after Mandy.

"Oh fuck!" Callan looked up at the sky as the helicopter hovered over the roof of the house. He was tempted to tell his men to shoot it down, but was well aware of the devastation that would be caused by a helicopter crashing into a residential suburb. He spoke urgently into his radio. "Hold your fire!" he barked, "No one shoot at the helicopter or anywhere near it. I repeat no one shoot at the helicopter. If it crashes, we are all done for."

The thundering sound of the rotor blades filled Mandy's ears, her copper hair blowing back and forth from the helicopters downdraft. She stood on the roof with Vincnipovic. He raised his pistol and pointed it at her forehead. Should he kill her? He took a moment for one more appreciative look at her lean athletic body. He was not an animal. He gestured for her to sit as Harry emerged on the roof, the roar from the helicopter now no more than 50 feet above.

Harry saw Mandy kneel and Vincnipovic pointing the gun. It looked like he was about to execute her.

The sound of the helicopter revived Fox. He slammed another magazine into his rife giggling as he did so. He swept the roof opposite with his telescopic sight. TRENT! – IT WAS TRENT! –FUCK – WHERE'S HE GONE?

Fox needed greater elevation; he looked round, a chimney. He scrambled to the top of it oblivious of the 80 foot drop that lay behind. Precariously he took up position. *There was Trent, he could see him, breath him, his sight traversed Trent's body, head? Bollocks? Head? Bollocks?* 'I'm going to shoot his bollocks off' he softly groaned to himself.

Harry had never fired a gun in his life. Copying what he'd seen on TV, he held it at arms length and fired at Vincnipovic. The Law Society probably had some rule about him shooting clients. He doubted after today though, that he had much of a future as a solicitor. The bullet went wide of Vincnipovic by several inches, demolishing a chimney pot. Vincnipovic turned and fired back, causing Harry to duck. The bullet shot past and flew through the air striking Fox in the foot.

A wasp had bitten his toe? Fox looked down; a bright red pool of blood was oozing over the top of his boot. As he lifted his foot to examine the damage, the laws of physics kicked in and Fox tumbled backwards off the roof. He was still trying to grab the toe as his body struck the ground. He lay there momentarily twitching as the LSD had one final race round his system, before it leaked out with the rest of his blood in to a scarlet halo around him.

The helicopter came lower and as the rope ladder bobbed across the roof towards him, Vincnipovic grabbed it and began to climb.

Mandy took her opportunity and, jumping to her feet, leapt onto the ladder below him. The helicopter lurched downwards under the extra weight causing the pilot to instinctively take the helicopter upwards. Vincnipovic, surprised by the sudden movement, lost his footing and found himself hanging from the ladder by his hands. He could feel the presence of Mandy below, as he scrambled to get his feet back on a rung. He shouted to the men in the helicopter to shoot her, but they were more concerned about hitting him. A bullet grazed Mandy's knuckles. She let out a yelp and let go with her injured hand. The helicopter bucked and swayed, dragging Mandy across the roof top. She grimly held on with her other hand as the pilot struggled to keep control. Harry dived towards Mandy and grabbed her - as her grip loosened and she fell - pulling her on to the roof. He felt the roof slate slipping beneath him. Vincnipovic was pulled up by waiting hands into the safety of the cockpit, but almost fell out again when a sudden gust of side wind hit the chopper.

Mandy lay gasping for breath on the roof as Vincnipovic's men struggled to pull him back into the cabin. Harry started to feel fresh air beneath his feet. He let out a yell as he fell backwards. The rope ladder of the helicopter swung in front of his eyes and with a final grab, Harry fingers tightened round the bottom rung. The helicopter shot into the sky with Harry clinging on to its rope ladder for grim life.

Harry looked down at the ground rapidly disappeared below. He swayed wildly from the bottom of the ladder, the pain in his fingers slowly eating away at his grip.

As the helicopter swept across the London sky, Callan screamed into his phone for air support.

The force of the wind tore into Harry's face and body, slowly his fingers slipped from the rung and down he fell. If this was death, then it felt quite tranquil. He could hear the roar of the air in his ears. His muscles gently relaxed. By the time, he hit the cold dirty water of the Thames, Harry was feeling quite chilled out.

Chapter Ten

"Victor, this meat you bought, all the tins are labelled in funny writing."

"What do you mean?" snapped Victor Davis into his car phone. "Get out of the way, you stupid bitch!" Victor yanked on the brakes and skidded to a halt in front of the zebra crossing as the Lollypop lady showed the children across.

"Ron says it's Russian," said the voice at the other end.

"Well, Ivan's Russian."

"And, there's a picture of an army tank on the tin. Who puts a tank on tins of dog food?"

"That's because its not bleedin' dog food, is it, Einstein. These are ex-Red Army rations. Ivan tells me he's got 20 million tins of the stuff; we're going to make a fortune! All we got to do is re-label it and get it down the warehouse."

"Some of the tins are a bit rusty, and we found a newspaper in one of the crates which was almost 40 years old."

"So?"

"Don't you think some of this stuff is a bit past it's sell by date?"

"Bollocks! That Commie crap lasts forever."

"So, what label should I use? The Super Chunky or the Super Chunky Deluxe?"

Victor hesitated, could he describe 40-year-old Russian combat rations as a deluxe dog food? Perhaps not. "Better make it the Super Chunky," he said, viciously honking at the Lollypop lady. As he roared off, he looked mildly shocked at her two-finger retort.

Victor glanced anxiously at his watch; it was almost 4:00 PM. His sister Jane would arrive at 4:30, so that gave him half an hour to hunt for the will. Edith Davis was the widow of Don 'Doggie' Davis, the dog food magnate. Victor had run the business for the last 10 years on the understanding that on his aunt's death, he would inherit it. Three weeks ago, he'd found her surrounded by pictures of donkeys, she animatedly told him how wonderful it would be if they could have some nice new stables and blankets, and how she planned to leave them most of her money.

Victor was horrified. After 10 years of scheming and plotting he wasn't about to lose it all to a donkey! As far as he was concerned, the best place for a donkey was in a tin. He needed to find the will. If it named him as the main beneficiary, fine, but if everything now went to the donkeys, it would disappear.

He parked his car in the lane at the rear of his aunt's house and went through the garden gate. At this time of day, she was normally taking a nap. He put his hand on the knob of the back door and pushed. Nothing happened. He tried again and the door opened a fraction. Something heavy was lying against the other side. Victor put his shoulder against the door and heaved. It opened a crack allowing him to insert his head. He glanced down and saw a blue slippered foot leading to a stockinged leg.

Victor went around to the kitchen window and peered in. Edith Davis sat slumped on the kitchen floor, her body resting against the door. He swore under his breath. How was he supposed to get into the house? The old woman was losing it, why she'd chose to sleep on the kitchen floor was beyond him. It didn't occur to Victor that his aunt might not be lying there out of choice, but could be in need of medical help. If Victor had been asked, he would have said it was nothing to do with him where his aunt chose to sleep, except when it stopped him getting into the house. As for calling an ambulance, he had more important things to do. He looked at his watch, it was ten past four. He had 20 minutes.

Victor had one more go at the door, it wouldn't budge. He walked round to the back of the house and found an open window. Victor swung a leg across the window sill.

He breathed in as his stomach became wedged against the window frame. His legs dangling either side of the window, he had no real purchase. He tried pushing with his arms, but was stuck. The sweat rolled down Victor's face as he heaved and grunted in the window frame. Finally, to the sound of ripping trousers, he propelled himself into the room, landing in a tray of cat litter as he did so. Panting, he got to his feet and examined his torn trousers covered in cat litter. Snarling, he walked into the hall. He glanced at the kitchen door. Should he go and see if anything was wrong with his aunt? He looked at his watch and the state of his suit. No, he fucking shouldn't, it was 4:20! He had ten minutes.

He went into the study and began rifling her desk - where was the will? - it had so many hidey holes. He picked up a sheaf of letters and looked through them. His eyes shot to the silver and black letter head of Clancy Burns Solicitors. It was a letter from Michael Burns saying he would call to see her to discuss the will. But had he? He turned to another letter with a picture of a donkey on it.

>*Dear Mrs Davis,*
>>*Thank you for your generous gift...*

Victor made a gargled noise and grasped the side of the bureau for support. Oh god! It was true; the bloody donkeys had got it all. But, hang on, she wasn't dead. He read on *...of five thousand pounds.*

Silly old bitch! He heard a car on the drive. It was his bloody sister Jane! She was early! Victor stood holding the letter, gripped by indecision. It wouldn't look good if he was found searching the desk. The door bell rang. How would he explain his car not being on the drive? Victor bolted into the kitchen. He would go out the back door and into the garden. He skidded to a halt in front of his aunt blocking the door. He bent to grab her arms and drag her out of the way.

"Hello auntie, its Jane. Are you there?" It was his sister calling through the letter box.

"Eeeerhhhh." Victor looked down. His aunt groaned as she awoke.

Victor stood with his arms around the waist of his waking aunt, the sound of his sister at the front door getting louder. What should he do?

Edith Davis hadn't collapsed or fallen. Her unconscious state was the result of two sleeping tablets and three large brandies. She'd gone into the kitchen and, feeling tired, sat on the floor and fallen asleep. As Edith began to wake, she felt Victor's arms around her. It was many years since she'd been held by a man. Thoughts of her early years with her husband Don flooded back, "Oh, Don" she muttered softly.

Victor heard the sound of a key turning in the front door, his aunt kept one under a flower pot, what should he do? Victor panicked. He dragged his aunt into the pantry and closed the door.

"Auntie? It's me, Jane, are you there?"

Victor stood in the darkness, his aunt propped against his legs. What was he playing at? He realised he should have brazened it out, but now he'd dragged his aunt into the pantry he was sunk. He would have to stay there until Jane left. He heard her footsteps leave the kitchen and could hear her calling from another part of the house.

"Oh Don! Don! Take me!" babbled his aunt. Desperately he looked around in the dark for something he could gag her with. He stepped back, startled as he felt something touch his leg. Oh God! she was caressing it He tried to back away, but the pantry narrowed, there was no room to retreat. He was trapped. Trapped in a pantry with this aged hag who was pawing at his leg and using language he'd only heard on the late-night porn channel. He was going to be sick.

The unmistakable zzzzzzpppppp sound of his flies being undone was more than Victor could bear. He didn't care if Jane found him. He wasn't staying in the pantry at any price.

Chapter Eleven

Ray Mace tapped his pin number into the key pad and the entrance door to the East Cheam holding centre of the Utah Gun Prison & Pizza Company swung open. It was the most profitable unit of the UK operation and Mace had been sent to find out the secret of their success.

In the main holding area, Colin Stubbins and Tony Lockwood were trying to inject a prisoner with Ketamine, oblivious that the drug was a horse tranquiliser. They'd been told it was a sedative for prisoners who might prove troublesome during transport. As guards were often expected to transport prisoners, in their own car, they had no hesitation in giving it to anyone who so much as coughed when he shouldn't.

James 'Tiger' McGivens had been through their hands before. There was no doubt he would cause trouble, given half a chance. Lockwood had spent half an hour looking for a bigger syringe so they could inject an extra-large dose of the Ketamine into him. He'd discussed with Stubbins going home and borrowing his wife's icing gun. Stubbins pointed out that they would never get the needle to fit in the end and the average icing gun wasn't sharp enough to pierce human skin.

Although Tiger McGivens was quite partial to the out-of-body experience you got when taking ketamine, he objected on a point of principle to having screws sedate him. Although no legal genius, even the few remaining amphetamine soaked brain cells in his head told him that there was something illegal in what was going on. More to the point, he was scared of needles. This coming from a man whose body was so scarred from knife fights he was know as Tiger was something of a contradiction.

"You're not sticking that in me!" said Tiger.

"Come on Tiger, don't misbehave," said Lockwood.

Mace was walking into the holding area as he saw Stubbins approach Tiger from behind with the baseball bat while Lockwood distracted him with the needle. The first blow from the bat struck Tiger on the head. He looked bemused and rubbed the top ot his head as if he felt rain. Mace looked on in horror as the next blow to Tigers kidney sent him crashing to his knees. Lockwood had now picked up a pickaxe handle and the two men rained blows down on to Tiger until he fell unconscious to the floor.

"What the fuck have you done?" screamed Mace. "You've killed him!"

Both men looked up at Mace in surprise at his outburst

"It's Tiger," said Stubbins by way of explanation, a look of puzzlement on his face.

Mace took in the 'what is your problem look?' stencilled across both men's faces. They clearly saw nothing wrong in what they'd done.

Mace was in no mood to treat this as if someone had broken the office teapot. "You've broken his fucking skull!"

"Not him," said Lockwood. He looked across at Stubbins who nodded in agreement.

"What do you mean?" queried Mace, bemused by the men's lack of concern or guilt over what had occurred. He knew violence happened in the prison system, but normally there would be denial or an allegation the prisoner started it.

"Tough as old boots. It never hurts him," said Stubbins, picking up a cup of tea and dunking a digestive in it.

"You've done this before?" asked Mace, his eyes flicking between the comforting site of a dunked digestive and the prone figure on the floor.

"Oh yeah," said Lockwood, the tone of his voice having change from bewilderment to reassurance. "We done it lots of times. It don't hurt him. He's a tough old bastard, Tiger."

"Don't like needles though," mumbled Stubbins through a mouthful of biscuit. Lockwood nodded in agreement and held out the packet of digestive biscuits to Mace. He waved them away.

"No, thank you. What are you trying to inject him with?"

"A needle," said Lockwood ramming another biscuit into his mouth.

"I can see that. What's in the syringe?"

Lockwood looked to Stubbins for guidance. Stubbins picked up the syringe and peered at it in the hope it would help. The name of the German manufacturer was printed on the side, but Stubbins was fairly sure the contents were called something different. However, he was in charge of the injection, having done a St Johns Ambulance course, and didn't want to appear ignorant. "We're giving him a Muller," he said.

"A Muller?" queried Mace. "What does a Muller do?"

"Makes 'em sleepy," butted in Lockwood, keen to show that Stubbins wasn't the sole font of medical knowledge.

"Sleepy? What for?"

"You got to sedate them before you put them in the car. Company policy," said Lockwood. Stubbins nodded his head in vigorous support.

"Car? There's a van for transporting prisoners."

"What van?" asked a puzzled Lockwood

"Where's Johnson?" demanded Mace his patience finally snapping.

"In his office."

Mace strode towards Johnson's office leaving the two men to debate whether the ketamine was still necessary

"Is he unconscious?" asked Lockwood looking down at Tiger's body.

"Dunno. Give him a kick and see if he starts growling."

Lockwood's boot lashed twice into Tigers side, but he gave off no sound. "He's not moving. Let's give him the stuff to be on the safe side."

"Alright. We need to find a vein."

"What's a vein?"

Johnson was busily admiring the topless model on page 3 of his newspaper and wondering if he could persuade his Linda to have a boob job when Mace burst into his office.

"What the fuck is going on?" demanded Mace.

"What?" said a startled Johnson dropping his paper. "Who are you?"

"I'm from head office. I'm here to do the audit. I've just seen two of your men beat some sod senseless so they can inject him with a tranquiliser."

"Yeah, Tiger always puts up a bit of a struggle."

Mace couldn't believe what he was hearing. So much for it being the most cost effective unit the company had, it was run by a bunch of psychopaths. Head office would go ballistic when they found out. Mace struggled to keep his voice under control. "Why do you need to tranquilise him?"

"I'm not putting a prisoner in one of my men's cars without him being sedated."

"Car! We have a van for transporting prisoners. A large van. The local prison screamed blue murder when they had to hand it over after we won the contract."

"We sold it."

"Sold it! Sold it! Who to?"

"East Molsey prison."

"East Molsey. We're tendering for the transport contract for that prison."

"That's right, so we'll get the van back."

"So, you are now getting prisoners moved around in private cars?"

"Yes. We give them a quick shot first and they're no trouble."

"All the prisoners?"

"Only the ones likely to cause trouble."

"How do you decide that?"

"Well, anyone who objects to being jabbed with a needle I suppose."

"What are you giving them?"

"Depends what I can get my hands on. We used to take most of it off the prisoners. You know, I thought we'd be a bit environmental, do some of that recycling people always go on about. Trouble was we gave some bloke an ecstasy tablet the other week and it all went a bit pear shaped. So, I tend to use one of those date rape drugs or ketamine. I got a mate works in a stables. They use it to sedate the horses."

"But… we don't have a doctor."

"Stubbins is qualified. He's been on one of those first aid courses," Johnson sat back in his chair and started to relax. He could see Mace had run out of steam.

"What? The St Johns Ambulance course on how to inject horse tranquiliser into violent prisoners?"

"I'm only following head office policy."

"Policy?"

"Yes. The manual states that we can move prisoners in private motor vehicles where appropriate and there is little risk they will try and escape. Since they aren't going to wake up for 12 hours, it's not a problem, is it? Anyway, the van cost a fortune to run. And, we make the men use their own cars, so I've slashed our transport budget to zero saved the company thousands."

"Do all your men have cars?"

"They do now. We got rid of Jenkins as he only had a moped. Prisoners kept falling off the back of it. Difficult to hang on when you're sleeping."

Chapter Twelve

It had been a week since Victor Davis's aunt had grabbed his penis in the pantry. He still shuddered when he thought of it. There'd been a difficult telephone conversation with Jane who'd asked f he'd been to the house. Victor begun to burble when Jane recounted Edith's claim Victor had dragged her into the pantry and ravished her. Jane was worried her aunt was having such bizarre fantasies and wanted to know if Victor thought they should have Edith examined by a psychiatrist.

Victor vowed not to get himself in such a situation again and decided to confront his aunt over the will. She hadn't answered the door and Victor let himself in with the key that this time he'd remembered about.

He'd found her lying on the floor of the study and, after seeing the empty brandy glass, he'd started going through her desk. He only noticed the blood when he stepped in it.

The fact Edith Davis lay in a pool of blood didn't mean she was dead, or, seriously hurt. Victor Davis stopped, one foot either side of her prone body. Fuck! Even he wasn't that obtuse. It was unlikely an 80-year-old woman who lay bleeding on the floor was merely taking a nap.

Having said that, he'd been here before.   His eye then caught the red smear on the corner of the desk. Obviously soused again she'd hit her head as she'd fallen to the ground. *Fuck, fuck fuck! where was the will?*

He heard a car on the drive, Jane. Victor dropped the papers on the bureau and closed it. He stepped over the body and headed for the door, as his hand reached for the door knob, he stopped. Calm down Victor, think. He didn't have the will. Could he steer Jane away from the room and pretend his aunt was okay? Should he be found leaning over her looking anxious? He turned and looked at the fallen body. A small stream of blood had trickled under an arm chair, was it there before? Victor didn't like blood. He would head out into the garden and pretend he'd been having a smoke.

Shit! Jane's key in the door.

He couldn't walk out now- she would see him. He turned around and gnawed at the remaining finger nail he'd been saving. Taking a deep breath Victor went over to his aunt. He hopped hesitantly from foot to foot, trying to take a position which Jane would regard as compassionate, but didn't involve him standing in any blood.

As Jane entered the house, she heard Victor talking in low tones. This was not his usual manner. All she could see was his broad back, he was leaning over something.

"Victor? What are you........?" her voice trailed off as she saw Victor was stroking their aunt's back.

"There, there, Aunty, you'll be alright," crooned Victor.

Jane dropped her handbag and pushed past her brother. She looked down at the prone figure on the ground and the blood-soaked carpet.

"Victor! What's happened?"

Victor looked furtive - he always did - and said nothing.

"VICTOR!"

"Its auntie… she's had an accident."

"I can see that. When did it happen? Have you called an ambulance?"

"I just…"

"Call one now! The phone is in the hall."

"Right."

Victor walked into the hallway. He took out his mobile phone. No reception. An old Bakelite phone sat on a table with a dial no less! He looked back towards the door and wondered if Jane would be able to hear him. He picked up the receiver and dialled the number which took an age.

"Thank you for calling Clancy Burns…"

"Hello, put me through to Michael," he whispered.

"…if you know the extension number you are ringing dial it now. If not, then please listen to the following six options…" Victor's fingers tightened round the receiver, wishing it was the throat of the person who had invented option calling.

Michael Burns had a large office overlooking a garden square. His desk took up one end of the room, while Harry sat at a rather smaller desk pushed into a far corner. He'd been pulled from the Thames by a passing barge and found his face plastered across the newspapers. A television crew captured him saving Mandy from falling from the roof and his subsequent flight hanging from the bottom of the helicopter. Alex Small and Suzy collected him from casualty. Small milking the press for all he could, saying what a fine credit Harry was to the firm. Harry was given the rest of the week off to recover from his ordeal. He arrived for work the following Monday for what would only be his second day. He'd been shown to his desk in Michael's office, whom he was still to meet. After some ten minutes of sitting and twiddling his thumbs and wondering for the hundredth time what ever compelled him to be a lawyer, he became bored and decided to nose around Michael's desk.

It was littered with yachting and car magazines, not a legal document in sight. He was glancing through a copy of *'What Ferrari?'* when the phone rang. As he reached for it, Harry knocked a mug of cold coffee over sending a stream of it across the desk. Cursing under his breath and mopping up the mess with his hanky, he picked up the phone.

"Hello?"

"Michael!" whispered a voice. "It's Victor. She's had a fall! I think she's dead!" Harry recoiled at the breathless excitement in the voice. "Have you got the will?"

"Michael isn't here."

"Have you got the will? – YES, I'M JUST CALLING THE AMBULANCE!"

"We're solicitors. You've dialled the wrong number if you need an ambulance."

"Sod the fucking ambulance! That was Jane. Look, aunties had a fall. She's unconscious and bleeding. I've told Jane I'm ringing for an ambulance, but before I do, I need to know if she's signed the will?"

Harry was dumb struck. What do you say to a man more concerned about his inheritance than the fact his aunt is lying in a pool of blood?

"I… I don't know."

"What the fuck do you mean 'You don't know!!!!??'"

"Victor! Why are you swearing at the ambulance people?" a woman's voice said in the background. "You heartless bastard! You haven't rung them, have you!? Give me the phone." Harry heard the sound of a struggle then the woman's voice came on the line.

"Hello! Who is this?" she demanded.

"Harry Trent, Michael Burns' assistant." She let out a howl. A series of thuds and bangs followed. Someone was hitting the telephone receiver against something hard. From the accompanying screams of "No! Jane, stop it. You'll break the phone!" it sounded like Jane was attacking Victor with it. The line went dead.

Harry replaced the receiver as Michael Burns walked into the room. "Hello Harry," he said. "Sorry I wasn't here to greet you. Problem with the Porsche." Michael Burns- tall, lean, tanned and a Hollywood smile.

"I've just had someone called Victor on the phone. His aunt is dying and he wants to know if you have her will." The tan faded. Michael reached over the desk and pushed the intercom button.

"Suzy, where's the Davis will?"

"I don't know, Michael."

"Well, haven't you typed it?"

"No." The tan faded from French Riviera to a sunny day in Bognor.

"Give me a hand will you, Harry? I must have something about the will on my desk - somewhere. What's happened here?" queried Michael lifting a sodden magazine.

"Sorry, small accident." Harry could feel the coffee from the soaking hanky he'd put back in his pocket slowly dripping down his leg.

They looked through the attendance notes, magazines and pieces of scribbled on paper that covered his desk. Harry's eye finally caught the name 'Victor' scrawled over a naked bottom adorning a hi-fi catalogue. The note said; 'Victor the lot' with the words 'the lot' heavily underlined. He showed it to Michael.

"Well done, Harry." Michael pushed the button on the intercom again. "Suzy, I need a will straight away on the Davis file. We'll be the executors and the old love is leaving everything to Victor. Usual terms, and do a bill for fifteen hundred"

Michael turned to Harry, "Do you like hospitals, Harry?"

The smell of antiseptic and boiled cabbage hit Harry as he entered the hospital. He followed the signs to intensive care. Twenty minutes later, Harry found himself back in reception. His second attempt was more successful. "I'm looking for Mrs Davis," he said to the young nurse behind the desk. She looked up, pushing a lock of hair under her cap.

"Your grandmother is through there, she pointed. Room six." It didn't seem the time to argue. "Amy, can you take Mrs Davis' grandson through."

Harry followed the pink uniform and black tights through the swing doors.

The room held the echo of a long-forgotten party; tubes hung from the ceiling like faded streamers - pumping life in and out of its occupant - while green lights flickered across monitors recording the final moments of her life. Victor Davis, paced back and forth, alternating his gaze between his watch and the bed. Jane Davis hovered next to it, clutching a handkerchief.

"Mrs. Davis' grandson is here," said the nurse, hurrying from the room when she saw the reaction her statement had provoked. Harry was clearly the black sheep of the family.

"Who the fuck are you?" snarled Victor.

"Victor!" exclaimed Jane.

"What?"

"Aunty."

"She can't hear anything. Well, who the......?" He glanced at Jane, her scowl causing him to stop. "Look, Barbara never had any kids. So, who the effin' hell are you?" he asked, specks of white foam, dancing around his lips.

"I'm Harry Trent. Michael Burns sent me." Victor's face lit up and a large sweaty hand grasped Harry's.

"Magic! I'm Victor Davis. This is Jane," he said, dismissively. "You're just in time." Jane curled her lip and turned away. Victor grabbed Harry by the elbow and dragged him to the bed.

Harry looked at the face of Edith Davis, grey skin stretched tightly over a skull, a beard of soft downy hair around her sunken mouth. He looked up at Victor, his eyes expectant.

"She seems to be.... dead?" said Harry. BANG! Light the blue touch paper and retire a safe distance.

Victor went off like a rocket, Harry's head cannoned into the wall as he threw him against it.

"WHAT DO YOU MEAN SHE'S DEAD?!" he cried. Victor grabbed the lapels of Harry's jacket and slammed him back against the wall, his head ricocheting of it. "SHE ISN'T DEAD! DO YOU UNDERSTAND!" he bellowed. His hands grabbed Harry by the throat. Harry kicked him in the shins, causing Victor to spin Harry round and lose his balance. They crashed to the floor Victor on top, his large bulk knocking the air from Harry's body. As he gasped for breath, Victor tried to wring what little breath remained from him. A strong sense of déjà vu hit Harry as his second client tried to kill him.

"Victor!" screamed Jane. BONG! "GET OFF HIM!!" BONG! As Harry and Victor wrestled on the floor, Jane struck Victor around the head and shoulders with a bedpan. They rolled towards the bed; Harry's face becoming enveloped in a plastic bag half-full of wee. His nose was pushed into it, causing the sides to balloon. The blows to Victor made him loosen his grip and he seemed content with grinding Harry's head into the ground. All Harry could see was murky yellow pee.

"YOU BASTARD!" yelled Jane. There was a sound like an axe splitting wood. The pressure on Harry's face relaxed and he heard a slow shuffle as Victor toppled backwards.

Harry looked up at Jane holding the bedpan and breathing heavily. It was severely dented and smeared with blood.

Chapter Thirteen

Jane Davis had a pretty face when she smiled. "Will he be all right?" she asked.

"The doctor said it's mild concussion," replied Harry.

The medical staff finally cottoned on that all was not well after Jane knocked Victor out. A heated discussion followed in which a semi-conscious Victor accused Jane of trying to murder him and Harry of impersonating a grandson. They dragged Victor from the room screaming, "She hasn't signed the will!"

Harry and Jane sat looking at the still body of Edith Davis.

"Pity. I've wanted to do that for years. He won't be so quick to patronise me in future. That's the second time I've hit him today."

"Yes, I heard you attack him with the telephone."

"Oh, that was you." Her smile grew broader. "I've spent years with dad and then Victor saying how useless I was. People tell you that for long enough and you believe it. I never knew I could get so angry. But, when I discovered Victor was ringing you instead of for the ambulance, I got so mad. He won't think I'm useless now... do you think they'll let me keep the bedpan?"

Alan Bentley saw the sign for intensive care. Should he go there? He looked down the corridor, he wasn't going back that way! Alan pushed his hands deep into the pockets of his white coat and felt for something comforting to hold. They came away empty. He felt the stethoscope, hanging from his neck and let out a deep sigh. He didn't want to be a doctor. If only he could be at home with his stamp collection.

The door behind him burst open, and a nurse rushed through.

"Oh, er… excuse me, could you…?"

She was gone. It had been the same all morning. Chaos reigned as doctors fresh from medical school began their supervised year. Supervision was not always what it should be. If it were, there wouldn't have been the incident with the enema or the sunburn diagnosed as leprosy. The General Medical Council had refused to register him.

Normally he would have been thrown out, but his mother was determined he would be a doctor. Her cousin was a junior minister in the Government. 'Strings were pulled'. Alan tried to rebel, but his mother threatened to flush his stamp collection down the toilet. The thought of his prize Penny Black whizzing round the U-bend was more than he could bear. He would try again. They'd known he was coming. Nobody wanted him. He'd spent the morning being screamed at by doctors and nurses, going from one department to the next, arriving late for each presentation and being screamed at again and ordered on his way. Enough was enough. He would go home, wait until nightfall and smuggle his stamp collection out of the house.

Victor Davis was another man at breaking point. A nurse had bandaged his head and left him to cool his heels in matron's office. After twenty minutes, he tired of waiting and walked into the corridor, a gnawing pain at the back of his eyes. He would get the will signed if it killed him. He winced- the way he felt, it probably would. He reached up with his hand and ran it tenderly over the plaster that held the dressing in place, stars danced in front of his eyes. He saw the white coat as his vision cleared. A doctor. That's what he needed. Someone who could make auntie better so she could sign the will. He lurched down the corridor towards Alan Bentley.

"Excuse me, doctor?" said Victor.

Alan turned to the bruised and battered Victor. "Are you OK? Do you need a doctor?

"No." Victor touched the top of his head self-consciously. He grimaced a smile, "Bit of an accident. Jane gets excitable sometimes."

"I see," said Alan. Victor looked at him expectantly. Alan said nothing.

"Women," said Victor.

"Women," parroted Alan.

"It's my aunt. Could you come and look at her, please?"

"I'll go and find you a doctor."

"Aren't you a doctor?"

"Well, yes, but…"

"I only want you to have a quick look. She's in here. It won't take a moment."

Alan shrugged his shoulders. Why not. It couldn't do any harm just to look at a patient. He followed Victor into the intensive care unit.

Harry glanced at his watch. The morning was getting on.

"No need to wait on my account," said Jane.

He looked up slightly embarrassed. "I'll give it five minutes and then call Michael." Although, what he was waiting for he didn't know. Okay, a doctor had come in and said she wasn't dead, but the chances of her regaining consciousness were slim. Harry wasn't keen on renewing his acquaintance with Victor Davis, but he figured it wouldn't look good if he went back to Michael with another failure. Michael had been instructed to prepare the will for the last two months and done nothing about it. If Edith died without signing, things would become unpleasant.

"I've found a doctor to look at auntie," proclaimed Victor as he came into the room.

They stood round the body expectantly. The minutes ticked by. Finally, Victor spoke. "Well doc? How is she?"

Alan looked at the old woman. He screwed up his eyes hoping for inspiration. She looked dead. He didn't think such a diagnosis would go down well. *Think! Think! Come on, you must remember some medical training. A pulse! Yes! See if she has a pulse.* He lifted up her arm and placed two fingers on the parchment like skin. The veins bulged outwards, kept in place by a scintilla of flesh. *There was the faint flutter of a pulse.*

"She's got a pulse. It's not much, but I can still feel it," he said.

Beeeeeeeeeeeeeeeeeeeeeeeep!

They all looked round as the flashing green monitor emitted a high-pitched wail. Harry had seen enough hospital soaps to know this meant trouble.

"Doc! What's happening!?" screamed Victor.

"She's..." he mumbled. A nurse ran into the room and dragged the doctor over to the monitor. Heated whispers followed.

Victor began to hyperventilate. "The will..." he gasped, collapsing on the floor. Jane looked at him, a mixture of contempt and sorrow in her eyes. She emptied her handbag and put it over Victor's face. Harry edged towards the doctor and nurse and listened into their conversation.

"Who the hell are you?"

"I'm one of the new intake."

"I might have known!" The nurse picked up a lead and plugged it back into the back of the monitor. The sound stopped and she left the room.

Victor lifted his head from Jane's handbag and clambered to his feet. The doctor was feeling Mrs Davis pulse again.

"It's all right Mr Davis, your aunt is still with us," he said reassuringly.

"You've saved her life doc! It's a miracle."

Alan gave a brief smile.

"Can you wake her up now?" Asked Victor.

"I'm sorry?" said Alan his smile crumbling away.

"Can you wake her up? We need her to sign the will," said Victor. Jane snorted in derision and left the room. Uncertainty clouded Alan's face.

"Mr Davis, your aunt is seriously ill."

"I know, that's why we need her to sign the will.

"I'll come back tomorrow then," Harry mumbled.

Victor grabbed him by the shoulder. "Nobody is going anywhere until she signs the will." Harry glanced at Alan, they exchanged a look of despair. "What does that do?" asked Victor, pointing to a crash cart.

"It's a defibrillator". Said Alan. "We use it when the heart stops beating."

"What, like jump-starting a car?"

"Something, like that."

"Does it bring them round?"

"Sometimes."

"Give her a bit of that then!"

"Mr Davis! I must protest! The shock could kill her."

"She's going to die anyway, so what's the odds?"

"No, I'm sorry. I have to go now," he said, edging towards the door.

Victor barred his path. "Not so fast doc. We're conducting some serious legal business here." He poked him in the chest with his forefinger. "You're obstructing the course of justice." POKE. "You can go to jail for that." POKE "Isn't, that right?" he said, turning to Harry.

"Well, obstructing the course of justice is an offence, but..." Harry replied hesitantly.

"Do you hear what my solicitor's saying?" snarled Victor. "You're going to prison!"

Alan threw Harry a hunted look. This was getting out of hand, thought Harry. He wondered if he should get Jane and her bedpan.

"Mr. Davis," said Harry, one eye on the scene and the other on the door.

"You're going to be struck off!" jeered Victor. He backed Alan into the corner of the room. The pokes in the chest turning to sharp jabs. Harry could hear the scuffling of his shoes against the wall as he tried to back through it.

"Mr Davis!" said Harry in a louder tone.

Victor ignored him, feeding on the fear that oozed out of Alan.

"So, what's it to be, doc?" demanded Victor.

Alan's head flopped forward in submission. "OK," he whimpered.

Wearily, he pushed the crash cart to the bed. Victor smiled in satisfaction. He held out his hand and Harry gave him the will. With a flourish, he took a pen from his pocket. He nodded at Alan to begin. He put the twin paddles on Edith's chest.

"Stand clear" he muttered weakly.

The machine made a whining noise followed by a "CATAAM". Edith's body shuddered on the bed. Victor looked on and Harry closed his eyes hoping it was all a bad dream. When he opened them, Alan was applying the paddles again. This time her body jerked upright, saliva dribbling from the corner of her mouth. She had a distant stare, her eyes wide and glassy like those of a cooked fish. Victor grabbed her claw like hand and thrust the pen into it. He moved it across the page of the will, signing her name and then looked at Harry.

"Her signature needs witnessing," mumbled Harry his mind numbed by the horror show he'd become part of. Victor gave the will to Alan, who scribbled his name on it, and then to Harry, who did likewise. Victor snatched the will from his hand and looked lovingly at it.

"Yeeees!" he whispered, lifting the will to his mouth and kissing it.

Jane entered the room. Victor quickly folded the will and put it in his pocket. "Aunty has signed her will, you will be pleased to know," he said as he left.

Jane came over to the bed and gently lowered her aunt back down.

Chapter Fourteen

Harry dozed fitfully at his desk. He'd not slept well, his dreams filled with visions of elderly bed-ridden fish offering to leave him all their money if he didn't put them in the frying pan. The previous day Harry had told Michael what happened at the hospital. He'd been concerned until it became clear Harry was the only witness.

"What about the doctor?" asked Harry.

"Not really going to be in his interests for this to come out, is it?" said Michael with a knowing smile.

"But Michael, it's not legal is it, if she's dead?" said Harry.

"Legal can be a very difficult word, Harry. At Clancy Burns we try and avoid using it."

Michael's voice floated towards him. "Harry, can you see Ben and Tim for me?"

"Who?"

"Ben and Tim, they're nephews of Lord Farrington of Farrington Industries. I was supposed to see them at 11.00 to discuss the formation of a company. Something to do with trees. Their uncle's a good client, so they need looking after. I've just got the chance to test drive the new S-class Mercedes. So, could you see them for me?"

"Sure."

"Be a tad careful. They've both recently come out of some high-class loony bin after burning their old school down. Something to do with an obsession for fire engines."

He saw the concern in Harry's eyes. "Don't worry. If they cause any problems, Suzy will sort them out. She's met them before."

Ben and Tim Farrington were both six feet tall, boyish looking but slightly gaunt. They wore identical dog-eared Barbour coats that looked like they'd been slept in. Wendy, the firm's receptionist was being chatted up, as Harry walked into reception to meet them.

"Harry," simpered Wendy. "This is Ben Farrington and his cousin Tim."

"Harry, thank you for taking the time to see us," said Ben. He gripped Harry's hand and gave him a radiant smile. They walked up the stairs to Michael's office and sat down.

"How can I help?" asked Harry.

"It's Grandpa Joe's trust fund," said Ben. "In order to qualify for our share, Tim and I must have a job when we turn 25. It's my birthday in a fortnight and Tim's in about six months."

"I see," said Harry, not seeing anything at all. Were they hoping Michael would give them a job?

"Uncle Maurice suggested we form a company and go to," said Tim, miming quotation marks with his fingers, "'work' for it. Apparently, he did the same thing in '62 and the lawyers didn't bat an eyelid."

"We think that's a tad dishonest, though," said Ben. "And Tim's got a great idea. Have a look at this, Harry," he said, excitedly.

Harry had wondered why they were carrying a double bass around with them. Ben opened the case to reveal an enormous chainsaw. The blade had more teeth than Jaws. As Harry looked at their beaming faces, the penny rolled across his head and dropped into his brain. He was alone with two mad men and a chainsaw.

The muddy brown waters of the Thames lapped gently against the side of Falcon View Heights. Bernie Doyle stood on the terrace of the penthouse flat and looked out at the sprawling mass of London. Fucking poncy name for a block of flats, he thought. He could hear the oohs and aahs of his wife Bianca coming from inside, coupled with the warm oily voice of the estate agent as he explained the latest benefits of Swedish kitchen design. Christ, it sounded like the silly cow was having an orgasm!

The staccato of her heels crossing the wooden decking of the terrace made Bernie turn around. Bianca Doyle had been *Golden Thighs of the Month* in 1994.

22 years later, she could still wear the skin-tight jeans she'd been ever ready to climb out of in the nineties. A broad smile spread across her face, her latest set of breasts heaving and straining against the leather bodice, which fought to keep them in place as she bubbled with excitement.

"Oh Bernie!" she purred. "Its lovely, we've got to have it!"

The estate agent stood in the doorway, his eyes tracking every sway of Bianca's leather clad buttocks as she sashayed towards Bernie. He looked up momentarily and shivered as he met the stare of Bernie Doyle. Doyle glanced over the edge of the railing and back at him. The estate agent gulped as the image of being thrown over the balcony flashed in front of his eyes. Bernie saw the agent had got the message and allowed a smile to cross his lips. The agent almost collapsed in relief.

"Very nice. How much is it again?"

"£3,999,500."

Bernie turned and looked back over the balcony. Four million quid for a flat! What would his old man have said? Most he ever had was the two hundred quid he'd won on the pools. Poor old sod thought he was a millionaire. Sweated his bollocks off in that tanning factory for 50 years from the age of 10. What did he have to show for it in the end? A two up two down council house with no bathroom and an outside loo.

Not for Bernie. He left school at 14 and went around breaking up snooker clubs until they paid him to stay away. He'd taken a few cars early on but that was a mugs game. Armed robbery was where real money could be made in the Eighties and early Nineties Then in to a bit of property, prostitution, protection, drugs, a couple of clubs and now, at 55, he was a self-made man. A respectable businessman. From up here he felt at the top of the world. Down below his empire, stretched from his brothels in Dartford to the casino in the West End.

Bernie turned to face Bianca and the agent, both had an expectant look on their faces.

"Yeah, we'll take it." Bernie's face split into a broad grin. He couldn't help himself. He'd made it. He'd arrived!

Harry looked into the grinning faces of Ben and Tim and back to the wicked looking teeth of the chain saw. "Very nice," he said, a hesitant smile on his face. Harry's gaze crept towards the door as he considered making a run for it.

"Would you like some chutney?" said Tim.

Harry turned his head back, and looked at Tim who was now holding a jar towards him. "Sorry?"

"Chutney. Lime and coriander." Tim handed Harry the jar and proceeded to take a small case from his pocket from which he extracted a silver spoon.

"Here you go," he said, handing Harry the spoon.

It was not every day Harry was offered chutney by a lunatic with a chainsaw. He stared nervously from one to the other of them.

"I think we're frightening Harry, Tim." said Ben. "It's OK, Harry. Dr Schultz said we were completely cured."

"Oh, good."

"Suzy!" shouted Tim. Michael's secretary came into the room.

"Hello boys. Oh! You've got some more of that lovely chutney with you. Let's have a taste." She grabbed the spoon and jar from Harry's hands, and perched herself on the corner of the desk. "Lovely," she said taking a spoonful. "I hope you two are being nice to Harry?"

"Harry thinks we're mad," said Ben.

"And dangerous," added Tim. "You haven't met Alice have you Suze?" said Tim pointing to the chainsaw.

"Too bloody true. You're a right pair of nutters. What on earth are you doing with that thing?"

"We're going to become tree surgeons."

"And, what do you know about trees?"

"Not much. But Ma's got lots of friends with big gardens and lots of trees where we can practise," Ben replied.

"Is the Golden Tandoori still open?" asked Tim.

"Why?" asked Suzy, suspicion creeping into her voice.

"I'm dying for a curry."

"Do you know what time Michael's due back, Harry?" asked Suzy.

"What?" mumbled Harry trying to make sense of what was going on.

"Where has Michael gone?"

"Oh, he's gone to… road test a car."

"Good. He won't be back for hours. I can take an early lunch and go for a curry with the boys. Do you want to come Harry?"

"Eeeer?"

"Harry, if you are going to be our solicitor then the consumption of large amounts of curry is essential," said Ben. "Besides, we're paying."

"It's all right Harry," Suzy whispered in his ear. "They are quite harmless, except when it comes to choosing other people's curry."

Chapter Fifteen

Ron James looked nervously at the sleeping prisoner in his car. "When's he going to wake up?" he asked. Lockwood turned to Stubbins for guidance.

"Won't be for ages yet." Said Stubbins.

Ron got into the car next to the sleeping Tiger McGivens who was handcuffed to the door. Gingerly he closed his door and started the engine, glancing anxiously at McGivens as he did so. Ron's car drove slowly out of the Croydon holding centre and headed for the magistrates' court.

Mandy Brighton stirred the spoon in her coffee. She was due to give evidence in a shoplifting case which should have started an hour ago. She finished the coffee and wandered back towards the courtroom. The barrister who was prosecuting came towards her. "PC Brighton, I know it's not your job, but there seems to be some problem in finding the accused. Would you mind going down to the cells and seeing what you can do?"

Ron parked his car next to a large white prison van which dwarfed his Vauxhall Astra. He turned and looked at the sleeping McGivens. No one had told him what to do if the prisoner was still sleeping when he got to court. The obvious answer was to wake him up. McGivens was twice Ron's size and he didn't fancy doing it without some help.

Ron showed his pass and was let into the holding area. A large warder sat behind a desk busily ignoring him. Ron coughed and the man looked up.

"Yes?"

"I'm from the Utah Gun Prison & Pizza Company. I've got a prisoner outside."

"Well, bring him in then. He might catch cold if you leave him outside. Or escape! Haven't they taught you bunch of useless nurks anything?"

"That's why I need a hand. He's handcuffed to my car door at the moment, but he's a bit large. He's called McGivens."

At the mention of the name McGivens, the warder rose and followed Ron outside. The car was empty. McGivens and the inside panel complete with door handle to which he'd been handcuffed were gone. The warder raced back inside and pressed the alarm.

Harry Trent was leaving one of the holding cells as the alarm went off. "Excuse me officer, what's happening?"

Mandy Brighton turned "Oh... hello," said Harry, "how... how are you?"

"Mr Trent..."

"Please, call me Harry."

"Harry, you should go back upstairs. We've got a prisoner on the loose. It could be dangerous." Mandy turned to go

"Can I....... see you again sometime" said Harry to her departing back, but she didn't hear and hurried on her way. Harry headed for the exit. It was locked. He poked his head into the office to the left and saw a fat man in a uniform that seemed to be made from bin liners anxiously searching for something.

"Excuse me can you let me out?" asked Harry. Ron James ignored him and went on with his frantic hunt. Harry went into the office and repeated his request, Ron looked up.

"Sorry, I've lost something, half a tick."

Harry looked at his watch. He hadn't realised the time. He was due in court with Dave Squirrel in 10 minutes. After the previous fiasco, he had no wish to be late. "I've been told to leave because of the escaped prisoner."

Ron halted in his tracks. "Escaped prisoner? Who told you?"

"The alarm," said Harry pointing to the flashing red light on the wall.

"It's Tiger... he's got my car door. You haven't seen a pie, have you?"

Harry didn't know how to respond. His mind trying to come to grips with tigers, car doors and pies. He saw a pork pie sitting on a pile of files and held it up. Ron's eyes sparkled as he grabbed the pie and forced half of it into his mouth.

"Marvellous," he spluttered through a mouthful of flying pastry.

Tiger McGivens was unsure where he was. The sound of the alarm bell was magnified ten times by the ketamine which was busily disagreeing with the remains of the ecstasy in his system. He'd woken in the car and easily ripped out the plastic door panel he was handcuffed to. Holding the trim, he'd run into one prison warder who he head-butted and then escaped into the warren of cells that ran below Croydon Magistrates' Court. Although the alarm was intended to alert all personnel that a prisoner was loose, the biggest contingent of guards' present belonged to another private security company. Upon being asked to join the hunt, they said they weren't allowed to pursue escaped prisoners they were not contracted to carry without a full health and safety assessment first and locked themselves in one of their vans. This left two HM Prison Warders, Mandy and Ron.

Harry looked in amazement at the speed with which Ron devoured the porkpie. Ron gave him a greasy smile. "That was close. Thought I was a gonna then."

Harry looked at him questioningly.

"I suffer from claustrophobia. The pies help keep it in check."

"You're a security guard and you suffer from claustrophobia?"

Ron tapped the end of his nose. "Best keep it quiet."

"Right, can you let me out?"

Ron shook his head "Sorry mate. I don't know how to". Further discussion was prevented by a growl and a cry of "Let me out you fucking maggot or I'll fucking kill you!" Ron let out a whimper and retreated further into the room. Harry turned and saw a large man with a shaved head clutching the internal panel of a car door. Tiger went to enter the room but found the plastic panel he was holding was wider than the door. He stepped back and dropped the panel but was only able to enter the room as far as the end of the length of his arm and the handcuffs.

Tiger stepped back into the corridor and ran into the room. As his arm and the chain became taut he crashed to the floor in a torrent of expletives.

The sound of Tiger's swearing and the smashing of the plastic door into the wall brought Mandy running. At this moment, the two cells in Tiger's brain sat down for a chat and it occurred to him that if he held the panel sideways he could get into the room. He charged in and grabbed Harry by the lapels of his jacket. "Keys!" he barked.

Tiger could hear his own voice, which had slowed down like a tape stuck in a machine and become muffled as his vision turned green. He heard a distorted voice behind him and winced as he felt a pain in his kidneys. He ignored it and tightened his grip on Harry. The second blow Mandy delivered to his kidneys had more of an effect. This was coupled with the large spider Tiger saw crawling out of Harry's face. The drugs in his body were now causing him to hallucinate – Tiger hated spiders- he let out an almost girl-like scream and collapsed to the floor.

Harry staggered back and looked into the face of the baton wielding Mandy. "That was close," he said with a grin. "He could have got really hurt if you hadn't intervened."

A shadow of a smile flitted across Mandy's face. She quickly cuffed Tiger and handed him over to the two prison officers who appeared now that the drama was over. They left the room with Ron scuttling after them clutching the prisoner release form, which neither officer showed any inclination to sign.

Mandy and Harry stood in the sudden silence, neither knowing what to say nor wanting to leave. Was he smirking or smiling at her? She wasn't sure. Mandy had been thinking about Harry since the siege. He had saved her from falling off the roof and wanted to thank him. Shift changes and exasperation at getting through the call waiting system at Clancy Burns had prevented her.

"Can I buy you a coffee?" asked Harry.

"Thanks. That would be nice."

Chapter Sixteen

The office was the size of a tennis court. On the right-hand wall hung a large oil painting of the founder Don "Doggy" Davis. Victor sat at the far end of the room, feet on the desk, a cigar almost as big as his ego clamped between his teeth.

"Where's Michael?" he asked, looking up at the ceiling as Harry entered the room. That was a good question. Harry received a call from Suzy as he climbed out of the taxi in front of what was now Victor's factory to be told he would be late and would Harry start without him.

"He sends his apologies and will join us later."

Victor grunted. "I needed to see you anyway. You know Jane is challenging the will?"

Harry had heard about it. Dr Bentley, racked with guilt after his 'Bride of Frankenstein' performance, had gone to see Jane and confessed all.

"Some bollocks about the will being invalid because Auntie was dead when she signed it."

"Oh, well..."

"WELL FUCKING WHAT!" screamed Victor leaping to his feet, froth gathering around his mouth. Harry had been down this road before, and he was on Victor's territory. There was no way he was going to say the 'D word'.

"...we will just have to fight it." Harry glanced towards the door.

"Yeah, yeah," said Victor pacing back and forth like a caged tiger. "There was nothing wrong with her, was there? She was as bright as a button."

A vision of the cold grey skin and glassy eyes flashed before Harry's eyes. "She was fine," he gulped.

"You'll testify, won't you?" he said looking directly at Harry for the first time. Harry hoped his look of guilt would be taken for agreement.

The cigar bobbed up and down in Victor's mouth as he chewed it. "It was that doctor. He should never have given her those electric shocks."

"No.... he shouldn't"

Victors face brightened. He pushed the long strands of hair back into place over his baldhead and sat down. He nodded to a chair. Harry perched nervously on its edge.

The phone rang. Victor glared at it and pushed the loudspeaker button

"YES?"

"It's Mr Jenks from the council," came a voice through the speaker. "They want to come tomorrow."

Harry didn't know you could go purple so quickly. Victor let out a strangled noise and picked up the receiver. "Put him through. ALFIE! ALFIE! WHAT THE FUCK IS

GOING ON? YOU AREN'T SUPPOSED TO COME TILL NEXT MONTH!" Victor's knuckles turned white as they strangled the receiver. The voice at the other end tried to calm him down.

"What do you mean he won't take the money? He's not bent! Alfie, everyone is bent. WELL, YOU'LL JUST HAVE TO GIVE HIM SOME OF YOURS WON'T YOU." He slammed the phone down, his face fading to a gentle puce. "Fucking health inspectors!"

Harry smiled lamely

"Read this." He threw a letter across the desk, it was from a firm of solicitors.

> *Dear Sirs*
>
> *We've been consulted by Mrs Marianne Wheatley, who instructs us she bought a tin of Poochie dog food manufactured by you...*

Harry looked up at Victor. "I thought you just made biscuits?"

"I diversified. Met this bloke called Yip in Bangkok and he put me on to this source of cheap meat that we ship in." Harry read on.

> *...on Wednesday of last week. On feeding the food to her dog, Trixie Bell Ya Ya IX, the animal began to choke. Mrs*

> *Wheatley was able to remove the of-*
> *fending item from the dog's throat and*
> *found it to be part of a dog collar. On*
> *further examination of the tin's contents,*
> *she found the remains of the collar and*
> *a name-tag bearing the name Trixie*
> *Bell Ya Ya VIII. Apart from being best*
> *of breed for two years running at Crufts,*
> *Trixie Bell Ya Ya VIII was also the mother*
> *of Trixie…*

The letter went on for several pages with frequent refer-ences to cannibalism, Oedipus and the very expensive medical treatment Mrs Wheatley was undergoing as the result of having fed her own dog to her own dog.

Harry put the letter down. "Well?" demanded Victor.

"They're threatening to sue you for five million pounds."

"I can read! I need a lawyer, not a fucking optician!"

"Is it true?"

"What?"

"That you stuck Trixie Bell Ya Ya in a can of dog food?"

"It's all bollocks! I get all my dog from Korea."

"So, you make your dog food out of dogs?"

"Yeah. That's what it says on the tin doesn't it."

They sat in silence for a moment. The remnants of Victor's cigar hovered on his bottom lip. He made a strange gargling noise as he tried to avoid swallowing the burning end. Almost failing in his efforts, he lapped greedily from a glass of water on his desk and then spoke from between singed lips.

"Look, I met someone in a lap dancing bar up West. Yip isn't always reliable with his shipments and this bloke said he could help me out. He works for the council and is responsible for rounding up stray dogs and sometimes those not so stray if you get my meaning. Apparently, he used to do a lot of business selling mince to butcher shops, but after all that food hygiene bollocks things tightened up. You can get a lot of meat off a St Bernard."

And thus, poor old Trixie had ended her days on a supermarket shelf.

"I want you to go to Thailand," said Victor. "Yip is willing to swear all the affidavits you need that I get all my dog from him."

"But that's not true, is it?" said Harry naively.

"Are you my bleedin' lawyer or not? And, I also want you to sue those fuckers who installed my mincing machine. They guaranteed it would mash up anything I put in it."

Chapter Seventeen

Red
Amber
Green
Amber
and back to Red.

The roar of the horns became muted as the lights turned back to red.

Amber
Green

BEEEEEEPPP!!! Smiling George sat behind the steering wheel, mesmerised by the changing lights, oblivious to the roaring tide of noise that surrounded him. Apart from his love of driving and fixing engines, little penetrated the silent world that his 30-year-old mind inhabited

"What's going on?" asked Tim, looking up from the stained and tattered Good Curry guide sitting on his lap.

"Dunno. Someone must have broken down," replied Ben. They were four cars back in the queue behind the black Mercedes driven by Smiling George. Tim looked at his watch, they'd twenty minutes to get to the Pride of India. If they sat down to eat before 7:00, the food was half price. Not an opportunity to be missed by two men whose appetite for curry was often larger than their bank balance.

"Come ON! Come ON!" screamed Simon Lawson as he again pressed the horn of his Land Rover Discovery. "Right!" he growled leaping from the car and striding towards the Mercedes that blocked his progress.

In the back of it, Bianca Doyle slowly came awake from where she had been dozing, woken by the growing noise from outside. "Georgie? What's going on?" she asked, her mind foggy from the mix of alcohol and pills taken earlier in the day.

"Pretty lights." Bianca let out a groan. Her brother's habit of sitting and watching traffic lights change had caused problems before.

"Oh George, not now baby, please! Let's just go home." As George's hand reached for the handbrake, his door flew open and a large hand grabbed his jacket. He looked up into the raging face of Lawson, the smile, for which George had received his nickname, fixed as ever across his face.

"You think this is funny do you!" shouted Lawson. He grabbed George with both hands and dragged him from the car throwing him against its side. George could not react, his mind trapped in its separate world. The crooked grin across his lips, like so many times before, seen as a taunt and not the trauma of birth that it was. Lawson's fist crashed into the side of George's chin, rocking his head backwards. The second blow ruptured the veins around his gums and tore the tooth from its root, expelling it from his mouth. Bianca shrieked as the blood splattered across her window.

The fists flew into his body, which flopped right and left under their impact. Bianca tried to open her car door, desperate to help her baby brother, but the weight of his body being flung back against it defeated her. She grabbed her handbag scrambling through it for her mobile phone as the car rocked under the impact of George's body.

"You can't make Mung Dal Na Poora without using turmeric."

"Can't see it adds anything replied" Tim, his eyes scanning the section on Curry houses in Kentish Town. "We moving yet?"

"No, seems like a fight has broken out."

George's body slammed back into the car blood pouring from a cut to his ear.

"Well, what are you going to do about it?" asked Tim.

SLAP the hand ricocheted of the side of George's face.

"Me?"

BANG the knuckles drove into George's nose.

"Ben we're going to miss the seven o'clock menu."

RIP the heavy signet ring tore through the flesh above George's eyebrow.

"Alright, alright, I'll see what I can do. Ben climbed wearily from the van. "Oh Christ!" Tim you'd better come with, I think this is a two-man job- and bring Alice."

"Okay, okay, I told you we should have gone the other way." Tim grabbed the case containing the chain saw and trotted after his cousin

Lawson stood back panting, his hands bloody and sore from their vicious assault. George swayed against the car his jacket trapped in the door as Bianca tried to open it. His left eye was puffed and closed, blood streamed from half a dozen wounds. Lawson couldn't believe the fucker still had the balls to smile at him. He was about to renew his assault when he felt the tap on his shoulder. He turned and saw the broad smile on Tim's face. Another fucker who thought it was funny. He raised his fist, Tim ducked and Lawson hit the double bass case that Ben was holding. Lawson let out a yelp followed by another as Tim trod heavily on his instep. As Tim moved aside Ben drove the bottom of the case into Lawson's kneecap and he went down.

"Ben, he's still moving!" shouted Tim. Lawson rolled on the ground clutching his kneecap and swearing profusely. Ben held the top of the case in his two hands and swung the side of it into Lawson's head as hard as he could. Lawson subsided into an unconscious heap on the ground.

Bianca burst from the far door of the car "GEORGIE!" she shrieked.

Chapter Eighteen

Harry was leaning against the bar of the White Lion when Mandy entered. She wore a faded denim jacket, white jeans and a close fitting black top that stopped just short of a pierced navel. She smiled as they made eye contact and walked towards him. The coffee had been a long one and they agreed to meet again

"Hello Harry," she said. She lent in and kissed him lightly on the cheek. "How are you?"

He'd been thinking a lot about Mandy and received some strange looks when he dropped her name into the middle of a conversation. Suzy demanded all the details when Harry asked for some 'Mandy's" to put in his stapler.

He brought her a drink and they found a table.

"I hear you've met Ben and Tim?" she said.

"The Farringtons?"

"Yes, they're good friends of mine."

"Really?"

"What? I don't look like the kind of bird who has posh friends?"

"No, I didn't mean…" Harry felt a trickle of sweat run down his back as Mandy's eyes burned in to him.

"I don't need this, Harry." She was half way to the door before he could stop her.

"Hang on a minute." She shrugged his hand off her shoulder. "Mandy, please. My foot doesn't live permanently in my mouth you know."

Mandy smiled. "Sorry, I'm just a bit uptight."

They sat down and sipped their drinks in silence. Harry kept silent whilst he tried to think of something that wouldn't cause further offence. Mandy tried to bring her temper under control and not see offence where none was intended.

"They're clients," said Harry hesitantly.

"Who are?"

"Ben and Tim Farrington?"

"Why are you staring at me like that, Harry?"

"Am I?"

"Yes."

"Sorry."

"Do you say 'sorry' a lot, Harry?"

"Yes, I mean no... that is..."

"Have a drink Harry."

He drank. The nutty brown liquid flowed smoothly down his throat. Was that amusement in her eyes at his babbling or something else?

"So how long have you been in the police?"

"About 2 years... but not for much longer." Harry raised a quizzical eyebrow.

"It's all a bit of a joke, and I'm fed up being the butt of it. I'm handing in my notice…. So, would you like to have sex?"

Harry choked, as a mouthful of beer went down the wrong way. "That would be nice," he croaked.

As they lay back in the candlelight, Harry slowly savoured the Rioja Mandy had poured for them. In the flicker of light, Harry's eyes slowly surveyed the warm, moist body that lay next to him- a body which minutes before had been tightly rapped round him as they'd enjoyed hot and torrid sex. Sex? Not love? Could something that intense be love he wondered? There hands and mouths had avidly explored each others bodies. Mandy had flicked a switch that he didn't know existed and he had rewarded her kindly for it. It was a fine line between pleasure and pain, and they had danced along its edges. Freed from any normal constraints, they had pleasured each other until they were both fully sated.

"What are you thinking about?"

"Oh, that you're a natural red head."

She giggled, "Was that all?"

"Well, that and whether I'll ever have the energy or the nerve to do that again."

"Oh, I'm sure you will. You can't take me into that kind of 'sweet shop' and not let me go back for a second helping. I tell you what, I'll make you one of my special omelettes so you can get your strength back and then you can have me for desert."

He followed her naked into the kitchen. Her firm breasts slightly swaying as she beat the eggs.

"You mentioned in the pub leaving the police?"

"Yeah, it's full of wankers."

"Lucky for me."

She turned and swatted at his penis with the wooden spoon she was using. "Watch it, mister. They don't all play with their own truncheons."

Mandy turned and leant against the counter oblivious to the egg that was now dripping from the spoon onto the top of her thigh.

"I could live with that, but it's just as if they don't care. Roper's the worst, its all about appearances with him, getting convictions. Whether we've got the right person or even if they committed the crime, doesn't seem to matter. It's all about clear up rates. We had one guy admit to 143 burglaries last week half of which had been committed while he was in the Army based abroad."

"So, why did you join?"

"All I ever wanted to do was help people, stop the bad guys."

"You won't achieve that by leaving."

"Don't know."

"My old granddad used to say if you want the trains to run on time don't give up driving the engine."

"Your old granddad! What else did he say then?"

"He always taught me never to waste food," said Harry kneeling down in front of Mandy, "have you seen where that egg is going?" his tongue snaking towards her.

Chapter Nineteen

A thick layer of Brylcream kept Arthur Bytheway's hair permanently plastered to his head. He tapped the end of a pipe between the gap in the front of his teeth. He wasn't allowed to smoke it in the office anymore but claimed that sucking it was better than nothing at all. "So, Michael's got you acting for Bernie Doyle on his new house?" Harry nodded. Arthur sucked on the end of his pipe. "Have you met him yet?"

"No."

"Interesting man, our Bernie. He will happily sit and talk to you about which vineyards you should visit for the best Bordeaux. He also employs a man called Billy the Blow Torch. Rumour has it that some bank manager got greedy and tried to make off with some of Bernie's money. Bernie nailed him to a table and Billy roasted his feet to find out where the money was."

Harry gulped. "So, I get to act for someone who nails people to tables."

"Well, I don't think he does it personally anymore. He has Norman the Suit to do that sort of stuff these days. No, outside these four walls and those of Paddington nick, he's a respectable businessman."

"Who's Norman the Suit?"

"A tale for another day my lad, it's almost lunch time, let's go for a pint." Arthur and Harry left his office and walked through reception.

"Harry?"

Harry turned. It was Michael Burns. He had with him a barrel of a man, five foot seven, short powerful arms and a face that said, 'peel me a wasp, I'm feeling hungry.'

"Glad I caught you. This is Bernie Doyle. Bernie, I'd like you to meet one of our rising stars Harry Trent."

"Oh, the lad from the helicopter."

Harry nodded bashfully.

"That was a brave thing, my son."

"Harry's a real asset to the firm, he's helping me with the purchase of your penthouse."

"Nice to meet you, Harry. So, you're the one who's going to sort out the new place for Bianca and me?" A large hairy hand shot out and grabbed Harry's, shaking it up and down like a dog with a rat in its mouth. He pulled Harry closer "This house is very important to my Bianca. We want to get in it as quick as possible. So, don't let anyone take any liberties."

"No Mr. Doyle, I won't."

"Call me Bernie. Come on Michael, let's go for lunch." He gave Harry's hand a final squeeze. "Remember- no liberties"

Harry and Arthur watched them leave, "I think you've earned that pint now," murmured Arthur.

They sat in the bar of the Dog and Sixpence. Arthur drank half of his pint, Harry took a couple of sips from his and looked around. It was an old-fashioned place with red velour seats, the bar and surrounds were done in the dark brown wood he only tended to see in his grandparent's house. It was obviously a favourite haunt of Clancy Burns; two or three tables being occupied by people he vaguely recognised from the office. Harry lifted his pint from the beaten brass table and took another swig. A barmaid came over and placed plates bursting with chips and burger in front of them. Arthur spotted a token lettuce leaf lurking under the corner of his chips. He sniffed, pulled out the leaf and put it on the side of the table.

"You having another?" asked Arthur. Harry looked at the glass in his hand; his was three quarters full.

"I'm fine for now, thanks." Arthur went to the bar and returned with another pint. He sat and took a large bite from his burger; licking the tomato sauce and grease, which oozed out of its sides from his hands.

"So, what do you think of it so far?" he asked.

"Good burger," said Harry through a mouthful. Arthur raised his eyes towards the ceiling.

"The law lad, Clancy Burns, our Mickey."

"Mickey?"

"Michael, your new principal. I call him Mickey sometimes to wind him up."

"He doesn't like it then?"

"Oh no, he's very much Michael." Arthur took a large swig from his glass.

Harry's mind replayed recent events.

"It's a little different from what I imagined."

Arthur pushed his empty plate to one side and got his pipe out. He reached for the wallet of tobacco in his pocket and scowled as he remembered he was no longer allowed to light up inside.

"Well, getting yourself arrested on the first day didn't help. Mind, that stunt you pulled with the helicopter put you back in good favour" he added with a grin. "Then, what have you had to deal with; that maggot Victor Davis, those barm' pots the Farrington's and, now Bernie Doyle. Michael doesn't believe in breaking you in gently does he? Not his style. If there's shit to be shovelled, Michael is always the last one to reach for a spade."

"Is it always like this?"

"Most of the time. It's the kind of clients Michael attracts. He doesn't mind if they're mad, bad or just a total pain in the arse, as long as they've got enough money to keep him in hand made shoes and flash motors. Michael might be a total arsehole, but he employs some good lawyers and knows how to make money. I had an old client say to me the other day that coming to Clancy Burns was like going to a VD clinic. Useful thing to have, but you don't want anyone to see you coming out the front door."

Norman 'the Suit' looked on in bemusement as Bianca Doyle chopped the fruit and put it in the blender. He lifted the mug of tea to his lips and took another sip. It wasn't making his stomach feel any better. Norman hated flying. The thought of 14 hours on a plane, even in first class, filled him with dread.

"What's it called?"

"Bermuda Honeymoon Surprise, it's very good for you Normie, you should try some."

Norman wondered which he hated more. Fresh fruit or being called Normie. He couldn't see the point in fruit. If he was hungry, he had his dinner or brought a Mars bar. You could leave half a Mars in the glove box and come back and eat it the following week, fruit just went rotten.

"If you get the chance, pop into Disneyland and get one of those big Mickey Mouse's. Our Theresa's just had another, and it would make a nice present."

"I don't think they have them in South America."

"I thought they had them all over America."

"It's a different country."

"Oh. Why's this not working?" Bianca's long taloned finger pushed the switch of the blender in and out. Norman stood up and plugged the blender into the wall. The contents whirred into a bright red frenzy as Bernie Doyle walked into the room.

"Bleedin' Ada, it's the man from Del Monte," chuckled Bernie as he took in Norman's white suit and Panama.

Norman shrugged self-consciously. He'd planned to go in his pinstripe, but Dolly his wife had convinced him he'd be 'sweating like a side of bacon' in no time. The little poof in the shop had told him he looked a million dollars in the suit, but Norman felt a right ponce.

"Bernie, you said you where going to America?" said Bianca.

"We are."

"Normie just told me you were going somewhere else." Bernie gave Norman 'the Suit' a questioning look.

"I was trying to explain, that we're going to South America and that a different place to America."

"How can that be then? That's like saying your going to South London and that's not London." Bernie and Norman exchanged knowing grins and said nothing.

"Oh Bernie," said Bianca putting her arms around him. Don't go, it's such a long way. You might not come back.

Bernie placed his hands on Bianca's bottom and gave it a squeeze. "Look, there's nothing to worry about. It's just like Spain, but with jungle."

"Jungle! You never said anything about jungle. They have tigers in the jungle; you could get eaten alive."

"It's not bleedin' Africa, you dopey cow. They don't have tigers in Columbia."

"India," chimed in Norman.

"What?" said Bernie.

"India, it's where they have Tigers, not Africa."

Bernie glared as he reached into the pocket of his blazer and took out a white envelope, containing the locker key. He handed it to Bianca. "Call a courier," he said "and get this taken over to Michael straight away. The sooner that money is out of the locker and in his hands the better. I'll call him from the airport to make sure he has it."

Bianca held up her hands and looked at the nail polish. She wasn't sure tangerine was her colour. She shook both of them and blew on the nails. She started as her gaze fell on the envelope. She'd forgotten to order the courier. Bernie would go mad if the envelope wasn't with Michael Burns when he called him. She looked at the phone and then her wet nails and let out an anguished wail. At the sound of the Bill and Ben theme tune from the next room, she rushed in and found 'Smiling' George entranced in front of the TV.

"Georgie. Be a love and ring for a bike will you."

"I used to have a bike, Ding ding." Bianca looked at George's distorted face the bruising now a dark blue. When Bernie had seen it, he'd gone berserk. It was with great effort that Bianca dissuaded him from having George's attacker killed. It was not that Bernie had any great love for George, it was the idea that anyone could attack someone who was - in Bernie's mind - a 'fucking idiot' who couldn't help himself. Bianca had told him of the actions of Tim and Ben, men she hadn't known, who had sorted the attacker out. Now she needed George to make a call. For fuck sake, he was her brother but some times.......

"Yes, I know love. Look, here's the Yellow Pages," she said walking over with the book clasped between her elbows. "I'll just find a number," she added turning the pages with her teeth. "Here we are- couriers, come on Georgie please."

"But I'll miss Bill and Ben."

"It's a DVD darlin', we can pause it."

A surly look on his face, 'Smiling' George came over and looked down at the phone book. "Look! A picture of a motor bike... brum brum."

"Just pick a number and dial it, will you baby? I'll tell you what to say when the man comes on the phone."

Michael Burns looked glumly through the post on his desk. He'd managed to ignore it for most of the day, but thought he should at least look at it before he went home. The papers had come in on the Delfco share sale. With Roger Clancy on holiday he would have to deal with it. God, he hated the law. His face brightened as he picked up this month's copy of, the Bugatti Owners Club magazine. He put it to one side in the must deal with pile. He let out a loud groan as he took in the next item. The picture of a fat comic that Michael vaguely recognised and a smiling child in a wheel chair told him it was the annual invitation to the Southdown's

Charity Golf club classic. The invite was halfway to the bin when he remembered, to his horror, that Bernie Doyle was sponsoring the event and that he wanted Michael to play on his team. He would have to go. Was it too early in the day, he wondered for a spot of Charlie?

"Bernie, we're going to miss the flight," yelled Norman 'the Suit'.

"I know, I know. I need to call Michael before we go." Bernie looked at his mobile, there was no reception in the airport. He ran to a phone booth but was beaten to it by a middle-aged businessman. Bernie was about to hit him when Norman touched his arm and pointed at the armed police walking by. They really would miss their flight if Bernie got in a fracas. Another booth came free, Bernie punched in Michael's private number. It was engaged. He let out a howl of rage and beat the phone against the glass. The man in the next booth stared at him in alarm.

"Bernie, for God sake!" cried Norman 'the Suit'

"He's on the bleedin' phone!"

"Call Suzy, she can interrupt him."

"Did you like them?" asked Michael speaking into the phone, a large leer on his face. "The latest thing in silk." Suzy jumped up and down in front of him as Michael made love to the phone.

"What is it?" he asked in annoyance.

"Bernie Doyle's on the phone."

"Tell him I'm with a client, no better still- tell him I'm out at a meeting"

"Michael he's going mad, he's about to miss his flight he said if you claimed you weren't here, he would rip your liver out and make you eat it when he got back."

Michael sighed, "You better put him through." He took his hand from the mouthpiece of the phone. "Nikki baby, urgent call from Moscow, got to go babe. Ciao."

"Bing bong, the gate for flight 7593 to Columbia is now closing."

"MICHAEL! MICHAEL! HAVE YOU GOT IT?" Bernie shouted down the phone.

Michael held the golf invitation distastefully between two fingers. "It's just arrived."

"Well don't sound so enthusiastic. Its not the first time you've had to do it." Growled Bernie. "You know what to do, don't ya?"

"Bernie the plane is about to take off," howled Norman in his ear. "Come on"

Michael looked at the phone in some surprise. What was Bernie going on about? He played off a handicap of 7.

"Yes, of course, I know what to do."

"Good," said Bernie, "I'll see you when I get back in about 10 days."

The line went dead. Michael replaced the receiver.
He contemplated whether he could be sick on that day.
Bernie hurried red faced towards the departure gate.

Chapter Twenty

The pages of the lease swam in front of Harry's eyes. The penthouse flat that Bernie Doyle was buying came with paperwork as thick as a telephone book, he'd spent most of the afternoon trying to understand it. He looked at his watch, 7.30, time to call it a night. Harry turned out the light and left the building.

Steve Casell grinned at the blare of the horn behind him. He accelerated the motorbike and shot through a narrow gap between a taxi and a Jaguar, the rain bouncing off his leathers. He loved working in the rain. While the traffic ground along slower than ever, he would slice through it like a red-hot knife through butter. Momentarily, his front wheel skidded on the wet surface and a bus loomed towards him. He regained control and cut up a Ford Fiesta. Yes! Yes! He was King of the Road. One more package to deliver to some poxy solicitor and then home. Victoria to Archway in less than seven minutes, a chance to set a new record.

The buzz of the alarm faded as Harry locked the front door. He could feel a distinct chill on his back. As he turned he saw a thick curtain of rain ricocheting off the pavement and parked cars. He stood on the portico and shivered. Pedestrians sloshed by in waterlogged shoes and plastered down hair. Their faces forlorn as the rain remorselessly sought out any remaining dry patch or crevice.

Fuckin' hell, he could hardly see! The white columns of the buildings flashed by Cassell as he shot past. The orange of the traffic light ahead spread out in a blur across his visor. He accelerated as the light turned red.

Harry ran into the rain and stopped. Run for the tube? Try and find a taxi? Buckets of water cascaded over him.

Claremont Square. Casell didn't brake, using the weight of his body to affect the turn. The woman getting out of the taxi leapt on to the pavement to avoid being hit. Reluctantly he slowed as he approached the office of Clancy Burns.

Harry was about to run for the tube when he had to jump back onto the pavement to avoid being hit by Cassel's motorbike. He squealed to a halt and thrust up his visor.
    "Clancy Burns?"
    "Yes."

Casell thrust a thin envelope into Harry's hand, and Harry pushed it into his pocket.

"Sign here." Casell stuck a clipboard and pen under Harry's nose. Harry added his signature to the fuzzy blue writing on the page.

Casell leapt back on his bike and pulled away with a roar. As he did so, there was a squeal of brakes, followed by the sound of a large wet fish being slapped against a counter. Casell came flying back through the air towards Harry, his right boot catching Harry a passing blow that sent him spinning to the ground. Harry winced as his coccyx smacked into the pavement. He heard the crumpled thud of the biker hitting the ground. A car door slammed shut, feet scurried on to the pavement. "Oh Christ!" came a disembodied voice. "I'll call an ambulance." The feet moved away.

The courier lay twitching on the pavement. Harry couldn't see his face; the inside of his visor was covered in blood. Harry knelt beside Cassel's moaning and twisted frame. The human body is not equipped for being struck by a Toyota Land Cruiser and then flung through the air with only concrete to break it's fall. Harry lifted his head and undid the helmet strap. Warm blood ran over Harry's hands. He sat there holding Cassel's head, not wanting it to be in contact with the cold ground. Through the hammering rain he heard the sirens approaching.

The voice came back. "He just pulled out. I didn't get a chance to stop. Is he going to be all right?"

A sticky warm glow spread across Harry's groin as he rested the head in his lap. It was the one part of him that wasn't numb. He could hear Cassel's slow struggled breathing as his life seeped away in a carpet of red all around them.

Chapter
Twenty-One

"There's no Anardana in these Samosas." Said Ben.

"No, it's not that, they've used dried coriander." Said Tim

"My throats on fire, they're taking for ever with those beer" said Harry. "Can I have a swig of yours Tim?" Tim nodded - as Harry eagerly gulped down his lager – keen to continue his conversation with Ben of what was wrong with the samosas.

Vindaloo Vindaloo was the home of the post-modern curry, so the newspaper review had said. Tim thought its vegetable samosas were crap.

"Tastes alright to me," said Harry as he downed the newly arrived pint of lager. The evening wore on with the pair of them arguing whether frozen or fresh peas made the best samosas. Harry was busily compensating for eating a hot and undercooked curry by drinking copious amounts of King Fisher.

When the bill arrived, the figures did a jig in front of Harry's eyes. Tim gently prised it from his hand and paid. Harry staggered to his feet grabbing the table for support. "I, I'll leave a tip" he said with a loud belch. Harry pulled a handful of change from his pocket and left it on the table.

The night air hit him like a smack in the face with a wet towel.

"You going to be okay, Harry?" asked Tim.

"Fine," he hiccupped. Harry said his goodbyes and began to slowly weave his way down the road.

"Sir! Sir!" Harry looked round as one of the Indian waiters from the restaurant ran up to him. "You left this with your change," he said handing him a key.

"It's not mine."

"We only take money," he said planting it in Harry's hand and walking away. He looked at the key, sitting down on the pavement to give it greater attention. It was a locker key, number 103, but what was he doing with it? He placed it in his suit pocket and staggered on to Victoria. The suit was just back from the dry cleaners. Most of the courier's blood had come out apart from a faint stain only visible if you held his groin up to strong daylight. Harry figured not many people went around staring at his flies, and what the hell, he only had two suits.

The bright lights of Victoria beckoned him. As he entered the station he took the key from his pocket. How had it got there? Harry's stomach rumbled in a warning fashion, had all that lager been a good idea? Slowly he proceeded through the station, halting now and then to let the pillars stop moving in front of him. He missed the entrance to the tube altogether and found himself amongst the left luggage lockers. "Oh look," he belched dropping the key and spending the next five minutes crawling on the floor to find it.

Locker 103. Sodding key won't go in. God, I need a pee. Harry leant against the lockers as a wave of nausea washed over him. He was going to be sick. He yanked down on his tie, which hung like a twisted piece of string. Harry pulled his hand away as it encountered the mango chutney that adorned it. The nausea subsided. *One more go.* The key jiggled left and right. He tried it upside down. Took it out, looked at it, squinted at the lock and the number. Tried it once more and it slipped smoothly in.

It was a large shiny case. The kind photographers use. Harry pulled it out and let it fall to the ground; it weighed a ton. He went to open it but his bladder intervened. Open the case or wet himself? Harry hurried to the gents dragging the case behind him.

At the third attempt, Harry made it up the stairs to his bedroom. He opened the door and collapsed on the bed. A feeling of triumph swept over him; he'd made it home without puking. He put the case next to him and eagerly pressed the locks. The lid sprang open revealing a field of flfty-pound notes neatly stacked and bundled. He picked one up and counted. A thousand.

The case was about 30 cm deep, there must be......
UUUUuuuuuuurrrrgggggghhhhhh. A thick mush of la-
ger and curry shot from his throat and over the money.
Harry collapsed on the floor and passed out.

Over the next 8 hours Harry discovered every crack
and crevice in the back wall of the loo as he puked and
wretched until it felt like his ribs had been kicked in. The
case sat on the bedroom floor buried under his discarded
clothing.

"Harry, are you okay? Can I come in?" The concerned tones of Harry's landlady Gemma drifted towards him. Her head peeked around the door, "I've
brought you a cup of tea."

He sat upright, feeling a dull pain across his midriff.
He looked at the clock it was 10.00 AM.

"Harry, you are pale. Here, try this."

He sipped the warm tea. The liquid passed soothingly down his throat dislodging the dried vomit stuck to
the inside of his mouth. Harry felt a strong need to brush
his teeth and shower. He tottered to the bathroom.

Twenty minutes later Harry emerged with a minty
taste in his mouth and a body that felt human again. He
sat on the bed and looked at the crumpled clothing on
the floor. Something silver and shiny was poking out
from underneath it. THE MONEY!!! - He pulled the case
out and opened it, wincing as the smell of stale vomit hit
him. He backed away and considered the situation from
the corner of his bed. The red of the notes was quite

distinguishable through the yellow goo, which covered them. He had an awful lot of someone's money and he'd puked all over it!

Harry stayed at home that morning, telling the office he was sick. He'd not often had the chance to spend so much time with his own vomit. It took a pair of Gemma 's rubber gloves and a lot of hanging his head out of the window to get the job done. Some of the cash looked more like Vindaloo than cash and went straight into a bin liner. He tried scraping the vomit off the rest with a spatula but gave up and put all the soiled money in the sack.

Harry counted what was left. Nine hundred and fifty thousand pounds. He had fifty encrusted bundles in the bag making a round million. He sat and looked at the most expensive bag of vomit in history. Why had he taken the case? It seemed a good idea at the time. That was the trouble with eight pints of lager inside you. It made the most lunatic idea look inspired.

Whose money, was it? It didn't take the work of a genius to realise it was 'bent'. Harry had been told all about money laundering at law school. He had a million pounds that belonged to drug dealers or terrorists! He clasped his hands to his mouth and just made the loo in time.

Harry sat at his desk that afternoon pondering over the week's events and the conversation he would have with his dad when he called on Sunday.

"Harry, how's the job going? No more hanging from helicopters, I hope?"

"Just great dad. I had another client try and kill me last week and guess what? I've now got a million quid that belongs to Al Qaeda"

He was contemplating another visit to the loo when Wendy breezed into the room.

"Can you sign this cheque for petty cash please Michael?" she said, waving it at him.

"Sure, give it here," he said picking up the phone as it began to ring.

"Michael, DI Nolan on the phone for you," said Suzy down the line.

"Put him through, will you? Brian, how are you? Have I heard about Melvyn Godson? No, why?" Burn's face turned a sickly grey as he listened. "Oh, my Christ! No I hadn't seen him for a few weeks. If I think of anything I'll let you know. Thanks, thanks Brian. If they find anymore, I mean if you hear anymore, let me know." He put the phone down and flopped into his chair. "Fucking hell," he murmured under his breath.

"What's wrong, Michael?" acked Harry, forgetting about his stomach.

"Poor old Melvyn Godson, he was a manager for Allied Scottish. Bernie and I have known him for years. They say he's been murdered. They found three of his teeth, a credit card and a badly burnt toe in a batch of chicken and mushroom pies.

"How do they know it was murder?" chimed in Wendy.

"Christ almighty! You don't end up with your toes in a chicken fucking pie by accident. The poor stupid fucker, I told him not to mess with..." he stopped in his tracks. He needn't have bothered, Wendy was half way out the room in floods of tears and Harry could guess the name he'd been about to mention.

Harry stomach felt like it was on the move again. "Do you think Billy the Blowtorch had anything to do with this?"

Michael narrowed his eyes and frowned. "Who's been talking to you about Billy?"

"Arthur."

"I might have known. Arthur likes the sound of his own mouth too much. It's not wise to repeat anything he tells you. Certainly, not outside these offices, understand?"

Harry nodded; "I need the toilet," he groaned.

After five minutes of retching, Harry sat on the cubicle floor. It could all just be a coincidence? Arthur had told him about the man who had his feet burnt, the charred toe- Christ, just the toe! Where was the rest of him? Teeth and toes of a dead bank manager had been found. A bank manager who knew Bernie Doyle and he had a million pounds that belonged to someone. Was it all connected? Oh God, he hoped not. He didn't want to end up in a chicken pie!

Harry sat in the kitchen, the black bin liner on the table in front of him. He peered into the bag, the smell sent him reeling. He was supposed to be on a course but had decided to stay home and have a go at cleaning the money. The sooner he could get it all back in the luggage locker, the better. It was 10 am and everyone he shared the house with had gone to work.

It was a big old house set on three floors. Empty of everyone it filled with a wonderful stillness. Harry's eyes wondered round the kitchen. The sink was full of last night's dishes. The lid of the swing bin sat precariously astride a sea of teabags, baked bean tins and empty cereal packets. Like many shared houses there was a 'rule' that the bin wasn't full until the lid was a good six inches clear of the rim! Once this happened you didn't need to empty it as long as you could find a carrier bag to use as a mini bin. The occupants of a house tend to split into two camps: Those who get fed up with emptying the bin and those who believe in the 'bin fairy'.

He went over to the sink, a thin layer of what looked like dandruff floated on top of the cold greasy water. Harry pulled the plug and gingerly stacked the dirty dishes on the table behind him. Well, it wasn't his washing up. He found a pair of bright yellow rubber gloves two sizes too small, which he managed to pull on to his hands with surgical tightness. Hot water splattered into the sink. Now washing up liquid or soap powder? He had a choice of three: *Fairy*, a packet of *Bold* and some hand wash that went by the name of *Morning Dawn.* The latter had a picture of a woman having an orgasm with a towel on the front. He plumped for the hand wash. Start gentle and work up to something industrial if he needed to. Harry opened the bin liner and shook a handful of curry stained fifty-pound notes into the sink. They lay on the surface between the white frothy bubbles like leaves floating on a pond. Little flecks of diced carrot drifted away, swirling over the surface. Leave to soak for half an hour, it said on the packet.

Harry decided to shave, while the soap powder worked its magic. He'd just got a nice lather on his face when he heard a radio. Someone else was in the house.

Harry tore out of the bathroom looking like Father Christmas and thundered down the stairs sending the cat hurtling for cover. The foam in the sink had turned a disturbing pink. He pushed his hands into the bright red water and pulled out a cleanish, but decidedly white looking piece of paper. He fished out three or four more in various degrees of pink. Harry jerked his hands out as he realised that this so-called hand wash was full of industrial strength bleach. If it stripped a banknote clean, what would it do to his hands? He did a quick finger count. Harry picked up the box and for the first time saw in the small print- it was made in Bulgaria. The radio was getting louder someone was coming down the stairs!!

They went into the bathroom and the door shut. Harry picked up a spatula; fried egg dangling from its tip, and scooped the money out and on to the draining board. Limp white and pink notes built up in a pile. He heard the toilet flush and the tread of feet on the stairs. Harry pulled open the door of the washing machine and threw the money in. He sat down with a newspaper and tried to look casual.

"Morning Harry," said Maurice. "We got any bread?" We? thought Harry, since when did he and Maurice go shopping? But then, that was Maurice. Why buy your own food when you could eat everyone else's? Harry put the paper down. Maurice's arms were full of washing.

"There's some brown in my cupboard. You can leave that washing, if you like, I've got some of my own to put on in a minute." Harry said, trying to sound nonchalant.

"Got a full load, Harry."

Maurice opened the washing machine and pushed in his clothes in one solid mass. Harry watched mesmerized as he added powder. The water whooshed into the washer as it rumbled into life.

Three slices of toast and half an hour later Maurice decided to leave. Harry's nerves lay round his ankles in tatters. Every now and again a fifty-pound note had bobbed into sight and waved cheekily at him from the other side of the glass. Any second he expected Maurice to notice what was happening, but he seemed more interested in eating Harry's jam and toast and telling me him ought to get some decent marmalade and not the organic shit Harry had brought.

"Oh fuck! Would you look at that!" said Maurice as he got up to leave. Harry fell off his chair. "You all right Harry? You seem a bit jumpy."

"No, I'm fine," said Harry from the floor, his stomach dancing the polka. He looked up. The water in the washing machine had turned a distinct red. A pale pink lather clung round the side of the glass. Harry gulped and looked at Maurice expectantly.

"Look what's happened to my Man United jersey. The colours ran."

"Isn't that Matt's jersey that you borrowed last week?"

"Oh yeah. Never mind, aye."

Maurice picked up his coat and left the house as the spin burst into life.

Harry spent the next half-hour picking bits of mashed up fifty pound notes out of Maurice pink y-fronts.

Chapter
Twenty-Two

Harry glanced at his watch, he was going to be late. He thrust money into the cab driver's hand and leapt from the cab, running the last quarter of a mile to the High Court. Marianne Wheatley's solicitor was trying to get an injunction to freeze the distribution of tins of Poochie while they searched for the rest of Trixie Bell Ya Ya VIII. Victor had screamed blue murder and demanded Michael get the finest QC money could buy. When Michael told him how much that would be, there was a long silence. They ended up with Jarvis Squires QC, who was more Volvo Estate than Ferrari when it came to the best money could buy. As a Queen's Council, he had to be accompanied by a junior. This was another barrister who wasn't in the least bit anyone's junior. Squires totally ignored Harry's existence when he arrived at court, leaving all contact with him to his junior- a barrister in his mid forties called Brian Wilson.

"Where is Mr. Davis?" asked Wilson.

"He's not here, then?" gasped Harry trying to get his breath back. Wilson made a great pretence of looking right and left and then up at the ceiling.

"I don't see him, do you? Do you have his affidavit?"

"Sorry, no. When I spoke to him yesterday he said I needn't worry about affidavits."

"I see. Well, I'd better inform Mr. Squires. You wait here," he added as Harry started to follow him.

Wilson walked over to Squires and said something Harry couldn't hear. Squires glanced briefly in his direction and they exchanged further words. "Not now, later will do," he heard Squires say. What they were talking about, Harry had no idea. From the looks they gave him, Harry could only conclude they were deciding when to kill him. Why not thought Harry, everyone else was.

Further paranoid contemplation was interrupted by the appearance of Victor Davis clutching an attaché case. He saw Harry and pointed to the case slapping it on the side.

"See, I told you- the answer to all our problems!"

As Victor had arrived, Wilson signalled that Harry should approach. He took Victor over and introduced him to the two barristers.

"Nice to meet you, Jarvy," said Victor, oblivious to Squires wince of pain at the term of address.

"Have you brought your affidavit, Mr. Davis?" asked Squires.

"Don't worry, Jarvy. I've got everything we need in the case. Look." Victor opened the case. It was full of money. Harry looked at the two barristers, who stared at the contents in bemusement. Neither had twigged what Victor's 'answer to all our problems' was.

"I don't understand, Mr. Davis. Why are you showing us this money?" asked Squires.

"It's for the Judge," said Victor.

"The Judge?" said Squires, still unable to comprehend. Harry looked at Wilson, whose face was black as thunder. He hustled Squires off to one side. Squires gave out a loud gasp as Wilson explained to him the purpose of the money.

"What's going on?" said Victor in bewilderment. "Isn't it enough?"

"Mr. Trent. A moment of your time, please."

Harry walked into the icy tundra of Wilson's presence. Squires sat on a bench chewing on the end of his wig, temporarily unhinged at the suggestion he should bribe a Judge. Wilson saw Harry taking in this pitiful sight.

"Jarvis!" ho hissed at him. Squires stopped eating his wig and settled for a facial tick.

"If that bag of offal," continued Wilson glaring in Victor's direction, "opens his mouth or his case again then Mr. Squires and I will walk straight out of court. Do I make myself clear, Trent? I will have you and the rest of that ragbag of cocaine snorting pimps you work for drummed out of the profession. Understand?"

"Perfectly."

"And, tell Burns that my clerk will be in touch to discuss a significant increase in our brief fees."

Harry walked back to Victor. "What's going on?" he asked. "There's fifty grand in the case. If it's not enough, how much do you bung a Judge?"

There are rocks and there are hard places. It was Harry's day to be caught between the two.

"MURDERER!" they heard from down the corridor; a large middle-aged woman was being restrained by her solicitor and barrister. They were having a tough job.

"DO YOU HEAR ME DAVIS? MY DOGS ARE GOING TO CHEW YOUR BOLLOCKS OFF! AND THATS ONLY FOR STARTERS!"

This was the sickly Mrs. Wheatley, who according to correspondence had been confined to bed with grief since opening the tin of Poochie. Harry looked round for Davis who was cowering behind him.

"She's not right in the head," he whined. "You heard what she said. You're my lawyer what are you going to do about it?"

"Wheatley -v- Davis Dog Biscuits. Court 3," called the usher.

Harry wrestled the case full of money from Davis's grip. "I'd better look after this."

"Good idea, you can slip it to the Judge after the hearing."

The bad news was that Lord Justice Poppins was a dog lover. The good was he couldn't stand women. If he thought the law was an unsuitable profession for Jean Bevan QC, appearing for Mrs. Wheatley, he was appalled at the suggestion that they had the slightest idea how to breed dogs.

"So, what sort of dog was this Trixie Bell, Miss Bevan?" he sneered. "Some sort of poodle?"

"A Great Dane, my Lord."

The grey hairs poking out of his Lordship bulbous nose did a can-can across his top lip. "Are you trying to be humorous?!"

"No, my Lord."

"What kind of name is that for a hunting dog?"

"A very good one, before that bast…!" yelled out Mrs Wheatley before her solicitor could clamp his hand to her mouth and pull her back on to the bench.

"I WILL HAVE SILENCE IN MY COURT!"

"Aaagh." screamed Mrs. Wheatley's solicitor as he snatched his now bleeding hand away from her mouth.

"SILENCE!!!"

"My Lord. With respect, the name of the dog is irrelevant. The fact remains it was found in the defendant's dog food."

"Is that not your problem, Miss Bevan? As I understand it, none of the dog was found in the tin."

"By the time the collar was discovered, my Lord, half of it had been consumed. The presence of the collar and name tag are strong evidence the dog ended up in the tins. That is why we need to have the remainder of them impounded."

"You wish me to impound thousands of tins of dog food on the basis of a collar and name tag?"

"I do, my Lord."

"Well, I'm not satisfied. Application refused. Good day to you."

"He's good, isn't he?" whispered Victor. "Well worth the 50K. You tell him there's lots more where that came from."

Harry was half way back to the office before he realised he still had Victor's fifty grand.

Chapter
Twenty-Three

Harry felt the warmth of Mandy's back against him as he dozed. There was nothing nicer than being snug under a duvet knowing you didn't have to get up for half an hour. Mandy rolled towards him.

"What's the time?" she murmured sleepily.

"About 6:30."

She let out a low groan. "I'm on a course today. Got to get up." A rush of cold air came under the duvet as she threw it back. "Have you got a briefcase I can borrow, Harry? I need something to carry my notes in."

"Have a look in the wardrobe," he yawned. Somewhere in the deep dark basement of his mind, a nagging thought let out a shriek and ran up the stairs to his consciousness.

"HOLY SHIT!!!"

Harry sprang upright as the nagging thought hollered at him. "DON'T LET HER LOOK IN YOUR WARDROBE! THAT'S WHERE YOU'VE HIDDEN THE MONEY!!!".

It was a scene Harry wouldn't forget. Mandy na- ked holding packets of fifty- pound notes. There was something sexy about a naked women and large amounts of money- two of the main things men spent most of their lives in pursuit of. His eyes flashed from the money to her breasts and then to the look of alarm on her face.

"HARRY, WHAT HAVE YOU DONE!!?"

"I HAVEN'T DONE ANYTHING AND THERE'S NO NEED TO SCREAM."

A gentle knock at the door. "Harry is everything OK?" It was the voice of Gemma, Harry's landlady. Defensively, Mandy covered her breasts with fat bundles of fifty-pound notes. *There's nothing like keeping the fact you have a million quid in your wardrobe a secret, and this was nothing like it.*

"We're fine, Gem. Mandy's just seen something, and it's got her a little excited."

"Lucky old Mandy," they could hear her footsteps as she walked away from the door. Mandy sat down on the edge of the bed, the money tightly clamped to her chest.

"Harry! Where has all this money come from?"

He sat bunny like, staring into the blazing headlamps of Mandy's eyes as her accusing stare hurtled towards him like an oncoming HGV.

"It... erm... it... erm... isn't mine," he burbled. Mandy's eyes went up a couple of hundred watts. "I didn't steal it. I found it," he added rather lamely.

Mandy removed the money from her breasts and her eyes went from main beam to dipped. Harry clutched the duvet defensively to his naked body.

"Harry, you don't just find..., how much is there?

"A million... a... um million pounds. But, I was sick on some of it. It belongs to Bernie Doyle, he's a... gangster client of the firm and he's going to... to... make me into a chicken pie when he finds out I've got his money."

"A chicken pie?"

He gave Mandy the potted history of how the money had come into his possession and told her of the fate of Melvyn Godson. She pulled him towards her, her soft breasts enveloping his face. He felt a stirring between his legs. They fell back on the bed and for the next half hour forgot about the money.

"You've got to give it back," said Mandy

Harry lay on his back hot and sweaty, one hand resting on her stomach.

"What about the fifty grand?"

"Chuck it away. Let Doyle think someone else has stolen the fifty grand. He won't have put the suitcase in the locker himself. Let him think one of his heavies has taken it."

He didn't mention Victor's 50K. There's only oo much stolen money you want to own up to in one go!

Bernie sat back in the soft leather upholstery of the Mercedes as it pulled way from Terminal 4. It was good to be back in England. As they drove out of the airport they passed a police car, two officers were questioning a West Indian by the side of an aged Ford.

"You don't know how lucky you are, mate," murmured Norman.

"I've heard it all now," said Bernie with grin. "You'll have your Vic joining up next." Norman turned towards Bernie grim faced.

"They might knock him about, but they ain't going to leave him dead in a ditch!"

"Yeah, live and learn," replied Bernie ruefully.

Columbia had been a searing experience for both men. They were used to and capable of quite extreme violence, but it was always with a purpose in mind. Neither could understand the casual and random nature of the killing they'd witnessed. Bernie had struck a lucrative deal with Gavuria for the supply of cocaine but was half hearted over the whole project. *Come on Bernie, get a grip of yourself.* The trill of his mobile phone broke further thought. Bianca 's name flashed on the display.

"Bernie, Bernie are you okay, darling? I was so worried," burbled Bianca' s voice into his ear. He felt a glow as her warm words cascaded over him. He would not tell her of Columbia. She'd been frightened enough of him being eaten by tigers without letting on he'd been machine-gunned and shot at by a tank. He sat back and listened as she told him of a shopping trip she's been on with her sister. "I took her to see the Penthouse as well. When we going to complete on that, Bernie?" The mention of the Penthouse made him sit up with a jolt. Christ, he'd forgotten all about the million.

"We're going to do it soon baby. Look I need to speak to Jules, we'll be home in half an hour. I'll see you then." He scrolled to the number of Jules Dupigny, the assistant manager at his Jersey bank.

"Jules, its Bernie. Did you get the package from Michael okay?

"Hello Bernie, what package?" I haven't spoken to Michael for over a month.

"Don't mess me about, Jules."

"I promise you; I haven't had anything."

Bernie broke the connection and called Michael.

The Ferrari accelerated as Michael's foot touched the pedal. The salesman sitting next to him began to count the noughts on his commission cheque as he saw the large smile on Michael's face. The ring of Michael's mobile and the consequent swerve towards an on coming juggernaut as he reached for it, wiped the thought of money from his mind.

"Hello?" said Michael, as the Ferrari swept past the truck with no more than a few feet to spare.

"Michael, where's my package?" growled Bernie.

"Hi Bernie! Guess where I am!"

"I know where you fucking will be if you don't listen to me Michael." Michael took his foot off the accelerator and pulled over towards the kerb.

"Sorry, Bernie. What's the matter?"

"I sent you a package. We spoke about it before I flew out."

Michael thought hard. Bernie would never refer to money or drugs by name over the phone. It would always be a package. What had Bernie sent him? As the high he'd got from the Ferrari floated away, the remains of the one he'd got from the previous night's cocaine hit him between the eyes, dulling his senses.

"Michael! You still there? I rang you from the airport and you told me you'd got it."

"The golf invitation?"

"WHAT?"

"You asked me if I'd got the golf invitation."

"Michael. I'm not talking about a fucking golf invitation."

"Bernie, I swear- apart from the golf invitation, I've not had anything from you."

Doyle looked at Norman. "He says he didn't get the key." Norman shrugged his shoulders.

"Perhaps Bianca didn't send it."

"No. She can be a dopey cow sometimes, but she's not that dopey." Doyle put the phone back to his ear. "Michael, this was a package I sent you by courier."

"Bernie, I'm sorry but I haven't had it." Doyle ended the call and rang Bianca.

"Bianca."

"Hello Bernie darlin', what would you like for your tea?" Bernie bit his lip; it didn't do to swear at Bianca. When he did, expensive things were broken.

"Bianca. That envelope I asked you to get couriered to Michael. He says he hasn't received it."

"I sent it by bike."

"What firm did you use?"

"I don't know. Georgie rang them for me."

"GEORGE!"

"Sorry, Bernie. I had wet nails."

Bernie terminated the call. "What's the number of the locker Melvyn put the money in?"

"Don't know. It's on the key."

"I don't have the fucking key!"

"We're fucked then, aren't we?"

Chapter
Twenty-Four

Harry walked down the concrete steps that led to the cells of Finsbury Road Magistrates Court, the once whitewashed brick of the walls yellowed with age. At the bottom, he was greeted by the rolling stomach and greased back hair of a security guard.

"Yes?"

"I've come to see, Mr. Crawford."

"WE GOT A CRAWFORD?" There was no response. He turned and lumbered down the corridor, Harry followed. They came to the door of an office, three equally rotund and scruffy security guards sat at a table playing cards. "We got a Crawford?" One of the guards picked up a clipboard.

"We got a Collins."

The guard turned to Harry, "You want to see Collins?"

"I'd rather see my client."

"I haven't got all day you know," he muttered turning away.

"Come on, Stan," said one of the card players. "It's your turn to deal."

"Yeah alright, alright," said Stan, rifling through a sheaf of dog-eared papers on the table. "Where's today's court list? You seen it Don?"

"No good asking me mate, I normally do building sites me." Said Don.

Stan turned to Harry, "Look, best I can do is Kamuzu. Do you want to see him or not?" Harry looked into the reddening impatient face of the custodian of law and order. Perhaps this was par for the course, if they hadn't got your client then you took the nearest to him. He debated for a moment asking to see Collins on the basis that sounded more like Crawford than Kamuzu did.

"Well?"

"Er..."

"Look, if you don't know what you want, then fuck off and stop wasting my time."

We all have our breaking point and Stan had broken Harry's.

"I'll go and tell the Magistrates, then."

"What?"

"I'll go and tell them you won't let me see my client."

Stan grabbed the clipboard from the table and gave Harry a look that said avoiding dark alleyways for the rest of his life would be a good idea.

"What the fuck does this say," he snarled almost taking Don's nose off as he thrust the clipboard under it.

"Crawford, he's in cell 6."

"Why the fuck didn't you say!" Don stood up, his shaved head brushing against the ceiling. If Harry ever went down any dark alleyways it would be with Don. Even his tattoos had muscles.

"Do you want to make something of it?" said Don.

"No, no, you know, you could have said."

"Well, I'm saying now."

"Yeah alright, alright Don keep yer hair - I mean, yer know, no offence like I'll err just show this brief where to go."

Stan wobbled down the corridor in quick time glancing nervously over his shoulder. In his newly found fear he was even polite to Harry.

"This way." A row of steel doors was set in one wall, the names of the occupants chalked on the outside. "You need to watch out down this end, we've had a bit of a flood. Always happens when it rains. We try not to use these two cells, but we've got a full house today. Trouble is with all this water about, it allows the dirty little bastards to piss wherever they like. Careful where you're walking," he said with a grin. Harry hop scotched round the pools which lay on the floor.

Stan turned his key in a metal door that opened with well-oiled ease. The cell had the smell and decoration of a car park stairwell. A small man head bowed sat huddled on top of a bench bolted into the far wall. The laces were missing from his shoes and he was holding up his trousers with his hands. Harry looked quizzically at the officer.

"We have their belt and laces in case they feel like hanging themselves."

The man's head shot up. "Hang me fuckin' self?! I'm more likely to fuckin' drown. Look where they put me." He pointed at the large puddle of water, which covered half of the cell floor. "How much longer am I going to be down 'ere Captain Nemo?"

"Watch your lip Crawford, this is your brief. Give me a shout when you've finished," he added turning to Harry. The door closed with an airtight thud.

"If I wanted to go to sea I'd have joined the fuckin' navy!" shouted Crawford in a last outburst of defiance. He turned towards Harry grinning, one hand buried deep within the folds of a dirty and torn green puffer jacket busily scratching away at his armpit.

"Bastards. You got a fag? You my uncle Norman's brief?" He said, spitting the questions out in quick succession.

"No, sorry I don't smoke. I'm from Clancy Burns. Mr Doyle asked us to represent you. I understand you are the nephew of his, err... colleague, Norman Crawford."

"Good old Bernie. I used to do some gardening for him. Did a course when I was in Youf detention. Like being outdoors."

Harry edged round the puddle of water on the floor and sat on the edge of the bench. A grimy nail bitten hand reached out towards him.

"Davy Crawford, pleased to meet ya."

"Harry Trent." He flicked open his case and took out the file. "You're charged with one case of breaking and entering on the 15 April at 14 Grove Mansions and on the same day breaking into 16 Grove Mansions and attacking Phyllis Brown with a hammer thereby occasioning her grievous bodily harm."

"NO, I NEVER! The burglary is down to me, but I never touched the old lady. They're tryin' to pin that on me coz they found my prints in the house and both got turned over the same day."

"Well, today is just the committal. In view of the GBH charge, the case will go to Crown Court."

Crawford's hand scurried back into his armpit. "Am I going to get bail?"

"I don't know. Do you have somewhere to stay?"

"I can live at my sister's. She does cleaning for Bianca Doyle. Christ, she gave our Sharon a right mouthful the other day. She and Bernie been havin' a row about some money. So, of course she comes and takes it out on our Sharon."

Harry's mouth went dry, the cell closed in around him, it's fetid smell slithered over his body burrowing down into his boxer shorts. He felt a sharp pain in his groin as if someone was twisting his testicles off. Harry emitted a low groan.

"You all right, Harry?"

Harry swallowed and managed to restore some lubrication to his mouth.

"Did... erm... Sharon hear what the argument was about."

"Well, it seems Bernie gave Bianca some money to deliver and she got her brother Smiling George to do it."

"Smiling George?"

"Yeah, he's called that as he's always got this daft smile on his face. He's a bit soft in the head. Didn't get enough air or somethin' when he was born and that left him a bit spazzy. Anyway, she give the money to George and he can't remember where he put it."

"Did Sharon say how much it was?"

"Ere why do you want to know? Nosey bastard int ya."

"Oh, you know," said Harry smiling lamely

Crawford leant forward and grinned through teeth that only had a dim and distant memory of a toothbrush.

"A million-fucking quid! Fuck me! Fancy losing a million quid! If George wasn't his brother-in-law, Bernie would have strung him up by his dick and that would have only been for starters. As it is, he's had to go into hiding till Bernie cools down or gets his money back."

Harry had the happy thought of being nailed up by his willy all the way back to the office.

Chapter
Twenty-Five

The dildo sat precariously on the pile of pornography. Harry put the magazines on his desk and it rolled off and across the floor towards Michael. He reached down and picked it up, a broad grin on his face. "Yours, Harry?"

"Mrs. Perkins."

"Ah, the infamous Mrs. Perkins."

Hilary Wheeler, the firm's family solicitor, was on maternity leave, so Harry got Mrs Perkins. As it was their first encounter, she'd been able to tell her story anew with too much relish for Harry's liking. Her husband, a bus driver, would hang round the local girl's school trying to pick up sixth formers who he thought would get turned on by a man in uniform. Mr. Perkins also liked pornography and sex toys. His wife would regularly bring in both as evidence of her husband's perversion. She seemed oblivious to the black eyes and bruises she wore - cheerfully stating that 'her Tony had caught her a right one' - regarding his reading of *Spanking Monthly* as a far more serious offence. One of her children however, took a different view of his violence and was caught putting rat poison in his tea. Reluctantly, Mrs Perkins agreed he would have to go. An injunction was to be obtained putting him out of the house.

"There's no more room in Hilary's office for this stuff."

"Sorry Harry, you can't leave it here. Take this box and put it in storage." Harry loaded the magazines in and headed for the door.

"Oh, Harry."

"Yes?"

"That incident with the courier."

"Yes?"

"Are you feeling OK about that now?"

"Fine."

"Good. He didn't give you anything, did he? It's just with the accident and him bleeding to death all over you, it might have slipped your mind?"

Bang on the nail Michael. What could Harry say? Oh yes, I've had a million pounds in my wardrobe for the last 3 days but I thought it best not to mention it as I didn't want to end up in a chicken pie.

"No. He just flew through the air... died in my lap."

"Yes, of course, very tragic."

Harry raced for the gents, leaving the box of porn outside the cubicle door as he entered. Five minutes later, his breakfast having taken a journey round the u-bend, he sat and pondered his fate. The sound of someone singing *All Things Bright and Beautiful* made him lift his head. It was Dominic King, the firm's senior partner. He suffered daily torments at having taken up the law and not the church. He was the last person Harry needed to see. He waited for him to leave. We had just got to "all things wise and wonderful" when the singing broke off.

"What's this?" Harry heard him exclaim.

Oh God! He'd found the porn, some of which was more 'under the floorboards than under the counter'. Harry heard the sound of pages rustling then a sharp intake of breath, *that was probably 'Bare and Bouncy' he had found,* this was followed by a "NO!" *that would be 'Shaven Babes',* the strange gurgling noise meant Dominic had got to the Latvian section. Harry hadn't looked inside, the cover picture of a fat naked woman sitting astride a donkey holding a large wire brush had been enough.

He heard the scuttling of feet, a shout of "I don't care if you want a piss, this toilet is closed!" followed by a louder scream of "MICHAEL!" It was unfortunate that Michael had sent a memo round the office that morning stating he was having certain improvements made to the gents and would staff bear with him whilst they were implemented.

The streets are strangely silent at 5:30 AM. The slam of the cab door was the only sound to break the quiet.

Harry looked down at the silver case, it was still missing fifty grand. He'd toyed with putting in Victor's fifty, but Victor knew he had it. If he didn't give it back, he was only storing up further trouble. He'd had enough of clients' money to last him a lifetime

Harry walked under the glass roof of the station towards the luggage lockers. Funny, he could see right across to *Burger King*. Perhaps he'd come in the wrong entrance. An elderly West Indian pushed a broom methodically across the floor.

"Excuse me. I'm looking for the left luggage lockers?"

"They're gone. We've closed them during the building work."

Harry picked up his chin from the floor. "But, I need to store my case."

"Sorry, son. The sign's been up for over a week."

He needed to sit down. Obligingly his legs gave way and he collapsed in a heap.

"Don't sit there son, I'm trying to clean up." At the edge of his broom, he ushered Harry gently out of the station. Some days you can't give away a 'million'.

Light streamed through the bank of windows that ran along one wall of the courtroom. It swept over the aged rows of wooden benches that filled it and up into the high corniced ceiling. On the walls, old and tarnished brass lamps gave off an ineffectual glow. Now mere

decoration, their original function fulfilled by large fluorescent tubes suspended from the ceiling. The faint
hubbub of traffic could be heard from the street below.
At the far end of the room hung the coat of arms bear-
ing the lion and unicorn, signifying the power and presence of the English courts.

There were five of them in the room; Mrs. Perkins,
Harry, Jonathan Whitehead (the young barrister instructed to represent Mrs. Perkins), the clerk of the
court who sat in front of the judge on a lower podium
and His Honour Judge Raymond Black. They filled a
tiny portion of the vast courtroom, the sea of empty
benches behind, like rows of wooden sentries, bear-
ing silent witness to all that went on. Mr. Perkins had
been summoned to attend but was absent. Harry
couldn't fathom why he was needed there when there
was a barrister. Harry had been told he was the 'instructing solicitor' and his presence was required.
The fact that he didn't feel capable of instructing any-
body was neither here nor there.

He glanced nervously at the million pounds sitting at
his feet. Any minute he expected someone to ask what
was in the case. After the debacle at Victoria, he'd had
no choice but to bring it with him.

The judge was in his early sixties and wore half-
rimmed glasses on the end of his nose. His head- normally bewigged was bare, revealing short grey hair.
He rolled back the purple sleeve of his robe and stared

ostentatiously at his watch. He'd made clear at the outset of the hearing they would finish by 12:00 as he would
not get caught in the Friday afternoon traffic and wanted
to reach his country cottage before dark.

"Your honour, these are serious allegations of bug-
gery," said Jonathan Whitehead.

The Judge raised his head from the book in which
he had been making notes and stifled a yawn. "Not really, Mr. Whitehead. It used to be an accepted means
of contraception amongst the lower orders. Still, it's
half past eleven. I can see from her affidavit that Mrs
Perkins has had an unfortunate time. I shall make an order excluding her husband from the matrimonial home.

"Does that mean he has to be gone when I get
home?" piped up Mrs. Perkins. The Judge looked at
her, acknowledging her existence for the first time.

"Your husband must be served with the order first,
Mrs. Perkins. As it's a Friday, that may not be possible
before Monday."

"What am I supposed to do until then? I've got six
kids."

The Judge, halfway out of his chair, stopped in annoyance and glared at Harry.

"Mr.?"

"Trent, your honour."

"Mr. Trent, cannot someone from your firm serve the
exclusion order?"

"I don't know, your honour"

"Well, can't you do it!" he barked.

"I'm sure he can, your honour," butted in Whitehead.

Great thought Harry. *A million quid at my feet and now I've got to go and serve a court order on some violent pervert. That's just what I need.*

"Be happy to, your honour" he said.

"Good. Get the order written up straight away, will you?" he muttered to the clerk as he left the room.

"Yes, your Honour," came the weary reply and then to Harry, "You'll have to wait."

"I'll go around me sisters until school finishes, then I'll go and collect the kids. You'll have him out by then, will you?"

"I'll do my best, Mrs. Perkins."

87 Ludlow Road was a Victorian terrace, hidden away behind privet hedge. Harry stepped over the broken toys littering the path. The garden was choked with thistles, a rusty pram wheel poking out from amongst them. There wasn't a doorbell so he knocked. The door swung open as his knuckles made contact. "Hello...? Mr. Perkins?" Tentatively he walked into the hallway. The faded and stained paper on the walls hung loose in strips revealing large blackberries of mould. Harry shivered in the dank atmosphere reluctant to proceed further. "Hello?" It was getting darker; the front door was closing behind him.

"Don't move," said a voice from the growing gloom. Harry felt the sharp jab of a shotgun between his shoulder blades.

Chapter
Twenty-Six

The Johnson brothers were small time villains with large ambitions. They thought the armed robbery of an illegal casino would be an easy affair. They also thought the man they would take with them was a good idea, as he was handy with a gun. They didn't know Bernie Doyle owned the casino or that their accomplice had a loose tongue. Word quickly reached Bernie of the plan.

As the Johnson's entered the casino, the lights went out sowing confusion amongst them. When they came back on, a hail of bullets tore into them sending all three spinning to the ground in a bloody heap. Killing them had been easy. What to do with the bodies was more of a problem

"What about the motorway extension?" suggested Bernie.

Norman shook his head. "No. We let Donny Phillips put two bodies there last week."

"Ginger?"

"He's not in the patio business anymore."

"I met this bloke in the pub, he sells meat for dog food," said Razors. "Says people he sells it to don't give a toss what they put in the tins. We get it chopped up nice and small who's gonna know?"

"All right, Razors. We can drop the bodies off with Jimmy the Knife on the way to my place."

Like a triumphant football manager Bernie had invited the team back to his house to celebrate. He was looking forward to a long hot shower and a cold beer.

Don Meadows pulled his silver Astra to a stop in the front drive of the Doyle's house. He'd already sold it for them but if he could find a buyer willing to pay more he found few sellers who wouldn't be happy to gazump the previous buyer. Bianca had been quite explicit he could only bring people round by prior appointment. He'd called and got no reply. These buyers he knew had more money than sense and he needed to get his figures up for the current month. He still had the key so who would know.

The Oliver's car pulled up behind him. He turned to greet them as they approached.

"It's smaller than I imagined," said Mrs. Oliver as she stood outside the house.

Ken Oliver snorted. "It's double fronted, triple car garage. What more do you want?"

There's also a double garage and workshop at the rear," chimed in Meadows.

"Has it got a pool?" she asked.

"No, but there's room at the rear for one," said Meadows

"There's no pool, Kenny."

"What do you want a pool for? You can't bleedin' swim!"

Sharon Oliver went red. "Course I can," she tittered, "Course I can. Don't be silly, Kenny."

"Shall we go in?" said Meadows ushering them towards the front door.

The Range Rover and Mercedes drew to a halt at the rear of Bernie's house. He held up the remote and the gates swung open. The vehicles drove in.

"Right," said Bernie. "I'm letting you in my house, so best behaviour. And no one is sticking their arses on my furniture until they've showered and changed. 'Ere." He threw a couple of plastic bagged tracksuits at Razors and Dublin Dave.

"What are these?" asked Dave.

"Track suits. Put them on once you've cleaned up."

Dave looked at the packet. "What's all this funny writing?"

"Your supposed to wear it, not read it!" snapped Bernie.

"I was only asking"

"Saudi World Cup squad," butted in Razors. "You remember we did that warehouse?"

"Oh yeah."

Bernie rolled his eyes to the ceiling. The warehouse raid was supposed to produce 5,000 England World Cup tracksuits that could have been sold at £50 each. A quarter of a million pounds of easy money. And what did they do? Nick the wrong boxes. They'd said World Cup 2014 on the outside alright, but none of the pillocks had noticed the Arabic script below.

Bernie opened the back door and pointed to the right. "Razors, you and Dave get cleaned up in the boot room. Once you're done, there's beer in the fridge and we'll see you in the snooker room." Razors nodded, Bernie and Norman disappeared into the main part of the house.

"The boot room?" asked Dave turning to Razors.

"Yeah, it's a place to keep yer boots, innit?"

"And this is the snooker room," said Meadows showing the Oliver's into a large book lined room, a snooker table taking up the centre of it."

"But Kenny, you don't play snooker," chimed in Sharon Oliver.

Razors removed his puffa jacket, the shirt underneath stiff with the congealed blood of Ronny Johnson. Dave was in a similar bloodied state. Bernie had not wanted them in the car in such a condition and only relented after Norman spread bin liners everywhere and they both sworn a solemn oath not to touch anything. Dave leant the two shotguns he was carrying against the wall and his clothing joined the bloody pile, on the floor. Both men stared at their bloodstained appearance.

"Fuck me!" said Razors. "We look like we've been in a car crash."

Dave sat scratching his groin staring at rows of Wellington boots and walking shoes as Razors showered. Most of them looked new.

"Why they got so many pairs of wellies?" he shouted to Razors over the noise of the shower.

"Bianca started watching all them country vet programmes. She kept dragging Bernie off for weekends in the country until she stood in some cow shit and they haven't been back since."

Look at the state of my fucking hands thought Dave. *I can hardly see my tattoos.* He was very proud of the "Mumm" and "Dadd" painstakingly written on his fingers. The backs of his hands were now dark red and little of his artwork could be seen.

"And, through here is the boot room," said Meadows his hand reaching for the door knob.

Bernie threw his jacket on the bed and started to remove his clothes. *What's that noise? Must be Razors or Dave. If they get any blood on the carpet I'll murder them. Was this wise, Bernie, everyone coming back in such a state? Well, who is going to miss the Johnsons or bring in the old Bill? At least here I can make sure every-thing is cleaned up properly and disposed of. Anyway, not often Bianca 's away and I can have the lads round for a few beers.* Bernie stepped into the shower and closed his eyes as the jets of water cascaded over his face and body.

"Is that the kitchen?" queried Sharon Oliver.

Meadows removed his hand from the doorknob and followed the Oliver's into the kitchen. Oliver turned to Meadows as they walked in.

"Christ knows why she's interested in the kitchen! Dopey cow can't even make toast without burning it!"

Dave walked to the sink, which stood in the corner of the room. He lathered his fingers from a tub of liquid soap. He turned the tap but nothing happened. He banged the end of it angrily, but still no water. Dave squinted underneath the spout but could see nothing. He stuck his finger up feeling for a blockage. He felt something against the tip but it moved backwards as he touched it. He tried pushing but his finger would go no further.

He scowled at the tap and twiddled it right and left in the vain hope it would make a difference. The tap stared back at him defiantly. Dave's eyes darted to the shotgun as he contemplated blasting it. Bernie, he thought, wouldn't take kindly to having his sink shot up.

Dave rubbed more soap on his finger and pushed it up the tap again. With extra lubrication, he managed to get his finger in further but could feel nothing. He tried to pull it back but it wouldn't move. He yanked violently backwards and the taps shuddered, but his finger was stuck.

"What the fuck are you doing?" asked Razors, stepping dripping from the shower.

"I'm fucking stuck! What does it look like?"

Razors burst out laughing. "You prat! Come here." He grabbed hold of Dave's arm and yanked it viciously. Dave howled in pain.

"You're tearing my fucking finger off!"

Razors stood behind Dave, reached over his shoulder and grabbed Dave's wrist with both hands.

"Right. On the count of three, we both pull" he said.

Meadows opened the boot room door and blinked. The house was supposed to be empty, which was surprise number one. Surprise number two was to see two naked men, one leaning over the other.

"Careful!" screamed Dave. "It's fucking jammed! You'll rip it off if your not careful!"

Meadows' eyes took in the bloodstained clothing on the floor and the shotguns propped against the wall. Christ almighty! What had he walked in on?

"It's not my fault Kenny, I didn't know it would make the microwave explode," whined Sharon Oliver as she walked into the room. Her eyes locked on to Razor's hairy, pink and naked bottom.

"Pull you silly bastard!" shouted Razors "I can't stand like this all day".

Bernie was stepping out of the shower when he heard the scream. He dropped the towel and grabbed the shotgun.

The sound of someone pounding down the stairs caused Meadows to look backwards. The sight of a third naked man, this one holding a gun, convinced him his end was in sight. Sharon Oliver turned to her husband in the hope of reassurance and let out a further piercing scream when she saw Bernie.

There was a loud slurping pop as Dave's finger came free. He turned with a broad smile on his face. "Thanks Razor's."

Bernie rammed the barrels of his shotgun under Meadows' chin, forcing him back against the wall.

"Don't kill me!" gurgled Meadows. "I'm only an estate agent."

Chapter
Twenty-Seven

The door to the Perkins house slammed shut and they stood in semi darkness.

"Mr. Perkins?" ventured Harry.

"Who wants to know?"

Good question. Telling a man with a gun that he'd come to throw him out sounded a bad idea. "I'm Harry," he said playing for time.

"What you doing' in my house?"

"I- err- wondered if you wanted to buy some double glazing."

"Move," he said poking Harry in the back with the gun. "Door at the end."

Harry pushed open the door in front of him. The kitchen table was littered with dirty cups, plates and the remnants of long forgotten meals. A sheet of plastic flapped over an empty window frame. On the floor, next to a brown stained sink sat a spilled tin of bake beans, the bright orange sauce the only spot of colour in the room.

"Sit."

Harry side stepped the remains of a curry and sat down. Tony Perkins was 45, receding hair and holding the tube of a vacuum cleaner! Perkins saw the look on Harry's face and let out a loud guffaw.

"Had you goin', didn't I?"

"I've got this for you." Harry reached into his case and gave him the court order. Perkin's face scanned the page.

"Not to molest? Servants or agents? Leave the house forthwith? What's forthwith mean?"

"Straight away."

"So, what?... I've got to leave the house and... then what?"

"Not come back."

"You havin' a laugh?" Perkins face had slipped from a smile, to bemusement, and now menace. "You're that slag's solicitor!"

"Well, I have to go," said Harry rising from the table.

"You're fucking going nowhere!" Perkins waved a rather long and rusty looking bayonet in front of Harry's face. "My old man dun in a few Krauts with this in the war. Just right for killin' rats after I've trapped 'em. Especially big ones like you." Harry sank down in to the chair. Perkins glanced at Harry's case sitting on the table. "What you got in that shiny case?"

It contained the money; Harry had carried it around all day.

"You got my magazines? Open it!"

Harry looked from the bayonet to Perkins. He'd only been in the law a few weeks and this was the third time he'd seen his end in sight. *Perkins was a man at breaking point - in the process of losing his wife and now some shiny suit fucker was telling him to get out of his house. Every man's home is his castle. In Perkins case, more of a rubbish skip, but now didn't seem the time to point that out - sticking a bayonet through Harry's head might not be the answer, but it was one way of telling people Mr. Rainy Face was in town.*

"Aaah!!" Perkins let out a violent scream as he brought the knife down in an ark. Harry dived to the left to avoid the plunging blade, he rolled across the floor and as his feet came up over his head, his bottom landed in the pool of baked beans.

Harry sat on the floor, nerves jangling. It seemed fitting somehow that having come into this arse hole of an existence he should have a taste of what it felt like. Harry looked round the room, the will to do anything in it had long since died. The decay eating away at the Perkins marriage oozed from every corner. Perkins sat at the table, his face sunk in to his yellowed stained vest. His pale white shoulders quivered as he wept.

Trembling Harry got to his feet and picked up the case. The court order lay crumpled on the floor, its corners now a vivid baked bean orange. He stepped over a child's sweatshirt lying on the floor and headed for the door. As he walked through it, he could hear Perkins saying, "I love 'er, I love 'er" in between his sobs.

Michael picked up the contract from his desk and discarded it in favour of a golfing magazine. He was avidly reading about an exclusive golf resort when his private line rang. He picked up the phone. "Hello."

"Michael, what are you doing for lunch?"

"I'm a bit tied up today, Bernie."

"I've got us a table in the River Room for 1.00." The tone in Doyle's voice didn't brook disagreement.

"OK Bernie. I'll see you then." He replaced the receiver with annoyance and was returning to the magazine when his other phone rang.

"Yes?"

"Michael," said Suzy. "There's an Inspector Chambers to see you."

"Tell him I'm with clients."

"It's about Melvyn Godson."

"Oh. OK, send him up."

Chambers was in his late fifties and had a younger officer, who he introduced as Phelps, with him. They all shook hands and sat down.

"What can I do for you, Inspector?"

"Did you know Melvyn Godson?"

"Yes, I've known him for a number of years."

"I take it you know he's been murdered?"

Michael shifted uneasily in his seat. "Have you... found the body?"

"No, just the teeth, some toes and a credit card,"

"And part of a hand" added Phelps.

"Yes, we found that in a Cornish pasty. Someone had put a nail through it," said the Inspector emphasising the word nail as he said it.

"Jesus!" exclaimed Michael who'd gone very pale.

"I understand you act for Bernie Doyle?" said the Inspector, sensing he'd unnerved Burns.

"He's a client."

"Did he know Melvyn Godson?"

"I believe so."

"My understanding is they had a very close relationship."

"I couldn't comment inspector. Client confidentiality, you understand," replied Michael realising he needed to take some control over the way the conversation was proceeding.

"No Mr. Burns, I don't. We're investigating a brutal murder." Chambers angrily threw some photos on to the table. They showed three toes and part of a hand. The big toe was blackened and charred at the tip. Michael recoiled as he saw the dark black hole in the middle of the hand. "Someone nailed Melvyn Godson to a table and then took a blow torch to his feet. So, I'll ask you again. What did Godson do for Doyle?"

Burns looked from the photos to the officers and forced back the bile in his throat. He'd heard the rumours about Melvyn from Arthur Bytheway. To have them confirmed was another thing.

"Godson stole a million pounds from Doyle and was tortured to death to reveal where he'd hidden it," added Chambers, seeing the ashen look on Burns face. He knew that most of what he was saying was guesswork. Forensics revealed the hand had been nailed to a wooden surface and a blowtorch used on the toes. He also suspected Godson laundered money for Doyle. Added to this was the rumour Doyle was going mental because a million pounds was missing. It didn't take much to put it all together. The look on Burns face told him he wasn't far off the mark.

Chambers got to his feet. He indicated to the officer to leave the photos. "Thank you for you time, Mr Burns. We'll be in touch."

Michael sat silently screaming inside. Transfixed by the photo of the tortured hand.

He was still in a state of shock an hour later when he left the building to get a cab. He sat in the back and pondered his predicament. The police claimed Bernie had murdered Godson. A million pounds sat in a luggage locker, and the key to it was missing. When Doyle called from the airport, he'd given him the impression he had the key. His explanation of the golf invitation hadn't been believed. This was what lunch was all about. Should he run? He could go to Heathrow and fly somewhere Doyle would never find him. But, that would confirm his guilt and he didn't have the money for Christ-sake. Why should he spend the rest of his life hiding in some god-forsaken hole for something he hadn't done?

The Maître d' smiled in recognition as he entered the River Room.

"Mr. Burns. How nice to see you. Mr. Doyle is waiting."

"Has he been here long?"

"About 15 minutes."

Shit! That was all he needed. "Thank you, Robert." He walked across the room to the table. Doyle was sitting looking out the window at the Thames.

"Hello, Bernie."

Doyle ignored the greeting, leaving him in a state of uncertainty. Finally, he turned his head and smiled. "Hello, Michael, how are you?"

Burns collapsed gratefully into his seat. "Fine. What was it you wanted to see me about?"

"Plenty of time for that. Try the wine, its from a little vineyard in the woods just behind the village of Leognan"

Michael picked up the glass, the wine tasted like chalk.

"Why don't we order?" said Doyle.

The waiter came and took their orders. Bernie broke a small piece from his bread roll and buttered it. "I thought it would be nice to have a general chat about things. Haven't been able to catch up since I got back from South America."

"Great."

A silence descended on the table. Bernie with surgical precision dissected and slowly ate his roll. Michael fidgeted until unable to stand the silence any longer he spoke.

"How was... South America?"

"Bit hot for Norman. He got sunburn." The first course arrived, Doyle spread the pate on his toast. "Yeah, he never could stand the heat. Old Melvyn was just the same."

The snail Michael was removing from its shell shot out and hit his tie leaving a trail of garlic butter across his shirt. "Melvyn?"

"Melvyn Godson. He came out to my villa last year, fell asleep by the pool. Got himself well toasted. You seen much of him lately?" The image of the burnt toe flashed in front of Michael's eyes.

"No. Not much."

Michael tried to wipe the butter from his shirt angrily waving away a waiter who tried to help. Bernie ate the pate, placing his knife back on the plate when he'd finished. "Some very nasty people in South America. Things can get very bloody when they get disappointed. Would you like some red?"

The main course arrived. They watched as the waiter carved the Boeuf Wellington they'd ordered, the knife sliding easily through the pastry and meat. A large pink slice flopped onto the plate. Bernie smiled. "Lot easier to cut through meat when you don't have a bone involved." Michael looked at the pink meat and tried to gulp but was unable to swallow. A selection of vegetables arrived and the two men began to eat. Michael pushed the food around his plate finally placing a sautéed potato in his mouth.

"Look at the state of that" said Doyle waving a blackened vegetable in the air, "burnt to a crisp"

Michael choked on his potato.

"You alright?"

"Yes," croaked Michael taking a drink of water. "Went down the wrong way."

"You want to watch that. It can be very unpleasant when things get taken the wrong way."

Doyle ate another slice of the Boeuf Wellington. Did Michael have the key? He was clearly uneasy but that was hardly surprising. If Michael had it, he would need to be a little subtle in getting it from him than he'd been with Godson. It didn't do to have two of his professional advisers turning up in Chicken pies in the same week.

"We must have the fish next time. They have some very fine salmon. You fish?"

"No."

"I always wonder about the fish. That hook getting imbedded in its mouth. I mean if someone stuck a meat hook through your mouth and held you up by it, it'd hurt, wouldn't it?"

Michael pushed his uneaten plate of food away

"You not hungry?"

"I've lost my appetite."

The restaurant was quite full now. Waiters glided between tables baring plates of nouvelle cuisine and bottles of Château Neuf de Pape. The soft tinkle of jewellery against cut glass could be heard.

"I'll have the Crepes aux bananas, please," said Bernie to the waiter.

"Just coffee for me" said Michael.

"How's Harry coming along?"

"Fine. He and I have gone through most of the papers on your purchase. We should be able to exchange soon. Has the key turned up?

A look that would have curdled milk flitted across Bernie's face. "No. You haven't heard anything, have you?"

"Your Crepe, sir." The waiter ignited the rum on the bananas. A bright orange flame shot into the air.

"No," said Michael his eyes fixed on the flame as it stripped away the outer flesh of the banana.

"You will tell me, won't you Michael?"

Chapter
Twenty-Eight

"It's flat" said Tim.

Both men looked at the wheel willing it to re-inflate. After two minutes of staring they exchanged glances.

"Let's ring Mandy" said Ben.

Mandy was not meant to use police vehicles to provide a taxi service, but it was one of those days when she really didn't care about her future in the police. Five minutes later she picked them both up. As they got in the car they could see she was not having a good day.

"Thanks Mandy." Said Ben. "Could you drop us at the Star of Bengal."

"Why not join us when you've finished" said Tim,

Mandy just grunted as they drove away.

Harry's legs made a squelching sound as he walked. It wasn't easy to clean your bottom of baked beans on a suburban street in broad daylight. After he'd seen the third pair of curtains starting to twitch violently, he gave up. At the end of Ludlow Road, he saw a black cab and flagged it down.

"Finsbury Park, please." Harry opened the back door, put the case on the cab floor and began to climb in after it.

"No so fast, sunshine!" snarled the cabby, leaping from the cab and grabbing Harry's arm as he was half way in the cab. "Out! Now!"

Harry looked at the driver with anguish- all he wanted was to get home and change. He tried to shake his arm loose, but it was held in a vice like grip.

"You can't refuse a fare."

"I can if they've pissed themselves!"

"No, I haven't!"

"What the hell is that then?" said the cabby pointing at Harry's crotch. They both looked down at his damp trousers. *Was the cabby colour blind, who had bright orange piss?*

"It's beans, can't you tell!" said Harry indignant at the suggestion he'd wet himself.

"What?!"

"Baked beans. I fell in some baked beans."

"Where?"

They both looked up the street for the baked bean lake.

"Look, I'm a solicitor. I was in a house serving an injunction when I fell in some baked beans." It sounded as real as finding a baked bean lake in the middle of

Finchley. The cabby wasn't interested. He pulled Harry from the cab and sent him spinning to the ground.

"Bleedin' pervert!" he shouted as he drove away. Harry sat on the pavement and buried his head in his hands. He could have wept. The sound of tutting from behind made him look round. Two elderly housewives were staring unable to decide whether he was a rapist a pervert or both.

THE CASE!! OH GOD! IT'S IN THE CAB!!! Harry leapt to his feet causing the women to scatter. The cab was vanishing into the distance as he ran after it. *Thank God! A red light.* He was gaining on it. He reached out and grabbed for the rear door as the lights turned amber. Instead of pulling it open he banged on the window. Why he thought the cabby would now welcome him and his baked bean laden bottom he didn't know, but you can't always think straight when a million pounds is about to disappear. One glance at Harry and he locked all the doors.

The cab pulled away with Harry hanging on. "YOU'VE GOT MY CASE!" As the taxi accelerated Harry crashed into the road. He looked up in despair trying to remember the number plate, AX13. BAAHHHH!!! A large red bus loomed towards him. He didn't care- Harry got to his feet and stood trance like as it bore down- it was a cleaner death than ending up burnt and chopped up in a chicken pie. The bus driver thought differently. He was clawing at his steering wheel as if his life depended on it.

Fortunately, it was lamp post he demolished as the bus skidded to a halt.

You couldn't blame the bus driver for thumping Harry. Most would have done the same. He climbed from his cab shaking like a leaf and saw Harry standing in the middle of the road with a broad grin on his face. As the bus smashed into the telephone box, Harry remembered the cab was done out for a Levi ad. How many 13 registered cabs could there be advertising Levi's especially as he had the first two letters as well. By now Harry was quite use to hitting the ground.

He heard a police siren behind him followed by the squeal of brakes. A hand grabbed Harry's shoulder and hauled him to his feet. "This way if you please, sir." The voice sounded public school and familiar. The next voice he heard was manna from heaven.

"Tim, for fuck sake pack it in and get back in the car." It was Mandy! He swivelled round and looked into the astonished face of Tim.

"Harry?" he said in horror and surprise at the sight that confronted him. Harry's suit was torn and covered in grime with splashes of blood and baked beans thrown in for good measure.

"That's him! That's the mad bastard!" said the driver advancing towards Harry, his arm and finger pointing vigorously as if it were a spear to impale Harry on. Tim stared at the driver in that public-school sort of way that's used to intimidate servants and horses. It pulled the driver up short. Tim picked a baked bean from Harry's suit and looked at it quizzically.

"Is this yours?" he asked holding it out to the driver.

"No," came the bemused, response

"It's evidence then," said Tim putting it in his pocket. "You," he said to Harry. "In the car."

"What's your name, my man," he said to the driver.

"Cussler, sir."

"Well done, Cussler." Tim held out his hand and shook the driver's. The man beamed.

"Thank you, sir."

"Oh, Chief constable." Harry looked over at Ben, whose face was contorted with tears of mirth. "Chief constable," he repeated in a strangled tone. "I think we'd better be going."

A look of uncertainty crept into the bus driver's eyes. Something was not quite right. He couldn't put his finger on it, but… Mandy caught the look and stepped in before Tim's megalomania was exposed. With a cool deft hand, she took the driver to one side for his details and saved the day.

Harry sat in the car with Tim and Ben as they rolled around trying to control their mirth. Mandy climbed back into the car her face black as thunder. Harry battered, bruised and smelling of baked beans sat in silence. Was this going to be the end of him and Mandy? He'd never seen her look so angry. It

was only as she drove away that he remembered he'd
lost the case.

Ronnie Becker backed his cab on to the drive. He grimaced as the discs at the bottom of his spine crunched
into each other; his back always felt worse when he
was tired. A stressful day made worse by the young lad
smeared in baked beans. It was getting dark. Ronnie
liked to be bathed and changed before the Sabbath began. In his anger, he'd forgotten to avoid the road works
and now he was late. There wouldn't be time to clean
the cab and his bath would be rushed.

He opened the garage door. Normally it was full of
household debris, kept on the off chance it might be
useful. On Sunday however he was taking the family
to Israel and he wasn't leaving his cab in the open for
two weeks. His wife had spent days moving the junk
stored there into the house. You could hardly move for
old lampshades, curtains, ancient stereos, carry cots
and other long discarded possessions. He backed the
cab in, closed the door and went into the house. Harry's
case lay in the darkness on the floor of the cab.

Mandy dropped them off at Tim and Ben's Pimlico flat.
She hadn't said a word other than she would be back in
an hour. Harry gratefully accepted Ben's offer of a bath
and a change of clothes. He dropped his suit in a tatty
pile on the floor and climbed into the steaming waters.

Tim came in with a gin and tonic in a tall frosted glass, a slice of lime gently floating in the top. Harry's shoulders slowly began to subside from between his ears. For 45 minutes, he was able to forget about the money.

The hornet like buzzing of the door intercom followed by the pounding of feet up the stairs heralded the arrival of Mandy. He could hear a low but angry voice coming from the next room broken now and again by a louder 'and don't you ever'. Harry emerged from the bathroom in Tim's slightly large sweatshirt and jeans. Tim and Ben sat on the sofa like two chastened schoolboys while Mandy prowled the room; a caged tiger, who'd spent the afternoon being poked with a stick. Harry's throat turned to carpet.

"Well?" she demanded.

He told her about the vacuum cleaner pipe and the bayonet, which brought a look of concern to her eyes and then the baked beans at which she suppressed a smile. When he got to the bus she burst into tears and threw her arms around his neck.

"But, you got the case back all right?" she sniffed.

"No."

Mandy leapt back as if he'd given her an electric shock.

"But, what about the million poun…"

Her voice trailed off as she looked around at Tim and Ben sitting with rapt attention on the sofa. Her mumbled "Sorry, Harry," was all the confirmation they needed.

"Million pounds!" piped up Ben.

"Case?" said Tim

"A million pounds in a case and you've lost it!" they chimed in together.

Harry collapsed like a deflated balloon into a chair. "I still have fifty thousand covered in vomit in my wardrobe," he muttered. "Oh, and another fifty grand that belongs to Victor Davis."

Mandy gave him a quizzical look. "Who is Victor Davis?".

"He gave me fifty grand to bribe a judge. But I didn't... I just... kept it," he said as Mandy's eyes got wider and wider.

"That's good," said Mandy in an abstract manner.

They sat in silence. Ben and Tim exchanged looks of bemusement. Mandy stared intently at the fire place. "Look, it's not as bad as all that," said Harry.

It broke the ice. Mandy let out a strangled hysterical laugh and demanded a drink. Cans were produced together with a large bag of cheese and onion crisps and a jar of chutney. Harry filled Ben and Tim in on the details they didn't know.

"We can speak to Andrea," said Tim through a mouthful of crisps, "she works for the add agency who have the Levi account. They must have details of the cabs involved and if we have half the number plate we're home and dry."

"Yes, but what if the cabby has just done a runner with the money?" said Ben.

"Or worse" said Mandy.

They all looked at Mandy expectantly. None of them could think of what was worse.

"What if he's handed the money into the police. I don't see Bernie Doyle wanting to go down to the police station to reclaim it, do you?

Chapter
Twenty-Nine

Harry had a sleepless night made worse by Mandy telling him it didn't matter that he couldn't get an erection.
It just lay there pink and useless. He knew exactly how
it felt. The trouble was he kept having mental images of
Bernie Doyle banging a nail through it. Mandy was on
early shift. She crawled out of bed about quarter to five,
dressed and left. He lay in bed alone; it felt cold and
empty without her.

"Murderer!" screamed the tin of baked beans from
the witness box. Counsel for the prosecution held up
his bean stained trousers and the jury chanted "guilty,
guilty". Harry looked up at the judge and from beneath
the wig beamed the face of Bernie Doyle. "Harry, you
have taken some liberties," he said. "Good job I brought
the blow torch." He tried to say he'd give the money
back, but he couldn't speak as a giant pastry case had
been put over his head. Harry awoke sweating.

Harry staggered into work that morning and sat at
his desk. The sea of papers in front of him bobbed up

and down. Michael was off at some boat show and was not expected in. The phone awoke him from his stupor.

"Harry, Mr. and Mrs. Oliver are here. They'd like to see you," said Wendy.

"Who?"

"Client's of Michael's. He's very big in sofa's."

He went into reception and met the sofa king. Everything about them looked fake from their botoxed foreheads down.

"Harry," beamed Ken Oliver holding out an armful of jewellery as he shook his hand. "We have a problem and need your help."

"What can I do for you?"

"It's Sharon's mother," he said nodding at his wife. "She's dead."

"Oh, I'm sorry. When did it happen?"

"About half an hour ago."

Harry had a vision of them standing over the body hoping she would die in office hours.

"Oh."

"We're on our way to the airport. Michael is her executor and we'd like him to do the business whilst we're away."

"Do the business?" Harry looked at Wendy for guidance - she shrugged her shoulders - and then back at the Oliver's.

Oliver glanced at his watch in alarm. "Oh Christ! Look at the time! We're going to miss the flight if we don't get a move on. We've got her in the car outside. Can you come and get her?"

"Your mother's in the car outside?" Harry parroted at Mrs. Oliver.

"Yes," she replied.

"But, I thought she was dead."

"She is," said Mrs Oliver, her plastic smile at breaking point.

"Is there a problem?" asked Oliver a note of irritation in his voice.

"But, what's she doing in the car?"

Mrs. Oliver snorted and turned to her husband for guidance. He raised his eyes to the ceiling.

"She's not doing anything. We've told you she's dead," she replied testily.

Harry stared at both Oliver's. His knowledge of probate was scant, but he was pretty sure that when your old mum died you didn't bundle the body in the car and drive it round to the solicitors to 'collect the winnings'. He could see the impatience rising on both their faces.

"Well?" demanded Oliver.

"We, um, don't do funerals," he mumbled. "Sorry, you will need an undertaker." Harry looked at his shoes and closed his eyes for a moment hoping this was just a bad dream that would go away. When he glanced up Oliver was sizzling.

"Look sonny, I'm supposed to be on my way to Barbados. Now I have her dead mother in my car. Michael is the executor of her will, so he's responsible."

"He's right you know Harry," butted in Wendy. "Do you remember that poor Mr. Green. He had no one in the world but us, so we had to get him buried."

Harry gave Wendy a stare that made her recoil in fright.

"But, you will want to come to the funeral?" he blurted out. They both shook their heads.

"No," said Mrs. Oliver.

"Not really," said Oliver.

"Don't look at me like that!" said Mrs. Oliver accusingly.

A surprised look came across Harry's face. Then he realised it wasn't him she was talking to but Wendy. He swivelled round and saw the look of disgust on Wendy's face.

"I don't have anything to wear for a funeral. I look terrible in black!"

"Listen," said Oliver. "It's quite simple. Her mother was supposed to look after our place while we went on holiday. I picked her up this morning and she was as right as nine pence. By the time, I got her to our house, she was dead. What I need you to do is to come with us to the airport. We'll catch our flight and then you take her to the undertakers."

The four of them in a Porsche heading along the M4 to Heathrow, there's not much room in the back, especially when you have no desire to sit next to a corpse. Harry sat with his head compressed into the window next to the very dead and very fat body of the late Mabel Evans.

They pulled into the unloading bay at the airport.

"Oh, my God!" exclaimed Mrs. Oliver as they got out of the car.

Harry and Oliver looked on expectantly.

"Look at me," she went on.

They did. Oliver in growing annoyance, Harry in the hope that a spark of decency existed in one of them.

She held her hands out towards Harry, "Look at the state of me." They started to shake. A tear appeared in the corner of a granite eye.

"What the fuck is the matter?!" exclaimed Oliver.

"I haven't done my nails!" she began to wail. "That's what happens when your mum dies," she said to Harry. "You forget all about the important things in life."

"What!" exploded Oliver, "What the fuck are you going on about your nails for at a time like this. We've got a plane to catch."

"But Kenny, we're flying Club! I can't fly Club looking like this."

The headline 'lawyer in triple murder' flashed in front of Harry's eyes.

"Never mind your bloody nails, we're going to miss the flight," Oliver replied.

They grabbed their cases from the boot. Oliver gave Harry a curt nod. "She needs a service".

"C of E?".

"Hey?"

"Was she Church of England?"

"I'm not talking about her! I meant the car. Watch your speed on the way back, the car needs servicing.

"Bye, mum!" shouted a disappearing Mrs. Oliver over her shoulder. "Have a nice..."

"Dopey cow," grunted Oliver running after her.

Harry drove back into London. Two firsts for one day; he'd never driven a Porsche before or had a dead body in his car. It was understandable therefore that he was speeding and didn't immediately notice the flashing blue light behind. When he did, and looked at the speed he saw he was doing 110 mph.

He sat and watched through the side view mirror as the blue uniform slowly walked towards him. The conversation to come ran through his mind:

> "Is this your car, sir?"
> "No."
> "I see, sir, and what about the dead body? Does that belong to you?"
> "No."

> *"I see. Stolen car, stolen corpse and doing 110 miles an hour. Not really your day is it, sir?"*

As it was, he was as nice as pie. Harry stepped out of the car as the officer approached.

"Good morning officer, can I help you?"

"Do you know how fast you were going, sir?"

"Yes, I'm sorry. I believe I was doing 110."

"Not a good idea with an elderly lady in the car, is it, sir?"

"No, officer."

He bent down and looked through the back window.

"Your grandmother looks a little unwell. Is she, all right?"

'As well as can be expected for any two- hour old corpse'

Then it struck him. "No, she's not well at all. I think she's had a stroke. I'm trying to get her to hospital."

"Right! Back in the car and follow me," and off they shot down the motorway. Harry watched his speed climb to 140 mph.

Leaving the old dear at a hospital was the ideal thing to do. It was perfectly plausible she had a stroke in the car and died before they could get there. Sadly, driving around with a corpse had rather dented Harry's sense of reality. All he could think of was that she was dead, and there was no point in taking her to a hospital. There would be big scene in which the doctors and 'Mr. Plod' would standing over him glowering, demanding to know why he'd taken a dead body to a hospital. There was also the question of how he'd get her back. Didn't you need a body to get a death certificate?

He lost the policeman as they came off the express-way. Harry drove into the maze of streets that surround-ed it zigzagging towards Victoria. This wasn't easy with the one-way system. On two occasions, he found him-self heading back towards the Marylebone Road. The first time he hit the brakes violently. Unfortunately, those on the car behind weren't as good, and he felt his neck whip forward as it hit the Porsche. He wasn't in the mood to swap numbers though and accelerated away taking any turn that appeared and found himself in a dead end facing a concrete mixer.

The Oliver's car took some further punishment as Harry tried to back out. The rear window of a Porsche doesn't give great visibility at the best of times, and he could see little with a corpse blocking his view. There was a sickening twang of the wing mirror flying off as he backed past a skip. He didn't care, the bloody Oliver's deserved it! He was a fugitive from the police, lost and stuck in a car with a dead body.

Harry jolted off across London - failing entirely in his state of funk to find the right gear - cursing the Oliver's and ducking whenever he saw a traffic warden. *OH, MY CHRIST, STOP! SHE'S CROSSING THE ROAD!!!!* Harry stamped the brake pedal through the floor almost tipping the car over. There was a soft thud as the body of Mable Evans toppled forward. He screamed as the cold tip of her nose pressed against his neck.

Harry looked through the windscreen fearing the worst and was relieved to see a young woman giving him a mouthful of abuse and a handful of flashing fingers. He mouthed apologies and sped on, every nerve jangling in his body.

He drove about a quarter of a mile and pulled into the first parking space he saw. Harry climbed out and slammed the door, forgetting all about the keys still in the ignition. His eye caught the ugly stump of the beheaded wing mirror. It matched nicely with the crumpled bumper and missing rear light. He needed a drink. Leaving a Porsche in the middle of London in broad daylight with the keys in the ignition probably wasn't a good idea, but then he wasn't having a good day and it wasn't as if the car was unoccupied!

Three scotches later Harry returned to the car. Or, where he thought he'd parked it. It took a good half hour for him to admit to himself it'd gone. It's not hard though to find a Silver Porsche in London. He ran up to two only to realise they weren't the right one. He had no idea what the registration number was, however the absence of a wing mirror and a dead body were rather a giveaway. Harry was really looking forward to giving that description to the police.

Eventually he admitted defeat. Harry walked down into Covent Garden to Bow Street Police station. He stood at the desk for about five minutes while the copper behind it did everything he could to ignore him for as long as possible. Finally, as Harry hadn't gone away, he looked up.

"Yes?"

"I, erm, want to report a stolen car."

"Stolen?"

"Yes, I think so." His smirk said it all so Harry added. "I parked my car, and when I came back it was gone. It could have been towed away, I suppose."

The officer gave him a look that said 'time waster' and then impatiently said, "registration number?"

"I'm sorry, I don't know."

Harry could see the steam starting to rise from the officer's head and thought it prudent to say why the number wasn't needed.

"The car should be fairly easy to trace. It's a Porsche with a missing wing mirror and a dead body in it..."

The officer dropped his pen as he heard the words dead body. He looked at Harry for confirmation of what he'd said. Harry nodded.

"Sarge!" shouted the officer as he ran from the room. He skidded to a halt as he reached the door and looked back at Harry, with a nervous smile.

"Don't move mate, all right? I'm just going to get you... a cup of tea. SARGE!" he bellowed as he galloped out of the room. *He would go far. What murderer would*

want to do a runner when he could stay and have a nice
cup of tea with the Sarge!

There were two of them. A young one with spiky hair and
an older one; a Sergeant whose dark brown eyes disappeared down twin burrows of flesh set into pink blotchy
cheeks. Short strands of curly grey hair poked out of the
corners of his balding pate. He rubbed his eyes with two
large hair hands as if he was struggling to stay awake.

"So, Harry, let's see if I've got this straight. You'd
taken the body to the airport dropped off..." He shuffled
through his notes.

"The Oliver's," said Harry.

"The Oliver's. So, is the dead woman a client?"

"Yes."

"Do you have many dead clients?"

Harry thought about this for a moment. The firm
had a fair-sized probate department.

"Yes, quite a few."

The two officers exchanged a knowing look. They
had a very narrow view of what lawyers did and had
taken Harry's claims of acting for the dead totally the
wrong way. This was understandable after Harry's con-
fession of having a dead client in his car.

"So, when did she die?"

"I don't know. She was dead when she came to see
me." Harry watched as the younger copper whispered
in the ear of the older one.

"Not necessary," came the murmured response.

Harry could see that he was rapidly losing the plot, but he was at a loss as to what to say other than the truth as he saw it.

"So, you had a visit from a dead woman?"

"No. Look, the Oliver's brought her in about her will"

"So, they brought her in to make her will after she'd died. Bit late, isn't it?"

"Look, it's all very simple. The Oliver's brought her in after she'd died, and they wanted us to bury her and collect in all the money."

"Okay Harry, calm down. Now, why don't you tell us about the money and your pal Oliver?"

"The Oliver's".

"Yes, the Oliver's. These were the clients who couldn't bury their mother because they were going on holiday?"

"That's right."

"But, you're not an undertaker?"

"No."

"So, do you get asked to bury many dead bodies?"

"NO!"

"Just this one?"

"Yes, No!"

"Which is it, Harry?"

Harry buried his head in his hands. "I want my solicitor," he mumbled.

"If that's what you want Harry."

They sat in silence for a moment. There was a knock at the door. A uniformed officer poked his head around it.

"Have you got a moment, Sarge?"

The sergeant rose and left the room. He returned seconds later a triumphant gleam in his tired eyes.

"We've just had a report you were stopped by one or our motorway lads this morning. It seems you told him your grandmother was suffering from a stroke, and when he tried to escort you to hospital you disappeared on him. I think its time you started telling us the truth, don't you, Harry?

Chapter Thirty

Bernie Doyle's Jag swept to a halt in front of the sales office of The Falcon Heights Development Company.

"You got the whisky?" asked Bernie turning to Norman.

"Yes."

Bernie climbed wearily from the car. The last thing he needed was to be nice to an estate agent. It was bad enough that the million was still missing without having to worry about losing the flat. He'd agreed to buy it, given the estate agent a ten-grand deposit that should have been enough, but they'd telephoned Bianca and wound her up about other interested punters. A hysterical Bianca then telephoned Bernie.

"BERNIE! BERNIE! WE'RE GOING TO LOSE THE PENTHOUSE!!!"

He yanked the phone away from his ear as if it'd bitten him. "Bianca, quieten down. What's the matter?"

"They're letting someone else buy our house, Bernie," she sobbed.

"What do you mean 'someone else'?"

"I had that Jason on the phone. He... said... they had another buyer," she sniffed "and if we didn't exchange right away... we'd lose it!!"

A frown crossed Bernie's face. Had he met Jason? They all looked the same to him; sharp suits and a smile as wide as a stripper's arse. Still someone was in need of a slap.

"Don't worry, Bee love. I'll send a couple of the lads to have a word." Bernie winced at the loud scream, followed by the sound of something expensive breaking and the wail of the cat.

"YOU FUCKING WON'T, BERNIE DOYLE! DO YOU HEAR ME!" Bianca began to cry again. Bernie looked at Norman who was driving. A look of desperation crossed his face.

"Try being understanding, Bernie," said Norman. Bernie scowled.

"I am fucking understanding," Bernie muttered back. He didn't like domestics, and this had the makings of a big one. All he wanted was to go home, have a large whisky and watch a bit of sport on satellite TV. He put the phone back to his mouth. "Don't cry baby, everything will be alright."

Bianca let out a loud sniff. "Let's do something like normal people for once Bernie... sniff... please."

Bernie bridled at the suggestion he wasn't normal. "Yes, OK."

"Go along... and see them... explain what's happened..."

"Oh yes, I can just see it! Look, I had this million pounds from selling heroin. Trouble is I've gone and lost it. Do you mind keeping the house for us until I find it or sell some more heroin?!" thought Bernie, his eyebrows doing the can-can.

"...and, be nice to them Bernie, take them a bottle of Scotch or something."

"Yeah, yeah, good idea Bee, I'll get something and go and have a word myself."

"I've got a nice steak for your tea."

"I'll be home in about an hour." Bernie closed his mobile and put it back in his pocket. "You'd better stop at the next off licence you see."

They walked into the sales office. It was a hive of activity. Young men and women sat at half a dozen desks speaking on the phone or talking to buyers.

"Remember Bernie, be nice," whispered Norman.

They stood there as a maelstrom of activity whirled around them. Finally, a young woman came free. Bernie hurried over, "Er... excuse me, love." Her phone rang. She put her hand up as Bernie approached and spoke rapidly into the phone. He saw another estate agent put his phone down and moved towards him, but was beaten to the desk by a middle-aged couple. He turned back to the desk he had just come from; the woman had disappeared.

Come on Bernie, you're a respectable businessman. Be nice be nice. Bernie hovered. He had never hovered before in his life. He glanced at Norman with a look of desperation in his eyes. Norman shrugged his shoulders. His normal answer to such a situation would have been to fire a shotgun into the ceiling and tell everybody to shut the fuck up. That didn't seem appropriate here. They stood like two little old ladies caught in the wrong queue at a supermarket checkout.

"Can I help?"

A wave of relief flooded through Bernie's body, which was rigid as a plank. He turned to face the voice. A young lad of about 25.

"I'm buying the penthouse." Bernie mumbled.

"The penthouse? And which penthouse would that be?"

Bernie was taken back. There was more than one! "The Falcon Heights penthouse."

"You need to speak to Jason." The lad turned away. Bernie blinked but recovered in time to grab the lad's arm in a vice like grip. The lad looked at him in pain and surprise.

"Which one?" hissed Bernie. The lad looked at him blankly. Bernie's eyes shot around the room. "Which one!" The lad felt as if the bones in his arm where about to break.

"Over there," he pointed. "Red braces."

Bernie walked towards Jason's desk. Norman followed. The agent rose to greet them as they approached.

"Hello, how can I help?" he said with a smile.

"I'm Bernie Doyle."

"Yes, how can I help you, Mr Doyle?"

"I'm buying the penthouse flat." Jason gave him the full smirk, as it was known in the trade.

"And which penthouse is that?"

"The Falcon Heights penthouse!" Bernie exclaimed.

"Let me just check on that." Jason rose and opened a filing cabinet behind him. He took out a file and looked inside it. He replaced the file and sat down. "As I thought, we exchanged contracts on that this afternoon." Bernie and Norman looked at each other in bewilderment.

"But, that's my house." Bernie blurted.

They showed Harry into a cell. The smell of BO hit him like a wall as he entered. A thin man, his face hidden behind a mass of hair, bounded to his feet.

"Can I go now?" asked the Hair.

"No," said the sergeant.

"You can't lock me up for watching TV!".

"It wasn't your TV, was it?"

It's not a crime to watch someone else's TV."

"It is when you break into their house to watch it. Now, shut up and sit down."

The Hair grumbled into his beard and sat down. Harry looked imploringly at the sergeant.

"You'll get used to it," he said.

"I want my solicitor," shouted the Hair.

"Well you're in luck, cus' he's one," said the sergeant shutting the door.

The Hair looked up. He parted the mass of greasy curls which hung in front of his eyes revealing pock marked skin that belonged more on a pizza than a face.

"You a solicitor?"

"I'm training to be one," Harry muttered trying not to breath.

"I want to sue my girlfriend. It's all her fault, the cow. If she hadn't got me so mad, I'd not have kicked our telly in."

"What happened?" asked Harry, giving up the fight and exhaling. The Hair scratched the side of his face causing an eruption of pus.

"Fucking bitch flushed my Charlie down the loo, so I gave her a right hiding. I fucking said to her I don't go out working my arse off all day knocking over post offices to have my hard-earned Charlie flushed down the loo. Fucking bitch! I was only watching telly, bastards!" His outburst spent, the Hair subsided and his face disappeared behind its curtain of dandruff. "Cow's hidden me shotgun," he mumbled under his breath. "How am I supposed to go robbin' without a gun?"

Harry looked around the cell and wondered if it was bugged.

"So, they arrested you for burglary?"

"Yeah. But I wasn't going to steal nothing. I only wanted to watch the telly. Do you watch *Neighbours*?

"No."

"I never miss it."

"Obviously. And, what about the armed robbery and the possession of cocaine."

"Aye?"

"Do they know about it?"

"No. Why should they?"

"Well you told me readily enough."

"You're my brief, ain't ya?"

Well every cloud has a silver lining, thought Harry. He'd been arrested for murder, but got a new client out of it. He sat on the bench as far from the Hair as he could. The Hair tried to engage him in conversation about who he thought was the father of Roxanne's baby, but as Harry's knowledge of the Australian soap didn't go beyond the theme tune, they didn't get far.

It was a small room dimly lit by an orange light imprisoned behind a thick wire mesh. Harry shook his watch and stuck it to his ear to check if it was still working. The Hair would get up every now and again, muttering a few expletives and bang on the door demanding a TV. When Harry told him that he doubted they allowed TV in police prison cells, the Hair gave him a nasty look.

Harry wondered about ringing the bell on the wall, but he subsided again and re-read the terms and conditions printed on the back of his dry-cleaning ticket.

His attempts to call the office for help had been frustrated by a lack of mobile reception, and when he did get through, it was to the replacement of Wendy on the switchboard who spoke broken English with a thick Eastern European accent. When he tried to explain the problem to the copper they left him with, he hadn't been interested. So, Harry sat in the cell and waited.

The cell door sprang open amid the sounds of a loud commotion. The charge room was full of rowdy football fans. A large man with a shaved head was pushed into the room and the door swung too behind him. A cold shiver ran down Harry's back when he realised it was Tiger McGivens. Would he be held responsible for foiling his last escape? How come he wasn't still in custody?

As it was, McGivens had been so off his head at the time he'd no memory of Harry. McGivens drug addled state had been skilfully used to cause the collapse of the entire case against him resulting in his release. The police had been suitably sanguine, knowing there would be every opportunity to arrest him again, as had quickly proved the case. The Hair looked up at his entrance.

"Hello, Tiger."

227

"Who's he?" demanded McGivens, pointing at Harry.

"He's my brief," said the Hair. "What they got you for?"

"Car hopping."

Car hopping, for those not in the know, is the football fans game of jumping from the bonnet of one car to another with the object of seeing how big a dent you can make in the process. This is a game usually played after your side wins!

"It was a good game then?" asked the Hair

"3-1 to us," replied McGivens.

"Do you know why he's called Tiger?" said the Hair, turning to Harry.

Harry looked at McGivens, 6' 4" of meanness with studs in both eyebrows. Other than he didn't fancy being in a room with either him or a Tiger, Harry couldn't see the connection.

"No."

McGivens lifted his union jack t-shirt and slowly turned around revealing lines of scars that ran around his body in varying thickness.

"Got this from some Chinks. We had a row over some DVDs. They sliced me up so I cut their bollocks off."

It was one of those conversation stoppers. "Oh," said Harry. "Nice scars," he added as an afterthought. McGivens grunted and pulled down his t-shirt. It hovered about two inches above a hairy navel, a tribute more to large quantities of lager than a desire to be fashionable.

"So, if he's your brief what's he doin' locked up in here?" demanded McGivens.

For the first time this thought seemed to enter the Hair's head. "Yeah, I normally have that git Deeley acting for me. Who are you?"

Things were turning nasty. "My name's Trent. Harry Trent."

"So, what they got you in here for?" asked McGivens.

"Yeah, what you doin' here?" said the Hair getting to his feet.

Harry glanced from one to the other; they both had the look of wanting to spill blood. There was little doubt who it would belong to.

Chapter
Thirty-One

Jason put his hands together and leant across the desk towards Bernie Doyle. "I'm sorry. The property isn't yours until contracts are exchanged. I'm sure that was explained to you and ... your friend when you made the offer." Bernie and Norman exchanged another puzzled look. "We have some more penthouse flats coming on stream in phase two of the development. I'm sure you and your friend will find them just as nice. Ideal for the modern relationship."

"Is he having us on?" said Bernie to Norman in a state of incredulity. "Are you having us on?" He repeated turning to Jason.

"I'm sorry?" That was the trouble with queens thought Jason, they could be so touchy. He wondered who was dominant. The little fat one getting hysterical, or the big silent one built like a gorilla.

"That's my house!"

"Subject to contract."

"Subject to what?"

"Would you like to put your name down for phase two? Or should we just refund your deposit? As you know, there's a 25% none returnable administration fee."

"Now look!" said Bernie. The phone on Jason's desk began to ring.

"Excuse me," said Jason picking up the phone. Bernie pressed down the leaver cutting off the call. The agent frowned, and Bernie's face started to go red. Oh God! thought Norman. He looked round the office checking where the doors were and how many other people were in the room.

"If you don't want to buy another property, you will have to excuse me. I'm very busy," said Jason through gritted teeth.

"You're busy, are you?" said Bernie. "You sell my house, call me a fucking poof and tell me you're busy!" Norman slid silently to his feet and took up position. He felt for the comforting cold steel of the gun in his pocket.

Jason saw a hand fly out and felt himself being pulled over the desk by his tie. Pens raked his chest as he was dragged across; his head crashed into the far edge with a painful thump. He felt the silk of the tie bite into his throat as his head was pulled up. He gasped for air. A blinding pain shuddered through his head as it cannoned into the desk again and again. He tried to cry out in pain and fear, but he was choking, choking. He couldn't breathe, he was dying! A warm trickle ran down his leg. He was still. He felt a sticky substance run over his face. All he could see was red; his throat burned.

Bernie relaxed his grip on the tie, which he'd wound around his hand. Breathing heavily, he looked across the room. A sea of eyes looked back in a mixture of fear and bewilderment. In the far corner a man scrambled for a phone.

"Put it down!" barked Norman, pointing his gun.

"Now..." said Bernie, "where's my deposit?" He let go of the tie. Jason lay silent on the desk for a moment and then scrambled backwards trembling. He staggered to his feet, a deep red gash over one eye.

"All cheques come from head office," came a voice from behind Bernie. He turned and saw a woman of about 30, her eyes blazing. Bernie tried to stare her down, but she wouldn't give way. A smile crossed Bernie's lips.

"What's your name?"

"Tracy."

"I might have known. So, head office will send my deposit back, will they?"

"Yes. Minus the 25% administration fee."

"Minus twenty-five fucking percent. Norman, put him in the boot," said Bernie, nodding towards Jason.

"Sorry, Bernie?"

"I said put him in the fucking boot. We'll take him with us- as - a - deposit. Mind you, we might keep 25% of him as an administration fee!"

When you're locked up with a coke snorting armed robber and a man who chops people's nuts off, it's important to establish credibility. It didn't seem a good idea to Harry to say he was in jail due to a misunderstanding.

"Murder," he blurted out. A visible note of tension went out of the air. McGivens, who'd been clenching and unclenching his fists, relaxed.

"Murder, aye?" said the Hair. "Shooting or stabbing?" Harry's heart crashed into his boots. He didn't like the way this conversation was going.

"I shot her," he said.

"Who?" said McGivens seeing the hesitation in Harry's face. This was tricky. Mabel Evans had been a little old lady. No one in their right mind was going to look kindly at killing a little old lady. But, who could describe these two as in their right minds? Inspiration struck him.

"Bloody slag I was married to. Cow had more men inside her than Wembley Stadium."

McGivens reached down and patted Harry on the cheek. "Well done my son," he said. As he leant towards him, he opened his mouth in a wolfish grin. Tattooed on his front teeth were the letters K I L L.

For the next half-hour, it was sweetness and light. McGivens showed Harry the correct way to head butt stressing how important it was to break the nose with the first strike. The he got to his feet and said "Right, I'm fucking off." Harry and the Hair looked at him in bemusement. "Roger, grab your guts and start yellin' your sick."

Harry looked around wondering who McGivens had been talking to and then realised it was the Hair. He was called Roger!

As with all good plans, keep them simple. Roger grabbed his stomach and began to moan. McGivens shouted for help and kicked the door as if it were an away fan. A young PC opened it and had his nose broken. McGivens was right- the sudden pain and face full of blood renders you defenceless to the follow up kick that puts your testicles between your ears. Harry looked on in horror at the blood-splattered copper writhing on the floor.

"Right, out," shouted McGivens. "What the fuck are you doing?" he demanded as Harry hung back.

"I, er, don't think I'll come, if you don't mind."

"Don't fuck with me!" snarled McGivens grabbing Harry by the ear. "Your breaking out or you're coming as a fucking hostage, but you're coming." As Harry was rather attached to his ears, it seemed sensible to follow.

They came out into an empty corridor and headed down it. A policeman came out of a door. McGivens grabbed him by the tie and yanked him forward for a head butt, but the tie came away in his hands and the PC bolted down the corridor. A loud siren filled the air. They ran around the corner and saw if not a sea then a very large puddle of police coming towards them. McGivens grabbed Harry's arm and threw him through a doorway.

Superintendent Franklin looked up in surprise as they crashed into the room. McGivens ran towards Franklin and smashed his own forehead into Franklin's face. Franklin fell backwards moaning.

"Oh great! They've got a telly," said the Hair running over to the set and reaching for the remote control.

"So, I said to our Trudy she should tell him where to get off. I mean it isn't right, is it Bernie? What do you think?"

Bernie nodded his head in assent, he hadn't been listening for the last twenty minutes as Bianca has gone on endlessly about the shortcomings of her sister's latest boyfriend. Bernie was not in a good mood. He hated food shopping and had only agreed to go in order to placate a tearful Bianca who'd been busily breaking all the crockery as a means of alleviating her distress over their lost house purchase.

The hazard warning lights of the Jaguar flickered as the doors unlocked and the boot slowly glided open. Bianca lifted the carrier bags out of the trolley and approached the boot.

"Don't hurt me," croaked Jason.

Bianca froze as she looked into the boot. A frightened and bloodied figure in a blue suit stared up at her.

"What? Who? What are you doing in my boot?" asked Bianca her voice quavering.

"I'm an estate agent…. Please help me."

"An estate agent?'"

Bernie's hearing tuned in on those two words, which he felt had been burned into his soul in recent days.

"I'll call him later, OK?!"

"Bernie!... Bernie!!!"

"WHAT!?"

"LOOK!"

"What! What is it now?" Bernie strode over to the car. The woman was totally bloody neurotic. *OH SHIT!* he looked down at the frightened huddled body in the boot. *Fuck Bernie! What is the matter with you?! How can you forget you've got a body in the boot of your car? Thank Christ it's not a dead one! Fucking hell Bernie! What are you playing at?*

Bernie looked round quickly and slammed the boot shut. "I'll be back in five minutes."

He drove the car up to the next level of the car park and pulled into a vacant bay. He turned off the engine and slammed his head violently into the steering wheel three times cursing himself as he did so. He sat back a violent pain now pulsating through his head. He looked round for something he could take his frustration out on. The car was all sleek lines and tightly fitted equipment, nothing for him to wrench out and destroy. "Fuck! Fuck!," he muttered to himself. There was always the estate agent in the boot. He could drive up to the roof and throw him off. He would feel a lot better for that. But, it was broad daylight and this was a busy shopping centre.

He yanked out his mobile and stabbed in Norman's number.

"Bernie?"

"I've got a fucking estate agent in the boot of my car!"

"What? Hang on. I can't hear, let me turn the telly down.'" Bernie's grip on the phone tightened as he heard the sounds of Norman hunting around for the TV remote. His wife Dolly hadn't seen it. Just as Bernie was about to throw the phone at the car windscreen, Norman came back on the line.

"That's better, now what's the problem with the car. I told you Jaguar were no bloody good you should have got..."

"Norman shut the fuck up! I've got a body in my fucking boot, do you hear?"

The line went silent. Norman searched his mind for the last time they'd killed someone. It had been Jimmy the Snitch. He'd been heard talking about the death of Melvyn Godson and they'd decided he should be silenced. That had been three weeks ago. They hadn't used Bernie's car, had they? Christ, the smell after 3 weeks would be terrible! Must be someone else, but who?

"Do you know who it is, Bernie?"

"What!?"

"Who you got in the boot?"

"I can't remember his fucking name! It's that fucking estate agent."

"Jesus Bernie, you didn't need to kill him."

"I haven't."

"So, you've got a live estate agent in your boot? Why?"

"You were supposed to get rid of him, Norman. I told you to dump him 50 miles up the motorway in his y-fronts and let the bastard walk home."

"No, Bernie, Dolly had her Bridge party, remember? You said you'd sort it. You dropped me off at the house."

Bernie was silent. What Norman said was perfectly true. He was losing it. What was wrong with him. He felt sick in the pit of his stomach.

"Bernie, you still there? Do you want me to come over with a couple of the lads and sort it out?"

"No, it's OK." Doyle ended the call and looked at his watch. He'd already been 10 minutes. Bianca would be 'doing her pieces.' He drove up to the roof. It was raining and luckily only two or three cars where present. He pulled over to a far corner of the roof and opened the boot. He grabbed the estate agent by the scruff of his neck.

"Out."

Jason stumbled from the boot blinking, smelling of fear, piss and sweat. Bernie looked about. He'd parked next to a fenced off service area. Bernie bundled Jason through a swinging gate and behind the building. As this was an area where no one was meant to go, the roof gave way to open sky. Bernie marched him over to the edge.

"Look."

Jason looked down at the people scuttling around like ants below. Fear sucked all speech from him. He looked pleading into Bernie's eyes. Bernie pulled him back from the edge and let him go. Jason crumpled to the ground and began to sob. Bernie walked back to his car and drove away to face Bianca.

"Grab hold," barked Tiger. They grabbed Franklin's desk and barricaded the door. Tiger rifled through the drawers and found a can of lighter fluid and a box of matches. "Yes!" he exclaimed. He ran over to the stunned Franklin and squirted the contents of the can all over his shirt. He then ripped one of the phones out of the wall and bound Franklin's hands and feet with the cable. Harry shuffled from foot to foot unsure whether he was one of the gang or a hostage. He didn't fancy being subject to the lighter fluid business.

"Oh fuck!" exclaimed the Hair, "It's bleeding satellite TV. How the fuck do you find BBC?" He turned and glared at Franklin. "Copper! How do I get BBC?"

The door shuddered as someone tried to push it open. Tiger ran over and pushed the desk back against the door. "Fuck off! I've covered your governor in lighter fluid. You hear me? Fuck off or I'll torch him."

It was five minutes before the phone rang. Harry decided the best bet was to become part of the furniture. The Hair was still swearing at the TV as he tried to find BBC and Tiger had spent the time gnawing his nails. His original plan of head butting his way out of the station having failed he now seemed stuck for inspiration.

Tiger and Harry looked at the ringing phone. "Answer it," he growled. Harry picked up the phone.

"Hello."

"This is Chief Inspector Allan," came a voice. "Who am I speaking to?"

"Harry Trent." The phone went silent at the other end apart from some muttering, and then Allan came back.

"Harry, we want to help. We need to bring this situation to an end."

Harry wasn't going to argue with that. He'd come to the station to report a lost car and was now a hostage- or an escaped prisoner depending on your perspective.

"Sounds good to me." He looked at Tiger who scowled back, not having taken kindly to use of the word good.

"How is Superintendent Franklin?" Harry glanced over at his second bloodied policeman of the morning; his face and white shirt streaked a vivid red.

"He's, err, okay."

"Harry, you shouted something about having covered Mr. Franklin in lighter fuel, is, that right?"

"No, I didn't!"

"So, he isn't covered in lighter fluid?" said Allan a note of relief in his voice. Harry felt a strong sense of déjà vu coming on. He held out the receiver to Tiger and gesticulated for him to come and take it. Tiger bared his teeth causing Harry to shudder as he saw the letters KILL. Harry put the receiver back to his ear.

"Hello, Harry? Are you still there?"

"Yes, I'm still here," he slumped into a chair. Tiger waved a box of matches at him and mouthed the word whoosh as he pointed at Franklin. "About the lighter fluid, Mr. Franklin is covered in it. And we have some, um..." Harry's remaining words were drowned out by the sounds of heavy metal blasting from the TV.

"Shut that fucking noise!" shouted Tiger.

"I can't find the fucking volume!" came the retort from the Hair. "It's fucking ON in two minutes!" The sound died down as a nature programme flicked onto the screen and a voice in German began speaking.

"Harry, Harry what's going on?" came the anxious voice of Allan.

"It's okay, its just the TV."

"The TV?"

"The Hair wants to watch *Neighbours*." As Harry said it he realised how flippant it sounded, but it was true. God help him, so much that happened just never sounded believable.

"Harry, are you using?"

"Sorry?"

"Look, if you are on something, come out and we can see what the police doctor can do for you."

The penny dropped. His talk of the Hair and *Neighbours* had convinced Allan that Harry was on drugs.

"No, its *Neighbours*. Listen." The Hair had managed to find it. The cheery signature tune reverberated around the room telling them all how we needed good neighbours.

There they were, England's head butting champion, the bloody and very combustible Franklin and Roger AKA the Hair- coke snorting armed robber and soap fan. Was there something about Harry that attracted them? Did he have a sign suspended above his head saying that if you are mad, bad, dangerous or just plain crazy, apply here. Harry put the phone back to his ear. There was silence at the other end. They'd obviously not covered how to deal with a hostage crisis during *Neighbours* at hostage school. Finally, Allan spoke.

"Harry, you know this is useless. Come out and let's talk."

Harry looked at Tiger. "He wants us to come out."

"Not until its finished," growled the Hair. "Now shut the fuck up. I can't hear."

Harry put the phone back to his ear. "You couldn't call back when *Neighbours* has finished, could you?"

He could hear Allan breathing heavily at the other end of the line. When eventually Allan spoke, it was slowly as he controlled his voice trying to not loose his rag with someone who was so evidently taking the piss.

"Harry, this is a very serious situation. Now, you were telling me you've covered Mr. Franklin in lighter fluid and you have some matches? Is that right?" Not quite right, but they needed to move the conversation on.

"Yes," he replied. "But, I didn't do it!"

"What do you want?"

Harry looked at Tiger. "What do you want?"

"A helicopter and a million quid."

"Darlene, I do love you. Rachel means nothing to me. You must believe me." The Hair had turned up the volume and the cast of *Neighbours* were now joining in the conversation.

Harry repeated Tigers demands down the phone.

"You bastard, you never loved anyone but yourself. I'm dying of a brain tumour and you go and sleep with my best friend?" The volume had got louder.

Harry turned to Tiger. "I can't hear him"

"Turn that fucking thing off!" shouted Tiger.

"I DON'T KNOW WHAT'S BEEN HAPPENING TO ME EVER SINCE I DISCOVERED THAT RAY WAS MY REAL DAD."

BANG! The TV exploded with a loud retort as Tiger put his boot through the screen. The Hair let out a scream of rage and leapt onto Tiger sinking his teeth into Tiger's nose. The blind covered windows exploded in a shower of broken glass and white smoke filled the room as dark figures came hurtling in. Harry hit the floor and felt the sharp prod of a gun barrel being pushed down behind his ear.

"Don't move!" a voice barked. "You so much as twitch and I'll blow you're fucking head off!"

"My name is Detective Chief Inspector Young. Sergeant Ives, you have already met."

It was two hours later. The sound of the exploding TV convinced the police they'd shot Franklin or where in the process of doing so, and they ended the siege. A bruised and battered Harry now sat in an interview room with two unpleasant looking coppers.

We've spoken with Duncan and McGivens. They tell us the break out was your idea and you told them you'd murdered Mabel Evans."

Harry presumed they were talking about The Hair and Tiger. "I'd like a solicitor, please." God knows how he was going to get out of this one!

Chapter Thirty-Two

The blue Mercedes purred slowly along the high street. Bernie Doyle gazed out absent-mindedly at the passing pedestrians. Old ladies doubled over pulling their shopping trolleys on wheels. His mum had one of those. He'd offered repeatedly to get one of his lads to drive her down the supermarket, she refused. Doggedly insisting on going shopping daily to the ever-diminishing number of High street shops she'd used for years. She didn't have a fucking fridge. Could you believe it? She shopped daily as she had no means of keeping food fresh. He'd tried to buy her one, but she refused to use it. He'd even got one installed in her house, but she switched the power off and left it sitting in the corner claiming it was a waste of electricity. God, she was a stubborn old bitch.

"We're almost there, Bernie," said Norman from the back seat.

Bernie stirred from his reverie and turned. He looked at the other occupant of the back seat, Steve Reynolds.

It was Reynolds who'd come to Bernie with the proposition to rob the bank. Twice a year a million in cash was delivered to the bank for collection by an Arab prince who when he went shopping, liked to impress everyone by paying them in large wads of cash. When the idea was first put to Bernie, he'd turned it down flat. His days of robbing banks long gone.

But then the million for the house went missing and Bianca was giving him such an earful over the loss of the penthouse. He needed to find another property quickly and had an urgent need for cash. He still wouldn't have done it, if it hadn't been for that night of reminiscing with Norman about their early days together as a pair of reckless young tearaways. The bank came up and both agreed the idea was absurd. Then that stupid old fucker Norman had got to add the throw-away line; *'Yeah, we're too old for that sort of stuff, Bernie.'* The words burned into Bernie's soul. He'd drunk most of a second bottle of scotch after Norman went home to try and forget them. The following morning, he felt like shit. Looking in the mirror he saw his father looking back.

To compound the problem, he couldn't sustain an erection. His doctor told him he shouldn't expect to be able to perform as if he were still 19. That was the final straw. He would show them he wasn't an old man, that he still had it in him. He agreed to rob the bank.

They burst through the door of the bank wearing ski masks and clutching a variety of sawn-off shot guns and baseball bats. Reynolds fired into the ceiling.

"Nobody fucking move!" he screamed. "This is a robbery!"

"Thank you for that. Nobody would have fucking guessed, Einstein" thought Bernie. *"Fuck, its blood hot under this ski mask."*

"Bernie, watch out!" shouted Norman.

Doyle looked up just in time to see an enormous mock chandelier hurtling down from the ceiling towards him.

"So, are you going to shag her or not?" asked Jim Basset.

Brian Fraser's hands gripped the steering wheel and his face went brick red. He glanced sideways at the half mocking face of Basset. Basset sat back in the cab of the wheel-clamping van, his feet on the dashboard, his mouth moving round and round with the gum he chewed incessantly. He knew he should never have told him about Davina. He had never found chatting up girls easy. To listen to Basset on the other hand, he was shagging a different girl every night.

"Bingo!" cried out Basset. "First one of the day."

Fraser glanced over to the curb and saw the blue Mercedes ahead of them parked illegally outside the bank. He pulled in behind it. Basset jumped out of the Transit's cab and pulled back the sliding door. He looked on admiringly for a moment at the thirty or so bright yellow wheel camps that sat in the back of the van.

"Come on, my beauty," he said heaving the clamp out. "Daddy's got to get to work."

Reynold's reckless shotgun blast into the ceiling neatly severed the metal chain holding the chandelier in place, sending it on its killing mission towards Bernie Doyle's head. Norman's last minute warning allowed Doyle to lunge to his left leaving him with a badly bruised leg where the chandelier caught him.

They all got distracted by the near death experience their leader suffered. When the dust settled and Doyle stopped effin and blinding at Reynolds incompetence they got back to the serious business of robbing the bank. It had only taken a few seconds, but it was enough time for one quick witted and resolute bank clerk to activate the security shutters.

The half a dozen customers glanced nervously from the grey steel shutters that sealed off the bank counter to the masked robbers who stood menacingly with their guns, masks and baseball bats.

Ray Stubbs, who minutes earlier was cursing the slow pace of service - it was always the same half a dozen windows but only one of them manned - looked on in a mixture of amusement and fear. He'd only ever seen bank robberies on the TV before. When ever he'd seen it, cowed bank clerks always handed over big wads of cash that were stuffed into holdalls whilst one of the robbers told them to hurry up. He'd never seen a situation where one of the robbers tried to kill another one and the bank had hidden behind three inches of armour plate. The body chemistry of the robbers told him that they were equally uncertain about what to do next. The masked faces looked at each other and then at the short stocky one who had almost been killed by the chandelier for guidance.

Bernie couldn't believe what was happening. His leg hurt like fuck. Where was fucking bank? All he could see was a wall of metal shutters and half a dozen middle aged people their hands half raised above their heads bobbing up and down, uncertainly whether or not to put their hands up or lie on the floor. Well, what did he expect? If you rob a bank, the customers are entitled to a little guidance. Put your hands up, lie on the floor- come on- what do you want us to do?

Reynolds walked over to a smartly dressed gray haired man.

"Give me your wallet!" he snarled.

This snapped Bernie out of his momentary reverie. What planet did that prat Reynolds come from? Bernie might have been at a loss as to what to do next. But, one thing he knew for certain was that now was not the time to take up a collection from the bank customers.

Oh, excuse me, as we can't rob the bank, would you mind making a small donation instead!? He knew what he would do. He would shoot Reynolds instead. He would blow his fucking head off.

Norman saw Doyle raise the shotgun in Reynolds direction. That was the last thing they needed now. Fine if Bernie killed him outright. But, with these modern hospitals you had to literally blow someone's head clean off to be certain they were dead. Last thing they needed was Reynolds with a new nose standing up in a witness box six months later screaming his head off and getting them all twenty years. Better to do it later when no nosy parker would be around to dial 999 and they could be sure the fucker bled to death in the proper manner.

He reached out a gentle restraining hand and pushed the gun down.

"Later. This is useless let's go."

Bernie nodded his head in agreement.

"Out now!" he yelled.

The three of them ran from the bank. As they did so, Doyle cannoned into Smiling George who stood in the doorway.

"WHAT THE FUCK DO YOU THINK YOUR DOING! YOUR SUPPOSED TO BE IN THE FUCKING CAR!"

"I wanted to watch."

Doyle pushed him out onto the pavement and goggled as he saw the get away car being clamped.

Basset slid the clamp over the front wheel of the car and began to tighten the first bolt.

"Get it off or die," snarled Doyle pushing the shotgun into his head.

The cold menace in the voice almost made Basset wet himself. When he turned his head, and saw the twin barrels of the shotgun he did.

Doyle wanted to kill him. He felt the need to lash out at something in response to the chaos which was happening all around. It was twenty years since he'd robbed a bank. This was not the way it was meant to happen.

Basset turned to the clamp his fingers scrambling over the nut which just seemed to spin in his hands. It wouldn't come loose he was going to die.

Norman pushed him aside, undid the bolt and lifted the clamp off. Basset lay on the floor his arms and legs curled up in the air in a half begging, half foetal position. George was already behind the wheel revving up the car as the others dived in and the Mercedes roared away.

They pulled their masks off as the car sped away. Doyle stared at Smiling George. His normal lopsided grin replaced with a rigid smile. His eyes had a strange distant look about them. Doyle turned to the back of the car.

"Have you fucking given him something?" he yelled at Reynolds.

Tight lipped Reynolds didn't reply. He'd given Smiling George some pills before the raid that he'd picked up in a night club. The couple he'd taken himself had had no effect on him and he suspected they were sugar pills. Clearly, those he'd given George were of a more potent variety. What they were, though he didn't know. They were purchased purely on the basis they would let him have a good time. What they were he regarded as largely irrelevant. Now however, was not the time to admit such things. He knew he was in deep shit with Doyle. The raid had been his idea. He had shot down the chandelier. If he came out of this with a good beating, he would consider himself lucky.

The car sped along the high street. They could hear the first sound of a siren. A police car appeared in front of them blue lights flashing and headlights on.

"Left! Left! Left!" yelled Doyle.

The Mercedes rocked slightly on two of its wheels as it shot through the No Entry sign.

George easily swerved round the two cars coming towards them as they shot the wrong way along the one-way street. The articulated lorry coming towards them seemed a different proposition. The sound of its horn and the glow of its lights flooded the car as it skidded towards them. Doyle could see the lorry driver raise one arm to shield his face as the vehicles got closer.

Doyle's head was jolted against the ceiling as the Mercedes hit the curb and bounced on to the pavement, scattering pedestrians right and left. The front of the shop loomed towards them as George, giggling, pushed the accelerator to the floor. Doyle looked on in a mixture of disbelief and horror as the car struck the display window. Exploding glass and flying kitchenware peppered the car as its three tons of speeding metal sliced their way into the store.

Tony Redmond patiently shadowed Eddie Paris around the store for half an hour. He'd watched as Eddie place a number of items into his pockets. Satisfied with his haul, Paris headed for the door. Redmond would arrest him as he stepped through it. He always waited until they left. There were no excuses then. Paris was stepping through the door, Redmond was reaching out with his hand to grab him when he heard the car engine. He looked to his right and saw the Mercedes coming across the pavement. A great shower of glass struck him as the car burst through the window, shredding his flesh, the pain died away as he felt himself fly through the air. Paris darted to his left as he saw the car approach. He heard the sound of screaming and out of the corner of his eye saw a man in a white overcoat flying through the air and slamming into the pavement with a sickening squelch. A metal wok landed at Paris's feet with a ringing thud. He picked it up and ran.

The Mercedes sped past the pick and mix counter, scattering shoppers and staff right and left. The police BMW behind followed them into the shop. It was a large store. The two cars careered around sending display stands and goods flying. The BMW struck an old lady not quick enough to get out of the way carelessly tossing her over its roof, the officers in it lost in an adrenaline rush.

I'm dreaming. I'll wake up in a moment and find myself in bed next to Bianca, thought Doyle. As they went past the 'Pick and Mix' counter for the third time, Doyle realized it was not a dream.

"THE BACK OF THE STORE! THE BACK OF THE STORE! There's bound to be an unloading bay we can get out there." The car rocked forward. The sounds of the following police siren loud in their ears. Two large doors stood ahead of them. They hit them at speed sending them flying outwards. The car nose-dived off the edge of the loading bay and struck the ground its back wheels crashing down and bounced up into the air. George giggled excitedly as the car sped away. The police following misjudged the doorway. The right wing of the car caught the door frame as they came through, spinning the car round and sending it crashing into a wall.

It was a cul de sac! The iron railings of the park blocking off all future hope of passage. The car braked to a halt with a jolt.

"OUT! OUT!" yelled Doyle. "Make a run for it."

They stumbled out of the car. The others ran off into the park heading in all directions. Doyle could hear the distant sound of the sirens. They needed some time. He removed his coat and thrust the arm of it deep down into the cars fuel tank. He could feel the ice-cold petrol soaking through the jacket and onto his flesh. He pulled the jacket out, the fumes stinging his nose. He jammed the collar of the jacket back into the tank leaving the sodden arm dripping onto the ground. An old and rusty Austin Allegro was parked across the road. Doyle ran over and rocked the back of it. He could hear the slosh of a half full tank. He looked into the car for something he could use as a wick. The brown furry car seat would do fine. The but of the shot gun shattered the window. Doyle reached in and ripped off the cover. He pushed one end into fuel tank pulled it out and laid a thin trail of petrol from the Allegro to the Mercedes. The sirens where getting nearer but it was worth it. With both cars alight, he would have created a barrier of flame which would keep the police at bay. He quickly thrust the dry end of the car seat into the Allegro's fuel tank again leaving the other end to create a dripping pool on the ground. He threw the shotgun into the back of the Merc. He had no plans to get involved in any shoot out. A running man with a shotgun tended to be a bit of a giveaway. If he could get a couple of streets away, then he would be safe and could get home at his leisure.

He threw a match into the line of fuel which lay on the ground. A bright orange flame leapt up into the air sniffing the petrol's 'sweet' scent. Momentarily the flame lunged towards the Allegro. Then remembering that the trail led in both directions, it split and the two ends raced hungrily for the mother load.

Doyle ran into the park. After he had gone fifty yards, he instinctively threw himself to the ground. He heard the booms as first one and then the other car's fuel tank exploded a hot rush of air over his ears. He looked up to see a tarnished wing mirror come flying through the air and bury itself in to the soft earth in front of him.

He looked round at the curtain of orange flame and billowing smoke that concealed him from the police. He had at least five minutes before the flames would die down sufficiently for any one to brave them, probably longer. Any pursuer would be concerned about the sympathetic detonation of adjacent car fuel tanks. They would have to evacuate the neighbouring houses. The police where going to have there hands full.

He looked around the flat expanse of park. He could see the others disappearing blindly into the distance. To the right stood a children's play area. Two young children and their mother were staring avidly at the flames. Ahead of him a solitary man was walking his dog. He wanted to run but knew he couldn't. The police, when they got through, would ask about running men. But, there had been a fire!

"There's been an accident!" he yelled at the woman. "I'll go and call the fire brigade." He set off at a jog avoiding the path of the on coming man.

Little droplets of sweat slowly rolled down the sides of Doyle's face. He could feel his trousers beginning to chafe his thighs as he ran. His breathing was getting heavier. He cursed himself as he ran: *You stupid stupid old fucker, how could you let you self get in this situation? Fucking Reynolds! He was a dead man when he got hold of him. And, as for the cause of all this- the fucking scrote who'd stolen his million- he would be begging to die by the time he finished with him.*

A low fence ahead, Doyle jumped over it and found himself flying through space. He struck the embankment with force and cannoned head over heels down it.

"Aaaaaahhhhh, fucking 'ell!!!!" he staggered upright, running as fast as he could to try and stop his feet from disappearing under him again. They skidded on muddy soil and he landed with a jarring thud on his coccyx and began to tumble again. A rusty pram handle raked his face as he flew past it, gouging away skin and sending a stinging pain across his head. His hand caught something sharp that sliced into his fingers. Something smelling of piss and vomit had rapped itself around his head he couldn't breath or see. A putrid rotting smell filled his mouth and lungs. Doyle felt as if he was going to die as he continued to cartwheel down the steep embankment picking up assorted detritus as he went like some magnetic force. It took about twenty seconds from the time he'd leapt over the fence until he felt his wild passage come to a sickening halt as his head struck something cold and metallic. It seemed like an eternity to Doyle.

He lay there gagging and screaming to himself. *Get this fucking thing off! Get this fucking thing off!* His finger clawed at his face finally pulling the rotting rags away. He gulped down the cold fresh air into his lungs. He staggered to his feet breathing heavily. His face felt itchy. He reached up to scratch it and something soft and slimy came away in his hand. A FUCKING MAGGOT! AAAAAHHHH!!! AAAAAHHHH!!! He staggered blindly forward, his feet slipping on the wooden railway sleepers he was obliviously walking on. The blare of a horn and the dazzling lights of the on coming train. Doyle flung himself aside.

It took him three attempts to scale the other side of the railway embankment. He had tried walking along the railway track, but after getting caught up in the slip stream of two passing trains, Doyle had had enough. Covered in mud and bleeding from numerous cuts he lay panting at the top of the slope. He looked up at the dark brown wooden fence in front of him. The smell of creosote from the freshly painted panels drifted towards him. He looked right and left. Fencing stretched in both directions. The boarded gardens of houses backing on to the railway line.

Doyle staggered to his feet and looked up at the fence which was about six feet in height. With the aid of an old milk crate, he was able to curl his fingers round the top of the fence. His feet scrambling against the boards Doyle pulled himself up and over the fence.

It was a low growl slowly rising in intensity. Doyle looked up at the bared yellow fangs of a dog's mouth, drawn back to reveal the full set of sharp and dangerous looking teeth which normally accompanied the mouth of a Rottweiler.

Chapter
Thirty-Three

It took the arrival of Michael Burns' oozing charm and Hugo Boss at the police station to secure Harry's release.

"It's very embarrassing, Harry," he said pacing to and fro in the cell and glancing at his watch. "I'm supposed to be at Tizzie's clarinet recital, you know. Bloody Vanessa will never believe I'm down the cop shop with you and a dead client. She'll accuse me of being off shagging Andréa again."

It was a tough life trying to keep a wife, mistress, hectic social life, the endless search for that perfect set of speakers, the never-ending road tests of the latest 'dick on four wheels' as his wife would call them, his daughters school concerts- oh- and an occasional bit of law on the go without having to get his trainee released from the police station.

"You know they wanted to see her fucking will, don't you Harry?!" he whispered angrily.

"Well, we hold it, don't we?"

"Of course, we do... somewhere. But, we've got hundreds of wills. You can't just find one like that."

"So, what have you shown them?"

"We had to type up a new one."

The sound of the key in the cell door brought their discussion to a close.

The detective sergeant who had questioned Harry earlier stood impassive in the doorway. Michael turned to him smiling and shot out a hand in greeting.

"Don! Long time no see."

"We've got better things to do with our time Mike than dealing with young lad's joy riding round town with corpses. Well, you've been lucky this time, young man," he said adopting his best headmaster tone towards Harry. "We've been able to contact the Oliver's in Spain, who've confirmed your story. Would you believe it, they wanted him done for criminal damage to the car," he said turning to Michael. "They decided to drop that however when I pointed out what a field day the local press would have if any of this ever came to court. Soon shut them up, callous bastards! Right you, on your way!"

The dog's small black nose was wet with anticipation. In it's eyes was a look he'd seen many times in men of violence, the joy and anticipation of battle. The chance to wreak havoc and carnage against a lesser foe.

Doyle looked desperately around for a weapon. There was nothing. He knew that to try and run was useless.

The only way to defeat a 'big bastard' was to show no fear, know no limits to what you would do, even if you had to crawl down the fucker's throat and choke him to death.

Doyle looked back into the dog's eyes and bared his teeth. He held his hands by his sides ready. He would go for the dog's throat to keep its teeth away. If he could get a good grip, he could throttle it to death.

"Come on then. Let's have ya!" The dog lunged forward. Doyle felt its hot rancid breath on his face as he was struck with a fine spray of saliva. The muscles in the dog's neck bulged with the strain of trying to get closer to Doyle, a collar biting deep into its neck. However, the rope securing it to the wall was tantalisingly short. The dog gave out a strangled bark almost asphyxiating itself in its need to get at Doyle.

Doyle's muscles relaxed as he saw the dog could not reach him. He sat back on the floor, his back resting against the fence. For the first time that day a small grin broke onto his face.

"Sorry mate, not your day, is it?"

He looked round the garden. There was no movement from the house, its owners at work. Next to the house was a gate leading out of the garden. He looked back at the dog and the rope tethering him to the wall. How long was the rope? Could he reach the gate without the dog getting to him? It would be close, but it looked a similar distance from where the dog was tied to the gate.

He edged slowly around the garden fence, the dog barking and straining on its leash to reach him. It let out a half-strangled whimper of delight as its nose momentarily brushed against Doyle's leg. Doyle scrabbled with the bolt on the gate. It was large and rusty and didn't want to draw back. He was halfway through the gate when a sharp stabbing pain shot through his leg like two metal hooks had sunk deep into his flesh. Doyle looked down at his leg. The mouth of the dog was firmly embedded in it.

The animals head was at a seemingly impossible angle. Through the pain, Doyle could hear its gurgled breathing. To get at Doyle, the dog was strangling itself. He brought the edge of his hand down with a hard-chopping motion on the bridge of the dog's nose twice, and it let out a whelp. He felt the grip on his leg diminish. He hit the animal again and the dog involuntarily opened its mouth to howl in pain. Weakened by a lack of air it relaxed its grip allowing Doyle to pull free and tumble into the passageway.

He held his leg gingerly and looked down at the two large pumping holes of blood which were rapidly merging into a single pool. *Christ, I could bleed to death. Fuck, fuck it hurts!* He closed his eyes and gasped as an arrow of intense pain shot through his body. He tried to focus on something to divert the pain. The scrote who has got him to this state - the bastard who had stolen his million - he wondered where he could get a big savage dog from to chew the fucker to death. With that happy thought in his mind, he tottered down the alleyway.

Blood was now pouring from the wound. He needed to apply a tourniquet. A pair of purple women's knickers came into view blowing back and forth as they dried on the line. He leant over the hedge and snatched them. As he did so, he heard the sharp tap of knuckles on glass. He looked up at the angry face of a middle-aged woman shouting at him through her living room window. Their eyes locked, the anger in Doyle's burning into the woman who hastily backed away from the window and ran screaming for the phone. She had seen the devil. He was in her garden stealing her underwear. Weeping she dialled the number of her parish priest.

Doyle staggered into the street. He needed to get home, to see a doctor, just to get away from this nightmare that was spinning out of control. He limped down the road, he needed to steal a car. *Steal a car! Bernie its thirty years since you've stolen a car. They've got all kinds of security on them these days. How the fuck are you going to know what to do.* He needed something old or Eastern European. A Mark I Cortina! He picked up a stone and broke the quarter light window. His hand shot through and opened the door, climbing in he felt under the dash board. His hand pulled down a tangle of wires, cutting through a green one with his pocket knife he pared back the rubber and brought the two wire ends together.

The car was filled with the sound of *Radio2* at full pitch. Doyle scrambled round for the volume knob his heart racing. The sudden silence as the radio fell dead allowed Doyle a flashing moment of despair. Bernie Doyle boss of London's docklands and he couldn't even steal a car! He breathed deeply and looked down at the spaghetti of wiring which faced him. Two minutes later the engine purred into life and Doyle drove away. He could feel the tension draining from his shoulders as the car became lost in a sea of London traffic.

The fetid smell of stale bodies and urine which had filled his mind and nose slowly faded away. He was not going back to prison. He would not be cadged like some animal in a cell 12' x 8' with some stinking low life and a decaying bucket of excrement in the corner to be used as a toilet.

He headed north onto the M1 motor way, stopping only briefly to tie the purple knickers in a tourniquet around his thigh. Coming off at junction three he followed a country lane for half a mile. He had no intention of taking a stolen car anywhere near his house. Doyle pulled out his mobile and telephoned Bianca. As Bianca's Mercedes pulled away from their drive to collect him, he could feel his eyes getting heavier and heavier. He remembered very little of Bianca struggling to get him into her car and the drive home.

Chapter
Thirty-Four

It had been a good day for Victor. All the remaining cans of Poochie in stock or that could be recalled were relabelled Granny Davis's Old English Stew and were now on the way to Uzbekistan. He would lie low on the dog food front for a while. He'd met a man in a massage parlour who told him there was a lot of money to be made in recycling toxic waste particularly if you didn't bother with all that 'European bollocks'. He had 50 tons of radioactive sludge arriving the following day.

He walked down the steps from his office and lit a cigar. There were two men standing by his car. Victor hesitated. They didn't look like his employees, but you couldn't be too careful. He made it a policy to avoid personal contact with any of the factory workers. He looked at his watch it was 6.00 pm. All his people finished at 5.00. He walked closer.

"If you're looking for work, come back in the morning and see my foreman."

They said nothing. "This is private property. If you don't leave, I'll have to call the police." Where was

Jenks his security guard? He should have been on the gate. Lazy git gone for a pee or some such bollocks on my time, thought Victor.

One of the men walked towards him. "Mr. Davis?"

"Yes?"

"Mrs. Wheatley asked us to give you her regards."

"What?"

Before Victor could say anymore, it all went black.

"Ouch!" went Victor. Someone was sticking a needle into his back. He woke up and felt behind him. It was a piece of straw. What was that doing in his bed? He was thirsty and had an appalling headache, he needed a drink of water. He felt around for the bedside light but couldn't find it. Why was he sleeping on the floor and on some kind of reed mat? Christ, he must have been pissed when he'd gone to bed. Slowly he staggered to his feet shivering, where were his pyjamas? He was naked! He walked towards the en suite. He'd only taken three steps when he felt something grab him round the neck and send him flying to the ground. He lay in a daze. Victor staggered upright. Something was round his neck. It felt tight and was biting into the skin. He explored with his hands, a leather collar? He felt further, something cold and metallic, a chain?

"AAAAAAAAAAHHHHHHHHHHHHHHHH!!!!" he was chained up by the neck! After 5 minutes screaming, he felt an overpowering need for a pee. Desperately he pulled on the chain to break free. As the hot urine splashed across his legs and feet, Victor came to the appalling conclusion he wasn't having a nightmare.

Half an hour of wailing and then feeling sorry for himself, Victor slowly began to recover some composure. It was as he rubbed his arms to warm himself that he discovered what nearly caused him to go insane. He had large lumps stuck to his arms. As he felt over his body, he found the lumps everywhere. He pulled at one and let out a howl as part of it came away with a tuft of hair. He held it to his nose and sniffed. The smell was familiar, CHRIST!!! It was one of his dog biscuits. Someone had glued dog biscuits all over his body!

Chapter
Thirty-Five

The fact that he was rich and about to become richer finally allowed Victor to claw his way back to sanity. The first grey of dawn was coming through cracks in the timbers. He could make out that he was in a large barn. Ten feet of chain lead from his neck to a ring in the wall. A padlock secured the collar around his neck. He looked down at his fat white body covered in dog biscuits. What was going on? MARIANNE WHEATLEY. That's what that man had said before he'd been knocked out. The bitch! She was behind this, some sort of perverted joke. Fucking hell, he would sue her for every penny she had.

The tinny sound of the 1812 rose out of the ground towards him. It was his mobile phone. It must have dropped out of his clothing as they had stripped him. Now he had the fuckers! Giggling he thrashed around in the straw until he found it.

"Hello," said Victor into the phone

"Is that you, Dave?" came a women's voice.

"No, fuck off!" said Victor pressing the end button. Quickly he dialled 999. He had the bastards now!

"Emergency, which service do you require?"

Victor hesitated. He wanted the Police. He also wanted rid of the biscuits. That would need some medical attention.

"Hello caller, which service do you require?"

Then it hit him. If any of this got out, he'd be a laughing stock. He pressed the end button again. He would call Michael. He dialled his mobile number.

"Your mobile's ringing," said Mandy her voice drugged with sleep.

Harry clawed round in the dark and found it. The name Victor throbbed at him in the green light of the phone facia. How did he have his mobile number? It was then he remembered he'd picked up Michael's phone by mistake. Harry pushed the receive button.

"Michael, its Victor. I need your help."

"It's not Michael, its Harry. What's the problem Victor, it's a bit early?"

"I'll tell you what the fucking problem is! That crazy bitch Wheatley has got me chained up in a shed somewhere and stuck dog biscuits all over me."

Harry lifted the phone from his ear and looked at Mandy who stared back through half closed eyes.

"Harry, it's the middle of the night."

"It's Victor. He says someone has chained him up and covered him in dog biscuits."

"He must be pissed," said Mandy collapsing back into her pillow.

He put the phone back to his ear.

"Hello? Hello? Harry! What's going on? Put fucking Michael on the phone."

Harry didn't know what to say, but then Victor Davis always had that effect on him. At least he wasn't close enough to attack him if he said something he didn't like.

"Are you alright Victor? You sound a little upset?"

"UPSET!!! You'd be fucking upset if someone had chained you up like a dog and glued biscuits to your bollocks."

"Woof, woof!" Victor looked around as the bark was joined by many more. There were a pack of dogs outside the barn. Then he heard her voice.

"Are you hungry? Would you like some breakfast? Aunty Marianne has got a surprise for you. Yes, she has. Who can guess what's in the barn?"

He could hear the sound of pawing at the door mixed with whines and yelps. Oh, sweet Jesus. He looked down at his biscuit covered body.

"Aunty Marianne was very naughty not giving you anything to eat yesterday, wasn't she? She wanted you to be extra hungry for today's big treat. The door started to shudder as the dogs threw themselves against it.

"HARRY! HARRY! GET ME OUT!" Victor screamed down the phone. In the background, Harry could hear barking.

"Is that a dog?" queried Mandy.

Harry shook his head. "I don't know. He sounds hysterical. I need to find out where he is and call Michael."

"Victor, where are you?"

"I'M IN THE FUCKING SHED! OH JESUS, THEY'RE COMING! FOR CHRIST SAKE, HARRY GET ME OUT!"

Harry turned to Mandy, who was now awake and sitting upright. She put on the light and they both screwed up their eyes.

"Harry, what's happening?"

He shook his head.

The door shuddered again. Victor looked down at his biscuit covered stomach. He dropped the phone and began clawing at his flesh.

"In you go! Breakfast!" came the bright and breezy voice of Marianne Wheatley. The doors flew inward and the dogs bounded in.

Harry could hear the sound of furious barking accompanied by Victor's screams.

The soft beige bubbles on the head of the pint slowly subsided leaving a creamy head. Harry lifted the pint to his mouth and felt the soft nutty liquid gently caress the walls of his throat as it slid down. Ben grinned at him and raised his glass in salute. "Cheers," he said. Tim returned from the juke box from which the sounds of Blondie burst into life.

"Granny grabber," said Ben.

"Not when she made this!" retorted Tim.

They sat down at a table.

"So, have you got it with you?" asked Tim.

Harry nodded and tapped the holdall lying on the ground with his foot. "It's in here, in a bin liner. Are you sure this is going to work?"

"Of course. You should see some of the curry stains Ahmed has got out of my coat," said Ben. The aged grey Burberry engulfed Ben's thin frame.

They drank up and walked down the dark street to Patel's dry cleaners. Ahmed Patel the Curry Cleaning King was not there. They were greeted by his brother Rajiv who seemed to be well known to Ben and Tim. A soiled fifty-pound note was produced and Rajiv held it up to the strip light in the ceiling. He let out a chuckle.

"How many have you got like this?"

"About a thousand," said Harry. Rajiv looked enquiringly.

"Mad Old Uncle Willy," said Tim. "Doesn't believe in banks. Poor old bugger suffers from the most appalling stomach complaint. Counting all his loot when whoosh diced carrots all over the place."

Rajiv nodded, "No problem we will get your Uncle Willy's money clean as new. Behold the Ashcombe 400T."

It looked like a giant washing machine only three times as big and in a metallic grey case. A large number of buttons ran down one side together with various gauges for temperature and nature of cleaning process. Ben and Tim looked at one another a little nervously. There were a lot of buttons.

"Shouldn't we wait until Ahmed gets back, Rajiv?" queried Tim.

"That's not be possible. He's gone to see our uncle who is unwell… in Calcutta. Don't worry. I have been running the business since he went and everything is running fine."

Harry looked uncertainly at Ben and Tim and tightened his grip on the holdall. Rajiv turned to Harry smiling and prized the bag from his hands. He removed the bin liner and tipped its fetid contents into the machine. Rapidly and seemingly without any thought Rajiv pressed a number of different buttons. There was a great gush of steam into the machine which instantly clouded up the glass window in the door.

"It will take half an hour. Come, let us go for a drink." He locked the shop door, and they walked back down the empty high street to the pub.

"I didn't know Ahmed was off to India," said Tim as they walked along. "When did he go?"

"He left this morning."

Harry could feel his insides dissolving as they walked through the door of the pub. Its warm air made him feel as if he were going to throw up. He headed for the loo and spent five minutes with his head perched over a foul-smelling toilet bowl. The cool air blowing through the broken and cracked windows slowly causing the feeling to subside. Harry unbent his legs, which were now stiff from where he'd been crouching, and sank back on to the grimy floor with his head resting against the metal wall of the cubicle.

Rajiv had only been running the business for one day. Harry looked at his watch, which confirmed what he already knew. It was Sunday!

The headlights cut through the darkness, seeking out the concrete wall as the BMW swung round and round slowly climbing to the top of the multi-storey car park.

Bernie Doyle stood on the edge of the roof looking out at the sea of light below. He turned at the sound of the car's engine and walked back to where his Jaguar was parked. The BMW came to a halt besides Bernie. Norman the Suit got out and went around to the boot. He and Knuckles McQueen, another of Doyle's employees, heaved a large bloodstained bundle over the lip of the boot and let it fall on the floor. They picked it up by its edges and dragged it across to Doyle. He could hear the bundle scraping along the floor as it was dragged. They dropped it at Doyle's feet and stood back panting slightly. Doyle pushed his foot into the bundle there was no movement. He looked up at Norman.

"I said bring him to me alive."

"He is alive. Look." Norman drove his boot viciously into the bundle. "Go on! Groan you fucker!"

The bundle twitched and a low moan was omitted.

"Stand him up."

Norman pulled the bin liner from the top of the bundle and he and Knuckles pulled it to its feet. They had to grab it more securely as its legs gave way letting out a howling scream as it did so. Norman clamped one of his hands over its mouth to prevent any further noise.

"Sorry about that, Bernie. I think one of his legs are broken."

The rush of cold air to Steve Reynolds's face and the jab of pain to his leg had revived him to a state of semi-consciousness. He could feel his hair being pulled away from his head, dried blood that had matted it to his scalp being ripped away as someone gripped a fist full of his hair and yanked his head upwards. He was about to yell out in pain when he found himself gagging on a warm sticky substance that filled his throat. As he retched he felt hair being ripped out from its roots as whoever was holding his head thrust it to one side.

His head was swung violently backwards again. His vision was clearing but he could only see out of his left eye. The lid of his right gummed firmly shut.

"Is he going to do that again?" demanded Doyle.

"I don't think so, Bernie."

"I'm going to have to burn this fucking suit now! Aren't I?". "The last thing I need is some fucking DNA wanker finding microscopic drops of his blood on it."

The tension in Reynolds's head relaxed as he felt his hair being let loose. His head dropped downwards.

"So, what did he have to say?"

"He gave George some tablets before the raid. Doesn't know what they were. Thinks they could have been E's."

The pain in Reynolds's scalp returned. He could feel a hot breath on his ear. Something warm like saliva dribbled into his inner ear sending a funny sensation through his body that was largely masked by the strong signals of pain it was sending out in all directions.

"You gave my fucking' get away driver drugs!" snarled a distant voice in his ear. The words reverberated in a muffled tone around his head. The second or third kick to his head by Knuckles had perforated one of his eardrums. Norman had had to stop Knuckles from administering further such blows.

A face swam into Reynolds vision. He thought he recognised it but wasn't sure.

Doyle surveyed Reynolds' battered head with a look of disgust. Most of his face was mottled with bruises and cuts. The right eye was swollen closed. Blood dribbled slowly out of one corner of the mouth and the bottom jaw hung unnaturally loose. The open left eye stared vacantly at him.

"Have you broken his fucking' jaw?" demanded Doyle turning to McQueen. "How is he supposed to bloody talk with a broken jaw?"

McQueen shuffled uncertainly and looked down at the floor. Doyle let go of Reynolds head and stepped back. *Well this is a fucking lot of use. I've told Norman before to leave them able to talk. That fucking Knuckles is a liability. The next motorway job we come across, he's going in the foundations.* He looked up at Norman.

"Sorry, Bernie. I let Knuckles get a bit carried away," said Norman sheepishly.

"Put him over," sighed Doyle getting back into his car. Norman watched as the Jaguar left the roof and began to descend in to the street below. He waited until the street was clear. Knowing his luck, if he dropped the body too soon it would be right on Bernie's car. He and Bernie had been together a long time, but there were limits to any friendship. He saw the car's rear lights disappearing into the night.

"Right," said Norman. He and Knuckles dragged Reynolds's body to the edge of the roof.

Reynolds could feel his feet scraping along the ground. The rhythmic motion reminded him of running a stick against railings as a child. The pressure on his under-arms suddenly disappeared and then a rush of cold wind on his face.

Harry knew what had happened as soon as they walked back in through the door. It smelt just like it did on damp autumnal evenings when someone lights a bonfire with wet leaves on it. The others were all smiling and laugh-ing. Their half an hour had stretched to an hour in which they all had three pints. Rajiv noticed Harry's stillness and then ran through into the back of the shop.

"Hey Harry, who do you think is better looking- that bird out of the Sugar Babes or Debbie Harry?" asked Ben, belching loudly in his ear.

"No, I'm not saying Debby Harry as she looks now," complained Tim lurching into Harry. "Here Harry, if your money is dry, can you lend us some so we can go and have a curry?"

Rajiv reappeared, ashen faced. Harry pushed past him into the back of the shop. The machine stood open, a small pall of smoke in the air. The bottom was cov-ered in burnt and blackened pieces of paper. Two or three pieces danced lazily in the air as they floated to the ground.

"HEY HARRY, CAN YO…" Ben's voice trailed off as he saw the contents of the washer. Tim came in and peeked over his shoulder. They all stood transfixed staring at the blackened remains as if they could will them back into fifty pound notes.

Chapter
Thirty-Six

The Jaguar glided to a halt in front of Harry. As he drew level, the rear window slid down and Bernie Doyle's face appeared.

"Harry, could you spare me a minute?"

Harry felt his bowels leap out of the bottom of his trousers and leg it down the street. "Bernie," he finally gabbled, "how are you?"

"Fine. Look, would you mind getting into the car for a moment?"

Would he mind getting into Bernie Doyle's car? If a lion invites you into its cage after its watched you eat its dinner, you mind. Harry climbed into the car. Doyle winced and ran his hand over his leg as he shuffled across the seat to let him in.

"Have you hurt your leg, Bernie?" Harry asked, keen to discuss anything other than the subject he knew was coming.

"No, it's all right."

They sat and looked at each other in silence. Doyle's eyes circled Harry like a TV detector van searching out an unlicensed set.

"So, how do you like working for Michael?"

"It's fine, just fine."

"Nasty business with the motorcycle courier."

"Yes... poor sod."

"Died in your lap."

"Yes, he...," Doyle looked at Harry expectantly, "...died in my lap"

"Harry, I have a problem and I need your help. That courier had an envelop on him which contained a key. No one found the key at the scene. Did you see any one picking an envelope or a key up at all?"

"No, no!"

Bernie Doyle looked at Harry for what seemed like eternity. Then he smiled and patted him on the knee.

"Thanks for your time, Harry. Sorry to have kept you."

Harry sat there, transfixed like a bunny staring into headlights. He knew!

"Alright Harry, out you get... Harry, I've got a busy day!"

"Yes, OK, Bernie. – See you soon."

Harry climbed out of the car and watched it disappear around the corner. As soon as it had gone, his legs began to wobble and he had to grab for the nearest railing to prevent himself from going over.

Bernie Doyle sat back in the car as it pulled away. His hand reached for his leg and he gave it a soothing rub. It hurt like fuck.

"What do you think, Norman?"

"Dunno, Bernie. He doesn't look the type."

"They're always the bleeding' worst. I tell you what. Take a picture of Harry and go down to Victoria with it. Pretend he's gone missing and see if any one recognizes his face."

Very slowly, Harry walked into the office. Michael Burns came down the stairs as Harry entered.

"Harry, I've just had a very odd phone call from Marianne Wheatley's solicitor. She's dropped her appeal to have the dog food impounded. He said his client didn't want to proceed in view of the fact that Victor had done a runner."

"Sorry, Michael, who's done a runner?"

"Apparently, Victor has, although how would Marianne Wheatley know?"

"He was certainly on something when I spoke to him, because he claimed Wheatley had him chained up and covered in dog biscuits."

"Yes, I remember you telling me. You don't think she's kidnapped him, do you?"

"Perhaps we should call the police."

"Oh no, Harry. We don't want to give the boys in blue the opportunity to come nosing through our filing cabinets. If Victor got to hear we'd let the police go through his papers, he'd throw a fit.

"Let's sit on it for now. Victor is bound to turn up at some stage. Anyway, I need you to go to Knightsbridge

Crown Court for me and meet counsel. Here's the file, cab waiting for you outside."

The cab arrived at the door of the court before Harry had even looked at the file. Thoughts of Bernie Doyle and his strange phone call with Victor Davies filling his thoughts. Victor had sounded very upset and weird. But he had heard him screaming and dogs barking.

"Knightsbridge Crown Court, governor."

"Thanks."

Harry scrambled up the court steps looking at his watch and the name on the file, R-v- McGee, to try and work out where he was going and how late he was going to be.

There is nothing like chasing round a cavernous court building trying to find both your client and the barrister who is to represent him for taking your mind off matters. Harry eventually found them both sitting outside court 14 waiting to go in. He introduced himself to the barrister who shook his hand and then disappeared.

Dermot McGee was a wizened little man in his mid fifties. He sat jauntily on the bench fixed to the wall swinging his legs back and forth and softly humming under his breath.

"Mr. McGee?"

"That's me," he said leaping to his feet. "Glad to meet you."

"My names Harry Trent. I understand you've already met Mr. Ames, the barrister who will be representing you today?"

"I have, he seems just grand."

"Good."

McGee looked at Harry expectantly, as if anticipating some confirmation of the legal attributes of Duncan Ames Barrister at law. As all Harry had got was a snooty good morning, he couldn't add anything. It seemed a bit churlish to dent McGee's optimism by commenting that the man had seemed a bit of a git.

They sat down and Harry opened the file. Dermot Albert Seamus McGee, born County Kerry, Eire, 1960, currently charged with arson and attempted arson. Harry glanced on through the file. There were three psychiatric reports. He looked up rather nervously at McGee who nodded and gave him a friendly smile.

"It says here you're very fond of seeing fire engines?"

"Red's my favourite colour."

"Okay."

"Will we be waiting long?"

"I don't know."

"Who's the judge?"

Harry shook his head and smiled back. "I'm sorry, I don't know."

"Well, as long as it isn't Judge Bream."

"Judge Bream?"

"Do you know the last time I came before that fella, he said I was raving mad and should be locked up for good? Still, I suppose he'd a point. I've been certified insane on two separate occasions."

"Right."

"Do you know what they call me in Brixton?"

"No."

He leant towards Harry and in a conspiratorial whisper said, "Mad Dermot!" He sat back a bright sparkle in his eyes.

"You know that Clint Eastwood fella? Plays Dirty Harry in all those movies. Well, he came to Dublin a few years back. And I thought he's played Dirty Harry, why not Mad Dermot? What do you think? Couldn't get near him though. He had all these bouncers round him, built like brick shit houses they were. Brick...."

His speech died off and he sat back, a subdued look on his face.

"Just think Clint Eastwood as Mad Dermot McGee, a true story. You know, if they'd made the film I wouldn't be here today. I ask you, labelling a fella mad just because he lights a little fire now and again. Where's the harm in that?

It depends, of course, where you light the fires. In McGee's case, it had been the Arndale Centre in Wolverhampton amongst other places.

"A man's entitled to keep warm, Harry. Would you not agree?

"Well, I suppose so. When did you light the last fire?"

"August Bank Holiday. God, it was a grand day. It was so hot me shirt was sodden with sweat. Half me matches wouldn't light. Ah, I suppose when it comes down to it, any days a good one to have a little fire. Is this your paper Harry?"

Harry looked down at the discarded copy of the *Guardian*, which lay on the seat between them.

"No."

"Well, if you don't mind then, I'll have it. It'll come in useful later.

Harry poked his head round the door of the court. Ames sat in the front bench chatting to the court clerk, he wandered towards him.

"Are we going to be long?"

"Judge has just gone for a leak," said the clerk. "Won't be back for a good 15 minutes."

"You may as well go get a coffee," said Ames. "There's a café on the first floor."

Harry went in search of coffee. McGee gave him a nod and a smile as he walked past.

Ten minutes later Harry walked down the steps and stared at the empty bench. Oh god! McGee had done a runner! He ran over to one of the ushers and asked them if they'd seen McGee.

"Runty little fellow about 5 foot nothing?"

"That's him."

"Yeah about five minutes ago. He borrowed my lighter and he hasn't brought it back."

"YOU DID FUCKING WHAT!!"

"There's no call for that language," said a grey-haired woman usher standing alongside.

"That man is a convicted pyromaniac, and you've just given him a lighter!"

A look of alarm seized the ushers face.

"But, I've just seen him go into court 14," said the woman usher.

The three of them ran pell-mell into the court. The library atmosphere and the low measured tones coming from the bench brought the first usher to a halt and Harry cannoned into the back of him. The Judge looked up with a scowl and both ushers shrank out of the courtroom. Under the Judge's baleful eye, Harry climbed into the bench behind Ames and tried to sit down, papers and a large brief case seemed to take up most of it. Harry put the case on the floor and sat down. He looked up at the court dock and got a cheerful wave of acknowledgment from McGee.

The hearing droned on. Harry was supposed to take notes but soon became engaged in a very elaborate doodle of £1,000,000. The sudden quiet made him look up.

The earlier scowl on the Judges face that promised heavy showers had now turned to a veritable tempest. Ames had broken off in mid speech unsure why his address was receiving such a negative response.

"Is there a problem, your honour?" he asked anxiously.

"Mr. Ames!" thundered the judge. "Is your instructing solicitor smoking in my court!"

"I'm sorry, your honour?" queried Harry sharing Ames bemusement. He didn't smoke. Had the judge gone mad? Harry glanced around to see if he could spot anyone else who might be the culprit.

"You heard me, Mr. Ames," growled the Judge "YOUR INSTRUCTING SOLICITOR IS SMOKING IN MY COURT!"

Ames turned around his teeth barred, having decided that if there was savaging to be done he would be running with the hounds not the hare. By this time all eyes in the court where focused on Harry. It wasn't him. He couldn't even inhale properly. This all seemed rather academic at the moment.

"I don't smoke."

It didn't matter. Harry could tell from the look in the judge's eyes that he was dead meat and it was dinner time.

"What the fuck do you think your doing!!!?" snarled Ames

A thin lazy column of smoke wafted its way in front of Harry's nose. He couldn't believe what he was seeing. He didn't smoke. Or, so he thought, but who was he to argue with such gob smacking evidence to the contrary? Harry looked down at the floor. The smoke was coming out of the briefcase he'd put on the floor.

"It's alright!" said Harry holding up the case. "Its not me - it's the case." He pulled the case open and a sheet of flame leapt out. "HOLY CHRIST!!!" he dropped the case like a stone. Burning chards of the *Guardian* flew through the air and pandemonium rained as barristers beat at their papers to put the flames out. Some enthusiastic court gopher ran forward clutching a fire extinguisher and caught Ames full on with a large spout of foam.

"It's all right your honour," sang out McGee from the dock, a mobile phone held high in the air. "I've already called the fire brigade."

Chapter
Thirty-Seven

"That's the house over there," said Tim.

Mandy leant over Harry's shoulder and nuzzled him with her chin.

"Well, we'd better get on with it then," she said. Harry stared at the house through the windscreen of Tim's minivan. There were just the three of them. They had left Ben at home on the basis that four burglars was rather mob handed. Harry had tried to talk Mandy out of coming, but she wouldn't listen and didn't seem to care about the effect it would have on her police career if they were caught.

It had been easier than they thought to get the cabbies address. Tim had spoken with his friend Andrea, who had been able to provide it and here they were.

"Where's the cab?" asked Harry.

"You see that little building next to the house? It's called a garage," said Mandy. "I rang the cab company and they said that Ronnie Becker was on holiday in Israel, so I think its fair to assume we will find the cab in the garage. Anyway, we don't want the cab, do we?

What kind of lunatic leaves a suitcase full of money in his cab?"

They climbed out of the van and padded through the night air to the side of the house. An ornate metal gate hung between the house and garage. Tim tried to push the gate open, but it wouldn't move.

"There's a bloody great lock on it!" he whispered. Harry looked up at the coils of barbed wire looped around the frame above the gate. Tim started to whistle the tune from the *Great Escape* under his breath. They both stood and looked at the dark silhouette of the sharp metal barbs just waiting to bite. Mandy let out a derisive snort. She pulled the thick woollen fleece she was wearing over her head.

"Harry," she whispered. "Get me up on your shoulders." He let out a slight grunt as she climbed up- Jesus, she was heavy. He'd never had her on top of him before. Well, not from that angle anyway, he thought with a grin. Harry tottered towards the gate, and Mandy wound her fleece round the barbwire and pressed it down. One foot on his head, she swung herself on to the top of the gate and jumped to the ground below.

"You two stay here, and I'll let us in."

They heard the soft tinkle of breaking glass. A few seconds later they were being ushered into the hall. Harry tripped over something on the floor, and the next thing he knew an avalanche of boxes fell on top of him.

"Harry, what are you doing?!" whispered Mandy, blinding him with her torch.

"I've fallen into the contents of someone's fucking jumble sale!" The beam of the torch left his face and danced around the hall. It was stacked with boxes of old lampshades, records and god know what else.

"I hope the whole house isn't like this," said Tim.

It was a fruitless couple of hours. Harry's hands were black and his throat parched from feeling on top of dusty wardrobes and looking under equally dusty beds. They stood in the kitchen, their shoulders hanging together in a mutual droop.

"Perhaps he put it in the bank," said Tim.

"No, he wouldn't have had the time," said Mandy. "The money was left in the cab on the Friday afternoon, and he flew off on the Saturday morning. It must still be in the cab."

The garage was alarmed. The wail from the siren bit into the night and next door's bedroom light came on. Mandy pulled the fire extinguisher off the garage wall and squirted its contents into the alarm box.

A window flew open in the house next door.

"Who's there?" a voice shouted followed by another hysterical voice that screamed "Gerry, are you crazy?! They could be murderers! Call the police!"

They were a two-minute drive from Temple Fortune police station. The garage light flickered on. Harry screwed up his eyes at the brightness.

"No point in worrying now about not being seen," said Mandy. She ran to the side of the cab and pulled the door handle. It was locked. "Tim," she said "go outside and keep an eye out for the police."

Tim trotted outside. He could hear the sound of a police siren approaching.

"Mandy, let's forget it. We have to go!".

"We are not going without the money."

Tim watched as the police car sped down the quiet street towards him. He ran out of the garden as it screeched to a halt. Before either officer could get out, he was at the side window hammering on it. The window slid down and Tim shone his torch into the interior, dazzling both policemen.

"The bastards have got all my mother's silver!" he yelled into the ear of the nearest officer. "They've just gone down the road in a silver Fiesta. I got the first half of the number. It's HDF3. Sorry I didn't get the rest. If you're quick, you should catch them."

The police car shot off. Tim ran back towards the garage.

The voice from next door rang out again, "Gerry! Where are the police going? GERRY! - DO SOMETHING BEFORE WE'RE ALL MURDERED!!"

Mandy picked up the fire extinguisher and struck the back window of the cab sending glass flying through the air. She put her arm through the broken window and opened the door. She had the case.

They ran down the garden and jumped into Tim's van, speeding off into the night to the distant sounds of Gerry getting a further ear bashing.

Both detectives were smiling as they came into the interview room.

Michael Burns reached under the table and tried to give Bernie Doyle a 'keep it cool' pat on the leg. Unfortunately, he chose the bitten leg. Bernie gave a noticeable wince followed by a blazing glare at Michael. Oops, thought Michael. Not a good start.

"Bernie, good of you to come in and see us," said Detective Inspector Long.

"What's this all about?" asked Bernie.

"We've had a very serious report," said Long.

"About a prowler," added Detective Sergeant Price.

"Now, this prowler was seen not a million miles from where the cars were dumped from that bank raid in the High Street."

Michael and Bernie looked at the officers with stony-faced indifference. Long knew it was a long shot to tie the two together, except for the fact that the description from the woman matched that of Bernie Doyle. Long knew from one of his informers there was a whisper on the street that Doyle was involved in the robbery. Long could hardly credit that a criminal of Doyle's stature would do such a thing. Still stranger things had happened. If he could nick a major villain like Doyle, it would be promotion city all the way. The chance to pull Bernie Doyle in for questioning over stolen underwear was too good an opportunity to miss. In the heat of the moment he might let something slip. Long waited for some reaction from Doyle. Bernie just sat there.

Long looked at Bernie and remembered the woman's initial description that it had been the devil himself who stole her washing. He knew exactly how she felt. There was something in Doyle's eyes that was very frightening. Long looked away and felt compelled to break the silence.

"This prowler was seen taking knickers from a clothes line in Ashcroft Terrace. We've had a rash of these complaints lately, but this is the first time anyone has been seen actually stealing the stuff. We need to catch this...," Long hesitated for a moment. He wondered if he dared to use the word pervert. Winding Doyle up was one thing. Calling him a pervert to his face was another. Doyle was not the kind of man to take such an insult without exacting some retribution. "...person"

Michael leapt in before Bernie blew a fuse and said something he shouldn't. He could feel the tension rising in the man next to him.

"Inspector, let me be clear about this. You have asked my client to come and see you over some stolen underwear. That is all you want to talk to him about?"

Long did not reply.

"Because, if it is inspector, then you have made a very serious mistake."

The two officers sat and said nothing. Michael's interjection and the look on Bernie's face had weakened their resolve. What had started out as a mixture of bravado and gamble now seemed an incredibly bad idea.

"My client is a very busy man. You have wasted his time and made a deeply insulting allegation against him. We are leaving now. Any attempt to stop us and I'll have a claim for false imprisonment and slander lodged with the High Court inside the hour."

Long said nothing. Michael and Bernie rose and left the room. As they did so, Bernie gave Long a look that sent a shiver down the man's spine.

The two detectives sat there after they had left the room. No, thought Long, I'm a DI. Doyle wouldn't dare try any thing on, but he knew that he didn't believe what he was thinking. A cold bead of sweat ran from behind his ear and down his neck. He forced a grin on to his face and looked at Price.

"Fuck him."

"Yeah, fuck him."

Michael and Bernie drove back to Bernie's house in silence. The car crunched to a halt on the gravel drive.

The two men sat in silence that was broken by Bernie. "Michael, this stops right now. I've had a million pounds go missing. A fucking dog has savaged me. I've had fucking maggots in my hair, and now some fucking low life copper accuses me of being a pervert!"

Doyle turned in his seat to face Michael. "The key went missing on your doorstep. Harry Trent knows more than he's saying. It's down to you, Michael. I want my money back, and I want the scrote who took it. And, when I get my hands on him I'm going to make the crucifixion of Charley Roberts look like a Sunday school outing."

Doyle got out of the car and walked into his house without looking back. Michael drove away his nerves dancing the polka. He well remembered the case of Charley Roberts, an East End gangster who had been found one morning nailed to a garage door, his face and feet burnt almost beyond recognition.

Michael punched his office number into the automatic dial of his mobile phone. "Suzy, where is Harry? Find him! Find him now! I want him in my office in half an hour."

"Hello Suzy? It's Harry. I've been up all night with a gippy tummy, so I'm not going to be into today. Can you tell Michael for me?"

"I've just had him on the phone, Harry. He's very steamed up about something. He said he wanted to see you in his office in half an hour."

"Do you know what about?"

"No. I know he had to go to the police station first thing this morning with Bernie Doyle. Perhaps it's connected to that.

"Oh, right. I'll see what I can do." Harry put the phone down on Mandy's bedside table and gave her a very worried look

"Harry, what's up?"

He turned and looked at her naked body now sitting bolt upright in bed.

"Michael wants to see me urgently. He's just been down the cop shop with Bernie Doyle."

Mandy leapt out of bed and swiftly pulled on knickers and a pair of jeans. "The money goes back now," she said as she dressed. Harry sat in bed a mixture of indecision and blue funk keeping him firmly nailed there.

"But, what about the missing fifty grand?"

"Sod it. If Doyle gets most of his money back, he'll be a lot less concerned than if the whole lot is missing."

"What, do we just drive up to his front door and give it back?"

"No." She sat down on the edge of the bed. "We need a plan. I'll call Ben and Tim."

They arrived half an hour later as Harry was emerging from the shower.

They sat in Mandy's living room. Harry gripped the cup of hot coffee in his hands feeling warmth and comfort from it. Mandy looked at her watch.

"I'm on at 2:00. That means I have to leave here by 1:15. Before I go, we need to have a plan to get the money back and it needs to be back today."

"What's the sudden rush, Mandy?" enquired Ben.

"Oh, nothing much, except it belongs to a murderous psychopath who knows I've got his money," chimed in Harry.

The conversation ranged back and forth on the possibilities. The hours ticked by. Mandy looked at her watch, frustration written large across her face. "This is useless. Look, at the end of the day we either deliver the money or Doyle comes to collect it."

"We should leave it at a drop," said Tim.

"Excuse me, have you...," the man brushed past Norman and continued along the rail platform. Norman resisted grabbing him by the collar and pulling him back. Although it would have been satisfying to have slapped the man around, it would not have aided his current task. He was also aware it would have been somewhat unfair to take out all the aggression he'd been building up that morning on one individual. Norman knew he was a violent man, but liked to consider himself fair-minded as well.

Wearily he trudged back towards the station exit, the new patent leather Italian shoes he was wearing biting into his ankles. Bleeding rubbish he thought. Always the same these days. You could never get your hands on a decent pair of stolen shoes.

An elderly West Indian was pushing his broom across the station concourse. "Excuse me, Pop," said Norman. "Do you know where I can get a decent cuppa round here?"

"Don's café. Out the station and turn right."

"Thanks." Norman walked past the cleaner. He halted and turned. He took the picture of Harry from his pocket, its corners bent and folded from its passage in and out of his jacket. "You haven't seen this bloke, have you? It's my sister's lad. Came down to London and disappeared."

The old man looked carefully at the picture. "Yes, I saw him. Couple of weeks ago when I was working late. I always keep an eye on those I think are about to puke all over the concourse. You see, it's my job to clean it up. As I'd already had three lots of vomit that night, I was praying he'd get off the concourse before he threw up. Once they get to the escalators it's Charlie Richard's responsibility. You should have seen this guy weaving all over the place dragging a great big case along behind him."

"What kind of case?"

"One of those shiny silver ones.

The Doctor removed the dressing from Bernie Doyle's leg. A large area of purple bruising surrounded the dark red wounds in the top of Bernie's thigh.

"How does it feel?"

"Hurts like fuck."

"Have you been walking on it?"

"I've got a business to run."

"I told you, Bernie. You want this to heal you need to keep it up in the air and your weight off it." The Doctor applied a clean dressing. "I'll leave you these stronger painkillers and remember keep off the bloody leg. Don't worry, I'll see myself out." The doctor rose and walked out of Bernie's living room.

"Thanks, Doc," said Bernie. He looked across the room at the bar and the bottle of whiskey standing on it. He could do with a drink. The phone rang.

"Bernie, we've got a positive ID!"

"Right, come around and pick me up. We will go and collect our Harry and take him for a little ride."

As Bernie put the phone down, it rang again.

"Hello."

"Mr. Doyle."

"Yes?"

"There is a grit bin on Seven Sisters Road opposite Finsbury Park tube station. Be there in half an hour and you will find something that belongs to you."

"Who the fuck is this?"

"Half an hour."

Ben ended the call and dropped the pay as you go phone into the litter bin.

"Do you think he bought it?" Said Mandy.

"Don't know. We'll have to see."

Bernie replaced the receiver. What the hell was that all about? Well only one way to find out. He picked up the phone again and tapped in the number. "Hello, Norman? Look, I want you to make a slight detour on your way back."

The silver Mercedes pulled to a stop by the side of the road. Ben and Mandy watched it through the window of the adjacent café in which they sat. Norman got out of the car and looked around. He opened the lid of the grit bin and removed the case. He got back in the car and it sped away.

Ben looked at Mandy and grinned, "there you go, problem solved!"

A worried look crossed Mandy's face, "I just hope its that simple."

"Count it again!"

Norman looked up exasperation written all over his face. "Bernie. I've counted it three times. There's only nine hundred and fifty grand, which means fifty grand is missing."

"Right. Well, we'd better go and pick that little toe rag up and find out what he's done with the other fifty grand."

"Sounds a bit odd to me, Bernie."

"What does?"

"That he'd take fifty grand and give the rest back. Doesn't make sense."

"None of it makes any sense, Norman. I don't normally expect my own solicitor to steal from me. Now, if he didn't take it, that leaves only you."

They exchanged odd looks with each other.

Bernie broke the silence. "Of course, I don't think you took it, you stupid old tosser."

"We've been together a long time, Bernie."

"Yes, I know. Look, losing this money. That fucking disaster of a bank raid, and my fucking leg," said Bernie with a wince.

"Yeah, I know. We're all getting a bit old for this game."

"Don't start down that fucking road again. Let's go and pick Trent up and find out what he's done with my fifty grand."

"Is it worth it Bernie? After all the trouble, we've had lately. The last thing we need is another body to get rid of."

"Worth it! Are you going soft on me Norman?"

"No, but it's only fifty grand and straight after the bank raid the last thing we need is someone to see Harry getting into your car and then his body being fished out of some lake."

"Do you know what that fifty-grand means to me? Well, do ya!!!???"

"No, Bernie, I don't."

"I'll tell you what it means. IT MEANS 50,000 KICKS UP THE ARSE! That's what it means and NOBODY!... NOBODY! Is taking that kind of liberty with me. Easter is coming early this year Norman. We are going to have ourselves a crucifixion when I get my hands on Trent."

Michael looked at his watch. Two hours since he'd spoken to Suzy. Where the hell was Harry!? He picked up *Country Life*- it had a special supplement on seafront villas in the South of France- and winced at some of the prices. It had been a good year for the firm. Would he ever live to enjoy it? At the thought of Bernie Doyle's anger, he threw the magazine down and stared glumly at the door to his office. It was so unfair; he'd never seen Doyle in such a state. He hadn't got his bloody money, but he seemed to think Harry did. He was Harry's boss. Would he be able to convince Doyle that he had nothing to do with it if it turned out Harry did have the money?

Had Harry's behaviour been unusual? That was difficult to tell. What was normal for someone like Harry? He'd been arrested twice, fallen from a helicopter, smashed up a Porsche, had a fight with Victor Davis, destroyed that maniac Pierce's garden and set fire to the court house.

The more he thought about it, Harry was a total liability. Any person capable of so much mayhem in four weeks was quite capable of stealing a million pounds from a major criminal. Anyone who did something like that had to be a lunatic and it was quite clear from what Harry got up to that he was a lunatic.

Had Harry signed his training contract yet? If not, it would be an easy job to get rid of him. He searched among the magazines and catalogues which covered his desk. He didn't know why he had so many. He really would have to speak to Suzy about keeping his desk tidier. Did he really need six different sailing magazines? Oh, here was that special edition of *What Car* on Lamborghinis. He'd been looking for that for weeks. Just look at these beauties with their 12 valve 8 cylinder engines. Oh! The '62 Coupe, what a classic, only 7 had ever been built.

Michael was engrossed in a magazine as Harry came into his office.

"Hello, Michael," he said nervously.

"What?... Harry, have you every been in a Turbo 5.8?"

"No."

Harry's blanking answer seemed to stir some life into Michael. He put the magazine down and stared at him. "Jesus, Harry, what have you been up to? Bernie Doyle thinks you've stolen a million pounds of his money."

"I know."

"So, have you?"

"Not really."

"What do you mean not really?"

Harry told him about the courier, which he knew, and the curry and throwing up over the money, which he didn't. When he'd finished, they sat in silence for several minutes, Michael looking like someone had just told him they'd closed Saville Row and from now on he'd have to get his suits from Budget Save. In the end, Harry could stand it no longer.

"Michael, are you OK?"

"Ha Ha Ha! You steal a million pounds from London's leading psychopathic criminal and ask me if I'm OK?

"But, I've given most of it back."

"Christ Harry! Bernie Doyle is not a man you can kiss and make up with. As a result of what you've done, Bernie has tried to rob a bank and had some dog take a fucking great bite out of his leg! And, you didn't hear any of that from me, right?!" he added seeing the look of surprise on Harry's face. "Before you ask, I didn't hear this from Bernie Doyle either. But, I know a lot of people and it's not hard to make four from two plus two. Okay, I believe it was an accident. Having regard to your record to date, it's all rather par for the course. Fuck me, you're a liability, Harry."

Michael stared into his knuckles and then looked up. We'd better get you out of London for a while. Dermot McGee is coming up for trial at Bangor Crown Court. You can go up with him on the train tomorrow."

"Isn't he in custody?"

"Yes, but they are sending him up by train hand-cuffed to some security guard so you may as well go with. The trials going to last about a fortnight. My uncle has a holiday cottage up there you can use. I'll try and speak to Bernie Doyle and see what can be done in the meantime."

Chapter
Thirty-Eight

Ian Skuse guilty of rubbing a violin? Was that a crime? It couldn't be, right? Harry looked at the page again as the words swam in and out of focus in front of him. Robbery with violence. He rubbed his eyes and closed the file. Enough was enough for one day. Where was Mandy? She was late. He turned out the lights and left the office.

It was a warm spring evening and it felt good to get the last rays of the day's sun on his face.

"Hello, Harry," he felt the jab of something hard in his side. He turned, and saw Norman the Suit. "Bernie wants a word," he growled. He hustled him across the road to the open back door of the Jaguar.

"Harry," said Bernie. "Good to see you."

Mandy swore under her breath as she ran towards the offices of Clancy Burns. She hated being late. She'd agreed to meet Harry at 6:30, and it was now almost 7:00. Unable to park, she abandoned her car on a double yellow line. Mandy turned the corner as Harry was hustled into the Jaguar. She saw his head disappear into the back and recognized Norman as he got in after him. The car sped past her. Quickly she turned and ran back to her old blue Fiesta.

Mandy leapt behind the steering wheel and gunned the car into life leaving what little tread remained on the tyres behind her. She could see the tail lights of the Jag disappearing around a corner about 600 yards in front of her. Mandy pushed the accelerator flat to the floor. She turned the corner and had to break violently to avoid crashing into the stationary line of traffic in front. Four cars ahead, she could see Doyle's car caught up in the evening traffic. Her hand scrambled into her handbag searching for her mobile phone. Her fingers crept over lipstick, loose change and god knows what else. Why did they have to make them so small? Mandy pulled the bag onto her knee and peered into it. The lights went green, and Mandy pulled forward. With her left hand, she emptied the contents of the bag onto the passenger seat. She stole it a quick glance and plucked out the phone. They were changing lanes. She dropped the phone again as she pulled into the left-hand lane to follow the Jag. A protesting horn came from behind. They were moving faster now. A yellow van and a red car between Mandy and Harry. She pressed numbers into the phone.

"No, *Denise Denise* was the first Blondie single," said Ben through a mouthful of rice. Tim snorted in derision and spread mango chutney on to his poppadum as if it were toast.

"The phone's ringing," he said, taking a bite out of the poppadum.

"Well, I don't have it."

"It's in your pocket."

"Oh yeah. Hello... Mandy?"

"Ben! It's Harry. He's in trouble. I need your help!"

"I'm in the middle of my vindaloo at the moment, Mand'. Can it wait?"

"No! Bernie Doyle, hang on their turning... has got him. Look, we are about to get onto the West Way. Where are you?"

"We're in The Paddington Tandoori. Its about two minutes from the West Way slip road."

"Good. Get in the van and come now."

"What's up?" asked Tim, scooping up a mouthful of chicken jalfrezi.

"We've got to go. It's an emergency."

"But, I haven't finished my curry!"

"Well, bring it with you." Ben placed two twenty-pound notes on the table and put an onion bhaaji into his jacket pocket. He headed for the door.

Tim piled his samosas and remaining poppadums on to the plate. "I hate soggy samosas," he whined following the disappearing figure of Ben out of the restaurant.

The car sped along the West Way. Bernie was looking out the window seemingly taking no interest in Harry's presence. Harry shot the odd glance at Norman the Suit who in return gave him a number of looks ranging from the baleful to the questioning, *You wouldn't? You didn't? Did you? I'd have never thought you had the bollocks?*

The latter was of considerable interest to Harry as he speculated whether he would still have his by the end of the day.

The van bounced on to the West Way sending a shower of yellow rice and a samosa flying on to the dashboard. There was a squeal of brakes as Ben corrected the van's direction as it shot along the outside lane. The engine omitted a high-pitched whine as if to say "Look, I'm a twenty-year-old minivan not a BMW. I don't go faster than 65 miles an hour so slow down."

"Where are they?" asked, Tim picking grains of rice off the speedometer and popping them into his mouth.

"Call Mandy."

"Yes!"

"Mandy, its Tim, hang on." Ben swerved into a gap that had appeared in the inside lane and then back into the outside lane to get around a Range Rover. Tim steadied his curry. "That was close. Where are you?"

"Just past Hangar Lane. Where are you?"

"About..." Tim's head struck the side window as the van swerved once more into the inside lane, "...two minutes behind you."

"Good. As soon as you can, get in front of me. If we use both cars, there's less chance of Doyle realizing he's been followed." Mandy put the phone down and let out a low sigh. It was reassuring to have the boys with her.

Ben continued to zig zag in and out of traffic. The faded blue of Mandy's Fiesta came into sight. He flashed her with his headlights and pulled in front.

"Ben, do you think they'll be armed?"

"Probably."

"Oh. We don't have guns, do we?"

"Who needs a gun when we've got Alice?"

They had come off the A-40 and were heading through the side streets of Ealing. Harry had an over whelming urge to pee. He wondered what the etiquette was in these situations. With the three of them in the back of the car, they were packed quite close and he had no idea how long they were going to be in the car.

"Bernie?" he said hesitantly.

Doyle turned and put his finger to his lips in a hushing motion.

"Bernie, sorry, but I need a pee."

"You what?!"

"I need to go for a piss!"

"Norman, sort him out, will you?"

Norman pulled a very large gun from the inside of his jacket and pressed the barrel down between Harry's legs.

"It's very simple, son. If you piss in Bernie's car then I shoot your dick off."

"OK," croaked Harry.

Doyle's car went straight ahead at the roundabout. The car separating it from Ben and Tim's van went left. Ben put his foot on the brake and slowed down.

"Give Mandy a call. She'd better go in front again," said Ben. "No, hang on they're turning into somewhere... Oh Christ, it's a cemetery!" He stopped the car. Mandy pulled up behind them and ran to their window.

"Leave the van here, we will go in on foot."

The Jaguar wound its way slowly through the cemetery. The three of them shadowed it at a discreet distance dodging between gravestones.

"This will do, stop her," said Bernie. "Nice and quiet. Gerry get out and keep watch. Make sure we aren't disturbed. Now Harry, about my money."

Bernie's driver got out of the car and positioned himself about 10 yards away. The three of them dived down behind a vault as they saw Gerry approach.

"What's happening?" asked Mandy.

"Hang on, I'll take a look," said Tim. He dodged off between the graves returning a couple of minutes later. "They're sitting in the back of the car talking. There's Doyle and one of his sidekicks."

"Norman the Suit," butted in Mandy.

"Yeah, Norman the Suit. He's holding something towards Harry."

"What? A gun?! A knife?!"

"I dunno."

"We've got to rescue him."

"We need to get rid of matey-boy over there first," said Ben. "If we could lure him over here, we could belt him over the head with something."

"How do we do that?" queried Mandy

"I've got an idea," said Tim. "Mandy could you have an orgasm?"

Gerry took a cigarette from his pocket and lit it. He sighed with pleasure as the first rush of nicotine hit his lungs. He cocked his head to one side. What was that noise? It sounded like a low moan. There it was again. A shiver ran through him. Bloody graveyards, he didn't like them one bit. Good job Bernie was doing this in daylight.

He took another deep drag on the cigarette and glanced back at the car. "UUUuuuuhhhhhhh…" Gerry's head swivelled back in alarm. He had definitely heard it that time. His eyes shot back and forth over the blackened sea of gravestones in front of him. "UUUuuuuhhhhhhh… UUUuuuuhhhhhhh." The sound was developing a rhythm. *Fuck me it's not a' ghost! Some dirty bastards are shagging!*

Gerry felt a stiffness in his trousers. A vision of a naked woman on a cold hard gravestone flashing in front of his eyes as they raked the cemetery trying to identify where the sound was coming from.

Mandy squatted behind the gravestone. It hadn't been easy to start with. It wasn't every day she tried to fake an orgasm in a graveyard whilst gangsters were beating up her boyfriend. Her first few attempts at a moan had sounded more like a cat being strangled than a woman in the heights of passion. Ben and Tim had looked on in despair.

"Think of Harry," Tim hissed.

"Perhaps she is," said Ben with a smirk.

Mandy closed her eyes. *Harry's bum. It was a bit hairy,* she smiled, *but small and firm!* Her hands slipped between her legs and gently caressed her thighs. *Harry turned around. Oh, my god!* She let out a long deep moan. Ben and Tim nodded enthusiastically.

Ben peered over the top of the gravestone. He could see that the man was unsettled. Behind him the rhythm of Mandy's heavy breathing starting to rise.

"UUh UUh UUh!!!"

He turned his head, "steady on Mandy, you'll wake the entire grave yard."

By now, Gerry was very interested. He had glanced back at the car and then skipped lightly over towards the nearest graves. Nothing.

"UUh UUH UHH UHH…" It was coming from his left.

"He's coming," whispered Tim. "Quick grab something." Ben looked around.

"What?"

"Anything."

Ben looked in desperation. Just bloody gravestones, not a stick, stone or anything he could hit someone over the head with.

"He's coming."

Gerry slowly crept through the gravestones towards where the moaning was coming from. He didn't want them to hear him coming, he wanted to watch.

Tim looked round. "Grab that bloody urn!" he hissed.

"It won't budge," said Ben as he vainly wrestled with the urn, which was clearly part of the grave.

The loud whispering caused Mandy to cock one eye open. A shadow fell over her. She looked up into the incredulous face of Gerry.

"What the fuck?!" he exclaimed.

"Hit him! Hit him!"

"It won't bloody move," said Ben as he continued to wrestle with the urn. His hands came away clutching a bunch of dead roses, which he proceeded to swat Gerry over the head with.

"Whaaat?!" Gerry turned in confusion as he felt the thorny rose stems scour the back of his head, the still scented blackened petals descending over his face. Where was the naked woman? Who was attacking him with flowers!!?

Mandy cannoned into the back of Gerry's legs and sent him toppling over her. As he fell, his head struck the corner of a gravestone stunning him. He tried to struggle up from the ground his vision foggy. He could see a face and something large and orange looming over him and then all went black.

Tim brushed his hands together as he straightened up. The earthenware flower pot he had brought crashing down on Gerry's head lay in pieces on the ground. Gerry lay still, his face partially concealed by soil and a chrysanthemum.

"Is he dead?" asked Ben.

"Dunno."

Mandy knelt down and brushed the earth from Gerry's face. A deep red cut ran across his forehead. She placed two fingers against his neck.

"No, but he could do with an ambulance."

"Pity we haven't got one," murmured Ben.

"Never mind, aye," said Tim.

"Still, if you can't get to hospital, the grave yard is probably the best place for you."

"Cuts out the journey."

"If you two have quite finished."

They sat in silence.

"So peaceful here," said Doyle. "I've just brought this place off the council. You know how much I paid for it?"

"No, Bernie."

"One pound. Can you believe it?"

"Sounds a bargain."

"It is. There are ten acres of prime building land attached to this cemetery. Once I've got planning permission to develop, it will be worth about £25 million. Course, I'm obliged to maintain the cemetery, look after its occupants. But, they don't ask for much so that's fairly easy. I like to think, Harry, that I am a reasonable man. But, I get a little irritated when somebody tries to rip me off for a million quid. Especially when it's my own bleeding solicitor."

"I've given you most of the money back, Bernie."

"I know you have, Harry. But, where is the missing fifty grand?"

"I don't have it."

"You don't have it? What have you done with it?"

"I burnt it."

"You burned fifty grand? Norman, bolt cutters!"

Norman reached down to the floor and lifted up a pair of black metallic bolt cutters.

"You can cut a three-inch steel bolt in half with one of these. Now tell me where the fifty grand is or Norman here is going to give you a pedicure with his scissors."

"I WAS SICK ON IT! THE MONEY WAS RUINED!!!"

"You what???"

"I'd been drinking. I didn't know I had the key. I found it on my way home from the pub. When I got the case home, I threw up. The missing fifty grand was all covered in vomit."

"So now your telling me you didn't burn it. You were sick on it? Norman pick me a finger."

"He's going to make a noise, Bernie."

"Well, use the gaffer tape."

Norman reached across with a role of tape and put a large strip across Harry's mouth, then he handed the bolt cutters to Bernie.

"Hold his hand out." Norman grabbed Harry's hand and held it out towards the bolt cutters. Harry rolled his fingers into a ball, but it was no use Norman bent his little finger out as if he was going to pull it off himself. Bernie raised the bolt cutters and brought the blade towards Harry's fingers.

"What the fuck!" exclaimed Bernie.

They could hear a high-pitched whine. Sparks showered down on top of Bernie as an enormous revolving blade came through the roof of the car. Bernie threw himself forward as it descended towards his head, dropping the bolt cutters. Norman dropped Harry's hand as he shielded his eyes from the flying sparks. Harry grabbed the cutters and caught Norman with a swipe across the bridge of his nose, blood and cartilage flew through the air. The car door on Norman's side flew open. Harry scuttled over Norman's body and rolled out onto the ground.

"Hello Harry, thought you might need a hand." He looked up into Tim's cheery face as he scrambled to his feet. Ben stood the other side of the car with the chain-saw in his hand, the blade smoking from its exertion.

"Come on, no time to hang around," said Tim. They ran from the graveyard.

Chapter
Thirty-Nine

"You've missed the turning," said Tim.

"What?" replied Ben. "I thought you were navigating?"

"I am. That's why I'm telling you you've just missed the turning."

"Oh, bloody hell!" Ben pulled the steering wheel viciously to the right and pressed down hard on the accelerator peddle. The minivan shot into the outside lane and across the central reservation to the sound of blaring horns and squealing breaks. It bounced onto the other carriage way narrowly missing an on coming HGV.

"Show off." The sign to Lower Malling appeared in front and the van turned left into a narrow bush lined lane.

"How do you know Uncle Max is going to be there?"

"I spoke to Ma. She said he'd just been kicked out of somewhere in Africa. Apparently, something to do with selling an aircraft carrier to Swaziland."

"I didn't know the Swazi's had a navy"

"They don't even have a sea."

"Tricky."

"Very."

The van turned down ever darkening country lanes canopied with trees interspersed with the occasional field and even rarer gate with a disappearing drive behind it. Finally, they came to a gate that proclaimed the name Spoons. Tim got out and pressed the intercom button set in the wall. A CCTV camera moved round and focused in on them.

"Yes?" came a voice through the intercom.

"Hi, Uncle Max. It's Tim."

"I can see that. What do you want?" Tim looked at Ben for guidance. They wanted guns. It didn't seem a good idea to blurt that out in public, even if they were standing on a deserted country lane. Ben shrugged his shoulders, grinned and shot Tim with his fingers.

"We need some stuff," said Tim finally.

"Do you, indeed? You'd better come in."

Great iron gates topped with razor wire swung open and the van roared up the gravel drive to a large imposing Georgian mansion.

"So, why is it called Spoons?" asked Tim as they pulled to a halt.

"Apparently, Uncle Max made a lot of money selling them to the navy."

"Ours?"

"Argentina's"

"I didn't know they ate so much soup."

"Neither did they."

The got out of the car and were greeted by a small man in his late fifties with close cropped grey hair and a bald palate.

"Hello, Uncle Max," they both chimed in unison. He looked them up and down whilst he considered whether or not to throw them out or hear what they were after. The last time they had visited had been for his daughter Jessica's 18th birthday party and the little sods had made off in the old minivan used by his gardener. He thought is best to see what they wanted first if only to make sure it was safely locked up.

"I see you've still got my van. If you plan to borrow anything else whilst you are here, would you mind asking first."

They both looked sheepish and stared at the floor. "We've got a small thank you for the loan of the van," said Ben.

Max took the bottle of Scotch that Ben proffered and saw with approval that it was his favourite single malt.

"So, who's drinks cabinet did you loot this from then?" He saw the hurt look in the boy's eyes and realised he had overstepped the mark.

"You'd better come in then, and tell me what it is you want."

"Thanks," said Ben.

"I don't suppose you have a key for the van do you Unc? It's a right pain starting it with a screw driver."

"I'm sure Jenkins will have a set somewhere. Whether or not he will want to give them you is another matter."

They followed Max into the house.

"Where did you get that scotch from?" whispered Tim to Ben as they walked behind him.

"Don't you remember? We picked it up at Jessica's party."

"You mean it's?"

Ben nodded.

They sat in Max's book lined study. They had both asked for a beer, and Max sipped a gin and tonic. He looked at the pair of them. They were both bright and highly personable. It was such a shame that both had lost their fathers at such a young age. This had led to a wild teenage period ending with the burning down of the school they both attended. A spell in the army he thought would do them both a world of good. Discipline was not their strong point, and both had failed the interview procedure for Sandhurst. The army had not taken kindly to having one of its tanks painted bright pink.

"So, what do you want?" he finally asked.

"We need some guns, Uncle Max," said Ben.

"Do you, indeed? And, what are you planning to shoot at? Pheasant, communists or is it the police?"

"Gangsters," said Tim.

"God, the company you pair keep. And, why exactly should I provided you with guns?"

"Well, you've got lots, and there is every chance someone is going to start shooting at us or at Harry, anyway."

"Firstly, I'm an arms dealer and secondly, who is Harry?

After they had told him what had happened, Max sat back in his chair and thought for a moment. "So, for once in your life you two are keeping company with people who have respectable full-time jobs, even if one is a solicitor who's stolen a million pounds and another a policewoman who is about to get chucked out on her ear".

"It's not their fault Unc," said Tim.

Max raised his eyebrows. "Well, at least you're not up to no good this time, and I never have had anytime for drug dealers. You're in luck. I've just got a new ship-ment for the CIA. Bloody yanks never could count, so I don't suppose they will miss one or two. You'd better come with me." He led them from his study down a long corridor. At the end of the corridor stood a heavy wood-en door. Max undid the three locks set in it, and the boys followed him down a flight of stairs that led to what appeared to be the door of a large safe. Max opened a control panel in the wall and concealing it with his body tapped a series of numbers in. The door swung silently open.

It was a well stocked armoury. The walls lined with rifles, light and heavy machine guns and enough other equipment to start a small war.

"So, what are you boys looking for?"

"Do you have anything armour piercing?" asked Tim.

A concerned look crossed Max's face.

"We just need something with a bit of oomph, an Armalite perhaps? And, something a little easier to conceal," butted in Ben.

"A bit of little and large," added Tim. "Is that a flame-thrower?"

"If you think I'm going to let you pair anywhere near a flame-thrower, you must be joking. Here try this for size." Max threw a pistol at Ben. It's a Heckler & Koch 42. The Germans are just about to issue it to their special forces. Has all the power of a Magnum 44 but a smaller dick."

Ben balanced the gun in his hand and stared along the sight.

"How many rounds?"

"Nine. Here's a box of ammunition and two spare clips."

They settled on the German pistol and an Armalite rifle.

"Right, that'll be £3,562. You can have them at trade seeing as your family."

Ben and Tim exchanged anxious glances.

"We were hoping we could just borrow them," said Ben sheepishly.

Max went red in the face. "What do you think I am? A bleeding library? I do not lend guns, I sell them. Here give them back." He reached out with his hands.

"I'm sure Ma would lend us the money," chimed in Tim.

"Well, let's get her on the phone then."

Harry arrived at Paddington Station about ten minutes before the train was due to leave. The station concourse was packed with holidaymakers, business people and the travelling public. His eyes joined the sea of others scanning the departure boards trying to work out which train and platform he needed. His search was interrupted by a loud interjection in his ear.

"Harry, tell him I don't have to carry his bleedin' pork pies!"

Harry looked round into the wizened face of Dermot McGee. In one hand, he carried a plastic carrier bag and in the other a small suitcase. Handcuffed to him was Ron James.

"You'll carry what I fucking' tell you to carry," said Ron. He turned to Harry. "Hello again," he said with a smile. "We didn't get properly introduced last time."

"I'm Harry Trent. Dermot's solicitor. Your office said yesterday it would be alright for me to travel with you."

"Ron James, security executive," he said proudly. Then as if to prove the point he said, "see…" and held up a badly crumpled card on which were printed the words "Utah Gun Prison & Pizza Company (UK) Ltd, Ron Jones Security Executive." The name Jones having been altered in biro to read James, "…this proves it."

Harry held out his hand and felt it being grasped by a warm sweaty palm. "Nice to meet you Mr…?"

"Call me Ron. Would you like a pasty? I'd offer you a pork pie, but I've only got three left."

"It's like feeding time in the zoo!" whined Dermot. "Harry, tell him it's against the Geneva Convention to make me carry all his food. The bag weighs a ton, and the plastic is fit to slice my fingers in two."

"Shut your yap, you! I've seen The Great Escape twice, and I don't remember nothing about not having to carry pork pies." He turned to Harry a smug look on his face. "All Utah Gun Prison & Pizza employees receive training in the treatment of prisoners, you know. It's part of the job. Of course, I do a lot of private study myself. I'm especially interested in foreign penal systems. Have you ever seen The Prisoner of Zenda?"

Ron started eating the minute the train pulled out of Paddington station. Food, he said helped him take his mind off his twin fears of train crashes and confined spaces or closet phobia. "You know that feeling like you've been locked in a closet?" as Ron described it.

"I can handle trains, but I go mental if they put me in the back of a van. So that's why I normally do the trains," said Ron through a mouthful of pasty.

They sat at one end of a carriage, separated from the public by an aged curtain on which the words 'Secure Section Do Not Enter' had been added under the old British Rail Logo. Ron had made a great ceremony of drawing the curtain before they had sat down.

"That's the security screen. No one can get in or out once that's drawn."

Dermot and Harry exchanged looks of bemuse-ment. "What's the little plastic window in the top for?" asked Dermot.

"Oh, that's very clever. I can't tell you what that's for." He leaned over and whispered in Harry's ear. "That's the security window for me to look through and make sure its safe before I let anyone through the screen."

Harry looked at the curtain. The plastic window was some seven feet off the ground.

"It's a little high, isn't it?"

Ron looked bashful. "That's the bloody manufac-turer's, that is. They're supposed to have provided us with a special plastic step so we can see through the window but it hasn't arrived yet. Anyway, I'm not ex-pecting any callers, so we can probably do without it. Screen's drawn, we're nice and secure."

"Tickets please," a small man in a cap burst through the curtain and waved a pair of clippers under Ron's nose. "Where's your ticket?" he demanded.

"You can't come in here. This is a secure zone."

"What you on about? The buffet cars down this end of the train."

The Swedish businessman unfolded the plans on Michael's desk. "This is stage one of the development," he said.

"He's got someone with him at the moment, you can't go in!" They both looked up at Suzy's shout as it came through the door. The door flew open and in walked Bernie and Norman, a red-faced Suzy behind them.

"Sorry, Micha..."

Doyle cut across her. "Where is he?" he demanded.

"Who?" said Michael rising from his chair. His mind still on the large fee he was going to charge the Swede.

Doyle's face darkened. "I haven't got time for this. Norman."

Norman walked round to Michael's side of the desk and struck him across the face. Michael fell backwards on to his chair, which under the force of the blow went over, throwing Michael to the floor. He got up, blood streaming from his nose on to the snow white of his shirt, a look of bewilderment tinged with fear in his eyes.

The Swede looked from Doyle to the two cherry red spots of blood that had appeared on his plans, his face a picture of incomprehension.

"You still here?" Bernie barked. "You never heard of solicitor client confidentiality? Can't you see I'm trying to have a quiet word with my brief?"

"Shall I call the police, Michael?" said Suzy from the back of the room.

Michael dabbed at his nose with a handkerchief. The five of them stood in the room, the limited edition prints that decorated the walls and the fine hand made furniture shrinking back into the walls from the violence they had witnessed. Michael could feel the eyes of the rest of the room on him. This was his manor. He was supposed to be in control. He dabbed his nose again and then looked from one to the other of the people in the room. Norman the Suit expressionless, seeing nothing out of place in sudden violence in everyday life, Anders Grunberg looking like a man who had suddenly found himself on another planet, Bernie a look of steely determination in his eyes that clearly said no was not a viable answer to any question he was going to ask. Suzy her eyes blazing with fire clearly just looking for the chance to kick Bernie Doyle in the bollocks. He couldn't help his lips crack in a thin smile as such ill-judged defiance.

"No, Suzy. It's OK." He turned to the Swede who was now busily folding his plans and putting them back in his case. "I'm sorry about this Anders. Let me call you later in the day." The Swede avoided any eye contact with Michael, snapped his case shut and scuttled from the room.

"Let me get you a cab, Mr. Grunberg," said Suzy chasing after him.

Bernie sat down in the vacated chair and Norman pushed the door.

"She's got some balls that one. What's she doing working for you?"

Michael picked up his chair and sat down. He looked at the bloodstained handkerchief in his hand and threw it in the bin.

"He's not here," he said slightly nasally through his blood blocked nose.

"I can see that, Michael."

"I mean he's not in London. I told him to get out of town whilst I tried to sort things out with you."

Doyle sat back in his seat and pursed his lips. "And, what exactly do you propose to sort out?"

"He told me about the money. It was all an accident Bernie. Harry had got no intention of keeping it."

"Funny that, because I lost the key on the Thursday and it was the following week on Wednesday before I got my money back and that was only after I threatened to chop Harry's fingers off. That reminds me, Harry seems to have kept fifty grand as a keepsake. So, you owe me fifty grand. Seeing as its you, I'll take a cheque."

"I don't have fifty grand, Bernie."

"Don't annoy me, Michael. Of course you do."

"What I mean is, I don't have that kind of money just laying around that I can give you. It will take me a couple of days."

"I'm sure if you write a cheque your bank will cover it. I want that now, and you can give me the rest later."

"What rest? I thought you said Harry gave the money back.

"He did. But there is the small matter of a new Jag. Those comedians and the slag he was with cut mine in two with a bleedin chainsaw. Who are they by the way?"

Michael looked at him in bemusement. "He's been spending a lot of time with the Farrington's Ben and Tim."

"Lanky looking? Posh accents?"

"Sounds like them. Harry mentioned they'd just got a chainsaw for some forestry business they were going into. They are the nephews of Lord Farrington who owns Farrington Metals."

"Good. Then he will have the cash to stump up for a new car. By the way, are they on drugs?"

"I don't think so, why? They're a bit eccentric but otherwise pretty harmless."

"I don't regard going around armed with a chainsaw and cutting my car in half as harmless. What do they do that's so eccentric?"

"They eat a lot of curry. They've also spent some time in psychiatric care after burning their old school down."

"So, I've got a couple of pyromaniac curry eating nutters to deal with, have I? And, what about the girl?"

"I think they are friendly with some PC called Mandy. Suzy has mentioned her a couple of times. Seems she is a bit wild, and is only hanging on in the force by her fingernails. I think she and Harry might have become a bit of an item."

"So, where is our Harry?"

"I told you, he's..." Michael voice trailed off as he saw the look in Doyle's eyes. "He's on a train on his way to North Wales. He's going to be staying in my uncle's cottage. I'll give you the address."

Bernie and Norman got up to leave the room.

"Oh, Michael," said Bernie.

Michael looked up, his face now an oily grey.

"You know what will happen, don't you, if Harry finds out we know where he is? Thanks for the cheque."

Ignorant of Burn's betrayal, things were beginning to liven upon on the train. As the ticket collector had informed them, passengers had to go through their part of the carriage to access the buffet car. The prison carriage was meant to be the last one, however once again the railway company had forgotten. Normally it wasn't an issue. Most of the security guards employed by Utah

Gun Prison & Pizza were big enough for it not to be a problem stopping people coming through the train except when they put the buffet car on last. Ron said this had happened once before and there had almost been a riot.

He managed to turn back the first couple with only a grumble and "this is outrageous I'll be writing to the managing director." Dermot had gone to the loo and was half way through whatever it was he was doing when the curtain began to twitch for a third time. Ron began to start back into the carriage. Dermot was of course handcuffed to him.

"Aaah, what are you doing!" he yelled, "I haven't finished." Ron found his arm being pulled out behind him. The chain separating the cuffs, which was about three feet in length-European specification apparently–went taut, and Ron found himself pulled to a stop. Ron gave the chain another hard tug that brought another anguished howl from Dermot.

"For the love of sweet Jesus, I haven't finished yet. Harry! Help me! It must be against the Geneva Convention to stop a man from taking a piss."

Ron's face went a deep red. "If he mentions the fucking Geneva Convention again I'll do him, I swear."

A small man in a flat cap had meanwhile come through the curtain and was witnessing what appeared to be two men chained together, one of whom was screaming from somewhere out of sight.

"If I don't get to finish, I swear to God I'm going to burst!"

"What's going on?" said the man. "There's women and kids on this train."

"Sod off," said Ron. "Can't you read? This is a restricted area."

"Read what? Our kid's hungry. He wants a sandwich."

"What's written on that curtain."

"Yeah, I can read it, but there's nothing written on the other side." As it turned out, he was right. The curtain had been drawn back when they got on. Seeing the wording on their side of the curtain they naturally assumed it was repeated on the reverse.

"Look, I'm the law, and I've told you to sod off."

"You don't look like a copper to me. More like a traffic warden. Why you chained to that bog door?"

"Haaarreeeeeeeeeeee!" came the scream from the loo. Harry decided it was time to say something.

"He's a security guard taking a prisoner to court. I'm his solicitor."

"What, you need to have a solicitor present before they'll let you take a piss? It's a fucking police state we're living in."

Harry stuck his head round the toilet door. Dermot stood with his trousers round his ankles, precious inches from the toilet with his legs crossed. He'd managed to loop the chain around the top of one of the taps thus preventing Ron from pulling him out, but by a similar fate Dermot could do no more than stare at the toilet bowl.

"Ron, you've got to back up a bit and let this bloke go through." Realising the hopelessness of his position, Ron walked back towards the loo. Harry unwound the chain and a grateful Dermot sat down.

Harry had never been good at goodbyes. Things were getting pretty hairy, and he figured it wasn't fair to have Mandy involved in his problems anymore. So, he'd left a note saying he was leaving the country for a while– well, Wales *is* another country– and that he'd be in touch.

When Mandy got the note, she called the office. Suzy picked up the phone.

"Suzy, where's Harry?"

"Michael has sent him off to Wales on a case. But look. Bernie Doyle's been here asking for Harry, and I think Michael has told him where he is. He's shut himself in his office for the last hour with a bottle of scotch and won't talk to anyone."

"I'm coming over. See if you can get hold of Ben and Tim for me and ask them to meet me at the office."

Mandy had called into her flat whilst still on duty and had therefore been able to blaze over to the office in her squad car siren screaming. She abandoned the car in the middle of the street outside Clancy Burns's office, and raced up the three flights of stairs to Michael's office.

Michael had consumed two thirds of the bottle of scotch and had moved from feeling sorry for himself to deep despair and now towards a hatred and contempt for Harry. "Own fault, silly tosser," he mumbled to himself. He looked up in a daze as Mandy burst into the room. *Oh Jesus! Raided by the police. That's all I need to finally flush the practice down the toilet. I hope to Christ they don't find the coke in my draw.*

"What can I do for you, officer?" he slurred

"What have you said to Doyle?"

"Hey? What have I said to Bernie Doyle? What's that… what's that got to do with you?"

"I'm Mandy Brighton. I want to know what you've told Doyle about Harry."

"Oh, the flaky copper," said Michael staggering across the room towards her. "Nice tits." As the words left his lips, Mandy kneed him in the groin. His face contorted, his hands rather lately but instinctively reaching for his balls, he fell to the floor and threw up over a Persian rug.

She left him to groan on the floor for a moment looking down at him in grim disgust.

"What did you say to Doyle?"

"Fuck off and leave me alone," groaned Michael curling into a foetal ball.

Mandy knelt by the side of Michael and wrenched his arm viciously behind his back. He let out a squeal, which brought Suzy and several other Clancy Burns staff running to the open door. When Suzy saw, it was Mandy, she gently ushered the others away and closed the door. "The police are just asking Michael a few questions, nothing to worry about."

As the people in the corridor dispersed, she saw the familiar figures of Ben and Tim loping up the stairs towards her.

"Hello, Suze," said Ben. "I hope this is important. We were just on our way to have a curry."

"Oh, I think you'll find the trip worthwhile," she said with a smile on her face. "Mandy is in there," she pointed at the closed door "talking to Michael."

The two boys entered the room, Michael Burns lay face down on the floor, Mandy had her knee in the small of his back and his right arm bent upwards at a sharp angle.

"Morning Michael, Mandy" they said as they went in. Tim sat in Michael's chair and put his feet on the desk. Ben sat on the front his feet dangling in the air.

"Ben, tell her she's breaking my fucking arm," whined Michael.

"He says your breaking his fucking arm, Mand," said Ben swinging his legs back and forward.

"While you've got him down there Mand, get him to tell you where he keeps those naughty photos he took of Suze," said Tim as he busily rifled through the draws in Michael's desk.

"I'll rip his fucking arm off if he doesn't tell me what he told Doyle."

"Ooh! Look what I've found," sang out Tim waving a small plastic bag of coke in the air.

"Oh, fuck," groaned Michael "Let me go, and I'll tell you everything."

They walked down the steps from the offices of Clancy Burns. The patrol car sat where Mandy had left it door wide open, blue light silently flashing.

"Don't you think we need to make a plan, Mand?" said Tim.

"Let's drive around the corner," said Ben. "Best not to let anyone hear what we have in mind."

They got in and drove the car 600 yards down the road.

"Why don't we just give Harry a call on his mobile?" said Tim.

"He dropped it down the loo last week," said Mandy. They both gave her wide eyed stares. "Just don't ask," she added. "The security guard he is with must have a phone or radio. We can contact Harry through him. He's safe for now. The train is an express and doesn't stop till it gets to Bangor. Doyle will either have men waiting at the cottage or at the station. That gives us two hours."

As lunchtime came, the flow of people through the carriage became irresistible. Ron had to sit and tolerate it.

Harry didn't pay much attention to the two men the first time they came through, other than to notice that one of them had a union jack tattooed on his neck, and the other told Ron to "feck off" in a strong Irish accent as he tried to stop them coming through. It was about then that Ron gave up trying to prevent people coming through. These two in particular where not the kind you wanted to have an argument with. The tattooed one was wearing only a vest and had arms like tree trunks. The other just had a look about him that had you dialling 999. They spelt trouble with a capital T and even Ron could see that discretion was the way forward.

When they came back a few minutes later, the one with the tattoo gave Dermot a very long stare and when Dermot saw him, he took an instant interest in what was happening out the window.

After they had gone, Dermot looked back and was chewing on his bottom lip as if it where a deep pan pizza.

He leant against Ron and whispered in his ear.

"What?" said Ron. "Bollocks. They can't do anything, we're on a train. Anyway, how do you know it's him?"

"I tell you it is. You see that red in his union jack. He did that with his own blood. I tell you he's mad as a hatter and twice as nasty. The man's like a pit bull on them 'C's'."

"What are C's, you daft bugger? You mean E's?"

"What does it matter what letter of the alphabet they're named after when yer man is ripping yer head off."

The ring on Ron's mobile phone cut off further conversation. The tinny sound of rule Britannia filled the carriage.

"Ronald James, security executive speaking," he said in a voice that filled the carriage. "You want to speak to who? Oh. But, this is official equipment."

Harry couldn't hear what was being said to Ron down the phone other than he caught the word "prat". He handed Harry the phone in the end with a terse "Be quick. The office may need to contact me urgently."

"Putting you through now, officer," he heard a voice say and then "Harry? Is that you? It's Mandy."

Harry felt a little taken back at this. "Hello... Mandy, look, I'm sorry about the note." Out of the corner of his eye, he could see Tattoo Neck and his mate coming back down the carriage towards them. The both stopped about 10 seats away and Tattoo pointed at Dermot.

"Harry, are you still there? Can you hear me?"

"Sorry Mandy, there's two guys coming towards us, and I think there could be trouble."

"Quick, Harry. They're Doyle's men. You have to get off the train now. Burns has told him where you are going."

The Irish one had grabbed Tattoo Neck by the shoulder and was trying to lead him away. Tattoo Neck threw off the arm. "It wasn't your feckin van!" he shouted at him.

"It's not me they're after Mandy. I think its Dermot. Look, I've got to go."

"I'm coming up to Wales with Ben and Tim. You can't go to the cottage. Where can we meet?"

"I don't know! I don't know the place."

"COME HERE YOU LITTLE FECK!" roared Tattoo Neck as he advanced towards Dermot. Ron took the pork pie he was eating out of his mouth.

"Here, what's going on?" he said "AAAHHH my nose!" Ron's hand went to his face as Tattoo Neck head butted him.

"Bangor High Street, coming from the station, last pub on the left. I'll meet you there at 6:30 tonight!" he yelled down the phone.

Harry could see streets flashing by outside. They were entering a town. He grabbed the emergency cord and pulled a fire extinguisher off the wall. Tattoo Neck had his hands around Dermot's throat and was bouncing his head off the window.

"Blow up my caravan, would you? You feckin Taig!" he shouted as he tried to put Dermot's head through the toughened glass of the window. Harry brought the fire extinguisher down with a crash on the back of Tattoo's neck. It bounced off. As he spun around, Harry ripped the pin out of the fire extinguisher and gave him a face full of foam. He now joined Ron in clutching his hands to his face.

His Irish friend- from the sound of it they were both Irish- decided to join in. Harry heard a loud growl, and as he looked round, saw a fist hurtling towards his head. He felt a sharp pain in his face and then it all went black.

Chapter Forty

The ceiling light swam into and out of focus as Harry regained consciousness.

"Harry, you're alive," said Dermot with relief. Harry sat up on the hospital trolley and looked around. Apart from his neck feeling rather stiff and a certain wooziness, he felt OK. Slowly he climbed to his feet.

"Where's Ron?"

"They're fixing his broken nose. When he started all the screaming I managed to slip the key out of his pocket and un-chain me-self."

"Where are we?"

"God knows. Some place in Wales with more l's in its name than a fella could every hope to pronounce."

They were in Llandidrod Wells, which was about 30 miles outside Bangor. When Ron emerged, he had a large plaster across his bloodied nose, both eyes which were set in a sea of purple skin. He'd had enough.

"I'm going on the sick." He handed Harry his mobile phone and dog-eared business card. "Can you give them a ring for me, Harry? They'll need to send a replacement out to take over."

Harry dialled the number and was greeted by a cheery pre-recorded voice:

"Welcome to the Utah Gun Prison & Pizza Company. Feed and protect your family with UGPPC. In order that we can more quickly respond to your call, please listen to the following 8 options."

They slowly went through the eight and established that Harry neither wanted to buy, rent, have built, or acquire a time-share in a prison or buy a pizza. Having exhausted all eight, he was then put on hold while a voice told him periodically how his call was important to them and was now of priority importance.

He looked at Ron. "Don't you have a direct dial number?"

"Mean bastards make us go through a call centre."

The number began to purr and an American voice came on the phone.

"Hello my name is Sandy, how are you today?" Before Harry could answer she went on, "The Utah Gun Prison & Pizza Company is dedicated to your every security need. With 10 Pizza coupons, you can get a rocket propelled grenade launcher for only $50.00. Local taxes and currency charges may apply."

"Can you put me through to personnel, please?"

"Who's calling, please?"

"My name's Harry Trent. I'm ringing on behalf of one of your employees, Ron James, who has been injured."

"And, how can I help you, Mr. James?"

Bernie put his overnight bag on the kitchen table and poured himself a cup of coffee. He heard the distant ring of the doorbell and yelled at Bianca to answer it. She tottered into the kitchen on her five-inch stilettos followed by Norman.

"It's Norman," she said. "How long are you going to be gone, Bernie?"

"Just a couple of days."

"Where did you say, you were going?"

"Wales."

"Oh, that's nice. We used to go there on holiday when I was a kid. Norman, what do you think off ocean spray blue for a bathroom?" Norman looked at Bianca in bemusement. "You know, for our en-suite in the penthouse. Half a sec, I'll show you the colour chart." Bianca clit-clattered her way out of the room.

"Haven't you told her about the flat yet?" Norman whispered to Bernie.

"For the tenth time of telling Norman, it's a penthouse not a fucking flat. I got a call from Jason this morning. He's found me another one."

"Oh, so a night in your boot made him see sense then."

"He was all over me like a rash. Right, let's go before Bianca gets back with those bloody paint charts."

The two men walked to the Ranger Rover parked outside. In the dark, Bernie could see the two figures inside.

"Who've we got?" he asked Norman.

"Dave and George."

"Good. We'd better take two cars. George and me will take the Merc, and you follow in the Land Rover. We tooled up?"

Norman nodded. The two cars pulled out of Doyle's drive and headed for the motorway.

Ben and Tim sat in the front seats of the minivan, singing out of tune with the *Blondie* CD they were playing.

Mandy's blue Fiesta swung onto the car park of the London Gateway service station in front of them. The boys scrambled out of the van and gave her a big hug. "It's going to be alright, Mand," said Tim

"I know, I know," she opened a car atlas on the bonnet of the mini. "We take the M1 and then the M6. If we get separated, we are heading for Bangor. I've arranged with Harry that we will meet him in the last pub in the high street on the left, coming from the train station."

They both nodded. Mandy looked at her watch. "It's 12:30 now. That gives us 6 hours to get there."

They climbed back into their cars. Mandy sped off with Ben and Tim behind. As the van shot down the exit ramp, Tim grabbed a large heavily stained paperback from the side pocket and began leafing through it.

"Well?" asked Tim from behind the steering wheel.

"I'm looking, I'm looking," said Ben, his eyes scanning the pages of their dog-eared but treasured copy of the Good Curry Guide. Tim drove onto the motorway without looking; the sound of a blaring horn from behind them caused Tim to look up from Ben into his mirror, which was filled with the front grill of an articulated lorry.

"He's getting a little close, isn't he?"

"I know, I know." Tim pressed his foot down on the accelerator but the car didn't respond. The blare of the horn now filled the car as it sped along, its rear bumper inches from the front of the truck. Tim glanced into his side mirror as an Audi shot past. The lane was clear. He yanked on the steering wheel and pulled into the middle lane. The giant truck shot past, buffeting the little van in its slipstream.

"Thank Christ for that!" said Ben. "I've found one!" He began to read out loud the review of the Bangor Balti Bar.

After being put on hold half a dozen times and passed from one person to another, all of whom expressed great confidence in being able to help Harry before passing him on, he was finally put through to Brad.

"Good morning, sir. How are you today?"

"I'm fine, thanks. I'm ringing about one of your employees."

"Sir, if you want to make an allegation of brutality by one of our employees then I'll have to put you through to our legal department. I should warn you though that injuries of a non-life terminating nature can often be incurred when our security executives are exercising reasonable restraint and do not give rise to a cause of action."

It obviously said a lot about the company that when you rang to speak about an employee they automatically assumed it was to complain about being beaten up.

"So, are you saying that any injuries sustained short of death are perfectly legitimate?"

"That would normally be the case, sir."

"I'm not ringing to make a complaint. I'm with one of your employees who wants to report in sick."

"Is he capable of motion, sir?"

"Well, he has a broken nose and is complaining his vision is rather blurry."

"I see, sir, but is he capable of forwards and backwards movement."

"Do you mean can he walk?"

"Not necessarily walk, sir. If an employee is capable of operating a wheel chair or has a friend or relative who is willing to operate it for him, then he is capable of motion and does not fall within the company definition of being too ill to work."

"So, in order to report in sick, you need to be in a comma?"

"If an employee is in a comma then he should notify us in writing to that effect and- subject to suitable medical certification- then sick leave will normally be allowed. All requests for sick leave must be signed personally by the employee, however."

Harry looked at Ron who sat forlornly on a chair. The front of his plastic looking uniform darkly splattered with blood. Dermot sat next to him handcuffed to a chair. The reinstatement of the cuffs had been, Ron declared, the last thing he was doing.

Harry put his hand over the phone and said, "They want to know if your capable of motion, Ron?"

"What?" groaned Ron.

"Motion? Isn't that one of those clever medical words for having a shit, Harry?" chimed in Dermot.

"Aye?" grizzled Ron, "Why do they want to know if I can still go to the lav for?"

"No, it's not that kind of motion. They say if you can still move you have to work."

"Jesus, they're hard fellas," butted in Dermot seizing the wrong end of the stick, "fancy that, if your well enough to have a shit, your well enough to work."

Harry put the phone back to his ear.

"Is there anything else I can help you with today, sir?" asked Brad.

Perhaps, reflected Harry, Dermot wasn't that far off the mark after all. The Utah Gun Prison & Pizza Company obviously had some very novel ideas on injury and sickness and poor Ron with just a broken nose and blurred vision wasn't going to get anywhere.

They were about 50 miles from Bangor with no trains until the following day. Dermot and Harry steered Ron out of the hospital towards the cab rank. He was in a semi conscious state from the painkillers he'd been given and sat in the back of the taxi softly mumbling to himself about pies.

The driver gave him an anxious look. "What's wrong with him? I don't want no drug addicts in my car."

"Don't worry, he's just been in a bit of an accident."

The driver gave Harry a look that said if anything happens I'm holding you responsible. "There will be a five-pound supplement as there's three of you."

"Fine." They pulled out of the hospital grounds in the white Peugeot and headed along the coast road. They drove through a fine mist of rain past steep green banks that rose up to craggy hilltops, interspersed with the woollen dots of sheep. Harry felt snug inside the nice warm cab away from the damp and chilly weather outside.

"Nice day," said the cabby. "We don't normally get weather as good as this. It's normally piss... oh, bugger." The seemingly fine day in Wales suddenly took a decided turn for the worst as hail the size of ping pong balls began to bounce off the car. The noise brought Ron back to full consciousness.

"Where are we?" he asked.

"In a taxi heading towards Bangor."

"A taxi! I need a pie," Ron's head disappeared into the large black shoulder bag sitting on his knees and emerged chewing nervously on a pork pie. Three pies later Ron sat back, his cheeks and lips smeared in grease and crumbs.

"Its alright," he said turning to Harry and giving him a grin through teeth decorated with pie crust. "I'll be OK as long as I've got me pies."

"How many do you have?"

"I normally carry about 20 for snacks and the like, and then I have the extra 10 in my other bag for emergencies."

"Other bag?" Harry glanced over at Dermot who shook his head. They had no other bag.

"Why don't you try and take a nap, Ron."

"Yeah, good idea."

They continued to wind their way through barren hilltops and valleys the windscreen wipers fighting a losing battle with the deluge outside.

"Jesus. It's worse than Ireland," moaned Dermot. "How can a fella ever get a fire going in weather like this?"

Harry gave him a knowing scowl.

"Just joking, Harry," he said with a smile.

Ron dozed fitfully, his snoring reverberating around the cab. They were just outside Port Dinorwic when trouble struck. Ron jerked awake with a start. " No! I wasn't asleep, just resting my eyes for a minute," he said. He looked nervously round the cab, scrambling round in his bag with a hand. It came up empty. He glanced around for his other bag. "You seen my other bag, Harry?" he asked his voice anxious and edgy.

"No, sorry Ron, you, err, only had the one bag when we got in the car."

"My pies! My pies! Ron's hands probed left and right, not that there was much room to conduct a search with the three of them jammed in the back of the car.

"Get off!" shouted Dermot "I'm not sitting on your feckin pies" as Ron's hands lifted him off the seat and pressed his head into the ceiling.

The cabbie's eyes looked at them uncertainly through his driving mirror. Harry needed to calm Ron down or they where going to have a problem.

"You don't happen to have any food on you, do you?" he asked the cabbie.

"No!"

"My pies! I need my pies!" moaned Ron. He turned the bag inside out in case a pie was hiding in some concealed corner. He picked the crumbs from the lining and sucked them off his fingers. Then in growing desperation, he began to lick the inside of the bag for any elusive crumbs that had evaded him.

Dermot and Harry searched their pockets and the floor of the cab for signs of any food they could use to pacify the rumbling volcano that was about to erupt from within Ron. Harry found a rather hairy toffee stuck to a bus ticket and Dermot peeled a piece of chewing gum off the floor. Unquestioningly, Ron swallowed them, but they were a momentary diversion not food.

"It's alright, Ron, we'll be there soon. Bangor has some great pie shops. Just sit back and close your eyes," said Harry trying to sound reassuring.

Ron's fingers nervously pulled at the dirt-smudged collar of his shirt. "Its hot in here. I need some air." He reached across Harry belching loudly as he did so, the smell of old school dinners shrivelling Harry's nostrils

The open window brought momentary relief from the eau de pork pie, but the driving wind that blew out Ron's gases brought in a torrent of rain.

"Shut that bleedin' window," growled the cabby "it's genuine Bry-nylon tiger skin on these seats!"

Harry wound up the window and looked at Ron who was sucking in air faster than a goldfish on a sun bed.

"I can't breathe! I can't breathe!" he gurgled.

The car window shot towards him, Ron could feel the car closing in on all sides, he would be squashed flatter that a hedgehog doing press ups on the M25. His tie bit into his neck and as he looked down he could see that it was not a tie, the large head of the snake raised its head and fixed its eyes on the great fat mouse it was about to devour. Ron felt its coils tightening round his throat. He screamed.

If you can imagine a pig that has swallowed a 500-megawatt amplifier trying to shit a grapefruit twice its own size, you would still not have the faintest inkling of the noise that came out of Ron's mouth. The taxi swerved violently left and right across the road, the cabbie having lost control from the shock of the sound.

Harry could hear nothing now but a high-pitched whistling. He looked at Dermot, his face the colour of a blanched grape left out to dry in the sun. The taxi bucked from side to side and a car flashed by. The taxi swerved to a halt in the middle of the road. Rain hit the side of Harry's face as the door came open and large bony hands pinched his neck and arm as he was dragged out on to the road, which he hit with a thump. The cabbie was saying something, but all Harry caught were the muffled words "out" and "bastards". The cab screamed away leaving the three of them in the middle of the road.

It was the sound of bleating sheep floating towards him that told Harry his hearing was back too normal. He looked through the wire fence into a little black face that stared at him for a moment and then proceeded to amble back up the steep hillside. His eyes followed its progress up the grassy slope that quickly gave way to a rock outcrop interspersed with heather. Harry looked around at the sweeping hills surrounding them. If the middle of nowhere had a dead centre, then they were in it.

"What pretty little lambs," said Ron. Harry looked around. Ron was sitting in the middle of the road as

happy as a sand boy. "I love the countryside," he added, his face set in a jowly smile. Harry glanced over at
Dermot, his face had now recovered from its pallor and
was turning crimson.

"You fucking moron!" he screamed. "Look what
you've done."

"Don't worry, we can't be far from town," said Ron.
"It's almost lunchtime, so we need to find somewhere to
eat soon anyway."

They'd been walking for about half an hour. By now
they were soaked through and indifferent to the down-
pour. The sound of the soft phut phut of the engine
preceded a tractor as it slowly came into view over the
brow of a hill. It was being driven at no more than walking pace.

Rhodri Evans hated everything. The rain, his life, the valley where he lived, his stupid fat ugly slag of a daughter of his that he just called Girl. She had a name, but
Rhodri had no idea what it was. He had never used it
and had always referred to her as Girl. His wife had
used it, but she had run off 10 years ago with Griffiths
the Sheep Shagger. Bastard! Rhodri had caught him
with his prize ewe. She had never been the same after
that. He was getting old and rheumatic. He needed
a strong pair of hands to help him on the farm. If only
the Girl could get a husband and give him a grandson.
Someone who could work the farm that he wouldn't

have to pay. He shifted sideways on his seat. His piles where giving him hell. He hated his piles. The only thing he hated more were the English, bastards!

He could see the three men coming towards him. The man in front was obviously English, the one following looked like a pig wearing a bin liner and a small 'ferrety' person was behind. A thin grimace, the nearest his face ever came to a smile, cracked his lips. As they came level, the English and the Pig beckoned him to stop, but he ignored them, save to swear under his breath in Welsh.

It was just after he had gone past the Ferret that the idea struck him. Perhaps he could get one of them to make the Girl pregnant. Probably not the English, but the Pig or the Ferret didn't look particular. If he got them up to the farm, they would never find their way back to the main road without his help. He could keep them all there till one of them had serviced her, or preferably more than one to give it more of a chance. Perhaps he could get them to leave him some sperm in a jar for use later should it be needed. He had heard of women who had made themselves pregnant in that way.

"He's stopping!" yelped Ron.

Harry looked back. It was true. The tractor had stopped. He ran back to it.

"Could you give us a lift to the nearest town, please?"

Evans lifted his head revealing a face weathered and beaten by the elements. The eyes had that look which Harry had seen on many a teenage date when confronted at the front door by a girl's father, which said 'my daughter is a princess and you are a rapist. I have a jar all ready for your bollocks in my shed and never forget it.'

"I'm not going to town."

"How far is the nearest town?"

"It's over that way."

"Is it far?"

"I wouldn't walk it myself."

"Do you have a phone?"

"There's one back at the farm."

"Would you mind giving us a lift to your house and letting us use your phone?"

Rhodri grunted approval and nodded towards the trailer attached to the back of the tractor. The three men gratefully climbed onto it. Rhodri allowed himself another grimace. They could use his phone as much as they liked. What for, he couldn't imagine. It'd been disconnected ever since his wife left.

As if a sign that things were getting better it stopped raining. They continued back the way they'd come for about half a mile and then turned onto a side road. The sun came out from behind the clouds and they began to dry out. Harry sat and took in the surroundings and for the first time that day began to appreciate the magnificence of the Snowdonia National Park. He was just beginning to wonder when they were going to get to the farm when thankfully they turned off the side road and onto a track. This was obviously the entrance to it. After bouncing along for about ten minutes, his first doubts began to set in.

"Is it far now?"

The farmer turned his head and shrugged.

The tractor went on past thick hedge and dry stonewall gradually climbing. Every now and again there would be a break in the cover, and Harry caught a glimpse of the land disappearing below. He looked at his two travel companions. Ron still seemed supremely content with life, Dermot's eyes were flicking nervously right and left. He caught Harry's glance and shuffled over towards his.

"Jeasus, Harry," he whispered "Where are we going!?"

Harry was beginning to share his nervousness when finally, ahead he could see a house, thin wisps of smoke lazily drifting from its chimney.

His feelings of relief skidded to a halt when he turned to point it out to Dermot and saw the look of abject fear on his face. Harry followed his line of sight. His first thought was they were ponies, but the shape didn't look quite right. As they got closer it became clear, they were dogs. Silently they fell in on either side of the trailer.

He looked down at the face of one, its head seemed to mainly consist of teeth. It glared back at him through small black eyes that said just one word: DINNER.

Megan Evans took a last look at the picture of the naked torso of the boy band singer, sliding her finger out of her mouth and across her cheek as she did so. She could hear the soft phut phut of the tractor as it came into the yard. Hurriedly, she pulled down the front of her dress and carefully slid the magazine into the gap behind the dresser. She took one last look in the oven. The pastry of the pies she had made was turning a burnished brown and were almost ready. Thoughts of the ribbed sides and throbbing motion of the Big John vibrator that had arrived in the post that morning filled her head as she distractedly opened the front door to greet her father. She couldn't stand him but wanted him fed and full of home brew as quickly as possible so that he would be asleep and out of the way so she could get on with the evening of solitary pleasure she'd planned. It was a pity the postman had been able to escape. Still, she would know better next time. She had acquired a thicker rope that would take more than teeth to cut through.

All thoughts of postmen and vibrators flew from her mind as she caught sight of Harry, she let out a soft moan and felt a warm tingle between her thighs. Megan ran to the trailer swatting aside the huge dog as if it was no more than an errant fly.

Harry didn't know if it was the mountain air or something in the vegetables, but nothing seemed to be of normal size. The pig-tailed woman who came out of the house was built like a rugby prop forward. She bounded towards the trailer and gave him a smile that he found almost as frightening as the look he'd got from the dogs.

"Who are these gentlemen then, Da?" she asked in a sing-songy Welsh lilt.

"I found them on the road," he grunted.

"Tea's almost ready," she said, her eyes fixed on Harry. "It's very nice to have some visitors isn't it, Da?" she said with a smile that offered far more than dinner.

"I've got to see to the goat," said the farmer to no one in particular as he walked off in the direction of the barn.

"Can I use your phone?" asked Harry. "We need to get to Bangor in rather a hurry."

"It's inside."

They walked into a stone paved kitchen, the room warm from the glow of the Raeburn.

Dermot dragged Harry to one side and whispered in his ear, "I don't think anything male is safe around here, Harry. Did you see that nervous look the dogs gave her?"

Harry looked inquiringly at Megan. "Sorry, we are in a bit of a hurry. Where is your phone, please?"

"Over in the corner. Would you like a pie?"

"They're bloody marvellous, Harry!" Their eyes turned towards Ron, who stood by a tray of pies next to the oven, one in each hand. "Sorry, but I was starving," he said through a mouthful of food."

"That's alright. I like a man with a healthy appetite," said Megan. "I hope they're not too hot, they haven't been out of the oven long," she said sashaying over towards him. "Mind, I quite like a hot filling myself," she added.

Ron eyed Megan with apprehension as she came closer to him. Why was she wiggling her bottom from side to side like that? As she came abreast, she lent in and whispered in his ear, "I've got very large nipples you know." He choked as the pie went down the wrong way and edged nervously away.

Harry hunted around in the corner of the room, finally unearthing a telephone thick with dust. He put it to his ear, but there was no dialling tone.

"I can't get a dialling tone?"

"No," she replied.

He looked at her enquiringly

"Would you like a pie?" she asked.

Chapter
Forty-One

They had pulled into the service station as Mandy needed more petrol and Tim was dying for a pee.

As Tim stood over the porcelain urinal, a look of contentment spread across his face as the hot yellow stream hit the bowl. He glanced to the left. A large man about 6 feet tall was standing three bowls along. He looked vaguely familiar.

Norman the Suit zipped up his trousers and looked up into Tim's gaze, which Tim hurriedly broke. Bloody queers, thought Norman as he walked out.

The hot coffee felt good and helped Mandy shrug off the edges of tiredness that were beginning to eat into her. She had been on the night shift and it was over 24 hours since she had last had any sleep. Ben sat opposite her busily chewing on a large burger, another one sat waiting for Tim. They'd made good time on the motorway and she'd agreed they could stay for a drink and something to eat as both Ben and Tim had begun to complain they were hungry. Mandy had turned down their offer to get her a triple decker with cheese, her stomach still doing the can-can.

She took another sip of the coffee and winced slightly. Ben seemed too engrossed in his burger to notice. Although the coffee made her feel more awake, it was not playing well with the twisted emotions busily churning up her stomach. She'd only known Harry for three weeks. In this time, he'd stopped her falling off a roof, found a million pounds in his wardrobe and was now driving to Wales to stop him from being killed? What was she involved in?

An excited Tim arriving at the table broke her thoughts. He sat down and lowered his head in a conspiratorial fashion.

"Look over there," he whispered. They looked through the latticework and plastic fronds that separated them from the rest of the restaurant. Mandy let out a gasp. Sitting at a table on the far side of the room were Bernie Doyle, Norman the Suit and two ugly looking bruisers.

"Is that them?" asked Tim.

"Yes," said Mandy tersely.

"Well, perhaps we don't have to go to Wales after all," said Ben. He put his hand into the deep pocket of his overcoat and felt the comforting cold steel of the gun that lay there.

Tim started whistling *The Good, the Bad and the Ugly* under his breath, his eyes shining. Mandy looked from one to the other of them, their faces full of that childish glow that she knew so well. A shiver ran down her spine. She didn't want to see either of them dead.

"What have you got in mind?" she asked Ben over the rim of her coffee cup.

"We take them out in the car park."

"They're moving," said Mandy. All eyes looked through the lattice. Bernie and the others rose from the table and headed for the door. Mandy and the boys shadowed them from the other side of the restaurant. As they all headed towards the carpark, one of Bernie's men peeled off and headed for the gents.

"We'll see you in the car, George," said Norman over his shoulder.

George disappeared into the gents and Ben and Tim followed him in.

George was just lowering his trousers when he heard the knock on the cubicle door. He stopped in mid stride and looked uncertainly at the door. Thinking he'd imagined it or it had been an accident, he pulled his pants down. A louder second knock followed.

"What?" grunted George.

"Can I come in?" asked Tim.

She held out a tray of pies towards Harry. They had spent almost an hour coming to the middle of nowhere to use a non-existent phone. *No, I wouldn't like a fuck-ing pie, you Welsh harpy.* He looked at his watch. It was 2:30. He was supposed to be meeting Mandy in four hours and had no idea where he was. Harry looked into the beaming face of the girl, her eyes a mixture of enquiry and rampant lust.

"Miss.. er?" he queried.

"Megan, Megan Evans," she panted. "Call me Megan. It makes a change from just being called Girl."

"Your father said you had a phone."

"We do."

"It doesn't work."

"No."

"How can I make a call, then?"

"Mr. Jackson has a phone. He's English like you. Da says all Englishmen are bastards."

"Where does Mr. Jackson live?"

"In the next valley."

"Excuse me, I need to speak to your father."

"I wouldn't bother him now. Not when he's with the goat."

"Will he be long?"

"It all depends."

"On what?"

She shrugged her shoulders. "Why don't I show you around the farm," she said with a smile. He counted to ten. They needed to get away, but he had no wish to walk in on some farmer who was 'busy with his goat.' He'd heard all the jokes. They walked outside. Farm was a bit of an overstatement. The farmhouse was set into the hillside on about an acre plot. Apart from the house, there was a rusting barn, a duck pond and in a far corner a large metal tank.

"What's in the tank?" he asked

"Diesel. Da always likes to keep a good supply in case we have any more of them shortages."

Oh, happy day, here he was imprisoned half way up a mountain with a nymphomaniac, an Anglophobe, savage dogs and now a tank full of diesel.

"If Dermot asks what in the tank, don't tell him."

"Why's that then?" she asked, giving him a coy smile.

"He's a pyromaniac."

"Reeeaaly! That little fella! I wouldn't have thought he had it in him. Mind you, I went out with a midget once, and he was always most insistent, four times a night sometimes. He said the reason he had to wear platform shoes was to stop it from dragging along the floor."

"No, Megan, a pyromaniac likes setting fire to things."

"Oh," she said disappointedly. "Getting a girl all excited. Are you married Harry?"

"No," he replied absent-mindedly.

"Oh good!" she said squeezing his hand and crushing three of his fingers in the process. He looked into the face of a woman who was plainly contemplating how many bridesmaids to have. He managed to prise his hand free his mind racing. What had he been thinking?

"I'm afraid I can never marry... I was involved in... a boating accident. I got too close to the propeller and..." he let his voice trail off and tried to look like a dog just back from being seen to by the vet.

The colour momentarily drained from Megan's face. "Oh, that's a pity. Worse things happen at sea, well not in your case I suppose." She gave him a smile, although this time more sisterly than salacious. "I'd better just pop back inside and see if Ron needs another pie."

Harry breathed with relief as she disappeared back inside. Now time to have it out with the farmer. If he caught him shagging his goat, it would be too bad. He wanted out of this place and fast.

Harry walked over to the barn. His hand hesitated though as he was about to turn the knob. Why had he brought them to his farm? Was it just as Megan said? He hated the English and this was a way of getting his own back, or did he have some other motive? Harry looked around him. Behind the house the grass and purple heatherd outcrops soon gave way to grey cliff face. In front of the farm a ragged fence gave way to a steep drop and the valley floor several hundred feet below. The only way off the mountainside was the track they had come along. You could have heard a pin drop, the only sound the occasional bleating lamb. Perhaps he had some other motive. Oh, sod this, he'd walk back down the track. He'd make faster time on his own. If it hadn't been for Dermot and Ron, he wouldn't have been in this mess in the first place. Harry strode purposefully away from the house.

The presence of so much testosterone had sent Megan's hormones into overdrive. Harry having cut himself out of the picture, she turned her attentions to Ron. She had dismissed Dermot for the time being. He might have been okay as an appetiser but she felt in need of some meat and two veg. There was no doubt that there was a lot of Ron and she liked something to grab hold of. It was also far more difficult for fat men to run away.

"I do like a man in uniform," she purred, offering him another pie. Ron's eyes flicked uncertainly from the pie to Megan. He found the hungry look in her eyes disconcerting. "Are you a policeman?"

Ron bridled slightly at the question. "No, I'm in security," he mumbled.

"Ooooh! You mean a secret agent? Like James Bond?"

"Yes, that right," replied Ron brightening noticeably. Megan waived a pie under his nose. Oh God, she was beautiful- that golden crust, that firm but delicate pastry- he had to have her. He reached forward and grabbed the pie. A fresh cascade of crumbs festooned his chest as he bit into it and swallowed oblivious to the hot filling scalding his mouth. Megan edged closer. She was working on the theory that the quickest way into a man's trousers was through his mouth and had a large supply of pies on hand to prove it.

Dermot sat at the table absentmindedly playing with the box. He'd been watching Megan stalk Ron, a hungry wolf with a frightened rabbit. He was in no great hurry to get to Bangor, but neither did he want to sit and watch Last Tango in Hippo Land. His fingers tumbled the box against the wooden surface of the table. He looked down at his hand. Christ! It was a box of matches! He dropped them as if they were red hot and pushed them to the far side of the table looking away. His eyes land-ed on the plump and squirming rear of Megan who was sitting on Ron's lap feeding him a pie.

"Oh, Ron," she cooed, "you're so brave."

Ron had been recounting the Darlington jail siege of 2006. His in-depth knowledge was largely based on the fact he and the other contract caterers he'd worked with had all been held hostage for most of it, a part of the story he thought best to gloss over. He felt a warm glow inside and was quite enjoying the attentions of Megan. For once he was not feeling nervous in the presence of a woman. He felt decidedly mellow as if lying in a hot bath, he felt sleepy. Megan looked into Ron's red face. His eyes were glazed. Had she put too much pot into the pie? They had been made for her consumption, and over the years she had built up quite a tolerance. By the look of things, she would need to work fast before he went to sleep. She wondered if they had any of those tablets left that they had fed to the ram when he wouldn't service the goats. They had such a remarkable effect that they needed a crowbar to prise the animal away in the end.

Dermot closed his eyes and tried to think of sea crashing against rocks. That was what the prison psychologist had told him to think about when ever he felt the urge to start a fire, but all he could hear was the crackle and snap of burning wood in his ears. Dermot grabbed the box of matches and headed for the door, oblivious to the sound of Ron's descending zip.

It felt good to be alone and in charge of his own destiny. He walked quickly towards the gateway between the dry-stone walls. Harry looked around at the sound of softly padding feet behind him. It was the two monstrous looking dogs that had escorted them in. He tried to give them a smile, as he took in their muzzles black and wet with saliva. If they'd been fed today, you couldn't tell from the look they gave back. His legs trembled as he stifled the urge to turn and run. All those wildlife programmes always talked about staring the animal in the eye and slowly backing away. Once you adopted the victim mentality then you might as well just climb in the pan and cover yourself with salt and pepper. He began to edge slowly backwards. The two dogs just sat down and watched him.

Rhodri stroked the soft hair of the goat's head as she lay on her side in the straw, her distended belly fat with the kids inside. The goat gave him a mournful look. Angharad was his favourite goat. The only living thing that had ever shown him any real affection. She was getting old though, and this was not going to be an easy birth. He held out a small piece of carrot and the goat nibbled it appreciatively.

Dermot walked quickly around the farmhouse looking for Harry and the farmer. He would just have a little fire, there would be no harm in that.

They stood outside the cubicle door waiting for George's reaction to Tim's request. Ben scowled at Tim, who shrugged his shoulders in a 'you think of something better to say then.'

George looked at the toilet door in bewilderment. "Who the fuck's there?" he demanded as he hovered over the loo in a semi squat.

"Put that man's cock down and come out now, you screaming big homo," shouted Ben.

The loo door flew open and the enraged, homopho-bic, George flew out having forgotten to pull his pants up. The boys darted right and left as he hit the ground.

Two middle-aged men standing over nearby uri-nals hastily finished and bolted for the door. George pulled up his trousers and got to his feet. Ben brought his locked hands down in a chopping motion across George's neck, but they bounced off.

"Hit him harder!" said Tim, skipping from one foot to another

"You hit him!" retorted Ben. Before Tim could do so, George had grabbed Ben by his coat collar and flung him against the wall of the washroom. They had not ap-preciated how big and strong George was. He'd lifted all twelve and a half stone of Ben as if he were a toddler.

"Your dead meat, you little fucker!" growled George as he advanced on Ben.

"TIM!" yelled Ben. "Now would be good!" Tim leaped onto George's back as his hands closed round Ben's throat. His weight pulled George backwards. George staggered and rammed Tim's body into a cubi-cle. Tim held on tight as George tried to pry his fingers loose from around his neck.

"Aaaahhh! You little fuckers! I'm going to kill both of you!" bellowed George.

Bernie Doyle drummed his fingers on the car steering wheel. He looked at his watch again with impatience.

"What's he playing at?" he demanded of Norman. Norman shrugged his shoulders.

"Dave, go and see what the problem is, will you?" Dave got out of the car and headed back into the service station.

"Of course, it's an emergency! I need a piss, and I can't get in the bog because it's being trashed by a bunch of hooligans!" said the man into his mobile phone.

Mandy put her hand on his arm and showed him her warrant card.

"Oh, it's alright, your lot are here already." The man put his phone back in his pocket and peered around Mandy. "So, where's the rest of you?" he asked.

"In there," said Mandy nodding towards the gents.

"What? The big one, or the two little un's? If it's the big bloke then I don't think he needs any help, but if it's the others, you better send for back up or an ambulance."

George careered right and left around the toilets trying to shake Tim loose, a breathless Ben staggered to his feet.

"BEN! BEN! THE GUN!" yelled Tim.

Ben took the gun from his pocket. Having given up trying to prise Tim's fingers open George was now trying to bite them and didn't notice.

"FREEZE! YOU BIG UGLY BASTARD!" shouted Ben. George looked up, at the sight of the gun he charged towards Ben teeth bared. Tim loosened his grip and slid from George's back. Ben sidestepped as George approached and brought the barrel of the gun down with a vicious swipe across the bridge of George's nose. George snorted as his nose was broken and in that split second, Ben pressed the gun into George's kneecap and fired. George collapsed like a fallen rhino and lay howling on the floor.

"He's a bit noisy. Can't you hit him?"

"What? Do I have to do everything?" replied Ben.

Tim picked up the metal litterbin and brought it crashing down on to George's skull.

Ben and Tim stood breathing heavily and grinning at each other.

"God, he was almost as bad as Bully Thompson," said Tim. For the first time, they became aware of the hubbub at the entrance to the loo.

"MOVE AWAY! THE NEXT PERSON WHO TRIES TO ENTER THE GENTS WILL BE ARRESTED!" the authoritative voice of Mandy came towards them. She came around the corner and into sight. Ben and Tim looked more dishevelled than ever as they stood over the bloodied heap that lay on the floor.

"We better get going, that gun shot is bound to bring more police along," she said.

"What about matey boy?" queried Ben.

"Is he dead?"

"No, just lost his knee cap and a few brain cells."

"Leave him. He'll be too scared of Doyle to say much."

Dave heard the gun shot as he'd entered the service station. He saw a large crowd was gathered around the entrance to the gents. He walked to the back of it and craned his neck forward.

"What's going on?" he asked the man next to him.

"Coppers, Special Branch, they've just shot some terrorist about to blow the toilets up," said the man, his fevered imagination working over time. Dave edged his way forward as he heard a woman's voice telling the crowd to move away. In the distance, he could hear the whoop of a siren. Bernie would want to know what had happened to George though. He peered around the corner and into the loo. A woman, who he recognised as Trent's bit of skirt, and two young men were in conversation. She stepped aside and he could see the body of George lying on the floor. Dave's eyes made contact with one of the men who tapped the other on the arm.

Ben followed Tim's gaze, raising the gun he still held in his hand.

Dave leapt forward as someone's scalding coffee hit his hand, hardly hearing the "Sorry, mate." The sight of Ben's gun, a dead George and a burnt hand robbed

Dave of what little rationality he normally possessed. Fearing his own imminent death, he pulled the gun from his pocket and let off two shots that flew wildly across the loo.

Chapter
Forty-Two

Dermot hunted around for somewhere he could have his fire without being disturbed. He had a keen sense of smell. Was that diesel? His eyes lighted on the tank.

Harry couldn't walk backwards all the way to the gate, so taking his courage in his hands he turned and walked on expecting at any moment to feel paws on his back as they knocked him to the ground. He was almost out and starting to feel a sense of relief when they silently slid past him and took up guard in the entrance. Harry hesitated for a moment and then pressed on. A slow but steady growl began to build.

Dermot had found an old paint tin that he thrust beneath the tap of the diesel tank and half filled. The fuel sloshed into the can giving off an aroma that made Dermot feel giddy with excitement. Flecks of rust floated to the surface and whirled around in the eddy. It was a very old can, with more than one hole in the bottom. Turning off the tap, but not fully, Dermot rushed off to the side of the barn where he had seen some old timber pallets propped against the side. Frenetically, he broke them up and poured the petrol on top. There seemed a lot less in the can than he remembered putting in. He ran back to the tank for some more. This time he filled the can to the brim, allowing the contents to spill over the side and on to his boots. In his eagerness to start the fire, he gave the tap a quick and careless turn and shot back to the barn leaving a growing puddle of fuel behind him.

Dermot's hands where trembling as he lit the match and threw it on the pallets which exploded into a ball of orange flame as did his shoes. "Oh, sweet Jesus," he cried as the flames licked around his feet. Dermot ran towards the duck pond in front of the house. The fire reached out and picked up the thin trail of diesel that Dermot had left leading back to the tank. The flame zigzagged its way across the ground.

Ron was so hot he could hardly breath. Something large and pink with a hard-knobbly bit on the end was being thrust into his mouth.

"Bite it, bite!" screamed Megan, so Ron did, somewhat harder than Megan had bargained for. She let out a scream of pain as Ron's teeth sank into her nipple. She jerked backwards grabbing Ron's lapels as she did so propelling them both onto the floor as part of the exploding diesel tank hurtled through the window above, showering them with broken glass and window frame.

Harry looked up at the sound of the bang and saw the flames licking at the sky. DERMOT!

The first bullet from Dave's gun severed a water pipe above the urinals sending a stream of water spurting into the air. The second hit a contraceptive machine setting off its alarm. Mandy and the boys dived left and right. Mandy cannoned through the door of a cubicle and found herself at the feet of a quivering middle aged man who'd become trapped as the fight erupted.

The man saw the water flowing in around Mandy and heard the loud klaxon alarm. "Oh, my God!" he screamed "we're sinking!"

Ben came up from behind a urinal and let off two shots at Dave. The bullets whistled over his head and obliterated the plastic filler tank Dave was standing underneath. The resultant waterfall swept him off his feet and hurled him into an empty toilet stall. He crashed into the toilet bowl and heard the soft plop of his gun as it fell into the bowl.

"THIS IS BLACK STALLION SECURITY!" boomed the contraceptive machine. "REPLACE THE PRO-PHYLACTICS IMMEDIATELY! DO NOT MOVE! A

SECURITY OPERATIVE IS ON HIS WAY TO TAKE YOU INTO CUSTODY."

In cubicle number 4, Donald Johnson glanced at his watch. Seven minutes, fourteen seconds and he had only three clues to go. He would get the Times crossword finished in under eight and a half minutes! What was wrong with his feet? They felt damp. No time for that, come on, Donald, concentrate- now 14 across.

Jimmy Brown raised the triple-decker mountain burger to his mouth and sank his teeth in. The phone vibrated in his pocket and began to merrily squeak the theme music to *The Sweeney*.

"Allo," said Jimmy through a mouthful of burger.

"Is that you, 517? Are you still at Gateway Services? We have a suspected break in, can you respond please?"

Jimmy's eyes lit up. This was his big chance. He had been there all morning as a packet of Spicy Ticklers were jammed in the machine and it took him an age to get them free. His friends had thought it a great laugh when he told them he was an armed response officer for The Black Stallion Contraceptive Company. The singing of 'Jimmy's in the Johnny Police' still rang in his ears. They hadn't believed him about the armed bit either, but Jimmy had got hold of a pepper spray, well, a can of his wife's furniture polish to be precise, but he reckoned a squirt of that in the eyes would be enough to subdue any

'Johnny Bandits' he came across. He stuffed the partly eaten burger in his pocket and headed for the gents.

Dave looked down at the gun he had retrieved from the toilet. He wondered if it would still work. Fuck, his hand hurt. A large blister was starting to balloon from where the coffee had struck. The siren of the mortally wounded contraceptive machine crashed all around him. He looked at the flimsy walls surrounding him, adorned with obscenities and phallic symbols. What did he do now?

Mandy was wondering the same thing. She could feel her feet turning from damp to soaking as the water swirled around her. She looked up at the man who cowered in the back of the cubicle.

"Don't worry, everything is going to be alright," she said.

The man nodded thinking, what is this crazy woman going on about? I come in here for a quiet shit and the next thing I'm in the middle of a gunfight and the place is filling up with water. What does she mean everything would be alright!?

The sudden appearance of Tim's head from under the side of the cubicle, did nothing to reassure him.

"Hello Mandy, Ben thinks it was time we were leaving."

"What about the guy with a gun?"

"Ben wants me to flush him out so he can get a clean shot."

Jimmy only heard the word "fire" as the screaming mob ran past him and into the car park. He grabbed one man as he went by.

"It's all right, it's just the alarm on the Johnny machine," he said. "There isn't a fire." The man gave him a wild-eyed stare and shook Jimmy's hands loose.

"Run for it, they're armed!" he shouted.

Jimmy advanced cautiously towards the gents, his can of furniture polish at the ready. Where was all the water coming from?

Tim began a rhythmic drumming on the side of the cubicle wall and started to sing his school song badly out of tune.

Dave heard the drumming, which was now competing with the alarm to see which could make the most noise. He wanted out and decided to make a break for it. As he ran from the cubicle ready to fire, Jimmy came around the corner. Dave spun round at the sound of Jimmy's voice. With more presence of mind than he would ever have again, Jimmy sprayed Dave full in the face with the furniture polish. The two men were inches apart, and although blinded Dave squeezed the trigger of his gun twice. Jimmy jerked backwards as the bullets struck him in the chest and neck.

Ben, trying to avoid Jimmy, fired low and caught Dave in the back of the leg. He went down firing wildly. As he hit the ground Ben shot him through the middle of the head.

Donald didn't see or hear the bullet as it came through the door, splitting wood and chewing through plastic. It shattered the left lens of his glasses and sliced through the thin layer of flesh covering his face before burrowing into his brain. It would be some hours later before anyone would notice the two neat little holes, one in the door and the other in Donald's lower temple.

Bernie and Norman looked on at the gathering pandemonium that was emanating from the service station.

"What the fuck is going on?" asked Bernie.

"Don't know, Bernie."

Two police cars and a van screamed to a halt in front of them and armed police jumped out.

"Were those two armed?" asked Bernie.

"George wasn't, but Dave might have had a gun."

"You don't think they've tried to rob the place, do you?"

The two men exchanged looks of incomprehension. They had both heard shots and Dave had a gun.

It seemed unbelievable, though, that they would carry out a robbery while travelling with Bernie.

"They must have got into some trouble," said Norman.

"Yeah. Come on, let's go. You take the Rover and I'll drive the Merc. We'll have to call up reinforcements. You got the keys?"

"Sorry Bernie, but George has the keys to the Merc."

"What! Are you telling me I've got to hot wire my own car?"

Sergeant Keffold carefully advanced across the foyer, sweeping the ground in front of him with the machine pistol in his hands.

"Freeze! Armed police officer!" he shouted as a sodden Mandy emerged.

"It's OK," said Mandy, holding her warrant card aloft. "Anti-terrorist branch."

Keffold had long ceased to be surprised at the strange looking specimens in the covert side of law enforcement. The wet and bedraggled Ben and Tim fitted the bill entirely.

As the three of them squelched past, Tim couldn't resist grabbing Keffold's hand and shaking it.

"Magnificent work, sergeant, well done. You'll find the suspects in there," he gestured, pointing back at the gents. "But be careful, I think we may have struck an iceberg."

Chapter
Forty-Three

By the time the fire brigade arrived, the flames were all but subsided and Dermot had disappeared. Megan was announcing to everyone that she and Ron were engaged. Despite the farmhouse being destroyed, she and Ron where remarkably unscathed- physically anyway. Ron didn't seem to know what planet he was on and went around addressing everyone as mother and demanding to know where his slippers were. The barn had miraculously not gone up, and the farmer had emerged with a kid in each arm proclaiming that he was a dad. Harry persuaded the firemen to give him a ride back into town and from there he got another lift into Bangor.

When they met, Mandy gave him the biggest hug he'd ever had. Her whole body shook as she held him. He gave her a potted history of his journey to Wales that brought a smile back to her lips. Mandy took him to the guest house where she'd booked rooms. They went to bed and made love.

They lay in each other's arms, Mandy's eyes heavy with worry. She told him about the gunfight at the service station.

"Where is it all going to end, Harry?"

"I don't know. Doyle is still down fifty grand, he's had his car cut in half and now Ben has killed one of his men. Perhaps we should go to the police."

Mandy snorted.

"Not a good idea?"

She sat up. "I know I'm somewhat biased, but Doyle has a very long reach and I don't think either of us would be very safe in custody."

This was true. Harry's story of being sick over the fifty grand and then burning it didn't get any better with the telling. They then had the breaking and entering to get the money back, and now a corpse and a shot up toilet to account for. The chances of them being banged up seemed fairly high.

"He isn't going to stop Harry. Not until we are all dead. If this story gets out, Doyle's credibility would be destroyed unless he has our heads."

So, there it was in a nutshell. Three weeks into his legal career and Harry was already contemplating killing one of his clients. It was a cracking start to being a solicitor.

He tried to distract myself by playing with her breasts, but it wasn't easy to think of sex when your girlfriend invites you to indulge in a little murder.

"So how do we do it?"

"We have to set a trap?"

Harry looked at her enquiringly.

"It's you he wants, Harry."

Bernie looked through the windscreen of the Range Rover. Norman and Knuckles has gone around the back of the cottage and were trying to find a way in. Billy loitered by the front door, a baseball bat in his hand. It had been a long drive and they had had to wait for reinforcements. Luckily Knuckles, Billy and Trevor had been in Liverpool and so they had been able to join them relatively quickly.

It was a nice old cottage thought Bernie, tucked away on the headland; he could hear the distant screech of seagulls. It was the kind of place you could retire to. He took the carefully folded letter from his inside pocket and read it again.

> *Dear Mr. Doyle,*
>
> *I am pleased to advise you that we have now completed on the sale of the last plot of The Four Winds develop-ment and have transferred the sum of £327,542.16 to your Jersey account as per the statement enclosed.*
> *Thank you for your instructions.*
> *Yours sincerely,*
> *Philip Diment*

Doyle smiled to himself as he looked at the copper plate signature. Diment & Sons, Solicitors in Wolverhampton for 150 years. The place reeked of respectability. He had not used Michael. He was too tainted with Bernie's past. The Four Winds had only been a small development of six houses, but it was a totally legitimate operation. None of his existing business contacts were used and he had made numerous visits to find local people. His absences caused awkward questions from his wife and mistress, both of whom accused him of having an affair. Hard work and effort for a very small profit. But, it was a start. Bernie put the letter away as Norman walked back to the car.

"Well?" Norman stood in the open doorway and shook his head.

"Place is empty. Doesn't look like anyone has been here in weeks." A rueful look came over Doyle's face.

"It doesn't look as though Michael is as scared of me as he should be. We'll have to sort that out when we get back to London."

"Where to now?" queried Norman.

Bernie pulled out a map book and looked at his watch. They were in Llanfairfechan, roughly half way between the two biggest towns in the area- Bangor and Llandudno. The train Trent would have been on stopped in Bangor. Bernie looked at his watch. It was 6:30.

"These two lads he's with. They're mad on curry, aren't they?"

Norman looked uncertainly at Doyle. "It's going to be dinner time soon, and they will want to eat. How many curry houses can there be in this poxy country?"

"I dunno, Bernie"

"Well, it's not bleedin Bradford, is it!?" Bernie glared at Norman who looked blankly back.

"What?" demanded Bernie.

"Bit of a wild goose chase, isn't it?"

"Have you got any better ideas?"

"No, Bernie."

"Right, let's get on with it then. You got those pictures of Trent? Give one to Knuckles and Billy and they can go up the coast to Llandudno. We'll take Trevor and work our way down to Bangor, and make it clear to Knuckles and Bill if they see them they call me first."

They could hear the sound of heated whispering outside the door as Harry did his trousers up. He looked across at Mandy who was pulling a sweatshirt down over her breasts, now firmly encased in a white bra. Her lovely flat stomach disappeared as the shirt slithered on to her hips. She smiled and shouted "Doors open."

Ben and Tim shuffled in, heads slightly bowed. "Hello Mand," said Ben. "We didn't want to... erm... interrupt."

"See, I said they'd have finished by now. I haven't heard Mandy squeal for at least twenty minutes," said Tim with a glint in his eye.

Mandy threw a pillow at his head. "You two are depraved."

Feathers flew through the air as pillows shot back and forth across the room. Harry sat on Ben's head as the room descended into a playground skirmish that went on until the gun fell from Tim's pocket with a resounding thud causing them all to stop and stare at it. The cold black steel bringing back the menace they all faced.

Tim retrieved his gun, and Mandy picked up the pillows. Ben walked to the window and peered round the edge of the netting. Mandy and Harry exchanged uncertain looks. Ben turned around.

"All clear outside. Tim and I had a walk around about 20 minutes ago and there was no sign of anything."

"Well, Doyle knows you were coming into Bangor but would have expected you to go on to the cottage," said Mandy, "so that where he will look first."

Their eyes flicked from one to another around the room.

"Mandy thinks we need to set a trap for Doyle," said Harry.

"Good plan," said Tim. "What do we use for bait?"

Harry pointed to himself

"Might be a bit of a problem digging a pit in Bangor High Street, Harry," interjected Ben.

"We could just tie him to a lamp post," said Tim.

Ben and Tim exchanged glances and shook their heads. "I think this calls for a curry," said Ben.

Chapter
Forty-Four

The poppadum stopped half way into Ben's mouth. "Oh dear, we have company."

Harry looked towards the door. It was Bernie Doyle. He had Norman the Suit with him, and a third man with a penchant for heavy stubble. They hadn't seen them yet and were in conversation with one of the waiters.

Bernie felt tired; this was the fifth curry house they had been to that evening looking for Harry.

Norman started to spout out his looking for lost friend's story again. Bernie tapped him on the shoulder.

"Come on, Norman I've had enough for…" their eyes met.

Mandy slowly crushed the samosa she held in her hand. Her eyes never leaving Doyle as she tracked his every movement.

Fuck! It was the tart from the graveyard! Bernie's hand bit into Norman's shoulder as he stared at Mandy. Norman turned his head and looked along Bernie's line of vision.

"Trevor, go and stand outside. Nobody comes in until I've had a little chat with Harry and his friends," said Doyle. "Oh, and give Knuckles a call. Tell him to come and join us."

The piece of chicken jalfrezi in Harry's mouth turned to clay. Trevor left the restaurant, and Bernie and Norman walked over to the table.

"Evening, everybody. Mind if we join you?" said Bernie. They both sat down at the table. Harry took the chicken from his mouth and put it on the plate. Doyle tutted his disapproval.

"You have been a disappointment to me Harry in so many ways, and now I see you leave your food as well."

He looked round the table. "Aren't you a copper?" he said to Mandy. She gave him a look that would have made milk curdle. "And you two must be the jokers who chopped my fucking car in half," he said to Ben and Tim.

"Ben Farrington"

"Tim Farrington. Cousins, not brothers, before you ask."

"I didn't come here for a family history. Harry and I need to have a little chat about expectations in life. So, you are going to pay the bill and leave with us."

"No," said Ben. "Sorry, but we haven't finished."

"Can't go until we've had all the poppadum's'," said Tim.

Mandy slipped her hand into Harry's under the table and squeezed it tight. Doyle didn't miss a beat.

"My friend Norman here first killed someone when he was 11. One of his teachers who thought it might be fun to introduce him to a new use for his arsehole. How many people have you killed since then, Norman?"

"Six," said Norman.

"So, it's a matter of mathematics. At the end of this evening, Norman can have killed 7 people, or it can be 10. Now, shall we go?"

Ben turned his face directly towards Doyle and gave him a broad grin. "Sorry, but Lucy says we don't go until we've had pudding."

"Who the fu..." Doyle stopped in mid-word. Ben had drawn a large gun from his pocket and was pointing it at Doyle.

"Norman," said Bernie.

"Sorry, Bernie."

Tim was holding an Armalite rifle against the side of Norman's head.

"Ben was the captain of the school rifle team, weren't you?" said Tim

"Yes, until I shot the headmaster. Didn't kill him so they were happy to put it down as an accident."

"Come on, let's go," said Mandy.

This seemed a damn good idea to Harry. Unfortunately, Trevor, having seen his boss held at gun-point, thought otherwise. He burst into the restaurant waving a shotgun in the air and screaming at people not to move. Then he shot a hole in the wall, a reasonable thing to do when a plate of boiling rice hits you in the face. The waiter's hands had gone up in the air as he had seen the gun and the laws of physics had done the rest.

They dived for cover as the gun exploded over their heads. Ben came up with his gun at the same time as Norman did with his. Three loud bangs from Norman's. Ben was lifted from the floor by the impact of the bullets and flung against the wall, his chest exploding in a mass of blood and gore.

"B-E-N!!!" roared Tim as he rose, hitting the edge of the table and sending plates of curry, rice and mango chutney flying through the air around him. His Armalite gave out a prolonged coughing noise and a diagonal line of red blotches made their way from the top of Norman's leg to his opposite shoulder. Norman spun backwards into a nearby table and disappeared into a pool of blood and chapattis.

Doyle looked on in amazement. *I don't fucking believe this. Norman, my best mate! WHAT THE FUCK IS HAPPENING!?*

Harry felt his hand being grabbed. "Harry, come on!" The voice was muffled, his ears ringing from the gunshots. Mandy dragged him to the door.

"Ben?" yelled Harry

"BEN'S DEAD! COME ON! WE HAVE TO GET YOU OUT OF HERE!" screamed Mandy.

Where's my gun? Doyle hunted feverishly on the floor, his hands and knees stained with the orange red and yellow of the curries that decorated it.

"NORMAN! WHERE ARE YOU? YOU STUPID OLD FUCKER! Where is my fucking gun?"

The restaurant had emptied once the firing had stopped. Norman lay dead on a pink tablecloth a mane of bright yellow rice strewn around his head.

Tim knelt in front of Ben's body delicately dabbing at the gaping wound between his neck and waste with a napkin. "Don't worry, don't worry," he cried in a hushed tone. "I'll go and get Matron."

Mandy propelled him towards the doorway. Harry glanced backwards. Trevor was clutching his face and complaining he couldn't see. If all he needed was a trip to the optician, then he had come off rather lightly. Mandy obviously of a similar opinion picked up a bottle of wine and broke it over his head.

She bundled Harry into the Fiesta and they disappeared in a scream of tyres.

The wipers flicked back and forth across the windscreen. Dry stonewalls and grey bushes flashed by in the headlights as they shot along the quiet country road. Harry looked at the speedometer- they were doing 90 mph.

"Bend coming up, Mandy." He looked at her pinched white face, her hands rigid on the wheel. "Mandy, slow down!" The brakes squealed as they hit the bend, the car spun out of control and came to a stop in the middle of the road. Harry eased Mandy on to the passenger seat and slipped behind the wheel, driving off at a slower pace. Two hundred yards down the road and he pulled into a layby and pulled Mandy into his arms. She collapsed into them shuddering. Deep racking sobs bounced of his chest. He squeezed her tight nestling his chin onto the top of her head.

"It's OK. Everything is going to be OK."

"I… I thought you were going to… to die!!"

He pulled her closer and nuzzled his face against her's. What could he say? She hadn't been the only one who thought his end was in sight when the bullets had started flying. After a few minutes, he wiped her face with a handkerchief. Dark lines of mascara ran down both cheeks. He kissed her gently on the lips.

"Let's get back to the hotel, collect our things and get out of here. OK?"

Bernie crouched over the still body of Norman the Suit. He wiped away a grain of rice from Norman's lips. Slowly he drew a napkin over Norman's face and got up. Bernie's body shook with rage. He looked at the carnage which filled the restaurant.

"Fucking hell! I only wanted to move house!" he muttered to himself. He hurried from the restaurant. As he did so, the Range Rover with Knuckles and Billy pulled up outside. Bernie jumped in the back. "Drive," he said. The car pulled away as the sounds of police sirens started to fill the air.

They stuffed clothing into a couple of bags in silence. Mandy's face was as white as snow. Harry decided to keep well clear of mirrors. They exchanged hurried Thank-God-you're-still-alive looks as they packed.

It only took five minutes, but Bangor isn't a very big town. Harry opened the front door of the guesthouse to leave and was confronted by Knuckles. He slammed the door in his face and was pushing Mandy towards the kitchen as he heard the sound of splintering wood behind him.

Mrs. Jenkins the landlady came charging out. Her eyes shot from Harry to the front door, uncertain for a moment as to who was the greater transgressor- guests who were obviously leaving without paying or whoever was breaking down her front door. As the lock gave way, she came to a decision. As Knuckles came through the shattered door, Mrs. Jenkins grabbed the mock antique coal shovel that stood against the wall and swung it full into his face.

"If you want to come in, you ring the bloody doorbell like any anyone else," she shouted

They ran through the kitchen and out the back of the guesthouse. Problem was their car was parked at the front. A bit of a giveaway but when your curry finishes with a gunfight you can be given a little latitude over these things. Harry grabbed Mandy's hand and ran around the side of the building. The Range Rover stood in the middle of the street unoccupied. He couldn't see Doyle or any of his men so they had to chance it. They were pulling away when Knuckles came running out towards them. Harry hit the accelerator and they shot past him. As Harry glanced in the rear-view mirror, he saw Doyle and the others climb into the car. They were facing the other way, and Harry gained vital seconds as they had to turn their car around.

They hadn't seen Bernie's headlights, but Harry took no chances and kept his foot firmly pinned to the floor as they streaked through the night. They hit the brow of a hill, and the drop on the other side was sudden and unexpected. Their moment of flight ended with an abrupt jolt as the car struck the ground. There was a loud snap like the sound of rotten wood breaking. The steering felt light and then they had none at all. Harry turned the steering wheel left and right in the vain hope that something might happen. It didn't. The leg bone was no longer connected to the hipbone, or whatever it was. His knowledge of car mechanics being akin to his knowledge of period pains;

he knew they both happened but he'd never seen the need to enquire into the finer detail.

They zig zagged crazily down the hill. Harry tried the foot break and the spinning around of the car that followed didn't seem to greatly help anything other than his screaming.

Mandy screamed in solidarity, "Harry!!"

She'd no need to scream. He'd seen the lamp post already. The left wing of the car cannoned off it causing the vehicle to swing violently to the right. Mandy's head slapped against the door fame. Harry glanced in her direction and saw her head flop forwards.

The hill bottomed out and the car pirouetted to a stop. Harry looked out at what appeared to be a sea-side front. To his left was an empty car park bathed in fluorescent light. To the right, he could make out amusement arcades and a funfair. He turned at the sound of Mandy's groaning. She had an ugly cut on her left temple that was oozing blood.

It was 2 o'clock in the morning, he was at a deserted Welsh beach with an enraged gangster somewhere behind and he had a girl friend in need of a hospital.

He got Mandy out of the car and staggered along with her in his arms. He needed to find a phone- he could get no signal on Mandy's mobile. Enough was enough. It was time to call the police. If they wanted to arrest him for stealing the money, then fine. At least he would still be alive. Christ, Mandy was heavy. It felt like his arms where being torn from his body. He heard the distant sound of a car approaching. Walking in the middle of a floodlit road suddenly seemed a bad idea. Harry staggered in amongst the amusement arcade buildings and lowered Mandy gently to the ground. She was shivering badly; he took off his jumper and rapped it around her. Her head was bleeding, his shirtfront wet and sticky with her blood. He pulled off his shirt and ripped in to strips that he wound about her head.

"Mandy? I'm going to leave you here for a moment and get help."

He poked his head around the corner of the building at the sound of squealing brakes. He could see Bernie's Range Rover had pulled to a halt where the Fiesta had been abandoned. Two dark shapes got out, looked hurriedly in the car and then jumped back in. The Range Rover shot forward and pulled up in the car park virtually opposite to where he was hiding. He saw the squat figure of Bernie climb out together with two men. Bernie pointed right and left and one ran in each direction.

This was getting serious. Serious! Harry's body silently racked in painful laughter. It had been serious ever since Ben had got himself pasted all over the wall of that curry house. But now he didn't have Ben and Tim, just an unconscious Mandy and three killers to deal with.

Bernie slowly surveyed the beachfront. He'd sent
Knuckles off to the top of the front and Billy to the bottom. The sea was at his back, which meant that Harry
and that slag girlfriend of his must be somewhere in
front of him, and at least one of them was wounded.
There had been blood in the car. He'd thought only one
of those public school ponces were shot, but obviously,
a bullet had struck someone else. He took the gun out
of his pocket and removed the magazine. He checked
it was full and slid it back into place.

"HARRY! I KNOW YOUR HERE. LOOK, I'VE HAD
ENOUGH OF THIS WILD WEST SHOW. COME OUT.
LET'S TALK."

Bernie waited for a response.

"LOOK, I KNOW ONE OF YOU NEEDS A HOSPITAL.
HARRY, BE SENSIBLE!"

Harry doubted if he walked out being sensible was
the first thing Doyle had on his mind. That was unless
you regarded being taken away in the boot of Doyle's
car and being dropped off the roof of a building somewhere as sensible. Still, he had to think of something
intelligent to do and quick. He made a mental list. Item
one, run away. Sounded good. But what about Mandy?
He looked down at her shallow breathing body. She
was in no condition to run anywhere, and he couldn't
outrun Doyle and his goons carrying her. He looked
around and spotted an old tarpaulin draped over a
child's ride. He manoeuvred Mandy sideways so that

she was leaning into the building wall and covered her with the tarpaulin.

Harry took a fleeting glance at what now appeared to be nothing more than an old tarpaulin bundled up against a wall and softly padded away. A sharp roll of thunder echoed in the sky, a light shower of rain began to fall. Shivering, he made his way through the back yard of the building. God, he was cold, he rubbed the flesh of his bare arms. Ahead was a brick wall. He scrambled to the top of it and was about to drop over the other side when a flash of lightening lit up the sky revealing a railway line about 30 feet below.

He was trapped. Bernie in front of him and his henchmen to each side. There had been nothing the way they had come and ahead lay the sea. That left him with only one direction to go in. He eased his way down from the wall and ran back the way he'd had come. Five minutes later he was alongside a bouncy castle. It was raining heavily and he felt the need to sneeze. He managed to suppress the first one but the second came out with a gigantic roar.

"Gotcha, you fucker!" cried Billy. He lumbered towards Harry moving with surprising speed for a man of his size. Harry dived sideward onto the bouncy castle. A large hand engulfed his foot and started to pull him off. Harry lashed out with his free foot. It made contact with something and from the subsequent yelp and release of his foot, he figured he'd made contact with his head. Billy had Harry's shoe though, and as he got to his feet he hobbled across the castle. Quickly he removed the other shoe. He could feel the motion of the castle as Billy got on to it.

"Come ere, Bernie wants you alive. *At least for now.*"

Harry leapt in the air as high as he could and came down with a crash. The ripple across the castle took Billy's feet out from under him. He shot backwards across the slithery surface and over the edge with an 'aah fuck.' Harry scrambled towards the front of the castle the driving rain stinging his face. Billy was up already though and blocking his escape. A shot whistled past Harry's ear. It seemed he'd forgotten Doyle's instructions. Harry dived to his left as Billy let of another round. A great farting sound hit the air from where the bullet hit the castle.

"You bastard, you've killed the bouncy castle," yelled Harry who was not thinking particularly straight. A rope net lay to his right and he began to climb up it. The castle killer wasn't far behind. Harry ripped off his socks to give him a better purchase and climbed the netting. He could hear Billy panting and swearing as he came up behind.

As Harry reached the top, the castle jerked alarmingly to the left as it expelled air, causing Harry to fall onto the bouncing surface below. He looked up, Billy was clinging to the rope netting for grim life as the castle bucked and weaved in the nigh sky. As he grabbed with his right hand, the gun slipped from his fingers and fell into the far corner of the castle. Harry dived after it, and Billy realising what he'd done, let go of the netting and plummeted down behind him. He hit the castle floor with a lot more force than Harry and went shooting off his feet. He tried to stand but as the castle lost air his large bulk caused him to flounder in the canyons, which yawned open as he tried to walk across the deflating surface.

The corner where the gun was looked like a beer drinkers gut. Harry dived in under the loose flaps of plastic blindly feeling around for the gun. He felt the surface vibrate underneath him as man mountain got nearer. Harry had disappeared under a sea of folded rubber. Mountain man came crashing down on top of him driving the remaining air out of his body. It was like Victor Davis all over again. Harry couldn't breath. He was being crushed A few more moments of this and he would pass out.

Luckily Billy staggered upwards and tried to grab Harry through the plastic, which wasn't easy. They floundered around like fish out of water, Billy's hand's grabbing handfuls of bouncy castle whilst Harry wriggled backwards and forwards to keep out of his grasp. It was getting hot under the plastic, frantically Harry contorted his body right and left, his fingers digging into the darkness in search of the gun. Suddenly the castle wall tightened around Harry' ankle.

"BERNIE! KNUCKLES! I'VE GOT HIM!" he shouted in glee.

"Billy? Where are you?"

"OVER ERE! THE BOUNCY CASTLE!"

"What the fuck! Where is he then?".

"E's under the fuckin' plastic! You pull it back whilst I keep hold of his leg. He's a slippery fucker, and I don't want to lose him again."

"What's happened to your nose?"

"Never mind my fucking nose. Let's just get him out. I'm getting soaked!

As the plastic was pulled away, cold air blew in under it and Harry caught a glimpse of sky.

"Ere he comes," said Billy in satisfaction.

Harry clawed at the rubber floor of the castle like a reluctant child being pulled from his bed. The night sky silhouetted by Knuckles and Bill came into view. Harry felt something cold and metallic against his stomach. As he was dragged over it, he grabbed the gun, his finger tightened around the trigger. Billy let go of his foot and leaned forward to grab Harry. Billy's head exploded as Harry fired at point blank range. Blood and bone rained down and his torso toppled back.

Knuckles let out a terrified scream and leapt back trying to scrape Billy's face from his own. Harry sent a bullet whistling over his head. Knuckles didn't stay around for Harry to improve his aim. He staggered upwards and shot off two more bullets at Knuckles rapidly disappearing frame. The gun clicked on empty, and Harry threw it down.

Bernie heard the shots and the distant shouting of Billy and Knuckles. He was cold and wet. What was he doing here? The week before he'd been at the Lord Mayor's banquet, he was about to start the construction of his next housing estate. Bernie climbed back into the car taking shelter from the rain. He took a flask of brandy from the glove compartment and lifted it to his lips, a warm glow ran through him. He should be at home in bed with Bianca. Or up West with young Sasha in her flat. Bernie closed his eyes and thought of the pert breasts and velvet skin of his young mistress. He opened his eyes and turned on the ignition.

The door of the car flew open driving rain into the warm interior. Knuckles, stood in the doorway his hair plastered down under a mix of blood, gore and rain, his eyes those of a frightened animal.

"FUCKING BILLY! - FUCKING DEAD! GOT NO - FUCKING – FUCKING - HEAD. NO FUCKING HEAD." The words tumbled out of Knuckles, garbled and laced with fear. "DO YOU HEAR ME, BERNIE? BILLY- HE'S GOT NO FUCKIN HEAD!" Knuckle's hands pawed at Bernie's coat.

Bernie's mind flashed back, the bank robbery; crashing through the shop window, the park, maggots in his hair, the dead face of Norman with his head crowned in a sunflower of yellow rice. His hold on reality was deserting him. He had to take control. It was how he'd got to where he was. He looked at Knuckles. The man had always been a liability. Bernie reached for the automatic on top of the dashboard and pointed it at Knuckles who was oblivious to it. The sound of the gun reverberated around the car as Knuckles crumpled to the ground.

Bernie sat there, the door of the Land Rover open, rain sleeting down all around. Knuckles lay on the ground, little rivulets of pink rain running out from under him.

It wouldn't end until Bernie killed again, killed both of them. He got out of the car and walked to the rear, removing from the boot a Heckler & Koch machine pistol. He put down the tailgate and pulled the collar of his coat tighter around him. Slowly he began to walk towards where he'd heard the gunfire coming from

The pain lanced into Mandy's head. Her eyes flew open but could see nothing, it was hot and humid and difficult to breathe. She reached out with her hands and felt a thick fabric. She tried to push it away but did no more than lift it upward. It still consumed her. She tried standing, and as she did so her head brushed against the tarpaulin. It felt as if someone had jabbed a red-hot needle into the side of her head. Screaming with pain, Mandy fell back and lay writhing under her canvas coffin.

The pain slowly subsided and Mandy explored outwards with her fingers, gently probing her surroundings. The floor was hard and rough; she was lying on
tarmac. Her hand felt further. It was wet, rain was falling on her hand. Gently she shuffled her bottom over
the ground toward the wet, holding up the canvas with
her other hand so that it didn't come into contact with
her head. Slowly she edged herself out from under the
tarpaulin.

Mandy shrieked as she went from its hot confines
to the cold rain falling outside. Staggering upwards, the
needle was jabbed into her head again. She grabbed
for the side of the building as her knees buckled under
her. Mandy knelt there breathing heavily, the rain beating down remorselessly.

The bouncy castle slowly subsided underneath him.
Harry stepped sideways to avoid the shattered remains
of Knuckles. As the rush of adrenalin subsided, the cold
numbness of the rain returned.

He looked up at the dull sound of a shot. *Oh Christ,
they've shot Mandy!*

Blindly he ran back to where he'd left her, she was
gone. All that remained was a small pool of blood.

Bernie knelt down by the shattered remains of Billy.
Poor old Bill, he'd been with Bernie since the early
days. What was it he'd said about the quiet ones to

Norman? Harry Trent was slowly destroying Bernie's empire. *You're getting old and soft Bernie. The world is not yours any more. It belongs to Harry Trent. The King is dead Bernie, long live the King.*

It was difficult to think straight when all that remained of the woman he loved was a bloodstain slowly being washed away in a disappearing eddy of lilac rain. An image of Doyle falling backwards, a large red hole in his head flashed in front of Harry's eyes. Then he could see the courier who'd given him the envelope, blood and rain. It was how it started and how it would end.

He needed a weapon. Opposite was a door leading into one of the arcades. Harry looked round for something to break the glass and found a brick. The sound of breaking glass disappearing into a roll of thunder as the storm intensified around him. Once inside he hunted around in the dark for a weapon. Any kind of weapon. He froze as the room was suddenly filled with light.

"Harry, a word in your shell like," said Doyle.

He stood about thirty feet away his gun pointed in Harry's direction. He started forward

"That's close enough for now. Where's that copper girlfriend of yours?"

"You should know you bastard!"

"If I knew I wouldn't be asking, would I? Now, it's late and I'm tired so stop pissing me about."

"You murdered her you bastard!"

A quizzical look flitted across Doyle's face. "Not me. Must have been one of the lads. Still, that leaves just you and me then. Bye bye Harry."

He raised the gun and sighted it at Harry's chest. As he pulled the trigger the lights went out and the bullet grazed Harry's shoulder spinning him sideways. Doyle let out a desultory laugh followed by a curse.

"You know, I should just fuck off and forget about this Harry. Twenty years ago, you would be dead by now. Trouble is when you get respectable you don't have much cause to use a machine gun, and you forget to check whether or not it's on automatic. What I should have done is this"

The room reverberated with a torrent of loud bangs and zinging noises as bullets whizzed right and left shattering glass, punching holes in some and ricocheting off more sturdy objects. Harry buried his head into the ground his arms tightly rapped round it as the carnival of death danced around him.

As suddenly as it had begun, it stopped. Silence bit the air. He could hear Doyle breathing heavily. Harry lifted his head. Doyle stood in silhouette his head moving from side to side. Slowly Harry edged his way towards the door. He was almost there when a piece of broken glass dug into his foot. He let out a muffled howl and a line of machine gun fire burst over the top of his head. Harry dived out of the door and zigzagged towards the sea. Stone, rock and asphalt flew up around him as Bernie fired in his direction. Harry dived over the concrete parapet head first into a pile of seaweed.

He lay panting and spitting out seaweed, his foot stung as if it had an angry wasp attached to it. He felt for it in the dark and pulled his finger away as he cut it on the charred of glass sticking out of the bottom of his foot. He pulled the wicked splinter out.

The beach was a mix of stones and shale interspersed with the odd patch of sand. Fortunately, he'd landed on a sandy part and avoided caving his brains in. It was getting towards high tide, great foam clad breakers roared up the beach and crashed down. With the fork-lightening in the air and the crashing waves, he couldn't help but imagine he was about to see some tall masted ship about to flounder on rocks out to sea. You mind does strange things when you're scared witless. If he was going to get through this evening, he had to block out of his mind the thought of Mandy lying dead in a pool of blood. He had to get through this evening as he still had one thing to do- kill Bernie Doyle.

The pale blue of the Fiesta danced in and out of Mandy's focus. Slowly she weaved towards it. All she needed was to get back to the car. Harry would be in the car and she would be safe. Why had Harry parked the car in the middle of the street? She was tired. All she wanted was to cuddle up next to Harry and go to sleep....

The warm sun shone in through the kitchen window. Harry sat at the table playing aeroplanes with
the spoonful of food he was trying to get to their baby
daughter. The baby giggled and clapped her hands together. Harry looked up at Mandy and smiled.

Bernie reached into his pocket and inserted the spare
magazine into the machine pistol. Bloody useless thing.
He had let of a whole clip and all he had succeeded in
doing was shooting up half a car park. He glanced at
his watch. The illuminated dial said it was 2:45. He had
been here just over half an hour. He wondered how long
it would be before the law turned up. True, they were
thin on the ground in this part of the world, but there had
been enough gunfire this evening to draw someone's
attention sooner or later. He needed to finish this and
fast.

Slowly he walked towards the beach, his eyes tracking right and left for movement. He walked up a concrete ramp, which led to the top of the wall and looked
down at the crashing waves. A small moon poked out
between the clouds to give limited visibility. Otherwise
the thick curtain of rain continued to fall and Bennie
could make out nothing but the foam white of the breakers. Nothing seemed to be moving on the beach.

A dark object flitted along by the water line. Bernie
pressed the trigger and a line of bullets danced across
the pebbles towards Harry.

Chapter
Forty-Five

Harry dived into the breakers as the first bullet zinged past his ear. It struck a pebble just in front of him tearing through the edge of his sodden trousers and raking the flesh from his knee. He came up gasping for breath. The next wave caught him smack in the chest propelling him backwards towards the shore. Bullets bounced off the pebbles all around like a swarm of angry hornets.

One struck him on the head and another on the stomach, their force thankfully spent by hitting both stone and wave beforehand. He fell backwards his vision going into freefall as his head struck something smooth and round.

The water felt warm and comforting. He pulled the duvet cover over his head and snuggled down. Abruptly the cover was pulled from him as he was slapped across the face with a wet fish. Someone was shouting his name down a tunnel.

"Wake up, Harry!" His head flopped from side to side as his face was slapped. Warm salty blood ran into his mouth. A double vision of Bernie Doyle swam towards him. The two visions shot sideward and then slowly melded into one.

"Come on Harry! There's no fun in killing you if you can't feel it! Oh fuck!"

He felt himself fly sideward as he spewed up a mixture of seawater and bile. Harry spent the next two minutes coughing up his lungs and then collapsed exhausted on the seashore.

As the vomit came from Harry's mouth, Bernie pushed him away and jumped to one side. Harry fell to the ground where he lay retching. Bernie looked down at his trousers where the contents of Harry's stomach had joined the blood and gore of Billy's head. It was a good evening for the dry cleaners he reflected. Not that any of his clothes would every see one. He would have to burn them. Probably have to torch the Range Rover as well. Fucking forensics, no wonder everyone's insurance premiums were so high. Bernie looked up at the sky, the rain had stopped. A pale moon had jostled the clouds aside and sat in the middle of a dark mauve sky.

It was very quiet. Even the pounding of the waves had dropped to a soft embrace of the shore. Bernie felt the tension drain away. He looked around all was still. *Oh, fuck it! I need a smoke. What about Harry?* Bernie glanced down at the prone figure that twitched every now and again as a small amount of water spewed from his mouth, it didn't look like he was going anywhere.

He sat on a rock and lit a cigar. As the first rush of nicotine hit the back of his throat, the jagged muscles of his chin creased into a soft smile. Bernie watched the fluorescence skipping over the sea. The air was filled with a lovely mix of ozone and tobacco smoke. He had gone fishing as a lad with his dad and Uncle Ernie off Southend pier.

Ernie, he hadn't thought of him in years. It was Ernie who he'd taken after, not his straight-laced father. Poor old Ernie had been a bit too fond of the sauce. He'd fallen asleep in the gutter one evening and someone had parked a car on him. Poor old sod had been crushed to death. Who can park a car on top of someone and not know? Bernie had asked that very question as he'd dangled the car owner out of a bedroom window by his neck. The man claimed he'd equally been drunk and not noticed. Bernie dropped him through the roof of his greenhouse.

What was his name- Ferris, Harris? He couldn't remember. Just another nameless face that crossed Bernie's path and paid the consequence. What had it all been for? He was 52, it was three o'clock in the morning and he was sitting by the sea, Billy's brains all over his trousers, and the body of his next victim lying at his feet. Harry would be the last. Time to move to his villa in Estoril and grow grapes. He was going to retire. The spat spat of rain on his face and the darkening over of the night sky broke Bernie's reverie. Harry groaned and began to raise himself.

419

Harry was cold and stiff. Random jabs of pain streaked across his body. A night of being shot at and bashing his brains in had taken its toll. He pushed his hands down into the wet smooth pebbles and managed to raise himself to all fours. Mandy was dead! A large knife tore through his guts twisting and slashing as it went. He threw up again.

"Fuck me, Harry, you must have swallowed half the Irish Sea."

He knew that voice but couldn't place it. Harry looked up at the face of the devil himself sitting there laughing and taunting him "*Your little bitch is dead! Was she a good fuck? Well, you won't be able to fuck her again, will you?*"

He threw himself at the devil and they went over in a roll.

Bernie was taken by surprise at the speed of Harry's movement. and the look of blind hatred in his eyes. He could feel Harry's fingers digging deep into his neck, trying to claw their way through the skin.

Mandy heard the sound of rain. Warm and asleep in her bed, she leaned over to nestle closer to Harry. She woke with a start as she pitched forward. Slowly the windscreen of the car swam into focus. Her head throbbed and she felt bewildered. She had been in bed with Harry. They were happily married; the baby was asleep next door. She let out a piercing scream as the realisation she had been dreaming hit her.

It came back in a tumble of vision. The escape and pursuit by Bernie. The crash! Harry carrying her in his arms and telling her she'd be OK. Now she was back in the car. Where was Harry? The sound of machine gun fire whipped along on the wind past her.

"HARRY?... HARRY?... WHERE ARE YOU?"

She ran stumbling in the direction of the gunfire, rain cascading around her.

In the distance, she could see the flash of light from the machine gun. Then the taunting shout of Doyle. She could see his outline standing on the beach wall. Then he disappeared out of sight. Mandy ran towards the wall and clambered on to it. White sparks darted in front of her eyes.

She came to and found herself lying at the base of the wall. "Harry?" Mandy whimpered. "Where are you?" she asked, her voice seared with desperation. Her body shuddered as the tears rolled down her face. Mandy clawed her way up the wall until she was standing, her fingers torn and bleeding from the effort. She was so tired, a single thought forced its way through the crowd of sleep that surrounded her: Harry was in danger! She had to save him.

Slowly Mandy pulled herself onto the top of the wall where she lay staring out to sea. There were two dark shapes struggling on the shoreline. She rolled backwards off the wall letting out a soft cry as her back struck the ground. She felt weak. She needed a weapon to make her strong. In the boot of the car was an axe. A birthday present for her father.

Harry pushed his fingers deep into Doyle's neck. He could hear him gurgle as Harry tried to force his Adam's apple through the back of his neck. Doyle grabbed his wrists and tried to pull them apart. Despite Harry's weight on top of him Doyle managed to roll to his side. Harry broke free and grabbed for a large piece of driftwood that looked ideal to beat Doyle's brains out with. He scrambled for the wood but Doyle was right behind. As he charged Harry scooped up a handful of sand and shale, which he threw in Doyle's face. His hands went up to protect his eyes and Harry butted him in the stomach, they crashed into the surf.

They came up coughing and spluttering. Doyle lashed out with his fist and blood flew from Harry's nose as he made contact with it. As Harry's head went back, he felt a sickening blow to his stomach and doubled over. As he did so, he was yanked upwards by his hair and thick metal bolts raked his face in a flash of gold and skin as Doyle struck him around the head. A broken tooth on Harry' tongue was soon joined by a second as the rings on Doyle's fingers tore into his face.

It was a big wave brushing them both aside like two angry flies. It knocked Harry into the shoreline, but as it retreated, it pulled Doyle after it.

Harry's face lay half in a pool of water. Through the other eye, he could see Mandy being dragged screaming down into it, then the pool clouded over with blood and he jerked upwards. Doyle was coming out of the water. Harry grabbed the driftwood and slammed it into Doyle's head sending him spinning into the waves.

Doyle started to gag as the salt water filled his nose and lungs. He tried to sit up but the weight of his saturated coat pulled him down. Greedily, the waves rushed over him and pushed him down. He gasped for air, but all he could feel was the acrid taste of salt. He felt himself floating. Momentarily, it went black. Then air, he could breathe air. His head came out of the water. He dug into the soft sandy floor with his legs and pushed himself up. A wave struck him in the back sending him crashing forwards. He stopped his fall with his hands, crawled out of the water and collapsed on the sand

Mandy staggered towards the beach trailing the axe behind her. It weighed a ton but she would not let it go. She would save her baby with it. "I'm coming, Harry," she sobbed. "I'm coming."

Harry lay motionless on his back staring up at the slate grey clouds above. The blow he'd struck Doyle with had sucked the final bit of energy from him. Out of the corner of his eye he could see Doyle's prone body lying half out of the surf.

Harry staggered to his hands and knees and tottered over towards Doyle. He stood motionless over his body. It didn't move. He knelt down and with some effort rolled him on to his back. Doyle's two large hands closed around his throat and began to squeeze.

Mandy felt the stones slide from under her feet she fell backwards, a jarring pain shot through her coccyx as she hit the ground. The axe flew through the air. She scrambled around in the dark feverishly searching for it. Her hand closed around its smooth rubber handle, and she staggered to her feet. Slipping and sliding over the stones, she made her way to the sea's edge.

He could see the concentration in Doyle's eyes as his hands grimly held on to him. Harry dug down into the wet sand, pulled up a handful and rubbed into Doyle's eyes. Doyle's grip relaxed, and Harry rolled away from him and to his feet. He hunted around for the driftwood. As Harry grasped it in triumph, Doyle crashed into the side of him and Harry went over with Doyle on top. He sat on Harry's chest grunting in satisfaction as his hands once more closed around Harry's neck and slowly tightened.

"It's over, Harry," he panted. "Do you fucking hear me? It's over!" He grunted again and his hands dug deeper into the flesh of Harry's neck. He felt the choking pain of his Adam's apple being forced backwards.

"NO!"

Mandy's howl pierced the night sky. The razor-sharp blade of the axe sliced through the air and crashed into Bernie Doyle's skull.

The waves, edged with white foam, ran around their bodies as they lay on the sand. Harry held Mandy so tightly she could hardly breathe. In the distance, they could hear the wail of police sirens.

"We've got company." Said Mandy.

"This could be difficult," replied Harry.

She stuck her head under his chin and nuzzled his chest.

"You're a lawyer, make something up!"

CHICKENS!

HD McTie

**Read on for the first chapters of the
sequel to Money Death Chainsaws and Curry**

Prologue

In the Woods

Harry Trent looked from the gun to the cocaine. The gun had just been used to shoot a policeman. Possession of cocaine got you a minimum 5 years in prison. Attempted murder of a police officer could get you life. He was sitting in a wood in the dark with the gun and the cocaine and the police were getting closer. This time he was in serious trouble.

Chapter One

'Bourbons or custard creams Jack?'

Jack Green looked up from the chair he was tied to. A large piece of silver gaffer tape stretched across his mouth. If the 11th Commandment was don't get caught, the 12th was don't steal from the Knapp brothers. Neville Knapp waved the biscuits at Jack, who looked back in mute terror. Neville walked towards him and tore the gaffer tap from his face.

'I ain't done nothin' Mr Knapp, honest,' blurted Jack.

'Well, let's discuss that in a minute Jack. First of all, I'd like to know what you want with your tea. Mmmm?'

Neville looked quizzically at the young man, but got no response. 'Custard creams it is then.' He sat down with the biscuits, which he placed next to two cups of tea.

'I swear on my mother's life Mr Knapp. It wasn't me.'

Neville took a swig of the tea and winced. He hadn't put in enough milk and it was too hot. Neville Knapp didn't like interrogating people. It was messy and loud. People would never admit what they'd done, until there was a certain amount of their blood and teeth on the floor. The amount would be influenced by a number of factors, including bravado, stupidity and ignorance of the crime they were being accused of. The Knapp's, like most criminals didn't possess any forensic scientists in their ranks and would therefore beat the living crap out of anyone they thought may have done them wrong until they confessed, or died.

Knapp sipped his tea and glanced at his watch. Where was his elder brother Gordon? Still busy with his roses, bloody perfectionist. Apart from armed robbery, drug smuggling, and prostitution, the Knapp's ran a successful garden centre and grew prize winning roses. Neville had an appointment with his chiropodist at four o'clock and hated being late.

'Now Jack, Gordon and I wanted a word with you, about the kilo of cocaine that's gone missing. Gordon thinks you might know something about it? He said I should have Donald discuss it with you....'

Jack glanced around nervously at the mention of Donald Knapp, the youngest of the three Knapp brothers. He didn't know much about him other than he was a fucking nutter. Spent half his time dressed in an old army uniform pretending it was still World War II.

Donald Knapp would have been mortally offended at the reference to an old army uniform. He wore a Saville Row tailored RAF uniform of a Wing Commander. Cut

in 1943 and only ever worn by Donald, its intended owner shot down over France. Wing Commander Donny
Knapp, as he thought of himself, liked to imagine he was
still fighting the Nazis. He'd only ever seen the Second
World War in old news reels and movies, but for Donald
the war could often be very real.

Donald was special, his mother would say, whenever
he threw one of his quite spectacular temper tantrums
as a child. Fifteen years younger than his brothers, he'd
never shown any interest in the family's main occupa-
tions of armed robbery and landscape gardening. His
father had thought him a 'fucking poof' and sought to
cure what he regarded as Donald's less acceptable
habits by beating him with leather belt.

'.....but Donald's got one of his headaches,' Knapp continued. 'So, I thought I'd have a word.' He picked up a
custard cream and took a bite. 'Good choice' he said
through a mouthful of crumbs waving the half-eaten biscuit at Jack.

'You couldn't untie my hands could you Mr Knapp?'

'I'd like to Jack, I really would, but then you might try
and do something silly. So, anyway, about the cocaine?

The sudden appearance of Donald Knapp in the
room halted Neville's questioning.

'Neville old chap. Can't lend me fifty quid, can you?
Need to get some ciggies,' said Donald.

Neville Knapp let out a deep sigh and took out his wallet. 'Donald, I've told you before. You should use the cashpoint, that way you wouldn't run out all the time.'

'Don't like to old boy. Cameras. You never know who's watching. Hello? He turned and looked at Jack. 'And who is this?'

'Its Jack Green', said Knapp. Gordon thinks he knows about the missing cocaine'.

A puzzled look crossed Donald's face. He knew the name, but from where? He rolled it round in his mind, his head groggy from the pills taken earlier. He'd got some new ones, from Dr Brown. Good old 'Brownie' could always be relied upon to provide Donald with the latest internet cures for Donald's many problems, real and imaginary.

Jack Green? Yes, he remembered. He was the chap trying to get the stolen V2 rocket plans back to the Nazis. Gordon wanted Donald to interrogate him. He'd mentioned the cocaine, but Donald had far more important questions to ask first.

For those who aren't students of Word War II, it was Gt. Britain against Nazi Germany. The Germans had a V2 rocket with which they planned to rain down death and destruction on London. Unfortunately, Jack's knowledge of the Second World War was limited to watching the porn movie, Nazi Lesbian Zombies III.

Donald swung his head down, his face inches from Jack's

'Jack old boy. Need to ask you a few questions.'

Neville, looked at his watch. He needed to go. 'Do you know anything about the Second World War Jack? he asked.

'I didn't do it!' said Jack.

'Well, I'll leave you with Donald.'

Donald sat down in the chair vacated by Neville. He took a cigarette from an engraved silver case and lit it.

'I didn't steal the cocaine Mr Knapp honest!' said Jack.

'All in good time Jack, I want to ask you about something else first.'

Donald took a drag from his cigarette and placed it on the ashtray which sat on the desk behind him. He saw the lump hammer lying next to it. A small tool but with a weighted head, used for driving fence posts into the ground. He turned back to Jack.

'How long have you been a double agent Jack?'

'A double what?' Jack let out a piercing scream as Donald picked up the hammer and brought it crashing down on to Jack's kneecap.

'When did you start working for the Germans?'

'I don't know any Germans!' Jack screamed again as his other knee cap was broken.

'I stole the cocaine! Fat Wu's got it. He promised to pay me five grand, but the bastard never.'

Donald put down the hammer and removed a pair of pliers from inside his jacket. He placed them on the table with the tea.

'Don't change the subject Jack, I'm not interested in the drugs. If you tell me where you've put the V2 plans, you can keep the cocaine. I'll tell Gordon you didn't have it.'

Jack tried to focus on what was being said, the pain in his legs was unbearable. Knapp had said something about V2 what the fuck was that? He'd confessed to taking the coke and been told he could keep it. Some how he needed to come up with an answer that was acceptable.

'Mr Knapp, I'm sorry about the coke, but I've got this mate, he gets tickets for concerts, he can get you some great tickets for U2.'

'Jack, I'm not interested in U-boats. We are talking about rockets. Now we have Clive,' he said pointing at the hammer, 'Or Gerald, indicating the pliers. What's it to be? Should I take out some of your teeth or break a few more bones?'

Jack looked at the hammer and pliers, he was a fan of the more gruesome horror movies. Slowly it was dawning on him he was now living one. He hadn't the slightest idea what Knapp was talking about and didn't know how to stop the pain he knew he was coming. Tears ran down his cheeks.

'Mr Knapp please'

'Ever played eeny meeny miny moe Jack?'

'Please!'

Donald started moving his finger between the hammer and the pliers, 'Eeny meeny miny moe, catch the nigger by his toe.' He stopped and looked up at Jack. 'Don't mind if I use the word nigger do you Jack?'

'I stole the cocaine' sobbed Jack.

'If it hollers let him go, eeny meeny miny moe, you are it. Look Jack, it's the pliers!'

'Please don't hurt me Mr Knapp.'

'I'm sorry Jack. I've got a war to win. Open wide.'

Chapter Two

As the music built to a crescendo the salesmen took up the chant 'Charlie, Charlie.' They roared as they say his carefully coiffured silver locks appear behind the platform, stamping their feet in unison. Charles Webster mounted the podium. He stood 5' 11" tall, immaculately tailored in a high collared suit, his eyes shining behind the round silver frames of his glasses. To either side hung a 12-foot photograph of his head and shoulders, flanked by black banners embossed with a red cockerel, the logo of 'Charlie's Chickens.'

The annual sales conference and awards were a well-crafted affair worthy of any Oscar ceremony. With his army of highly motivated and well-paid salesmen, Webster dominated the UK and European poultry business. One in three of all chickens consumed in the EU came from his plants. Webster raised his hands above his head in recognition of the cheers and the salesmen went into a frenzy. As he clapped them back they became ecstatic, the noise so loud the sound engineers hastily adjusted their equipment. Slowly the cheering and clapping subsided.

"Gentlemen…….. YOU!……… Make me proud. Without YOU…….Charlie's Chickens is nothing. YOU - ARE - Charlie's Chickens!"

"CHICKENS! CHICKENS! CHICKENS!" they chanted.

A CGI presentation began. Webster took them through the achievements of the previous 12 months. France had been the last bastion in Europe to fall. Proud of their long history of fine food, no market could be found for his highly-manufactured product until an outbreak of e-coli decimated the national flock. No one but Webster and a few of his closest aides knew that this 'tragedy' as he described it to *Le Monde* had been manufactured in one of his laboratories.

The presentation was followed by the awards ceremony. Several of the winners looking more like boxers than salesmen. Webster left nothing to chance when it came to sales. Former competitors could have testified to this if they were not in hiding or busy learning to walk again.

As the presentations ended, a hush fell across the room. The lights went down and a single spot light illuminated Webster. "Gentlemen, as you know, it is our aim to have every household in the UK and Europe eating our chickens. We shall not stop there. We have new markets in North America, Asia and the Pacific Rim. But, it is not just market share. We must always drive down price so that EVERYONE, EVERYWHERE can afford a Charlie's Chicken. our scientists working day and night to breed bigger, stronger, fatter birds.

The room darkened. Aron Copeland fanfare to the common man filled the room.

I give you K743!'

The entire wall behind Webster turned into a TV screen. A gasp went up from the audience.

"Yes, my friends, the bird you are seeing is actual size."

The chicken stood three foot six inches tall and had legs which looked more like a pig's trotters than those of a chicken. This was no surprise as a significant amount of the chicken's DNA came from a pig.

The spotlights dancing around the screen came back Webster. "This, my friends, is the chicken of the future. You will take this chicken and sell it across the land. No one will stand in your way. Everyone will eat Charlie's Chickens!" Webster drew himself up to his full height. "As you leave here today, remember this: There will BE only one supplier, there will BE only one sales force, there will BE only one chicken!" Webster pointed at the bird on the screen, his hand quivering "This chicken! Will conquer - the WORLD!" he shouted. He turned and raised his hands towards the heavens "I give YOU-One supplier! - One sales force! - ONE CHICKEN!"

Chapter Three

"What do you do for a living, if you don't mind me asking?" said the taxi driver.

Harry did mind, as he knew full well what was coming. "I'm a solicitor."

For the next 20 minutes, Harry was given the cabbie's views on the criminal justice system. It was very simple, cut the hands-off shoplifters and hang everyone else. Oh, except people who committed adultery, who should be stoned to death. It's never hard to spot a divorcee.

As they got closer to the Knapp's garden centre the cabbie went quiet. They drew up in front of the main building and Harry got out. Having no change, he handed the taxi driver a fifty-pound note. From inside the building he could hear the strains of a George Formby record, music he'd last heard at his granddad's as a kid. The taxi driver feverishly scrambled through his bag for change, muttering 'fuck-in-ell' under his breath as he did so. He looked up as the music grew louder. A door opened and a man dressed in an RAF uniform came out.

"Look, have the ride on me," said the taxi driver. He thrust the money back into Harry's hands and sped off in a cloud of dust.

"Can I help you?"

Harry turned to face the RAF officer. He was a man in his mid thirties with a pencil moustache and a slightly strange look in his eyes. There was something very odd about the uniform - It was the style – it looked like something out of a WWII movie.

"I'm Harry Trent. I've come to see Mr. Knapp'"

"I'm Donald Knapp, but I imagine its one of my brothers you want. Come this way."

He led Harry into an office that stood next to the garden centre. The Knapp's were yet to embrace the paperless office. Aged wire trays spilled their contents over a desk and ran into assorted box files, yellowing invoices and piles of old gardening magazines. An old record player sat in one corner, the strains of George Formby dying away as they entered.

"Have a seat."

Harry sat on a frayed and battered typist chair. Donald perched against a table opposite and took a cigarette case from his pocket.

"Cigarette?"

He held the case out. It bore the inscription 'To Jammy Jenkins from all the lads in 633 Squadron.'

"I don't smoke."

"Nasty habit, isn't it? Still, you never know when you're going to cop a packet."

"Err, no. Are you home on leave?"

He took a deep draw on his cigarette and blew the smoke out of his nostrils.

"Special ops," he said tapping his nose.

"Oh." They sat in silence. Harry looked at the cover of a magazine that promised to tell him what would be the best buy in greenhouses for 2004. Whenever he looked up, Donald gave him a knowing smile.

"Sorry to have kept you, Mr. Trent."

Gordon Knapp was a man about 50 of generous but muscular build. He wore a dirty torn jumper, Wellingtons and the appearance of a man who'd spent a busy morning gardening. Behind him stood his brother Neville who was of similar looks and attire.

"Thank you, Donald. Haven't you got things to do?" asked Gordon. "And, I've told you before about playing George Formby in here!"

Donald eased slowly to his feet.

"Must be off. See you later, Harry," he said sauntering from the room.

"Cup of tea, Mr. Trent?" asked Neville.

A day in the country Michael had said. Go and see the Knapp brothers to discuss the renewal of the lease on Four Acre wood. It was an area of scrubland and trees that backed onto their premises which they had rented for a pittance for 25 years. They regarded the land as theirs and were far from happy to discover the lease expired and the landlord planning to build houses on it.

"You must understand, Mr. Trent. We cannot allow strangers to dig on our land," said Gordon Knapp.

"Would you like another fondant swirl?" asked Neville offering a plate of brightly coloured cakes.

"But, the land is uncultivated. Why is it so important?"

"It's a very good source of compost," said Gordon.

It was only later after the Surrey police spent 2 weeks digging up the land that Harry discovered the source of the compost was the six bodies the Knapp's had buried there. Ignorance is bliss. So, after an inconclusive meeting he didn't object when they offered to give me a lift back to the railway station.

Gordon couldn't find his keys, and Neville's car was being repaired.

"We could get Donald to drive," said Neville.

Gordon gave him a pointed look.

"We've got to get my car from the garage," added Neville.

"How long has your brother been in the RAF?" asked Harry innocently.

Gordon snorted as they went outside.

"Its not Donald's fault, Mr. Trent. He doesn't have the fingers. Not a single green one to his name," said Neville bringing up the rear.

Like Donald's uniform, the car was World War II vintage. Harry climbed into the back and sat on aged and cracked leather. Neville and Gordon climbed in either side, squashing him in the middle. It was getting dark as they left the garden centre and Harry hadn't paid much attention to the route out in the first place. They'd been going for some time when he tried to look at his watch and realised he couldn't see a thing. As Harry looked forward he noticed the front of the car was equally dark and CHRIST ALMIGHTY they we're driving with out any lights on.

"Donald? Where are we going?" asked Gordon.

"Best to avoid the main roads."

"Donald! We don't have time for this. We have to get Mr Trent to the station."

"Erm, we don't seem to have any lights on," added Harry.

"Donald!" barked Gordon.

There was a loud tut as the car's main beam went on lighting up the canopy of trees that stretched over the road.

"I'm sorry about this, Mr. Trent," said Gordon. "Our brother is rather indulged."

"It's only what we promised mother," butted in Neville.

"Mother said we should look after him, Neville. She didn't say we had to encourage his fantasies."

Ten minutes and several country lanes later Harry felt Gordon stiffen beside him. "We're being followed."

Neville looked over his shoulder, Harry twisted his head. There was a car behind keeping a measured distance.

"Perhaps they are just lost like us"' suggested Harry.

"Lose them," growled Gordon. The car shot forward.

Harry was starting to feel worried. What on earth was going on? It was bad enough he was in the middle of a wood with these three and now someone was after them.

The pursuit lasted for about 5 minutes until Donald took a sudden side turn after a bend and they lost them. Harry only saw an antler and heard the thump. The car slewed off the road and came to stop. They climbed out. Donald was breathing heavily and had a cut across his brow. Harry looked back at the road and saw the fallen deer. It tried to stand but from the un-natural angle of its back leg and the blood you could see this wasn't going to happen.

"Well, this is most unfortunate," said Gordon. "Harry, have you still got that Dundee cake?"

"Cake?"

"Yes, the one we gave you for Michael."

"It's... err... in my case."

"Good. Michael will be very upset if he doesn't get it. Now I don't think we should hang around. I have a suspicion it could be the Robinson brothers in that car."

"They would be?" asked Harry

"Business rivals," said Neville. "Their Trevor was involved in a slight contretemps with Donald and a Stanley knife. He's been looking for his ears ever since. You must understand we deplore violence Mr. Trent, but gardening can be a dirty business."

The sound of a car engine made them turn and run into the trees. Harry needed no encouragement. "This way old chap," said Donald grabbing his arm. They ran through dense bracken and over ditches. Harry's foot hit something squelchy, he pulled it away cold and wet. Donald stopped ahead of him clouds of condensation coming from his mouth. It was then Harry realised Gordon and Neville were not with them. He was alone with Donald in a wood in the middle of nowhere being chased by a man who wanted his ears back.

Elvis was no ordinary chicken. At 3'6" and weighing 56 pounds she was the best genetically modified chicken that money could buy. It was debatable whether or not Elvis should be described as a chicken with 25% of her DNA coming from a pig. To the scientists who had invented it, the chicken was Subject k7432589/4/7/02. To the men who worked in shed 72 at Charlie's Chicken's, she was known as Elvis.

The two men looked apprehensively at the chicken shed. Its metal sides reverberated as the screeching cluck was heard again. It was followed by a supporting cacophony from the other chickens.

"That was Elvis," said Ray Crabshaw.

"Who?" asked Don Weaver his supervisor.

"Elvis, the King of all the chickens."

"What are you going on about? Elvis was a bloke."

"You don't call anything that big a girl."

A red plume topping her black feathers, Elvis strutted back and forth across the chicken shed. She had been bred for meat and the production of extremely large eggs. No one had bothered to consider what other characteristics such a large bird might have, particularly when the pig DNA in question came from the Senegalese Fighting Pig. Fergal McGee, Cage technician grade 3 had discovered two of them that evening.

He had been clearing a blockage by the automatic feeder when he heard the noise of bending and snapping metal. He looked up in incredulity as Elvis bent apart the bars of her cage and bit off the top digit of his index finger.

Fergal fled from the shed clutching the bloody stump of his finger and screaming that the Chicken from Hell had attacked him. Ray Crabshaw saw the fleeing Fergal and went to investigate. He shone his torch round the dimly lit shed wincing at the cacophony of noise the birds were omitting. The beam settled on Elvis who was playing with something on the ground. Ray shone his torch down to see what it was and recoiled as he saw the fingernail and bloody severed digit it was attached to. As the finger was lit up, Elvis let out a blood-curdling cluck and flew at Ray. He saw the wall of black feathers and wicked talons coming towards him dropped his torch and fled from the shed howling. As he exited, the crowing of the birds sounded like a collective jeer.

He now stood outside the shed with Don Weaver who, despite his mockery of Ray's claims that the chicken had gone for him, showed no readiness to enter the shed.

"Where's Fergal?" demanded Weaver.

"He's waiting for the ambulance."

"An ambulance for a bird peck!?"

"It's had his finger," said Crabshaw waving one of his own in Weaver's face.

"Bollocks," replied Weaver, his face set in an ugly grimace

"I saw it on the floor. Elvis was playing with it."

"Look it's a fucking chicken!" Weaver exploded, his arms wildly gesticulating right and left. "Not Elvis bloody Presley. How did it get out of its cage?"

"Fergal said it broke out," said Crabshaw retreating before the flaying arms.

"Bollocks."

"They're big birds. That Elvis is as big as a dog. I've told you before the cages aren't strong enough."

Fergal looked at the crimson topped bandage covering the remains of his finger. His bowling hand. He'd lost the top of his index finger to his bowling hand! Southern Counties champion two years running and the chance of a historic hat trick in two weeks' time, but how could he bowl now? Someone was going to have to pay for this. His cousin Dermot had mentioned a solicitor who was a good fella when they'd met at Grandpa Donal's wake last year. He would go and see Harry Trent.

In desperation Harry looked right and left for Gordon and Neville. "Donald where have your brothers gone?" he hissed.

"Don't know old chap," giggled Donald. "Seems they've done a runner."

Harry heard the sound of someone coming and dived behind a tree. Hiding didn't seem a good idea to Donald. As the flash-lights approached, he drew a gun and fired. Harry heard a scream and one of the lights disappeared. Donald turned, ran towards Harry, and pressed the gun into his hand. "You might need this Harry, now the shootings started," he giggled and then disappeared through the trees. Harry thrust the gun into his pocket and fled.

Harry didn't see the low branch. It caught him full in the face and sent him flying. He lay on the ground clutching his nose to stem the flow of blood. As he held a hanky to his face he heard the dogs. Harry pulled the gun from his pocket and crouched behind a fallen log, the gun shaking violently in one hand the other busily stuffing a hanky up his nose. They were getting closer. He looked round for somewhere to hide. His case was open its contents strewn across the ground. The brown paper packet containing the cake was torn and he could see something white poking through the paper. Harry ripped of the remains of the wrapping and stared in horror at the packet of white powder he was holding. When he heard the voices he nearly had a heart attack.

"Deeley, where are you?"

"I'm over here, sir."

"You okay?"

"Yes, but Sergeant Thomas has been hit. We need to get an ambulance."

Harry looked from the gun to the white powder. It didn't take a genius to work out it was cocaine – Michael Burns addiction was well known to him - that's why Gordon Knapp had been so concerned about him still having the Dundee cake. Fucking Michael, that bastard!

He hadn't done anything! The trouble was the police were a suspicious bunch and the recently fired gun and the cocaine might make them think different. When they found out he was a solicitor as well they'd be calling for a rope and looking round for a suitable tree. Harry furiously wiped the gun with his hanky to remove all fingerprints and threw it into a bush. He was busy doing the same to the bag of cocaine when the moon broke through and he noticed the red smears he was leaving all over it. As Harry removed his prints he left a trail of blood. The gun would be covered in it! He froze and began to babble to himself as the depth of his stupidity hit home. The sound of barking getting louder snapped him out of it. He dived into the bush where he'd thrown the gun biting his bottom lip as something sharp drove into his hand. He felt around blindly with his other hand, he'd gone and stuck his fingers into the decaying remains of a hedgehog. Harry could hear the swish of stick against bracken as the police line advanced. MY CASE! he'd left it out in the open. He crawled out of the bush and scrambled around putting the contents back in it. He hesitated over the cocaine, but couldn't leave it, not stained with his blood. The beam of a torch cut through the air above Harry's head.

Case in hand he crawled back into the bush sitting on the gun in the process. He pushed it into his pocket and began to pray.

Not being very religious, his nerve broke after some thirty seconds and he decided to run for it. He let off a couple of shots and then ran. He gained a few precious yards, but the sound of him crashing through the undergrowth quickly resulted in shouts of "over there" and as he legged it Harry could hear the barking getting ever closer.

His one advantage over his pursuers was he knew how much trouble he was in if they caught him. Harry tore through the wood like a man possessed, the dark outlines of the trees flying past in a blur. He could feel his chest getting tighter and tighter until Harry though it would burst. Ahead the trees were thinning out. Once he hit open ground he was a goner.

Before he'd time to think about this he was in the open. His feet disappeared underneath him as he rolled down the embankment. He hit tarmac and looked up into the lights of an on coming car. Harry managed to roll back onto the hard shoulder just in time. It's a frightening sight watching cars speed past at hedgehog level.

Harry scrambled to his feet and back on to the embankment. He'd come out onto the A3, a three-lane highway. He looked behind him as the first copper and his dog had emerged at the edge of the wood, the dog sniffing the ground like crazy. Harry's head shot back and forth between the edge of the wood and the oncoming cars. If he could get across the road they would never be able to follow. So that was his choice: 20 years of never being able to bend over in a shower or running the risk of becoming road kill.

The shout of "down there" made up his mind. The inside lane was clear and he had some distance on the truck coming up in the middle one. As Harry hit the fast lane he heard the sound of the horn and momentarily saw the horror in the driver's eyes. Thankfully he had the balls to accelerate and not brake. As he swerved round Harry his wing mirror clipped the back of Harry's leg. He heard the roar of the trucks horn and was blinded by his flashing lights as the car cut him up and accelerated away. Some how he kept his balance and hold of his case and leapt over the crash barrier. A car whizzed past him in the fast lane, but mercifully it was then a clear run across the other carriageway and he collapsed into a very wet and boggy ditch.

Chief Inspector Cullen stood at the top of the embankment. "Shall we go after him, sir?" Cullen turned to the dog handler standing next to him, struggling to hold back his dog

"No, I think we've done enough chasing for one night." He turned to his sergeant, Mortimer who had come up along side him. "Jim, how is Sergeant Thomas?"

"Just a flesh wound, Guv. They've taken him off to St. Hugh's, but he should be ok. We got any idea who he was?"

"No, didn't have the build to be one of the Knapp's regular lads. But we did find this." Cullen held out the muddy business card to his sergeant who read it.

"Harry Trent, Clancy Burns, solicitors."

About HD McTie

McTie lives and works in Suffolk England and can be contacted via his agent Nigel George ng@georgeandco. co.uk 01449 737281 / 07957 186297

84771686R00273

Made in the USA
Lexington, KY
25 March 2018